Past Praise for Hilary Masters

for *Last Stands: Notes from Memory*

A luminous consequential book.

—Jonathan Yardley, *Washington Post*

An elegant book.—*Los Angeles Times*

Recollections as fixed and poignant as family photographs.

—*New York Times*

A model demonstration of the use of memory. —*The New Yorker*

A lovely work.—*Publishers Weekly*

I doubt there has been a better written memoir, page for page, in the last twenty years.—Phillip Lopate

An American classic. —*Boston Globe*

for short fiction and essays

The richness of Masters's tales lies in an understanding of what occurrences in a person's life mean, for that person and for the community that person inhabits. —*Chicago Tribune*

Everything that needed to be said has been said ... Henry James with libido.—Rick Demarinis

Hilary Masters investigates relationships with such delicacy, he's like the hummingbird of short story writers. —Ann Beattie

for *Cooper*

Its truths resonate and book invites return when we finish.

—Richard Russo, *Philadelphia Inquirer*

A memorable book worth rereading as I have done with relish.

—George Core, *Washington Post Book World*

for *Elegy for Sam Emerson*

... brimming with a richness not merely of scene and detail but of life. Marvelous.—Stewart O'Nan

A novel of passionate intelligence and profound humanity.

—Margot Livesey

The world needs more books like this.

—Cynthia Shearer

Also by Hilary Masters

Novels

Elegy for Sam Emerson
Home Is the Exile
Harlem Valley Trio:
      Strickland: A Romance
      Cooper
      Clemmons
Manuscript for Murder (as P. J. Coyne)
Palace of Strangers
An American Marriage
The Common Pasture

Short Fiction

How the Indians Buried Their Dead
Success: New and Selected Stories
Hammertown Tales

Essays

In Rooms of Memory
In Montaigne's Tower

Memoir

Last Stands: Notes from Memory

Nonfiction

Shadows on a Wall:
      Juan O'Gorman and the Mural in Pátzcuaro

Post

a fable

Hilary Masters

BkMk Press
University of Missouri-Kansas City

BkMk Press
University of Missouri-Kansas City
5101 Rockhill Road
Kansas City, Missouri 64110
(816) 235-2558 (voice)
(816) 235-2611 (fax)
www.umkc.edu/bkmk

Financial assistance for this project is provided
by the Missouri Arts Council, a state agency.

Book design: Susan L. Schurman
Managing Editor: Ben Furnish
Editorial Assistant: Sarah Eyer
Special thanks to R. M. Kinder, Advisory Editor
Editorial Consultant: Elizabeth Uppman

BkMk Press also wishes to thank Karla Deel,
Elizabeth Gromling, Heather Inness, Deirdre Mikolajcik,
and Nicholas Sawin.
Printing: Macnaughton & Gunn, Saline, Michigan

Library of Congress Cataloging-in-Publication Data
Masters, Hilary.
Post / Hilary Masters.
p. cm.
Summary: "This literary novel (which combines narrative conventions
of the mystery, magical realism, meta-fiction, environmental writing, and
satire) is set in the future in New York and follows an investigator's efforts
to find the link between the state's late governor's ruinous redevelopment
policies, the governor's son-in-law, and the extinct passenger pigeon"--
Provided by publisher.
ISBN 978-1-886157-75-0 (pbk. : alk. paper)
1. New York (N.Y.)--Fiction. 2. Magic realism (Literature) I. Title.
PS3563.A82P67 2011
813'.54--dc22
2011003157

This book is set in GiantSizedSpectacular Std BB, and Garamond Pro
Typefaces.

Again and always,
Kathleen

ACKNOWLEDGMENTS

In addition to those newspapers and journals mentioned in the text, acknowledgement must be made to other sources that relate to the history of the passenger pigeon. Of these, the most important is the excellent book by A.W. Schorger, *The Passenger Pigeon, Its Natural History and Extinction*, the University of Wisconsin Press (1955). Of next importance is the contribution from J.J. Audubon's two volume *Ornithological Biography* (1831) and the *Birds of America* (1839). *Wilson's American Ornithology*, New York (1839) edited by T.M. Brewer was also consulted. Mention must also be made of Elon Eaton's *Birds of New York* (1908) and Dr. R.W. Shufeldt's article "Published Figures and Plates of Extinct Passenger Pigeon," the *Scientific Monthly* (1921).

Also, appreciation is hereby expressed to the staffs of several institutions for their generous assistance. They are the American Museum of Natural History, The San Diego Zoo, The American Geological Society and the Zoological Society of London.

And finally, the author wants to express his appreciation to the editors of *Sports Illustrated* who published a portion of this story when times were hard.

PROLOGUE

So many plaques hang on the façade of New York City's Chelsea Hotel to honor famous former residents that the old hostelry resembles the Black Knight's castle adorned with the shields of the brave, though foolish, warriors who dared to throw down a gauntlet—in this case a challenge to enduring fame.

These trials so honored make an indiscriminate collection that includes a compiler of Greek recipes and several anthologists of Eisenhower formalism, so it is difficult to understand why a small space could not have been found on the façade or over the doorway to preserve the name of Emil Nalbandian, the man who almost single-handedly revolutionized the no-trump opener in the game of bridge.

It is difficult to ignore the ugly suspicion that Nalbandian's ethnic background had something to do with his exclusion; that various historical committees and semi-governmental commissions only bestowed these bronze honoraria on their own constituents. This suggestion, at once unsavory as it is un-democratic, is given a sad credence by a review of the names that were cast in some permanence: Wolfe, Thomas, Davis, Moody, Hume, Slate, and Johnson—both father and son. And so on. The presences of a Behan and a Flynn only support the accusation while simultaneously paying tribute to the historical role of the Irish called upon to prove Anglo-Saxon fair play.

There is little doubt that Nalbandian's intimacy with Khalil Gibran prejudiced his standing with the establishment whose daughters may have run through the night screaming his harm-less odes to bread but whose prosodic pretensions were found to be seriously lacking by more seasoned minds. No need to mention that the Lebanese prophet himself was ignored by the historical marker committee though there are numerous authenticated reports that place him often at the counter of the drugstore that used to adjoin the hotel, sipping a lemon Coke.

Nor was it Nalbandian's murder that denied him a place on this grand façade of fame because the hotel's management took some pride in the slovenly fashion by which their famous clientele sometimes checked out. A few of the older clerks in their retire-ments established appreciable careers by becoming prime sources for journalists' inquiries into the sordid details of a poet's or a painter's death. One or two set up modest kiosks in corners of the hotel's lobby to offer full-color brochures describing the suicides, the alcoholic meltdowns and other unsavory demises of this particular academy. Their narratives decorate the rooms and halls of this Valhalla as the front of the building is distinguished by their names.

The details of these final deliriums assume the blood-flecked frenzies of an E.A. Poe, and their subjects were tumbled like bags of sodden linen into the service elevator and hauled away to take their cup of quassi in some obscure charity ward. Others took a more direct route to street level, crashing through the ailanthus branches to land among the parliament of cats that always convened in the back courtyard. The yowling debate would pause only long enough to accommodate the new refuse dumped in their assembly.

Thus the discovery of Nalbandian with a bullet in his heart in Room 242 was only a curlicue in the old hotel's baroque reputation. Moreover, the bullet had passed through the strong diamond suit Nalbandian had been holding, and we might reconstruct the pathetic gesture, a vulnerable defense by which he had attempted to shield his breast with the playing cards, as one more gratuitous demonstration of art's feeble play against reality.

The dashing Armenian supported himself by giving private lessons in contract bridge, and the assassin had surprised him in the course of one of these tutorials, which proved to be the bad luck of the young woman Nalbandian had been coaching in the basics of the no-trump opener. An honor student from Sarah Lawrence College, she became his companion in death upon the paisley throw. She had held a poor hand in any event. As for the no-trump opener, it is only one of the brilliant innovations his genius brought to the game, only to have it appropriated by lesser minds who will remain nameless.

The double murder was featured for several days in the newspapers (DEATH TRUMPS ALL), though it is evident from these reports of many decades ago that the hotel had not yet acquired the respect that was to make it into a national landmark. The *New York Sun*, for example, indicated a preference for the adjective *seedy* in its description of the place. Nalbandian's murder was never solved.

Police then were preoccupied with the opening and closing of speakeasies and leading different heroes and explorers down the pavement of Broadway, a near-continuous parade in those days, since there was still yet much to be explored and heroes were in abundance. Consequently, the identity of the person who slipped into a rundown West Side hotel and put an end to an obscure card player with origins in Asia Minor never received proper investigation. In fact, it would not concern us now, not even the wrong done to Emil Nalbandian by the fast-shuffling establishment, were it not for the proposed East-West spur of the Governor Kimball Lyon Expressway.

This last great dream of the late Governor Lyon, he who developed the Perpetual Parking Plaza, gives employment to millions, brings the fruits of progress to the doorstep of almost every site in the state, and sets the stage for a dynamic synthesis of rural tradition and urban energy. Indeed, we have yet to realize the full measure of Governor Lyon's promise, and few of us alive today will see the end of the road. The concept that the highway would never be completed but would remain "a growing thing" compounded magnificently with the idea of the Perpetual Parking Plaza—the one enhances the other. It was of no small consideration in the nominations made for his Nobel Peace Prize that the Perpetual Parking Plaza was the ultimate defense against terrorist attacks. "What can they do to a parking lot? Bring 'em on," was the Governor's quick retort that silenced critics while displaying that unadorned common sense that so ignited the electorate and swayed even the most austere intellectual.

So, ironically, it is the proposed new extension of the highway that has reopened the case of Emil Nalbandian, as new construction in an old and respectable neighborhood will sometimes unearth a grisly history long buried. The new East-West spur will connect the Hudson River Extension of the Governor Kimball Lyon Expressway with the Long Island Extension and downtown Long Island City. It is to parallel the spur that connects the Hudson River Extension with the loop built across the Wall Street area several years ago and which joined Fire Island with several exit ramps, some rather extreme. This new "grid access," to use the engineering term, is to join the loop at a point near Fishers Island utilizing a series of bridges and floating interchanges over Long Island Sound, the designs for which have already excited the acclaim of the world's engineering community. When completed, it will eliminate the long haul out to Montauk Point for the motorist who has only wished to go from Bronxville to Rye.

This new spur is to be built along what is now 23rd Street in Manhattan, its eight lanes incorporating 24th and 25th Streets to the north and 22nd and 21st streets to the south. Of course, all important buildings, historical sites, and national landmarks in this area are to be preserved and relocated, and this list will include not only the Hotel Chelsea but also the Flatiron Building and the quaint house farther east that had been the home of the author of Rip Van Winkle. The McDonald's food chain has successfully bid on Irving's cottage and plans to re-install the house with a typical garden of the nineteenth century in a suburb of Olathe, Kansas. The final bidding on the Hotel Chelsea has been especially heartening. A historically minded conglomerate has made the successful offer to relocate the hotel—shields of fame intact—to a large amusement park in Crawfordsville, Indiana, where a portion of the Grand Canal has already been preserved.

Imagine then the puzzlement and consternation when full-page ads against this proposed extension of the highway began to appear. Opposition (by well-meaning traditionalists) is always to be expected to progressive measures. But these published attacks, worded to excite the basest of emotions, carried the name of Leo Post. Not only is Leo Post the late Governor Lyon's son-in-law, and thus the widower of the beautiful and tragic Molly Lyon, but he is also a longtime confidant of the Governor's, an example of the man of letters who functions effortlessly in the political arena. In fact, it is Leo Post who is credited with the slogan that won the public's enthusiasm and support for the Expressway. Even today, some of us find ourselves humming "It's a grow—in thing," that little tune that is credited with putting over the Self-Propelled Expressway.

Consequently, this department has been activated, and I, B. Smith, a duly appointed agent of investigation, have been assigned to make this inquiry and report.

It was not easy to locate Leo Post. His appearances in the files come to an abrupt end subsequent to the death of his wife, the Governor's daughter. The last publication attributed to him, an article in *Military Age* titled "The Rhetoric of Georgian Verse as Found," was published fully a year ago and before the horrible accident on the Poughkeepsie-Elmira Access Grid that claimed Molly Lyon's life in the flaming wreckage of her sports car in that first year of the Mark Twain 500. Post's file contains no receipts for travel or living expenses, no credit-card carbons, no registers of any kind, and though it may be possible for some citizens to slip through their daily lives unaccounted for, it is highly unlikely for a man of Leo Post's habits and way of life. Indeed, the file folder that contains his speech accepting the Pulitzer-Jones Prize also has a pink tab that notes, "Possible Deceased. Save for Obit."

The newspapers could only produce the typed letter that had accompanied the advertisement's copy. (SAVE THE CHELSEA—WHY DOES INDIANA DESERVE THE CHELSEA HOTEL??...REMEMBER DREISER AND SISTER CARRIE... LET THEM HAVE ROCKEFELLER CENTER.) No return address, and cash money was used. Allowing for the effect of time, analysis of the signature compared favorably with the samples of Post's writing on file. Ultimate proof was made from the actual prose of the advertisement that produced identifying marks of style and language usage that were as unequivocal in their identification as a drop of DNA.

A phrase such as "Shall I permit the legacy of a madman to concretize the last grove, sylvan sliver of squirrel's retreat" contains many Postian traits. The deliberate usage of the near obsolete "shall" to achieve emphasis. Or, "Were it possible to out-maneuver the cumbersome yet merciless advance of the Self-Propelled Expressway, I should not ask anyone to join me in this venture" offers even more proof of its authorship. Though to be fair, an occasional critic suggested that Post's aristocratic tone could be a form of self-mockery.

But where was he? How could a man of his prominence and recognition disappear? Even Henry L. Blackman, who won the World Lottery, was uncovered on a beach in Texas by a purveyor of red-hots in just a matter of days after Blackman had declined the island of Puerto Rico. Post had clearly taken another name and assumed another identity. I, B. Smith, frustrated, ordered a complete Assimilator, testing all Post archives. The man's entire file. The file on the Hotel Chelsea, including the complete registry of its tenants since its opening in 1912, plus an index of the year's books, was put into the machine. The transmitter hummed and digested the material and carefully typed the name *Len Banal*.

Banal's most recent pornography was published by Ariel & Sloan, and these publishers, respectable as they were, provided us with Banal's current address. It was a postal box in the small village of Shadroe, upstate and just off of Exit 19-B of the Governor Kimball Lyon Expressway. I, B. Smith, the operational officer, instituted surveillance, and within a week we had a promising lead.

Mail addressed to Len Banal or Lenny B was picked up by a very tall man in Western costume, including high-heeled boots, and driving what appeared to be an old-model taxi. The car was painted black and was in need of new piston rings. Subject was six feet four inches tall, slim of build, dark hair and about sixty years of age. It was not Leo Post.

Surveillance followed the subject who turned north on the Lyon Expressway, exiting at the unfinished Access Grid near Catskill, thence going in an easterly direction, toward the river, driving expertly and fast. But beyond a sharp curve, the black taxi disappeared into thin air. Surveillance detected nothing but an empty country lane, the river to the right, and the handsome transportation viaduct of the Expressway on the left. A small wisp of blue smoke hung in the air.

This identical chase with the same dematerialization at this same spot on this country road happened several times. A survey of surrounding territory was made from the air, and it revealed no house or structure at the river's edge. Several hundred yards off the bank lay Pejon Island as it has been called on all navigational charts since those drawn by Henry Hudson. The site is more popularly known as Leek's Island, taking this name from the old river family whose holdings on both sides of the river were granted by James I. More particularly, locals call it by that name because of the bizarre castle built upon it in 1862 by Emanuel Leek, the munitions manufacturer to whom Lincoln turned in desperation during that tragic winter. The structure has been uninhabited for more that 100 years, its crenellated towers crumbled, the small lagoon at the entrance choked with weeds, and the iron grating of the portcullis rusted and hanging awry on one chain.

THAT MORNING

I, B. Smith, duly disturbed by this incomplete report by Surveillance, entered the investigation. On-the-spot interviews in the area suggested the island was not uninhabited. Residents spoke of strange lights moving within the castle at night. Fishermen reported the sound of gunfire, and some said armed guards patrolled the grounds with huge dogs. The dogs barked viciously and were presumed to have been pets that had gone wild after being left behind by summer renters. Pilots of boats passing on the river testified to seeing what appeared to be human figures on one of the parapets on the castle's walls. Evidence identified the tall mail courier as a regular customer of Alma and Fred's Everything Market in Athens. Groceries were paid for in cash. Catsup and peanut butter were prominent in his purchases.

I, B. Smith, ready to broaden the inquiry, took up a position on the bank opposite the castle. It was dark, an hour before dawn, and the island fortress was silent. The structure loomed, an intense

shadow in the rippling darkness of the river, as if its mass of blackness pulled all illumination into its depth. But not sound, for the
comforting hum of vehicles passing over the Expressway high
above was reassurance that goods and services were being carried
to that exchange down the road that fosters civilization. But at
the river's edge, the rippling of the current resembled a teasing, a
beckoning into a forbidden area. The shape of Leek's Castle had
gradually appeared as a photographic print in its chemical bath
slowly defines itself. The crenellation of its walls, the platforms
and towers and other architectural details slowly materialized until the whole resembled a huge raft on which some precocious—
that is to say, on their way to madness—children with unlimited
resources had reproduced their most ambitious summer fantasy.
I, B. Smith, absorbed in this spectacle and the resulting play of
metaphor, was taken by surprise.

"All right, ponder, keep your hands where I can see them. I
gotcha covered." The ominous clock-clack of an old-fashioned revolver being cocked enforced the command.

As Surveillance had noted, he was about six feet four inches
tall, with black hair, slim, and somewhere in his sixties. The pistol was considerably older, a frontier model of six-shot capacity.
However, as a piece of ordnance, it appeared to be functional. I,
B. Smith, on the defensive, followed his directions promptly. At
river's edge in a small cove, the black taxi idled smoothly. The
car had been driven upon a wooden float of ingenious design
that transformed the vehicle into a ferry, its rear wheels driving a
treadmill apparatus that turned a pair of small paddle wheels.

Our guide seemed to relax as this makeshift ferry moved away
from the bank. He returned the pistol to the holster strapped to
his skinny thigh and turned to navigating this curious craft. His
confidence in our captivity was justified by the dense fog that lay
upon the water only a few feet from shore, which made for a prison
as secure as a steel vault. Sound and sight were obliterated except
for the husky rasp of the taxi's engine and the wash of river water
against the ferry's hull. I, B. Smith, usually calm in most situa-

tions, experienced a momentary panic to be so divorced from the mainland. A perplexing sense of alienation prompted a clammy sweat, and this separation from identity caused uneasiness.

But we had neared the small lagoon that served the castle as a moat, and the sound of the taxi's engine bounced hollowly around the inner walls of the entrance. Rotted timbers poked above the surface of the water like the heads of monsters. Chugging through a circuitous route of an unmarked channel, we passed beneath a battlement just as a large piece of masonry fell into the ferry's wake. A moment earlier and the block of stone would have crushed us, but the tall man at the tiller showed no concern, as if near disaster always accompanied these passages. The buffeting of the car's engine noise, together with the wash of the ferry's passage, may have loosened the crumbling mortar.

Black iron sconces bracketed an arched entrance, a passage that took us directly beneath the heavy grid of the portcullis that seemed ready to fall like a huge guillotine blade. Inside, a courtyard was completely enclosed by high parapets that missed a few teeth here and there. Four long balconies, one from each wall, seemed to be bound by thick vines that grew over the entire structure. Enormous casement windows rose from the balconies. The taxi's engine idled, the paddle wheels stopped, and we coasted toward a small landing where a man dressed in a rumpled double-breasted blazer, dark trousers, and white buckskin shoes waited for us.

Scuffed and soiled as they were, these shoes shimmered in the gloom of the early hour, almost as footlights to cast a reflecting glow on the cherubic features of their wearer's face. Despite the monochromatic wash of the pre-dawn, the face seemed to intensify the illumination from the shoes and to pulsate with a startling pink of health. Expressive eyes, the color of ripe olives, made a somber note in this rosy countenance. I, B. Smith, do solemnly affirm, the man was Leo Post.

"Welcome, welcome," he was saying, extending a hand to help us to the landing. "I do hope Taylor has shown you every courtesy. You've not had breakfast, I'd wager. As you see, we keep early hours here, and we have not breakfasted yet either. I think our dear Lucy has prepared something special for us this morning. Come along, come along."

Note the multiple usages of the first-person pronoun, and these only in the initial moments of introduction. The taxi's engine turned off, a humid silence fell upon the courtyard, lightened only by the feckless lap of the river's current, and somewhere within the castle, water splashed, perhaps a first trickling alarm of a calamitous rupture about to happen. No breeze, yet the thick vines that embraced the walls rustled as if some creature worked its way among the leaves. Post had turned his back and led the way through a doorway set into a narrow squinch. Our footsteps led us into an immense gallery that had been adopted for several usages.

A heavily mantled fireplace, Italian Romanesque circa 1210, was a focal point, chairs of impressive size on either side. A narrow upholstered bench was before the hearth, and a table about twenty feet long and four feet wide was placed in the center of the room but by no means occupied it. With the exception of a few ordinary chairs, these furnishings constituted the appointments of this great hall. A row of large windows, the casements we had observed from outside, followed the worn bolster fixed upon a long stone divan; however, the ivy's screen was so thick at this point that the view of the river's mid-channel was nearly obscured.

The massive table, like the room, was apportioned to several usages. One end, clearly devoted to intellectual pursuits, bore stacks of large books, manuscripts, and periodicals. Crumbs and leavings of meals littered the opposite end of the table, and here places were set—a quick count made three—amid a collection of condiments, jars of jelly, a tub of peanut butter, and several catsup bottles, their necks with brown rings of age.

Within this brace of human sustenance—mind and body—were areas of other interests. The hobby of carpentry was represented by half-finished birdhouses, and as if to companion this interest, ornithology was represented by the sad proxies of two feathered carcasses—their pitiful beaks open and silent. A motion picture projector, pieces of leather, and saddlery were in the center of that table, and a portable typewriter, no doubt the one on which those subversive advertisements were composed, poked the end of its carriage out from beneath the different newspapers that had printed the poisonous notices.

A fearful clamor resounded from behind the plywood partition that formed the fourth wall of the room, a temporary division, for the other half of this grand hall lay on the other side. A chimney and mantle, duplicate to what is near the large table, could be made out in the distant gloom. A clang of steel, caballing clash of pots and pans, a scour of escaping steam was accompanied by a screech of oaths. Coincidentally, a large vessel passed, going up-river, and its large bulk completely filled the windows to give the sensation that the castle—the island itself—had been set adrift and was moving downstream. The tympany and curses behind the temporary partition contributed to the illusion of a ship weighing anchor, cantankerous machinery goaded to performance by an angry engineer.

"That's dear Lucy," our host said amiably. "She's preparing some delicacy for us now."

"Goddamn sonofabitch?" the cook's voice shouted in a contralto range.

"Well now," Post continued, as if he had not heard the outburst. "Let's warm ourselves at the hearth. These mornings on the Hudson can be deceptively cool. I had Taylor lay a fire for us before he left to fetch you." More lines seem to have been cast off, the shore had become more distant, and we were underway.

Small tree limbs the size of a man's arm had been cast into the cavernous hearth with a random placement that suggested the fire setter's complete confidence in his skill, or complete disinterest. No kindling, no stubs of paper, and the wood glistened with moisture as if it had only just been pulled from surrounding waters.

A thin snake of smoke coiled from this damp mass and Post held his hands to it, rubbing them together and chuckling content-edly, as if a roaring fire were in the hearth. The slant of his profile, the dark eyes downcast, recalled those moving photographs taken at the memorial service for his wife, when he was surrounded by luminaries of the poli-literary world, the fashioners of contempo-rary culture, as well as the entire membership of those devoted to motor sports. The calm mien of his image clearly pressed from a vineyard of suffering, to use the language of a popular internet blogger. Meanwhile, Post had turned his back to the enormous hearth and lifted the double vent of his blazer.

"Well, now, I suppose it was the Banal book that led you to us," he began. It surprised us to hear him pronounce his pseudonym, emphasis on the first syllable. "Just a little toss-off with which to buy groceries. Actually not all that lacking and well received in certain quarters. Did you happen to catch Pickett Sneat's review in the *Gross Almanac*? Strange fellow, do you know him? You'll meet him soon. Yes, he's here, too. You may remember he received a Lyon Foundation grant some years back and has been working on a special project unlike so many who have been so endowed. He wanted some solitude, and so he is here."

"Well, down to business, correct?" He chuckled once more and faced the smoke rising from the sodden wood in the immense hearth. "You are here to record why I have spoken out against the continuation of the Lyon Expressway—the Self-Propelled mon-strosity that I had a small part in creating. What I had thought to be the fine edge of Governor Lyon's Machiavellian thrust into the soggy posterior of a halting dense populi turned out to be the luminous fumes given off by the deterioration of his mind. He had a head full of foxfire. I did not know at the time that the Self-Propelled Expressway was the ultimate revenge he set loose on a world that never took his poetry seriously.

"When will we learn," Post continued, while moving to the table, "that it is far better to flatter the meager talents of this set of mind than to measure their tepid logorrhea against the stern disciplines justly reserved for the rest of us? How many more examples must history supply: Nero, Louis XIV, Winston Churchill? How history might have changed, one wonders, if those snobbish galleries in Vienna had admitted the work of the young Hitler. Surely, there must have been a corner—in a back room—where space could have been made for one of those prosaic scenes he favored, thatched-roof cottages beside a bridge festooned with climbing roses. It could have been a real lifesaver—hanging one of those mundane sketches. Well, what's done is done, and so it is with the Lyon's Expressway. The Perpetual Parking Plaza, of course, the harmless but obvious example of an ideologue out of his depth."

"SHIT!" The cry penetrated the plywood partition with the force of a heavy-caliber bullet. A utensil clattered upon the stone floor.

"Sounds as if Lucy is about to serve breakfast," Post announced cheerfully. He moved to the far end of the table and sat in the armchair apparently reserved for him. "It was Sneat, of course," our host continued, "who put me on to Lyon's poetry and how it connected with his mania for new pavements. The *Schoharie Review* printed the rave Pickett gave to Lyon's volume of verse—can't remember its title. Crist, Humphrey, and Beauty was the publisher, by no means a vanity press, though its integrity could be compromised by the fact that the Lyon Foundation owns the controlling stock in UMG, which in turn controls Crist, Humphrey, and Beaut—but you know all that, don't you?"

Reminded that the title of Lyon's book of poetry was *Sunspots*, Leo Post only nodded. We should record that the man spoke easily and without hesitation in that flat, inflectionless manner that had been familiar on national lecture platforms and that still can be heard on tapes and vintage records—*Leo Post Reads The Little Red Hen and Other Classics*. If there had been any suggestion of anxiety caused by our inquiry, it could have been his continual arranging and rearranging of the silverware and the jars of jelly and peanut butter, the bottle of catsup—the whimsical play of a chess master setting up the board for his own amusement. A further observation: The cuffs of his shirt were badly frayed, and while fooling with the knife and fork, positioning the catsup to put the mustard in jeopardy, he paused to pull down the sleeves of the blazer to click the metal buttons together like the counters of a nervous gambler. Another file speaks of the elegance of style concealing a threadbare substance.

"*Sunspots*," Leo Post murmured. "How could I forget? I had been on the outs with the *Schoharie Review*—they had completely ignored my biography of Sam Walter Foss and so when Pickett's article appeared—enormously long and shamelessly freighted I must admit—I immediately wrote him. I shudder now at the language and the tone of my note. The names I called him—this man who has since become my friend and confidant—such as hack, whore and toady just to cite a few—you know the rest. Fortunately for all of us, the letter has never been made public, and Pickett called me and in that generous way he has—that sprightly, roguish manner that so mineralizes the crushing weight of the affliction he carries with such grace that the underlying courage is often obscured."

Post seemed to have let his saltshaker be checked—grape jelly to spoon—but after a moment's pause and reflection, he moved peanut butter to catsup and checkmate. It was a brilliant tour de force and done with all the offhand bemusement of a brilliant mind.

"There," he said half to himself. Then raising his voice as he turned those somber eyes upon us, he continued. "Sneat told me what he pursued, which naturally immediately enlisted my support. Those of us in the intellectual community owed it to our fellow men—and of course women as well, but they are not fellows—to keep the excesses of a Kimball Lyon to a minimal horror, since he would undoubtedly be re-elected again and again. It would be our contribution to humanity, he convinced me, and one that would be of far more value than any of the egocentric assemblies some of us call works of art. I enthusiastically endorsed his scheme. I still had some contacts on the *New York Times-Tribune*. So my long and ambiguously favorable review of *Sunspots* appeared within a fortnight."

BLAM! A cannon-like roar sundered the interview—the castle could have been under attack.

"Do not be alarmed," our host said mildly. "Be calm. Nothing to fear. That's just Taylor practicing his fast draw—no longer very fast, I fear. Sometimes the arthritis crimps his fingers so that the gun drops to the floor and a cartridge explodes on impact. It just happens. He uses the portrait gallery on the other side of the courtyard, and these accidental discharges are probably the basis for the local rumor that Pijon Island is the site of a hunting and fishing club. No doubt, you have such a claim in your folder."

At this point, the door in the plywood partition was kicked open by a tall Afro-American female carrying steaming bowls of food on a tray. "Ah, here is Lucy with our breakfast," Post said eagerly, a sort of rubbing of the hands together in his voice. The woman approached the table. She wore white leather boots that came halfway up her thighs.

"What have you prepared for us this morning, good Lucy?" Post asked.

"Same old shit, hun," the woman replied. She was young and handsome.

"Splendid, splendid." The author sniffed the rising vapors of what looked to be porridge. His face was suffused with a blush of expectation. "Is Mr. Sneat up and about yet?" he asked as he spooned peanut butter into a bowl of the hot cereal. "Do see if you can be of some assistance to him, Lucy."

"That little freak can dress himself," the cook replied with a curl of her lips. "He took liberties with me yesterday and I'm not anybody's pet cushion."

"Certainly not!" Post exclaimed, seemingly as offended as the woman. He looked at her with appreciation. She fingered the cartridge belt that slanted over her chest from one shoulder. It was the urban renegade costume of an heiress. "What would we do without you, Lucy," Post said, as she turned abruptly on the stiletto heels of her boots and strode toward the plywood door. She kicked it open. "It was a lucky day for us," Post continued, "when that fine creature answered Pickett's advertisement. Oh my, we seem to be out of milk, but you'll find the catsup is a notable substitute. And probably more healthful as well."

"Imagine my surprise therefore," Post said after swallowing a spoonful of the reddish-brown mixture, "to receive an invitation from Kimball Lyon for dinner at his townhouse on Gramercy Square in New York City. He had yet to announce his candidacy for governor, and the plans for the Expressway were still in the drawer. The Perpetual Parking Plaza concept was still dormant in that burning slag he used for a brain. I immediately called to see if he had been invited also, but no— because Lyon did not read the *Schoharie Review*. If he had read Pickett's review of *Sunspots*—infinitely more pandering than mine—we could have all broken bread together. In any event, we agreed I should attend, just to see what influence ... well, this seems so long ago."

Post fell into a kind of musing. He ate in silence, spooning the porridge and tipping the bowl to scoop up the last bit. The pink crown of his head flashed in the light. The room had become silent but for a trickle of water in the kitchen. The black woman named Lucy may have been fulfilling other housekeeping duties in another part of the castle. Again, I, B. Smith, not finishing my porridge, experienced that curious sensation that we were afloat and that the island and the old stone castle had been cut loose and we were drifting downriver with the current.

"We are prone to put our own preoccupations upon a given situation." Post had carefully placed his empty bowl on the table, the spoon athwart it. "Several years ago, in a park, I found myself observing an old woman sitting a distance away and opposite a lagoon. Her hand would sometimes rise and fall upon the chair arm as she stared blankly into space. I took the gesture to be one of impatience—she may have just remembered a chore undone, or an urge to quit this place had needled her, but no other site was so extraordinary as to make her move. Or perhaps she observed a schedule for sitting by the lagoon, and the sun had become too hot to complete that regimen, yet she was determined to stick it out despite her discomfort. Or maybe those fingers tapping against the chair were signaling impatience with life itself. One more fancy—she contemplated leaving more than the park bench. When I left the park, I passed close by her. A small transistor radio lay in her lap and a program was playing Beethoven's Symphony No. 6. She had only been marking the music's rhythm."

A series of clanks and measured thumps echoed in the stone hall outside the gallery, and in this pseudo-medieval setting, one might believe an armored knight approached. Post leaned back in his chair, his countenance radiating a cheerful expectation as he looked toward a closed arras of an archway near the fireplace. The clang of metal had paused on the other side of this curtain, and a metal rod, not unlike the barrel of a rifle, had poked through the drapery. It seemed aimed at us and then sharply twisted to one side to sweep back the heavy hanging and reveal the noted book reviewer, Pickett Sneat.

I, B. Smith, with foreknowledge of the man's condition, was still shocked by the extent of the paralysis that immobilized him from the waist down. His torso and legs were encased in a framework of steel ribbing. He advanced slowly with the help of heavy crutches, the hinges and latches of the metal harness clicking off his advance like some antique counter as his powerful torso dragged his immobilized lower limbs. A grin was fixed to his face as if he were determined to make the best of the disaster that had befallen him, though as he got closer, it was clear the Herculean effort had washed his expression of any merriment and the residue resembled a grimace. The freckles across his snub nose, the reddish hair slightly touched by gray, and the absence of several front teeth gave him the near-comic mien of a man-sized doll.

"There you are, dear fellow," Leo Post greeted him.

"Have you confessed?" Sneat's husky voice asked. "Have you confessed?"

"Now, now—none of that," Post soothed him. "Here, let me help you." He teeter-tottered the critic toward a chair, as if the man were a heavy wardrobe to be rocked this way and that toward the table and a chair where Post reached down and loosened several wing nuts on the man's brace and then guided and folded him into the chair. Sneat's weight, combined with that of the apparatus, was more than Post could completely support, and the book reviewer finally fell into the chair with a resounding jangle and rapid bouncing.

"Oof," he exclaimed. The plucky grin remained unchanged. The braces and intricate framework that held him together were fastened over his clothes that had numerous stains and encrusted droppings of food and drink, suggesting the pants and suit coat were rarely removed. "What's he told you?" The rasp of his voice filled the huge chamber. The voice was not unpleasant but aggressive. "He's told you how we flattered Kimball Lyon on his poetry in order to save the world from his paranoia. Ha-ha—what nonsense. But he believed it. He believed it—Mr. Goody-Good." He choked on his laughter.

"Now, now, dear Pickett," Post said gently.

"What nonsense. Nonsense," he shouted into Post's face. "I was only currying favor with Lyon because I had applied for a Lyon Foundation Grant. That's why I had done that jelly-jam review of *Sunspots*. And by the way, Leo, that grape jelly we last got was rather thin. Not too much flavor."

"I'll make a note to tell Taylor," Post answered.

"But doesn't everyone do that?" the critic continued. "Put down a little sweetening on the path to success. But he—that one," he raised one of his crutches to point at Post, "refuses to believe it. He refuses to believe the whole thing is fixed. I even made an amusing essay out of it. You'll find it in *The Fieldstone Sensibility*. He insists on believing that crap about keeping Lyon's madness under control. Fool! Fool!" he shouted, his face becoming so red the freckles entirely disappeared.

"Now then, old friend," Leo Post said amiably, "we've been over that a dozen times before."

"But I got him. Didn't I, Mr. Goody-Good? I got you, didn't I?" He nearly choked on his emotion, and the grin had become a smirk. Post looked uncomfortable for a moment, unbuttoning and buttoning his double-breasted blazer. "My career would have been stopped dead if Leo the Good's article had been published." He had sensed our next question before it was asked. "I had to give him some rationale for my blatant dishonesty, had to convince him that there was some reason for praising Lyon's poetry other than to advance my career. I was desperate. So I invented this idea of quelling Lyon's madness by praising his artistic pretensions. And the fool believed me!" he bellowed. The metal carapace that enclosed him seemed about to fly apart.

"Well, of course, I believed you, old fellow," Post replied easily. "And I shall forever be grateful to you, too, for it was due to you that I met the great love of my life—my dear mully Molly. You will always have my gratitude for that, Pickett."

"Gratitude," the book reviewer nearly spit. Although he was immobilized, he seemed ready to leap from the chair to throttle his companion. But he took a deep, ragged breath. "Well, then, are you going to confess to this official or shall I?"

The challenge seemed to shake Leo Post. He had placed his hands to his face, collected himself and tugged at his shirt cuffs. He turned toward us.

"What he wants me to tell you is this," the author-politician said evenly. "I am raising objections to the new access grid of the Self-Propelled Expressway not because of any philosophical belief, nor any claim for ecology or misuse of public funds. I hope to defeat this proposal because the father whom I never knew was shot to death in his suite of the Chelsea Hotel, and his name was Emil Nalbandian. The murder weapon was never found—a .38 caliber Smith & Wesson revolver. After all these years it is still secreted in a spot in room 226 and still bears the fingerprints of my mother, the late and beloved Olivia Leek."

A Little Later

"It could be said that I was an accessory to my father's murder," Post remarked as we paced the parapet overlooking the river's mid-channel. Pickett Sneat had fallen into a stupor at the table, eyes half-closed and mouth rouged with the purplish stains of grape jelly. I, B. Smith, trained in logic, reasoned the weight of his harness made frequent naps necessary.

"It shall be a fine day," the author continued. "The mist is lifting, and Aurora waits to offer her dowry." The author paused and leaned against a merlon, his gaze upon the east shore of the river. It resembled a park, and the outline of a mansion was visible at the end of an orderly grove of oaks. He nodded his head toward the picturesque view. "There is the last of the Leek estate. It's been a recreation park for trade unionists for many years. Two aunts raised me there after my mother went west. This island was not part of the original domain that once extended from the Connecticut River to the east bank of the Hudson. My great-great-great-great grandfather, Emanuel, acquired this island in the 1850s, and built this castle as a storehouse for his inventory. He traded in armaments, selling guns and supplies to both sides during the Civil War, and some of his speculations brought the family to the brink of bankruptcy several times. For example, just before Appomattox, he invested the entire family fortune in black powder. But the U.S. government was phasing out the use of black powder in their ordnances—and they also owed grandfather Emanuel a lot of money. Family records, letters, and diaries suggest he may have contemplated suicide. But a grateful nation worked out a deal. If not cash, could not the account be settled with some other kind of goods, perhaps the surplus of goods left from the recent national calamity? So Emanuel Leek received three hundred thousand dollars' worth of used bandages and other surgical dressings, shipped as soon as they had been changed in the military hospitals around the country. Oh, he was ridiculed," Post chuckled as we resumed our stroll, "but he refurbished the Leek fortune with those old bandages, and the profits from selling them have carried the family up to the present day. Every family who had a beloved son or father in the conflict, a kinsman wounded or killed, wanted one of those blood-stained dressings, and grandfather Leek accompanied each with a printed statement describing the nature of the wounds they attended in an artfully ambiguous manner so the grateful recipients could claim they had assuaged a relative's agony. A particularly brisk business was done with men who had never been near a battlefield and even with a few draft dodgers. Thus the pitiful yen of the human to adorn the commonplace toil." He had winked broadly, and the dark expression of his inheritance was clearly witnessed.

"I suppose what I am preparing to say is that my mother was no stranger to violence, nor am I, I'm sorry to confess. In fact, all of the Leek women were experts with firearm and foil. It was part of their discipline and education. Even now, on certain nights when the moon is scarfed by a passing cloud, I sometimes think I can hear the wisp and slap of rapiers at play across the river in that old mansion. They were as tall as the Livingston woman; my mother, for example, stood six feet two inches in her Raymond Duncan sandals and was as handsome as any of the Chapmans. But within that great and majestic beauty there resided a disproportionate vulnerability, a softness of temperament that made her an easy prey for the likes of Emil Nalbandian, my father.

"You can imagine the effect on an impressionable young girl, still poring over Sara Teasdale in classes at Miss Chatte's Academy, of the sophisticated salon orchestrated by Nalbandian at the Hotel Chelsea. He had created a sumptuous Middle Eastern retreat in his suite with hangings of printed silk, overstuffed ottomans and tables of camphor wood. Exotic elixirs were sipped such as the apricot liqueurs his uncle would send down from Highland Falls, and long black Russian cigarettes were smoked, gold-tipped and of a distinctive fragrance. Stuffed grape leaves wherever the eye would light as well as hummus. Ah, the hummus. His acquaintances were equally seductive. Men and women of genius and artistic leanings, discussing the fashionable topics of the day. Has Man Ray lost his eye?—that sort of thing.

"A heady mixture for a young girl coming down the river to the big city. Nalbandian had been a part-time faculty member at Miss Chatte's, hired to teach the young ladies the rudiments of contract bridge—one of the several social skills offered in that curriculum. You can imagine the hearts fluttered by a glance from those dark, lustrous eyes—an inheritance, you can see, and one that I have been very discreet in using. No estimate would be fair to the goose pimples his soulful manner raised on the silky skin of upper-class maidens as he simultaneously raised their bids."

We had come to the corner of the battlement, and Post wedged himself into a corner of the tower's enclosure. Below, our guide from this morning—the man called Taylor—peered through a telescope set up on a tripod.

"Do you see anything, Mr. Taylor?" asked our host.

"Nope."

"Well, keep at it, keep at it," he ordered.

The author resumed our stroll along the parapet, turning to face upriver. On a far hillside, a tiny tractor and harrow slowly shuttled back and forth across the dark brown background of freshly turned earth. "Among my mother's effects are a cube of sandalwood incense, a few ribbons, and other memorabilia too moving to describe. Some notes the young girl had written herself, reminders hid among the envelopes of lavender sachet, to guide her deportment when in the presence of this evil mentor and his friends. One in particular comes to me with heartbreaking resonance. It read, 'When he gives me a jack opener, I must show him my dummy.'" Post had swung around to fix us with his large dark eyes, clearly to register our comprehension. Satisfied, he continued our way.

"However, this gentlest, most innocent of creatures—all six feet two of her—was turned a fury by the most common of causes. Betrayal can spur wild monsters in the most modest stables— hmm," Post paused. "That's rather good—I must remember that phrase. But to be a Leek betrayed is to raise a dragon fully fired, as I know all too well myself." His voice had trembled on a sob, and he nervously smoothed down the material of his blazer and reached out to grasp the stone molding before him as if suddenly blind. He took a deep breath and regained his composure as well as the narrative.

"It must be clear to you that, as I was born five months after my father's murder, I was present at his demise and therefore a post facto if not unwilling accessory to the crime. It always grieved my mother that the young woman who held that very poor diamond suit had held it across from my father, and therefore within the scope of my mother's aim. She was the daughter of a trader in municipal bonds and could not be left alive.

"My mother gave me the name Banal, a partial anagram of Nalbandian as your clever machines have already, no doubt, worked out. She affectionately called me her 'little bird' and Leonard was also her choice, though my nature could never be described as hawkish. Leonard or Lenny Banal became a nom de plume for those works that would probably have appealed to my progenitor's crude tastes but which, ironically, have supported me in a style that, while not up to Leek standards, is not altogether lacking in some grace. The world of more serious literature, the arena of public life, knows me as Leo Post—the name taken from my posthumous birth. The date of my birth: *Who's Who* puts it on July 4th, a pseudo-patriotic gesture for which I have no explanation, for it is actually 21 July that gave me Leo. As you may know, the sun enters the fifth sign of the zodiac on that date—the constellation of Leo. And there you have it," he said abruptly, "and to all this I attest."

The catwalk had terminated in one of the two towers that overlooked the small lagoon at the entrance. The west bank, yet shawled by mist and thick with underbrush and scrub timber, was also awash with the sound of traffic on the Expressway like the hiss of a sea falling upon an obscure shore. The pop-popping of a small outboard engine shattered the serenity. A small boat approached from upriver. Three figures were in the boat, and it suddenly turned toward Pijon Island. Leo Post motioned to get down, and we crouched behind the tower's outer wall. He peered through a small opening. Voices could be made out above the racket of the outboard.

"Snoopy fishermen," Post whispered. "The duck hunters are the worst. If they have a bad day, they empty their guns on the castle."

He held a finger to his lips. The boat was very near, the sounds of its ragged combustion beating the air as it rounded the small point and neared the lagoon. The engine was throttled down, then stopped. It became abnormally quiet; the voices in the small boat stimulated our hearing. Post became tense, alert. He carefully raised himself slightly to peer over the parapet. Despite the resonance of the water, the actual words of the men in the boat could not be distinguished but only teased our understanding. They carried a small portable radio tuned to a morning newscast, and its clamor further complicated comprehension. One of the fishermen said something to cause uproarious laughter in the others. Post turned pink in the face. "Intolerable," he muttered. "Intolerable."

He got to his knees, cupped his hands around his mouth, and began to bark in an excellent imitation of a very large dog, possibly a Doberman pinscher or a German shepherd. His own artistry was magnified by the reverberations of the castle's stone walls, so it could be believed that several fierce animals were about to be unchained. His performance was emulated by howls and ululations from within the castle, which, though no match to his authentic renderings, added to the temper of the concert. The husky baritone of Pickett Sneat could be identified giving it his all, taking the role of a Great Dane.

The ruse worked. The outboard engine was hastily started up, and the boat and its occupants, one of them wearing a bright yellow cap, continued downriver to disappear around a small peninsula just below. Post observed their leave-taking with an amused expression, almost disdainful as he stood and dusted off the knees of his gray flannels. But the wild lustrations of the bogus Great Dane continued, out of control, until the profundo timbre was abruptly slapped into a series of lap-dog yelps and then silenced.

"Poor Pickett," Post sighed. "He means to be of help, but he gets so worked up. Happily, Lucy can calm him, and it is almost time for his morning therapy." Post dimpled in that manner reminiscent of that beguiling manner familiar to the late governor's press conferences as he faced down obnoxious journalists. "You must admit," he continued amiably, "that Mr. Taylor and I compose an excellent pack of watchdogs to guard this modest Tartarus."

STILL LATER

I, B. Smith, investigating in the best interests of all, was left to explore the rest of the castle. Our host, satisfied we would not abandon his generosity, had excused himself and promised to meet again for lunch. He had business to attend.

The circular stairway within the corner tower led down to a large room, similar to the one in which we had breakfasted. But here the casement windows looked down on the courtyard and the boat landing. This area was a kind of portrait gallery, the interior wall completely covered by large oil paintings, frame to frame, from eye level all the way up to the dim altitude of the vaulted ceiling. We were in a museum. Stuffed animals and the preserved bodies of birds of unfamiliar species were displayed in glass cases or mounted in full-scale dioramas and seemed ready to pounce or take flight.

The costumes in the portraits roughly paralleled the loose chronological order of their hanging: several centuries of fashion in a counterclockwise parade around the room's walls, excepting the sides of windows. Men in the stiff-necked clothes of the seventeenth century accompanied women in brocaded gowns, and these couples were followed by others encased in the impervious breastplates of Puritan times. From floor to ceiling, the figures of the Leek dynasty silently reckoned the motes sliding down the slant of filtered light with a dusty regard and shared aloofness.

Farther along the wall, the unmistakable brush of Stuart could be detected in the portrait of General Benjamin Leek, aide-de-camp to Washington and the hero of Shokmeko. Next, a painting clearly of the Hudson River school depicted a formal family picnic at water's edge, the silhouette of the Catskills ominously rising in the background. A father, mother, and two children relaxed in the false security of a gazebo seemingly about to be overwhelmed by vegetation and bad weather. We noted the painter had included in the background the very island we stood upon, and the castle's walls were reflected in the romantic swirl of waters and cloud effects. Two of the four towers were incomplete, and an outside wall was represented by a stair-like diagonal, suggesting the family portrait had been commissioned during the landmark's construction.

However, the artist—yet to be authenticated as Frederic Church—may have devastated the place pictorially to satisfy a romantic taste for ruins. Tiny sheep had also been set loose within the castle's grounds and around its lagoon.

The work of an unknown primitive presented another family portrait, dated 1869. A stiff assemblage of children played with a spotted hound in a severe garden. The river and the completed castle were miniaturized in the background, and a boy—perhaps a grandfather or great uncle of Leo Post's—held up a cork-stoppered popgun for inspection.

Indeed, weaponry was as much a part of the costumes as were the ruffs and waistcoats. Richly inlaid muskets, silver-handled pistols, the gleam of a broadsword, flash of a saber: each implement marked the time of the portrait on down to the handsome twelvegauge shotgun held by Captain Ira Leek, the legendary wing shot. The gun was a full choke made by Gastinne Renette of Paris and presented to Captain Leek by Annie Oakley after their famous pigeon shoot in Gloucester, N.J., on July 30, 1888. The quality of light that struck the hundreds of grassed pigeons scattered around the competitors' feet is reminiscent of Thomas Eakins's *Max Schmitt in a Single Scull.*

This painting of the famous pigeon shoot was the last that could be credited to a well-known artist, for the rest of the portraits were the work of those promiscuous society painters who moved from one commission to another without a single original conception. The height of the Leek women seemed to be the easy target of these painters as they had been posed beside polo ponies, tall French windows, or within the colonnades of an ancient temple—crane-like creatures just settled to ground. Perhaps it is one of the maiden aunts who raised the young Leo Post who stands calmly beside a giant yucca. In several, the bluish burr of a flowering leek, the family mark, had been incorporated.

The place in this gallery where there might have been a portrait of Leo Post's mother—perhaps done by a smart stylist of the 1930s—was taken up by the thick, somewhat musty skin of a polar bear. Over the fireplace hung a portrait that compensated for this curious omission. Molly Lyon Post. The late Governor's daughter and wife of the subject of this investigation had been posed in a surrealistic garden by the artist, who is still alive and therefore unnamed. The mindless dabbles of his recent years are a collage of holy families in which the face of Mary closely resembles the face before us in this portrait.

The woman stands in a courtyard of infinite perspective, strewn with broken columns, fragments of statues, a wilted bouquet, a partially peeled orange. Her green velvet gown is simply cut, leaving arms and shoulders bare, and the string straps dent the flesh of the plump, rather broad shoulders deliciously.

The painter, even in the restraints of his meager talent, reproduced the haunting glamor of that face—so often the subject of

Sunday supplements. The wide mouth about to produce a toothy smile, the long straight nose with its round tip, the high cheekbones on either side. The heavy mane of reddish blond hair fell about her bare shoulders. But it was the eyes that pushed the artist to his outer limits.

Large and lynx-like, they stared from the canvas like those of a wild animal startled. Luminous, they looked out from the canvas and almost appeared to follow this observer from side to side as I, B. Smith, sought different perspectives. They were alive with a sheen produced by tears or madness and gave the image a disturbing vivacity. In the cave of an immense hearth below the painting crouched the preserved specimen of a white panther, faced turned in a silent snarl.

This portrait supplements our file reviewed before this investigation began. Following the usual thin folders containing accounts of childhood and education, subsequent material abruptly bulged the folders coincidentally with the time of her introduction to Leo Post. Clippings and reports of the couple's courtship appeased a hungry readership as the media followed them to dog races, garden shows, the opening of new ramps onto her father's Expressway, and political rallies—and always just in the near background would be Leo Post. His hand would often be on her elbow, tender and tentative as the smile on his face was assured. Her eyes, in all these pictures, would frankly address the camera, and her expression was not the pensive regard in the portrait before us but a glance caught in mid-flight of a joy that had tripped the camera's shutter by its very essence. The insertion detailing the couple's elopement was as brief as it was anticlimactic.

Additional folders held the details of the woman's mercurial career as a racing driver, and more than one pedant exercised his imagination in coupling her passion for the sport with her father's historical place in express-highway construction. Pictures from this period show her in trim coveralls, negligently holding a helmet among glistening trophies—the remarkable eyes ringed by grime and grease like those of a raccoon, which exaggerated their luminosity. Later, she appeared on the cover of *Sports Illustrated* when she was named manager of a professional basketball team, the Worcester Pelts.

Another file folder documented her scholarly pursuits: her appointment to the Soyer Chair of Culinary Science, her different papers presented on physical probabilities, and the archeological team she led to Tell el-Amarna. Finally, one sees a pink slip stapled to a manila envelope denoting the subject was deceased. Its contents described the circumstances of her death behind the wheel of her Moroni Special when it crashed into a mausoleum in Woodlawn Cemetery in Elmira, New York, on the last leg of the Mark Twain 500. She had been far in the lead.

I, B. Smith, leaving the gallery by way of a vestibule to the left of the fireplace, felt the eyes of the portrait follow my exit. The air outside on the balcony was no longer damp, for the sun had now fully risen above the eastern shore of the river, but its brilliance also revealed the sad state of the castle's condition. Walls heaved, the lintels of doorways were cracked, and great blocks of stone lay about the foundation like the torsos of warriors who had failed to scale the battlements.

Sparrows and starlings fluttered about the vines offering their morning lyrical tributes. A cock crowed on the far bank, where lines of laundry already hung like the signals of some fleet either at anchor or trapped in a sargasso. The fragrance of wild honeysuckle sweetened the morning air. The continuous hum of traffic on the Lyon Expressway pulled the landscape together as it put the whole scene within the parentheses of its steel construction.

The funnel and bridge of a tanker going downriver heaved into sight to glide across the castle's parapet, its lower decks and hull obscured. I, B. Smith, remembering Post's earlier covertness, stepped into an alcove and out of sight as a seaman on the ship, toothpick fixed in the corner of his mouth, leaned against the railing to survey the island and the castle casually. It was only one of many landmarks on the trip downstream. The black taxi on its paddle-wheel raft bobbed and nudged at its mooring in the inner lagoon, unseen by the sailor digesting his breakfast.

The wake of the tanker thundered against the castle's outer walls, sending tremors through the castle and shaking loose some mortar from around a gargoyle in the far corner. The sounds of an old Woody Guthrie ballad accompanied the boat's passage, and the song from a radio on board could be heard long after the vessel's superstructure had disappeared downriver. Leek's Island gradually resumed its mid-morning repose.

Doors off the canopied walk led to other chambers, perhaps sleeping quarters. The tall figure of the man called Taylor appeared and reappeared as he passed through a distant colonnade, his steps neatly measured as if he were stalking wild game in a grove of saplings. He disappeared into the corner tower.

I, B. Smith, followed him, passing through a heavy door thickly studded and fastened with large ringbolts. Sounds of muffled voices, garbled speech, and exhortations could be discerned but not understood. Nor did the occupants hear our knocking, or else they ignored our official herald. The bolt slipped easily and the heavy door swung open on its iron pinions. Pickett Sneat sat in a wheelchair of steel tubing pulled up beside a table piled with examples of antique recording equipment. Reels of magnetic tape had come unwound to spill like the gray festoons of a funeral cortege. The critic looked up as we entered with the expression of Puck caught midst some prank. It had been one of these tapes that had been heard through the door.

TWENTY THOUSAND VOLTS WILL COOK
MY SHIT! ... ZAP-BANG! ... GODDAMN!!
EAT OF ME SOCIETY—
IT'S ALL FREE
AND SO IS ME—AND SO IS ME—

He flicked off the tape deck, his mouth set in a jack-o'-lantern grin and a crafty glint in his eyes. A curtained alcove was to the right, apparently a bed within, and an electric heater glowed in a fireplace to the left. As we approached the table in the center of the room, a scurrying sound to our rear caught our attention, and the white heel of a boot was glimpsed just as the heavy door closed.

"That's not his best work," the book reviewer informed us. "No. 965122. A great talent. Raw talent, of course, but authentic. He had been found guilty of the murder and dismemberment of nine young women in Versailles, Indiana. But your inquiry concerns more mundane intricacies of the human drama." He shut off the tape deck. "Yes, the tyranny of Kimball Lyon." He whirled the contraption that carried him to the center of the floor, abruptly stopping for emphasis.

"Were it not for the great Lyon fortune, Kimball Lyon would have been committed. Instead, he went into politics and became governor. He would have become president but for his untimely end. Beware the politician with a pretension for art—he'll build a mausoleum of your bones." His voice rose out of control, and the warning was accompanied by whistlings through the gaps of his teeth. His body seemed to inflate and press against the cage that encased it as if to test its very rivets and clasps.

"You don't know," he continued, the deep baritone suddenly diminished as if he were talking through a severe congestion. "The Perpetual Parking Plaza, the Self-Propelled Expressway—they were just two of his responses to his fear and his distrust of big cities. Lyon's answer to urban problems was to pave them over. The silence that comes with concrete appealed to him.

"You remember the uproar when he restored the death penalty? You remember all of those commissions he named to study the question? All of those distinguished scholars who agreed to serve on the governor's review of the efficacy of the death penalty, all those philosophers wheeled into contemplating the morality of the death penalty: all those penologists, sociologists, morticians, criminologists, religious leaders, and playground superintendents— DO YOU REMEMBER? DOES ANYONE REMEMBER?" His bellow startled pigeons that had been roosting along one of the exposed beams of the room's high ceiling. They flared and flustered, quieting and re-landing as the book reviewer's voice resumed its cultured tone.

"None of that meant anything. Nothing. Those tons of reports, miles of opinions and judgments—they all meant nothing. They didn't matter, because Kimball Lyon had already decided to restore the death penalty. And why? Why do you suppose?" Sneat's face bunched up as if he were about to cry, and he slumped in his chair with the clamor of a stack of arms collapsing on the stone floor. His voice became calm, even. "Because he was a lover of poetry.

"Yes, yes. I can see by your expression that you think me quite mad. Perhaps I am mad but you must believe what I say. You are here, after all, to make this record, not judge its contents. I confess to be as much a part of this conspiracy as anyone. Mea-mea. Culpa-culpa. I was not mad when Governor Lyon grabbed the back of my wheelchair at the Pegasus Society, nor did it surprise me when I learned that one of his blind trusts funded the society. Nor was I mad when he trundled me into an anteroom during Lester Appledom's reading of his dreary ode to Henry Kissinger. You see," the critic paused to grip the wheels of his apparatus. His expression was both winning and coy. "I'm not always responsible for the direction I take. In any event, when he had pushed me into the next room, 'Listen, Bud,' he began, using a form of that nominative that was to become famous in his tenure. 'Lo-bud—Lo-bud—Lo-BUDDY'." Again, the metal harness creaked and snapped as his voice swelled uncontrollably. After several ragged breaths, he regained his composure and the freckles across his nose slowly reappeared. "Governor Lyon, the poet, had a theory. If the best work of men like Cervantes, Dante, Raleigh, and Pound was done within prison walls, what ultimate brilliance could be produced by the application of the death sentence? A staggering concept, you must agree. You've just heard an example of what that theory stimulated." He pointed to the tape deck. "No. 965122. Boy, did he sizzle and pop!"

He had removed the spool from the machine, placed it to one side, and clumsily picked up another to peer at its label. It was clear to I, B. Smith, observer and witness, that the machinery was dated, but no explanation was to be determined for this curiosity. Meanwhile, he had passed over the new tape spool, several yards of magnetic ribbon coming undone, and sorted through the pile at his elbow for another choice. "I'm trying to find one of the early ones for you," he said, "before they became mannered and burdened with recycled imagery. It is a sonnet, a breakthrough for the project—yes, I will say our project—done by a man who had clubbed his wife and children to death one Thanksgiving morn.

"So, *Songs from Sing Sing,* as the anthology was to be called, had its birthing, but that was to happen later," he went on. "That evening at the Pegasus Society, I thought I was only humoring one of those rich nuts that hang around the arts with the flies of their purses open. Oh yes, Kimball Lyon had already served on different commissions by the opposition party—one of those misguided gestures toward fair play, when there is no fair play. His own party never gave him a letterhead. They knew better, but now he had both his nomination for governor and a book of poetry. And he had pushed me into the next room—you get the picture?"

An excursion boat, playing on its PA system a merry melody, passed the island going upriver. The clear morning air accentuated the laughter and cries of passengers, but Sneat had continued talking, uncaring that his words were momentarily lost in the revel slipping by. Gradually, the latter faded and—"I was on wheels, after all, so he could push me around." The critic enjoyed his own wit sensibly. "Oh, I agreed. What harm could come of it since the death penalty had been long abolished? I could not guess that the people would support him dusting off the electric chair. Few of them read poetry. Before we parted that fateful afternoon, Lyon pressed on me his small volume *Sunspots.* Not privately printed but by Faller, Stubbs, and McAdoo. Of course, one of Lyon's interests owned the firm. And the selection of the *Schoharie Review* to print my puff piece seemed perfect. Nobody read that journal, and I must credit my cleverness just a bit in that my review was not all that favorable. I took my own advice as outlined in *The Craft of*

Artful Reviewing to cite one or two unimportant flaws in a work for stern admonishment before slathering the rest with excessive praise. Please pass the mayonnaise."

But there was no such condiment on the table, and the critic looked amusedly upon our frustration. He waved away our search and continued.

"Of course, Post saw my review. He reads all kinds of drivel in the cause of popular culture. His own review was even more dishonest because he believed my sentiments. What a fool! Imagine the damage righteous, honest idiots like Leo Post can do to the natural, dishonest order of things. And to top it off, Post's review meant more than mine, so he got the cushy job, and I was left lecturing the old cunts at the Pegasus Society. GODDAMN HIM!" The force of his curse sprung a gear in his braces, and his right leg snapped out straight and locked in that position. The man began to weep, and large tears ran down his boyish face and around his purpling mouth.

"He's always had an easy time of it," he said piteously. "His background. His knowledge of wines and those quaint resorts that bar me by their poor accessibility for cripples like me. Because he can walk. HE CAN WALK. I, not Leo Post, deserved that appointment. It's a given of artful reviewing to be nice to those who deserve good reviews. The handicapped of all persuasions, people married to insensitive mates, those who have worked at lunch counters, whose fathers toiled on assembly lines and mothers made fireworks, potential suicides, and drunks of various capacities. Surely, I have omitted some. Oh yes, all those in these so-called writing programs who guide the illiterate into deeper incoherence—one must be generous to them, and I always honored the principle. They got rave reviews from me," he whined through tears. "But when my turn came to be rewarded—nothing." The tears oozed through his fingers as he wiped his eye.

Sneat pushed himself around the end of the table, his right leg stiffly out like a guidon. He messed through the debris as he continued. "You know the rest. After Lyon was elected governor, he re-introduced the death penalty as a measure to protect society, withholding his real motive, which was to spur poetic creativity. That idea would have been rejected outright by the public, most of them poorly educated and ignorant of the finer things. Another demonstration of how one lacking encourages another. Immediately, I applied to the Lyon Foundation for a grant to study the effects of a death penalty upon the creative faculties of a condemned criminal. Of course, I cited the examples Cervantes, Raleigh, Dante, and Ezra Pound. Moreover, in my proposal, I also advanced that Thoreau could have been made infinitely more profound had he been condemned to death rather than those dinky few days he spent in the town lockup for not paying his taxes. Mind you, I did not definitely accuse Henry Thoreau of dilettantism, but the implication was there to read between the lines. Ah, here we are," he said, holding up another tape spool. He swept aside the clutter around the tape deck and pulled close to the machine.

"I confess to promoting the governor's state murders, but my infamy is nothing compared to Post's. Do you think that old story about his mother—Olivia Leek shooting to death her paramour in the Hotel Chelsea—is all he has to hide? Oh, I could tell you such a story! Why do you think we have been exiled to this foul island? And it was I who bagged him, put it to him, trapped him." He began to rock back and forth in his harness. His mouth twisted to one side, and he snorted and whippled. He had difficulty fitting the spool on the machine's spindle, so shaken was he by his repressed ire. "I promise you a full confession by Post before you leave. But first, I want you to hear this—the work of No. 290063. The guy finished off his father with a croquet mallet, and I got the governor to stay his execution twice because the poor fellow was having a hellish time with the final couplet." He leaned over the table to thread the tape through the different heads and onto the take-up reel. "Now listen to this," he said, and turned on the switch.

A crackling of electrical current accompanied the man's bugging eyes. His mouth was frozen in the grimace of a grin and his hand seemed stuck to the switch. The red hair stuck out from his head like copper wires, and miniature lightning bolts of bright blue played about the steel harness that held him upright, and the whole rig throbbed with the hum of high voltage. He resembled one of those elaborate machines seen at country fairs to entertain the local peasantry with a demonstration of electrical possibilities. Beneath the table and in the ganglia of wires, I, B. Smith, ignorant of such matters, endeavored to disconnect the apparatus. The sounds from Sneat's mouth became poignant in their resemblance to electronic music of a Modernist mode. Then, just as suddenly, it stopped, and the coils of the heater in the hearth darkened. The book reviewer blew a fuse.

A Moment Later

"**P**oor fellow, poor fellow," Leo Post crooned. He laid a cool cloth upon Sneat's brow. "He tries to play the caitiff, but he's too good for the part." The author took the book reviewer's hand in his own, patted it, and stroked the knuckles. Taylor and the black cook had helped us lift Sneat onto a four-poster bed in the alcove.

"I've warned him about using this antiquated equipment. His mania for authenticity, playing the contemporaneous of the device with the work recorded so as to sustain the purity of the moment, has caused similar problems before. But it's only a slight shock, nothing to worry about. It may have only done his digestive system some good. Pep him up—he's been depressed lately. Shall we go down to lunch? What little surprise do you have for us today, Lucy?" he asked the cook, who turned away silently. The man called Taylor followed her out the door, the wide cartridge belt and low-slung holster creaking.

We were about to follow them through the door when a motion from the bed caught our eye. The pale hand of Pickett Sneat beckoned. His eyes drew us to the bedside and then glanced apprehensively about the chamber. "Come back later," he hissed. "I shall tell you everything. Come back later." Then he fell abruptly into a coma. Feigned or real? It was impossible to ascertain.

In the hall, voices echoed hollowly and a heavy utensil clattered to the stone floor. An anguished cry. We took the opportunity to return to the portrait gallery—a half-remembered detail had led us there. A small photograph similar in size to those sometimes found on top of a grand piano in fashionable homes had nudged our curiosity. In it, a small child sat nestled in the niche of a heavily draped column, and there was no mistaking the broad, high brow and the sober appraisal in the dark eyes. A very young Leo Post.

But closer inspection disclosed the toes of a pair of shoes poking out beneath the drapery, and then it became clear. The child, Leo Post, was sitting in someone's lap—a person who did not wish to appear in the picture, not be identified, but yet wanted to hold the child on her lap. We use the feminine, for the shoes nosing from beneath the throw were clearly identified by the intricate tooling of the toe as from the Parisian collection of Emile Hausseur, circa 1926-32—a favorite of women of a certain class. What could have been a tablecloth had been thrown over this person, and the small lad, one leg folded under the other, had been placed on her lap. What appeared to be a clump of vegetation behind them was, on close inspection, revealed to be a bunch of scallions that the woman was holding out from the enveloping cloth.

Noon...

"We don't stand on ceremony here," Post told us. "Lunch is always buffet style." He stood to one side to allow us to make our own peanut butter sandwich. "No formalities to clot the free flow of collegial sensibilities," he said, chewing and swallowing as he observed a cloud of fruit flies swirling above a bowl of blackened bananas.

"Try a little of the grape jelly with the nut spread," he advised. "Lucy introduced the variation to us. A real gem, is she not? A lignite in the rough. Naturally it's old Pick once again whom we have to thank for her presence. He is almost always found at the bottom of our well of happiness. He had simply placed a classified ad in a journal, and Lucy appeared one day. We did not know how much we needed her until she joined us. She looks after us, but it is not the first time that Pick has introduced me to a woman who became important in my life.

"But more of that later," he said, facing us across the large table.

He had mashed one of the bananas into his sandwich, and brushed crumbs from the front of his blazer. "Now then, I want you to listen to something. Something extraordinary." He cranked up an odd-looking device as he spoke, then picked up a black cylinder and held it out for our inspection. We recognized the apparatus as an early recording device worthy of museum classification.

"Yes, yes," he nodded, accrediting our recognition. "A rare recording made by the Wizard of Menlo Park himself on May 15, 1906. An historic occasion." He clipped the Bakelite tube over the machine's spindle. "We know the specific date of this recording from the notes made by John Burroughs, a friend of Edison's, you will remember, who was present at the recording." He stood up and raised an emphatic finger. "In fact this recording was made near here, around Kingston. Both men enjoyed hiking in the Catskills, cooking over open fires—roughing it—that sort of thing."

Post had bent down and released the brake on the machine's motor, then set the needle in the outer groove of the cylinder. Only an innominate rasp came from the petunia-shaped speaker, and the condition of the sound seemed to deteriorate as it played out. The arm of the player moved from right to left. As Post observed us steadily, a speculative light in his dark eyes grew to an appreciative glint as he saw us realize that what we listened to was not the residential imperfections of an ancient methodology—their volume increasing with every revolution of the cylinder—but the precise renditions of strange cries.

"*KEE-KEEK KEE-KEEK KEE-KEEK*"

"*Columbia migratoria*," Post shouted over the ugly noise. "There must have been hundreds of thousands of them passing over that day. Burroughs reported the incident—his notes can be found in Elton Eaton. The flock was apparently a mile wide. Edison had been visiting his friend that day and luckily had lugged up his ingenious device to record some of Burroughs' nature poetry— all lost to us sadly, but not this. Not this!" Post's manner became highly excited, a glimpse of madness in his countenance.

"KEE-KEEK...KEE-KEEK...KEE-KEEK."
The cries of the long-dead birds smothered the author's words.
The flock had grown near, perhaps at the point of their immortalization on a plastic surface as the inventor and the naturalist stood by. Post raised his voice and continued.
"Lucky for us that we have this recording. The only known recording of the passenger pigeon in flight. Unlike any sound you'd expect, isn't it?" he screamed. "Not the coo-cooing of the ordinary pigeon or the inquisitive note of the mourning dove." The swarm must have been just overhead at the point of recording.
"KEEEEK-KEEEEK...KEEEK-KEEK...KEE-KEEEK"
"You see," he continued, his expression reddened, and his throat strained against his open collar as he made himself heard, "sometimes there would be millions of them flying together at once, and if they coo-cooed—" He had strained his larynx and fell to coughing. The cries continued so the chamber became a haunted aviary. The noise abated, and Post paused to allow it to lessen more. The flight had passed over.
"You see," he resumed, "there were so many of them, if they communicated in the usual pigeon coo-cooing they would not have heard each other—they would have lost their way. So they had developed this peculiar screeching. Unique. In their quieter moments, mating, for example," he looked away as he spoke, "they sounded like other pigeons." He wiped what could have been a tear from one eye.
"Kee-kee...kee-keek...kee-k..."
"There they go," Post said, looking down at the revolving cylinder. The needle had run its course, all the way to the left in the grooves. "Flying away, fly away, fly away forever." As if on cue, possibly rehearsed, the machine produced a final, distant peep, and the author lifted its arm with a smooth flip of one finger. "A tumultuous concert, wouldn't you say? And only eight years from extinction. Yes, just eight. Indeed, the following year, Burroughs reported only a thousand birds flew over his retreat, and the next year—only a few dozen."

He waved to the fireplace, one arm motioning us to follow, and sat down in one of the massive armchairs before the hearth. A stack of sodden wood smoked idly in the yawning hearth. The author carefully crossed his legs, adjusting the gray flannel slacks just so as we took the opposing chair. His arms fitted to those of the chair, hands upturned and relaxed. One white shoe rocked idly in the air. I, B. Smith, a duly sworn officer of record, noted the confessional mood of the subject and prepared to manage the interview.

"Let me first give you some material that might seem extraneous to your inquiry, which is to ascertain my motives for objecting to the extension of the Self-Propelled Expressway. You may have forgot that's why you are here." He paused and looked at us mischievously. "But it might be useful if your records had some personal recollections of the Lyon era in New York state politics, some insights and recall not to be found in the other oral histories.

"Let me begin by confirming the rumor as to Governor Lyon's height. Men in public display can often disguise abnormal features of their physique. How many at the time knew of FDR's paralysis, that from the waist down he had as much flexibility as that table top over there? The media at the time—even the newsreels—do not show handicaps as they are known today. Image is all; image is all, my dear fellow. The artful camera angle or the practiced fictions of a press agent can modify perception—not to mention how a forceful personality can make an observer see only what the subject wants to be seen—it crops the picture. So it was with the Governor. The rumor about his height is true—Kimball Lyons was only four feet six inches tall. But one was dazzled by the broad smile, the hearty handshake, and the familiar '*lo, buddy* salutation—every gesture and turn enwrapped in that schoolboy charisma, so even standing next to you the man seemed to be looking down on you. And of course he was.

"Being nearly the same height sitting down as he was standing up, he was usually photographed in a chair, behind a desk, signing documents or conferring with aides. A special podium was constructed for his public appearances—his speeches to the legislature, for example—a clever construction that incorporated a small stepladder. Height was also an important qualification for those men chosen as advisors and department heads—the shorter the better. Many a brilliant advisor was passed over because the expert could look down on the Governor. You may remember his lieutenant governor, Leonard B. Walsh, always in the hospital because of the damage done to his spine, all because he had to squat down whenever they appeared together. So, Kimball Lyon looked as tall as the associates around him, give or take a few inches, when they were photographed together in meetings or appeared in public. I can still hear the hiss of relief some made, the picture opportunity over, as they resumed their normal height in an outside corridor of the capital or within the fragrant aura of the men's room. Of course, the nature of my Leek length made me the exception, but I operated behind the scenes." For a moment the man's cherubic expression became the cunning leer of a satyr.

"Given these circumstances," the author continued casually, "you must imagine my bewilderment when the door of his townhouse on East 74th Street was opened by a lovely replica of Athena—his daughter, Molly. She could rise prettily on her toes to a full seventy-three and one-half inches in order to ace an opponent in tennis, and with no effort at all she could steady herself in a crowded subway train by pressing the palm of one hand against the ceiling of the rocketing car.

"Indeed, the beautifully proportioned dimensions of her person, together with expressive gray-green eyes, enforced the sense of peril she shared with other magnificent creatures put down by a perverse nature with the flaw of their being hidden within their great size. I recognized this aspect of Molly on first sight, that first night when Lyon had summoned me to his mansion. He had seen my review of *Sunspots*. The way she walked struck me immediately as I followed her down a long corridor faced on either side by the bubbling aquariums of her father's rare fish collection. There was a pliancy of the lower torso as she held herself in a queenly fashion, shoulders square and pulled back so it might seem she was deliberately emphasizing her bosom. Not the case, not so. Quite the contrary. The whole posture was meant to effect a defense of a vulnerable spot between her shoulder blades, an imaginary shadow where a leaf had fallen when she had been dipped in the preserving gel of the Lyons' fortune.

"How often I kissed that spot." His eyes rose to the portrait above the mantle. "To catch her *aux abois*, one might say as the position facilitated..." Post's words became muddled by the booming passage of an ocean-going vessel, and its sonorous rumbling obliterated the man's speech. A piece of masonry was shaken loose and plunked into the lagoon. "...or over the turnstiles of the old Liberty Street ferry, long abandoned and a domicile of sparrows," he concluded.

"Your reticence and reserve on hearing these details encourages me. I was testing your objectivity, and what seems to be your high threshold of discretion encourages me to tell you everything." He rose to poke at the smoldering mess in the hearth with an iron tool. The author bent stiffly from the waist, suggesting the effect of the castle's dampness on his joints. "But your mission is not to hear tales of my romance of the Governor's daughter. But one final note about Molly. She had inherited her father's toothiness, enhanced by full lips and the slight slant of eyes as you see in the portrait above, for which, in all probability, my own genetic reference made me an easy mark."

Post had replaced the fire tool in its holder and resumed his chair. "That first meeting, Molly had brought me into their parlor and introduced me to her father. As your records must show, after her mother had been institutionalized, she served as her father's hostess. And just to make one more digression from the straight narrative you have been instructed to acquire, this similarity in our parentage, a mother's abandonment, drew us together as well.

"Kimball Lyon had been standing before the large windows of his mansion that looked down on the park. He turned and advanced, his right hand extended, teeth glowing, and seemed to grow taller with each step. When he reached up to take my hand, that peculiar magic spelled me for it seemed our statures had been reversed, and it was I who looked up at him. I had a moment to study that egg-smooth face, the squinty eyes and full cheeks, to find some mark or crease, a healed crack in the forehead from which the motherless goddess standing next to me may have emerged. "Lo-there ol' buddy," Lyon said, wringing my hand and immediately plunging into the subject of my review of his book. He volunteered some insights that I did not acknowledge nor did I deny them outright. As Pickett had warned me, I was dealing with a madman posing as an artist, but I was aware of Molly following this fencing exercise between her father and me with a luminous intensity.

"It was not until after dinner, served on the roof terrace by three midgets in emerald livery, that he brought up the subject of running for governor. From sorrel soup, through a rather indifferent *flan des îles*, talk had ranged over a large *carte du discours*, not particularly profound; therefore, I was not prepared for the sudden shift when he began to outline his plan to sit in the governor's chair. I had been dazzled by the play of candlelight in the eyes across from me and distracted by the lush sheen of her bare shoulders—even excited, let me confess it, by the thought of the Louis Onze chair pressing its crude conformations into the impeccable nakedness of that back. Did I say she was wearing a backless dress that evening? She knew how to dramatize her best qualities." A racket commenced outside the large windows overlooking the lagoon—an engine had roared to life, and water splashed.

"That's Taylor setting off on the mail run," Post explained. "A fine fellow, and he comes into an interesting part of the story, which you will hear." As the sound of the taxi-ferry pulled away, the author seemed to fall into a reverie and had to be reminded of his situation—that he was being interrogated. "Yes, of course. Lyon told me that the reviews of Pickett Sneat and others had not surprised him with their tumultuous praise. Those guys, I can hear his inflection now, those guys are always looking for something. He knew all about Sneat's careerism, and he planned to reward him for it. A chilling smile had taken his face. He had already instructed the people at the Lyon Foundation to put Pickett on a lifetime grant. But when I, Leo Post," the author paused to smooth and set the lapels of his blazer, "had praised his poems, it had made him question his destiny. Should he forsake the people's service and enter the sequestered cloisters of high art?

"Then he became very serious, leaned toward me in a collegial manner. If he sacrificed his art for the greater good of the people, he asked me, would I join him in this mission in public life by making a similar compromise in my own career? He made it sound like two equals meeting on some sunny field of history. The hooves of mounted ambition stamped impatiently."

Post abruptly rose to stand beneath the heavy mantel. He nervously fingered the brass buttons on the sleeves of his blazer. "It is useless to dissemble before you," he said, after a thoughtful pause. "Not that I'm trying to hide anything from your inspection. It's just my style of narrative, and you have to accept the form with the content; and curiously, I was about to introduce a matter that may allay some of your puzzlement. But I must confess that joining Kimball Lyon on that pinnacle of power was an ascent I fully enjoyed. Intoxicating.

"When *A Year in the Country* won the Pulitzer-Jones Prize, the sides were drawn. I was damned on both sides and further condemned by the book's success, both critical and financial, so that now, a dozen volumes later, the term *one-book author* sticks to me like chewing gum. A meaningless phrase, of course, when one thinks of Cervantes, Chaucer, Whitman, Dante, and so on. But it is a quick identification for the glib and superficial. It originated by Reuben Slate who also had a book out that year, and picked up by that crowd at the Pegasus Society, broadcast by Otto Grubber, the anthologist. Some said that Grubber played Sherman Adams to Slate's Eisenhower, but the parallel is lost if those names mean nothing to you as I see they may not.

"There is nothing so superior than a minor poet, and there are so many of them. They set upon an individual like the furies, if he dares to rise above their knee-high standards. You say politics? The most ordinary essayist, the drabbest reviewer for *Stacks and Bins*, the meanest rhymer and verse tinkerer daily indulges in ploys that make the crassest courthouse hack resemble Thomas Jefferson.

"So after years of enduring the hee-haws and snide witticisms of the literary fraternity out of the blue, Kimball Lyon offered me a chance to slip on a mantle of power. Some beings live in one element and some in another but the trick of survival is to become amphibious and adapt to both. If nothing more, we humans have maintained our supremacy because we are able to breathe in the past as we exhale in the present, but there are some single-lung creatures among us for whom the past is oblivion and immediate respiration is everything. They look like the rest of us, talk and generally walk through the quotidian without a single gesture to betray their difference; yet they are strange to this planet, as if they had been set down on it in the dead of night from outer space. Their rates of propagation are frightful—something in the air perhaps. And they have no tolerance for the native residents."

The sound of a small motorboat rushed Post to one of the casement windows. He edged around the frame, peering through the thick lattice of vines. "Our fishermen friends again," he said softly. "Do you have some cohorts in your investigation, by any chance?" I, B. Smith, eager to complete the assignment, assured him the mission called for a single operative. He had eased the window open, and we expected his imitation of an attack dog, but the boat had passed upstream and out of hearing.

"Well now." Post returned to the fireplace in a jovial manner, holding and rubbing his hands over the smoking pile. "There's no need to repeat the details of Lyon's first campaign. They are fully documented elsewhere. Lyon's smashing defeat of old Governor Hastings came as no surprise. Having been appointed by Hastings to chair the Good Government Committee, Lyon merely turned all the examples of corruption and ineptness discovered against the incumbent. What that venerable patrician had thought to be a gesture of fair play, to bring under the roof of his administration the different elements of influence, only gave Lyon the means to tear down the structure. Basic Machiavelli. Of course, the Civil Liberties Union and League of Women Voters had applauded the appointment, saying Lyon's great wealth would make him incorruptible, and they were the first to desert Hastings in the campaign and to endorse Kimball Lyon when he announced his candidacy. Both organizations received heavy contributions from the Lyon Foundation, and that swayed their backing, but I won't go that far. Perversity of the human spirit is my choice of explanation.

"Then we ran into trouble in the second campaign. Lyon's passion for concrete began to raise doubts in the public mind despite the argument that the Perpetual Parking Plaza was a brilliant defense against terrorists. I will take a modest credit for some of that rhetoric. But as more and more of New York City and more and more of its boroughs were paved over, questions were being asked about the cost of this unique defense. No one could question its efficacy—not a single act of terror had been committed against any of the parking lots—but Governor Lyon was spending public funds as if they were his money. So went the criticism. Editorials fumed that without raising taxes economic chaos would result.

"'How can you sit there,' his opponent asked—of course Lyon had been standing up—'and say you will not raise taxes?' You will remember how Lyon smiled and squinted as if he was sorry to deliver the truth. 'I solemnly swear to the people of this state that I will not raise taxes.' We won by a landslide.

"But we were in trouble once again next month after the dedication of the Zenia B. Lyon Memorial Swimming Pool in Binghamton, New York. It was the tenth such pool to be named after the governor's grandmother. There had been ugly speculations about the money spent on these projects, and this controversy took the discussion into an unhappy turn when Tom Tabheimer, the Olympic diving champion, broke his neck during the dedication ceremonies. An investigation revealed that the pool's

uniform depth was four feet, and that the unfortunate Tabheimer, overcome by his place on the podium, neglected to test
the waters before launching into his famed four somersaults and
a jackknife. In fact, all of the new pools built across the state
were only four feet deep, and a study done by the American
Safety Bureau, a privately funded institution, provided statistics
to show that the great majority of swimming pool fatalities occurred at depths more than four feet. In fact, it was I, using these
statistics, who wrote the legislation for the law that prohibited
any swimming pool, public or private, to be deeper than four
feet. It was sad about young Tabheimer, but his film career—all
agreed—would have been limited by his stammer in any event."

Post stopped his testimony abruptly and placed a finger to his
lips. It was unearthly still. His dark eyes turned toward the curtained arch near the fireplace. He stood and tiptoed toward the
portal and then lunged to whip back the heavy arras. The archway was empty, nor was there any evidence that someone had been
eavesdropping. Leo Post stood with a whippet-like attention, his
large head cocked as if to catch the sound of a retreat. All was well,
and he readjusted the curtain and returned to the large chair by
the fireplace.

"I worked to restore Lyon's credibility with the public after
that unfortunate accident with Tabheimer. Molly and I had just
eloped and were happily collecting specimens of conch in the
Exumas. But one evening a small silvery seaplane landed in the
quiet lagoon of a deserted key where we had anchored our ketch.
The Governor had tracked us down, and he and I conferred on a
coral outcrop. The man's ability to reduce the most complicated
issue to single-cell simplicity was breathtaking. To solve the problem, the Department of Public Works, the agency responsible for
the swimming pools, was moved into the executive branch and
renamed the Committee for Recreation and Transportation, so
it would not be answerable to the Legislature, claiming executive

privilege. A semi-public authority would be established to under-
write the funding, selling tax-free bonds that were bought by
guess-whose banks.

"But Lyon was really concerned about the tax issue. He had
television time waiting for him to say something about taxes.
What could he say, he asked me in that tropical twilight? I remember the call of mockingbirds on that Caribbean atoll and
the faint glimmer of the anchor light of our small boat a hundred
yards away—the answering sparkle through the rigging of Sirius,
millions of light years distant. I thought of my bride, this monster's daughter, waiting for me in the snug cabin of the Galatea.
The man's presence was offensive to me—gratuitous. Why don't
you say, I told him, you have to raise taxes. The simplicity of the
strategy appealed to him, and unbelievably it worked!

"He went on television and said, 'Folks, I was wrong—I have
to raise taxes.' And then he disappeared, dropped out of view.
Actually, he had only stepped off the ladder behind the podium
but the effect, together with his announcement, was astounding.
The electorate bought the magic of it. The remaining fifty-six
minutes purchased on all the major networks remained blank;
viewers stared at the vacated podium with the seal of office
emblazoned on its front. It was a hypnotic moment, the public
mesmerized by the emptiness of the television screens and not
unlike the disappearing acts used by ancient prophets. No one
thereafter dared ask Kimball Lyon where the money was coming
from."

Leo Post paused to kick casually at the branches in the fireplace. He chuckled and then walked to a large lexicon on a stand
in the corner, the heavy book borne on the large, outstretched
wings of a black iron griffin. The author flipped several pages and
finally studied the text through a large magnifying glass.

"I was only curious to review the genesis of the word *wrong*.
Lyon had a singular way of using the word, emphasizing the con-
sonantal diphthong of its northern European dialect origins. I
can hear him now—'I was wraun-ngah.' This dictionary gives

more pages to the definition of right than it does to wrong—I've counted them. What does that tell us—that evil is easier to grasp than good or that justice and virtue are more ambiguous? For example, when someone says, 'Take a right,' you are not being asked to subscribe to moral excellence. So, the confusion is complex, and the simplemindedness of a Kimball Lyon becomes refreshing. He could do no wrong." Post took up his previous pose by the fireplace. "Surely we must side with Carlyle when he said, 'Man's gullibility is not his worst blessing.'"

"LIARY...LIAR...CHEAT AND LIAR...." These shouts came from behind the closed drapery of the archway by the mantel, and like a huge chrysalis bursting apart, the folds of the drapery split to reveal Pickett Sneat enveloped and supported by the material that entangled him. It is safe to say that he had dragged himself without crutches or steel braces noiselessly over the stone floor. He resembled an enormous soft larva precipitously ripped from its pod.

"Now, now, dear fellow," Leo Post said soothingly as he approached the critic. "Lucy," he called out. "Have you a minute, Lucy?"

"LIAR," Sneat continued to yell as his rust-colored bangs bounced against his round forehead. "He has told you lies. CONFESS...CONFESS...CON...Agghrh..." And just as quickly, he disappeared behind the curtain as if plucked from sight by a puppeteer who had just realized his mistake. Considerable commotion ensued behind the scenes; a slender black leg appeared, bent gracefully at the knee, and pulled aside the portière.

Her African origins were handsomely emphasized by the struggling white man she held in her arms, and Lucy stood in the doorway dramatically backlit. "I'll put him back up, boss," she told Post.

"Thank you, Lucy," the author said. Held tightly in the cook's arms, he resembled a demented Raggedy Ann doll as he nuzzled the woman's breasts beneath her tunic. His lifeless legs dangled, and his hands convulsively twitched in concert with the suckling sounds made by his lips.

"Poor Pick," Post said with a look that begged our sympathy. "He's been through a lot, and I'm afraid the strain of it has begun to tell on him."

The book reviewer began to laugh, and his head rolled toward us on the beam of his shoulders. "Prisoners," he said with a softened voice that was more startling than his previous hysterics. "We are all prisoners here. You as well. We are all prisoners. PRI..." He raised his voice but disappeared in mid-syllable, yanked from view by the black Amazon.

An ironic cast had come into Post's dark eyes, reminiscent of his progenitor perhaps when a double finesse was about to be performed. He turned to the windows just as the superstructure of a tanker passed by going upstream toward Albany. He pressed his fingers to the juncture of his brows and nose.

"He is correct," the author said at last. "We are all prisoners of one sort or another, and certainly it is the case here on Pijon Island. Do not try to escape. In the bowels of this old castle is a storehouse of several tons of black powder that Emanuel Leek, my great-great-great grandfather, failed to sell to the U.S. Army. The generals had switched to a more stable explosive. Black powder is risky material, and these long years in storage have not improved its stability. I am the only one who can access this storehouse." An ominous flatness had fallen over his voice. "If any unauthorized attempt is made to leave this island, a special mechanism will be triggered, and the Corps of Engineers will have to make new charts of this part of the river, for Pijon Island will no longer exist."

A MOMENT LATER

Following this melodramatic pronouncement, he conducted us to a small bedchamber in one of the towers with the instruction, almost a warning, that dinner would be served precisely at eight. The temporary imprisonment in this tower permitted a review of what had transpired.

Is Pickett a prisoner on this island or is he, as I, B. Smith, am, to facilitate this investigation, only pretending? What is the position of Lucy—cook, nurse, and mistress? Is she unable to leave? The man called Taylor is apparently trusted by Post to come and go, or he may be held captive by some information about his past, perhaps related to the antique pistol he carries on his hip.

But the key to all these questions is the fact of Leo Post himself on this island in the middle of the Hudson River. Why, at the peak of his fame, did he choose to retire to this mildewed oblivion? Was it grief that drove him here; the sudden, tragic death of his wife stripping him of that old, arrogant certainty, an armor that had been his character and defense? Were there darker reasons, as Pickett Sneat's outbursts suggested?

Two windows illuminated this cell of a chamber; one looked out on the west bank of the river and a very large mobile-home community. The other window looked downstream toward the Kingston-Elmira Access Spur where the mid-afternoon traffic moved over the handsome cement span that perfectly fills the omission made by nature between the Catskills and the foothills of the Berkshires. Contemplating this example of Kimball Lyon's appetite for symmetry, I, B. Smith, an accredited witness, initially failed to notice the floundering figure in mid-channel. The man's kayak had been tossed and turned over by the wake of the tanker that had passed previously, and the dunked sportsman was being carried off by the current. Meantime, reference is urged to Leo Post's file, most particularly excerpts from his acceptance speech of the Pulitzer-Jones.

"...must be room for error. We no longer have time to be wrong, and to survive is to have time for error, as perfection may be an integer of extinction. I'll not surrender the notion that griffins and dragons may have existed and that the human being's cleverness has made him an outlaw. In the isolation of spirit, as if on a laboratory slide, a culture has been grown more virulent than any other—Homo Perfecto. We have become the wild cell in the Earth's corpus, crowding out and destroying the healthy cells around us, killing off the host planet as we suffocate in our own perfect wastes."

Herein, further remarks made before the Association of American Linguists: "...fool ourselves that we can transcend time as the sailor who walks toward the stern of his ship underway may think he remains in one location. It is an illusion, of course, as both he and his ship move from one point to another, no matter where he stands or moves upon it...but there may be a purpose to the old illusion—a simple magic to transcend doom while moving toward that doom."

Another time, the Society of Ceremental Engineers heard him say, "Like the plastic bottles our technology exultantly extrudes, we humans are subject to no return: one more example of the mimetic instinct at work. However, unlike the formula for urethane, our chemical composition constantly changes. We deteriorate; we change our own matter to become different matter. *Subject to No Return while Alterations Are in Progress* is the sign we put out. We are no different, and probably not as successful, as the dinosaur was."

Further survey of the room revealed a chamber with minimal appointments though not uncomfortable. Along the inner wall were several glass-fronted bookcases faced by a dusty and dilapidated chaise lounge, one end of which rested on a stack of heavy volumes. Closer inspection identified one of them to be a rare edition of Wilson's *American Ornithology*, Philadelphia (1810). This preoccupation with birds was also represented by other titles in the bookcase: *Audubon's Birds of America*, London (1838), *Birds of New York*, Elton Eaton (1909), *The Histories of Travail into Virginia Britannia*, and so on.

A preserved heath hen perched on top of the bookcase, one foot poised in mid-air, slender neck and head turned to confront an unknown danger, attentive and with a glass-eyed acumen bestowed by the taxidermist upon the bird that the doomed species never knew in life. But even Audubon, it might be noted from a review of his engravings, put his specimens into positions, attitudes of flight, that were to accommodate the eye more than to realize a natural behavior. Or, to pursue a hypothesis advanced in some of Leo Post's essays, these stuffed carcasses, rigid in their unnatural contortions, were to suggest their contest for survival against mankind had been more equal. Fairer—a past-perfect effort.

The fourth wall of the room was covered by a tapestry of distinctive workmanship depicting a favorite subject of medieval fantasy, the Unicorn in Captivity. However, this weaving differs from other examples of the genre in that among the wildflowers blooming around the hooves of the mythical beast this loom had woven hardy clumps of wild onion, purplish burrs pricking the neutral background of the masterpiece.

Several paperbacked mysteries had been placed thoughtfully on the bedside table, perhaps as anodynes to the ponderous scholarship in the bookcase. Three of the pornographic works were from the pen of Len Banal, and these had makeshift bookmarks inserted in their pages as if to single out the more inflammatory scenes for a drowsy guest unwilling to plow through the obligatory exposition that sought to establish legitimacy for a sordid interlude.

However, the nature of these slapdash insertions drew our interest more than the contrived couplings they marked. In even a casual assembly, these scraps—but some rather large, even full typescript pages folded lengthwise—could compose a small manuscript, though all seemed to be excerpts from different works—a dismembered anthology of sorts.

In the novel titled *Stella's Phallus*, a statement attributed to Cotton Mather had been inserted in a passage describing a fanciful sexual encounter taking place in the foyer of Grant's Tomb. *"Yea, they sat upon one another,"* the Founding Puritan had noted, *"like Bees till a Limb of a tree would seem almost as big as a House* ... [their migration taking them] *far to some undiscovered Satellite, accompanying the Earth at a distance."*

A few pages later, interrupting a series of orgasms experienced by the heroine, a larger piece of manuscript had been inserted. A handwritten note claimed it to be from a publication entitled *The Jesuits' Relations and Allied Documents* (1636).

Among the birds of every variety to be found here, it is to be noted that the pigeons abound in such numbers that this year one man killed 132 at a single shot. They passed continually in flocks so dense, and so near the ground, that sometimes they were struck down with oars. This season they attacked grain fields where they made great havoc ... (And here in what is similar to Post's hand has been written,

Bishop of Quebec excommunicated pigeons in 1632 because of damage done to fields.)

Further into this steamy narrative, at a point where the heroine entertains a motorcycle gang, the reader encounters the typed copy of a poem.

The Wild Fowl
by John Holme

> *Here is such wild fowl nears to use resorts,*
> *I know not how to name you half the sorts.*
> *The pigeons in such numbers fly*
> *That like a cloud they do make dark the sky;*
> *And in such multitudes are sometimes found,*
> *As they cover both trees and ground:*
> *He that advances near with one good shot,*
> *May kill enough to fill both spit and pot.*

A second volume, its title more suggestive than the last, contained a full sheet of paper within its bound pages that had both typed commentary and handwritten notes, from Post.

Audubon a Plagiarist?

Wilson, American Ornithology, *clocked a flock of pigeons several miles wide and forty miles long near Frankfort, Kentucky, in 1800.* Speed est. 60 mph, three birds per sq. yard. Wilson watched the flock flying over for four hours! *He estimated a total of 2, 230,272, 000. (Yes, that's billions!) He figured this flock would daily consume 17,424,000 bushels of mast—acorns, hazelnuts, etc.*

Compare with Audubon writing much later. He says he encountered a flock in 1813, near his house on the Ohio River, while traveling to Louisville. (In Post's hand—*same locale.*) He watched for three hours and came up with an estimate of 1,115,136,000—exactly half of Wilson's number. (SPECULA-TION: Audubon borrowed his "observation" from Wilson but could not believe Wilson's figures or feared his readers and sub-scribers would not accept the Wilson figures so he halved them. So early on, the country's attributes are perverted, and by one of its most hallowed naturalists.)

> KANHI—Mohawk language for long poles used to knock down pigeon nests.
> TE HOKXATON ONTE—Mohawk for, "He has brought down a pigeon."

Dung droppings on the water of lakes and rivers like a shower or a hailstorm. Flocks would leave a wide, milky white, bluish path across the countryside. Pigeon excrement collected for fertilizer. Source of saltpeter for explosives. Dung mixed with molasses was a remedy for migraines and stomachaches. (Possible source of ex-pression, "This stuff tastes like shit.")

> *STOOL PIGEON—Live bird, eyes sewn shut, tied to a wooden stool-like contraption. Operated from a hunting blind. Hunter would jiggle a stick to dislodge the bird from its trapped perch. Flapping wings, rise into the air and re-settle, giving a false idea of security to passing flocks that would then land and be shot.*

Market price around 1800 was twelve cents per dozen. Live pigeons were fed buckwheat and corn to improve flavor. Later, costs would rise to twenty-five dollars per barrel, shipped railway freight. Freight agents would pass the word by their telegraph keys of migrations and nestings to professional netters. Then ship the barrels of processed pigeons to market. Thirty dozen pigeons per barrel. About fifteen hundred barrels could be shipped per day from the nesting site. That counts up to HALF a MILLION birds slaughtered per day.

J.F. Cooper, *The Pioneers, The Chainbearer.* Bumppo disgusted by villagers using small cannons to shoot down the pigeons. Technology raising its big muzzle.

State Legislature, Ohio. Report of 1857. Pigeon needs no protection: there are so many of them.

Ira T. Leek, my ancestor and one of the great wing shots, is quoted in Outing, LXIII (1913) to have recorded 27,378 kills in his lifetime. This does not count the number of "Not Birds"— those shot on the ground—or the number of "Lost Birds" that had to be clubbed by trap men after being only wounded.

During the nesting season in Sparta, Wisconsin, 1871, three tons of powder and sixteen tons of shot were sold to hunters. As the old Mohawk would say, that was a damn big KANHI.

The third tome of smut, *Over She Goes, a Girl's Guide to Internal Combustion Mechanics,* bulged with the inlay of the photocopy of a whole article from the journal *Forest and Stream,* May 1875. One paragraph had been underlined in the red ink that Leo Post seemed to favor.

Nowadays, fortunately, all such butchery of birds is removed. We now shoot at the best flying pigeons we can procure. We shoot them from five ground traps, five yards apart, giving them a good long start, and if they are wounded by the first barrel, the second generally gives them the coup de grace, or else the trapper instantly kills the wounded bird, ending his suffering. (And his life! Post's hand.) So that as a matter of fact, pigeons are much more humanely treated than poultry huddled up in coops, carried head down by the legs, eventually decapitated with a dull ax or saw-like knife. Pigeons are shipped in roomy crates, are well watched and fed, and on all first-class shooting grounds are given first-class care. (Post's hand in the margin: *Clickety-clack—all the way to Auschwitz.*)

The point: it was the telegraph and the railroad that doomed the pigeon, one alerting the professional trappers to the birds' location, and the second invention providing rapid shipment of large quantities to market. Each technological advance serving the other at the expense of a living creature. They might have survived everything else. Another example of the basic formula (X)XMan=Extinction.

Song, circa 1930s. "It's Not What You Do/It's the Way That You Do It."

Our investigation was interrupted by the creak of the chamber's door, and the figure of Lucy backed into the room on tiptoe. Satisfied that her entry had not been observed, she carefully turned around with a cautioning finger placed to her lips. With a toss of her head, we were directed toward the open window that looked downstream where we had earlier seen the unlucky kayaker. He had disappeared. Lucy had joined us with the swift grace of a cat.

"If we speak out the window," she said softly, "no device can pick up our words." The narrowness of the stone aperture forced us to stand close together, and the wholesome aroma of her black womanhood permeated our senses. As previously noted, Lucy was over six feet tall in her white-boot stilettos. "Was I glad to see you arrive this morning," she continued in a voice strangely neutral and devoid of the slurs and old-plantation mannerisms of before. "I was beginning to think headquarters had forgot me. But perhaps before we continue, you might want to see my credentials," she said, as she undid her blouse buttons and exposed the twin perfections of her breasts of a creamy, cocoa color. She lifted one breast for our closer inspection, a finger pointing to the place this excellent orb jutted from her rib cage. A serial number had been tattooed there in a spot usually concealed by the undulating fall of the mammilla.

"Yes," she said, coming to attention, "Sgt. Lucille Anderson, New York State Police." Her smile surely would assure a rapid rise in the ranks. Satisfied that I, B. Smith, a more-than-cognizant observer, had had sufficient time to inspect her credentials, Sgt. Anderson closed and buttoned her tunic and leaned against the parapet, a businesslike mien on her handsome face.

"My assignment here began last month," she said, answering our question. "BCI has kept the file open on Molly Lyon Post since the accident that took her life. Her body was never found in Elmira's Woodlawn Cemetery, and the Moroni Special had been completely demolished. We don't have enough evidence to feed the computer in order to punch out the usual pink slip—deceased."

The policewoman abruptly left the window and then returned with the pornographic *Coming on the Line*, an egregious usage of a blue-collar milieu. She tapped the cover of the book and looked significantly at us. "She had become an expert driver, and it is unlikely she would have missed that turn and piled into that mausoleum. And by the way," Sgt. Anderson mused, holding up the book, "old Post, aka Len Banal, does have a way with words. If you haven't read it, I recommend the scene where the union leader brings off the little laundress. But I digress." She became all business.

"Of course, BCI knew of the whereabouts of Leo Post all the time," she continued in velvety tones so different from the harsh sounds of this morning. "We have cross-reference facilities you do not possess. For example, that old revolver the man called Taylor packs has to be licensed even though it only shoots blanks. His address is in our files. His position as Post's chauffeur must have even been in your records." I, B. Smith, proud of my bureau, refused to be intimidated by Anderson's jibe. It was also understood, as we stood close in the window, that we would be working together.

"Moreover," Sgt. Anderson continued, "BCI had been waiting for an opportunity to place an agent in Post's domain. Then an operator who had infiltrated the underground press came across a classified advertisement with the same return address as that used for the man called Taylor's pistol permit. It was the lead we had been waiting for, and I was quickly dispatched. What was the nature of the advertisement, you ask?" Sgt. Anderson looked away in the direction of the Self-Propelled Expressway access to the south. She reached into her blouse pocket and pulled out a newspaper clipping.

BASKET CASE needs Black mammy
To feed him soul food.
Box 72
Sullivan Corners, N.Y.

"You wouldn't believe," the police officer murmured, shivering as if suddenly chilled in the glow of the afternoon sun, "the things I have had to do in the performance of my duty." For a moment her Amazonian stature seemed to have been overcome by a tremulous femininity. A touching display, just as quickly dispelled by a return to her militant manner.

A high crooning from the depths of the castle interrupted her narrative. She canted her head to listen; it sounded like a dog. The policewoman's nose wrinkled as if she had smelled something unpleasant. The high-pitched howls continued. "The electrical shock must have given him a temporary surge," she said. "I thought I had wrung him dry for the day. (Smile!) We shall talk again," she told us. "Come to the kitchen when you hear me preparing dinner—no one will disturb us. It is a suitable cover for my investigation, though I have no feeling for the activity. Until later, then," Sgt. Anderson said with a snappy salute and closed the heavy door behind her.

We reviewed this remarkable disclosure for several minutes until a knock on the door. It was Sgt. Anderson again. Her manner had changed completely, and before we could put to her some of the questions her revelation had spurred, she had clothed herself in the good-natured leer of Lucy, the cook.

"The Boss, he say for you to join him down on the tear-ass for some hooch 'fore I gives you the eats," the state policewoman said in a near-flawless accent.

THAT EVENING...

The flagstone esplanade that served as a terrace adjoined the main gallery and faced the east bank of the river. It must have afforded splendid views of the river in both directions but an abandoned growth of privet, part of which had been a formal garden, walled off the prospect. The vegetation was at least fifteen feet high and badly needed trimming. Evidence of a classically designed rose garden had become a thicket of spindly shanks, pip- less and shivering in the breeze. The heavily leaved branches of two gigantic willows hung over the terrace like great thunderheads, and their ubiquitous root systems thrust up between the stones of the terrace to heave the surface. Air rising from the river stirred these tendrils, or imagination could think them to be blind organisms feeling their way around the ruptured mortises.

"There you are, old chap," Leo Post greeted us. He waved to a grouping of iron chairs around a glass-topped table. He had changed for dinner, wearing Bermuda shorts in a dark plaid pattern, black knee socks but the same white buckskin shoes, and the familiar blazer. A jaunty yachting cap was set over one ear.

"It's cool here this time of day," he continued. "The sun is on the other side of the Catskills, and the river currents freshen the air. The wild honeysuckle is especially piquant tonight. Can you imagine what it must have been like for Henry Hudson and his crew coming up this waterway—just over there? Some of his sailors kept diaries that described the aromas, the perfumery of fruits and flowers that overwhelmed them even at sea a hundred miles or more from the river's mouth. The overpowering fragrances of the wilderness as they approached the river and sailed up it. Some described the atmosphere as the frankincense of paradise and others as the musk of hell. It's an ambivalence we have yet to resolve."

He had half raised from his chair, his athletic figure near-comically poised like some great bird considering flight. The black eyes and the long beak of a nose contributed to this appearance. His arms, disproportionately short, were bent and held close to his sides like vestigial wings.

"I hope you like daiquiris," he said, turning toward a small banquette that held glasses, an ice bucket, and bottles. "Daiquiris were our drink here on the river. That is, the Leeks, the Delanos and the Dows always drank daiquiris. Probably something to do with the family rum trade in the old days. The Chapmans and the Aldriches always drank gin, in all probability a taste acquired from the painters they patronized. The Livingstones, I'm sorry to say, went to vodka toward the end, and the Roosevelts had a nose for sour mash. Freddy Vanderbilt was a teetotaler, but he came very late here. Here you are." He passed to us a frosted glass of the cocktail.

"Of course, they're long gone and their mansions have become commercial ventures or religious retreats. Elaborate bed-and-breakfasts and trailer parks. The whole valley is an abandoned aviary. Like those birds you may have been reading about earlier and, by the way, are your quarters comfortable? Good. I mean, the notes on the pigeons that may have turned you away, in all modesty no great loss, from my pitiful attempts at light fare—something for an idle hour.

"Yes, extinction. Whether it's birds or a class of people or a way of life. It's a new idea relatively speaking. Such disappearances have always occurred—they haven't been conceived of until Darwin. Survival is only half of the equation, the other half being extinction. It had been usually believed that a species had merely changed its grazing grounds, some pampa so remote that it is off the maps. Thomas Jefferson ordered Lewis and Clark to keep their eyes open for the mammoths that some said they heard roar in the depths of Virginia woods. Oh, yes, fossils. Fossils were believed to be fragments from a distant exploding planet that had fallen to Earth, carrying the imprint of the strange life that had flourished on it. The dark side of selection no one thinks about, that you and I may not be the ultimate citizens in this neighborhood." He paused to smile over the rim of his glass, a boyish image. "I would bet on the cockroach, if I were you."

The scrape and clang of metal announced the appearance of Pickett Sneat. Lucy—now known to us as Sgt. Lucille Anderson of the New York State Police—escorted the critic, guiding the positioning of the steel crutches and the braced legs. The man's expression was marked by the usual jack-o'-lantern smirk, and his popped eyes stared at one of the chairs as if he pulled himself along by that line of vision. Lucy undid the various screws and wing nuts of his fastening and folded him into the chair. We avoided Sgt. Anderson's look.

"There you are, Pick." Post addressed his colleague with a pleasant expression. "We've just had a sip. Dinner in an hour, Lucy?" But the woman had already disappeared. "Here's a daq for you," the author said, presenting a frosted glass.

"What have you been talking about?" the book reviewer asked petulantly.

"Nothing much. Extinction mostly."

"I suppose you have boasted about giving me my start," he said. Some of the drink gurgled down his throat. Some of it ran over and dripped off of his round chin. He seemed calm, subdued.

"No need of that, no need of that," Post said, with just a trace of admonishment. He had taken the other chair and crossed his legs. The heavy calf muscle of the one leg bulged through the black knee sock to remind us that his mark for the high jump still stands.

"It happened many years ago," the critic began. He had slipped sideways in his chair in a pose suggesting a confiding gesture of casual discourse, but the weight of the steel cage around him had pulled him over and held his torso stiffly aslant. His red hair gave him the appearance of a channel buoy tipped over by a swift current. "Mr. Goody-good here doesn't like to talk about that history. We were both fresh out of school, and Jocelyn Van Horner was running the book section of the old Sunday *Journal*. That is when she was sober and not screwing some emigré poet. Ever get any of that, Leo?" the book reviewer asked the author.

"No need to be sordid," Post admonished Sneat. But his expression had been sportive, suggesting schoolboy banter between the two men.

"In any event, Horny Van Horner handed him a copy of Reuben Slate's *Visions and Revisions*, and he wrote a wickedly damning review of it. As it deserved. However, Jocelyn was putting out to old Reuben—the picture of her easing his arthritic eminence on top of her is too much to ponder—so she—"

"Not true, Pickett. You keep promoting that error. It was Jocelyn's niece who was having an affair with Slate then—"

"Well, *vaginem per extendo*." He shrugged.

"I think you mean *extentum*, don't you?" Post corrected his friend.

"Will you kindly shut up," Sneat snapped. He took a steadying breath and tried to right himself but to no avail. "In any event, Old Horny wanted a favorable review for Reuben, so she asked you to do it over to sweeten it up a little. But, of course," the man's eyes engaged us with a humorous light, "the virtuous Post would not change a word of his thunderous prose. So she gave me the assignment, and my effort wasn't completely dishonest. I tell the story in my *The Craft of Artful Reviewing*—how I put the negative opinion in the final paragraph, knowing the compositor would lop off the last part to make room for an advertisement. So, you see, I had given an honest opinion, but commercialism had eliminated it."

"Cleverly done," Post said, sipping his cocktail. "I wish I had thought of that."

"No you don't," Sneat replied, holding out his glass for more. "Such craft is not in your nature. You're so goddamned honest. What a bore you are—you and your principles. Always putting the best face on everything." He had paused to sip some of the new drink that Post had poured him, but he could only pour the liquid into the upper corner of his mouth due to the sharp angle of his posture. That he missed his ear amazed us. Some of the daiquiri spilled over his chin, and he tried to catch it with swipes of his tongue. Post came to the rescue by striding to him quickly and forcefully pulling him upright in the chair, wiping a napkin over his face and adjusting and tightening the braces on his legs as if the critic was a piece of furniture with loosened mortises.

"Let's change the subject, shall we?" Post said lightly. "We shall have a movie after dinner, Pick. Mr. Taylor brought a film that was in the afternoon mail. It's the one I ordered from the Archives."

"That's the story we should tell our guest," Sneat said, looking wistfully into his now empty glass. "Tell how you met that extraordinary clown, Taylor."

"Not much to tell," Post said, though his expression suggested his pleasure with the invitation. He poured a fresh round from the crystal pitcher and resumed, with a tug of his knee socks. He got them just right.

"Now then, about Mr. Taylor." Affection sugared his voice. "He is a superb horseman, but his horse was killed in an urban riot in Poughkeepsie a few years ago. Pathetic event. He is also one of the fastest draws with a pistol in the Western world, but arthritis has modified that skill—dare I call it an art? He's still a crack shot when he has a few moments."

"A broken-down rodeo clown is what he is," the book reviewer interrupted, smacking his lips. "The seedy icon of a false
and nefarious history. But you met him long after that affair in
Poughkeepsie. Long after he gave up playing Natty Bumppo. It
was that dinner at Kimball Lyon's house, if I remember."

"Yes, that's correct." Post had squeezed the bridge of his nose
as if to press out a pain. "I admit to no other reason for joining
forces with Lyon but to be near his daughter. My attraction to her
was instantaneous, overwhelming—a spontaneous combustion
of my very being. You know what she looked like. Her voice was
honey and lemon. Her movement—a lioness lazing through high
grass. To look into those clear green eyes was to regain the wisdom
lost in that fire in Alexandria."

"Saints preserve us," Sneat said and rolled his eyes.

Post continued unruffled. "The feeling was mutual. We were
made for each other in intellect and appetite, soul and body, and I
think I might add without being tasteless, she was no novice to the
amatory arts. She fully knew the paradoxical truth of conquering
by way of absolute surrender."

"Oh boy," Sneat said and tried to kick his legs, "get a taste of
that!"

"So as I masterminded, as the popular press would have it,
Governor Lyon's first campaign, I was also courting his daughter.
It was a delirious moment in my life; looking back it seems un-
real—an affair conducted within a well-organized, well-financed
and hotly successful political campaign which in itself produces
a kind of sexual heat. So the two charged atmospheres inflamed
each other."

"The prick behind the throne, so to speak," the book reviewer
said and leered.

"Permit me to limn here," Post continued hurriedly to forestall
more interjections from his colleague, "a small outline of myself at
that time. Sired by a Bohemian cardshark of Middle Eastern origins, then born illegitimately into one of the grand old families of
the Hudson River aristocracy—I was unacceptable in either world.

Moreover, my first book was so easily successful in every way," the author lowered his eyes in artful modesty, "that it angered those colleagues who should have praised its small accomplishment. Moreover I had not worked on the assembly line at Ford Motor so my credentials were not acceptable to the blue-collar Puritans, nor had I attended Exeter or The Hill, Stanford or Iowa, so I slipped through the network that sustained the numerous mediocrities who, in those days, fell into the lap of the national oeuvre."

"Tsk, tsk," his companion muttered. "Imagery like that tells all." He shot us a dark look and blew at the russet bangs on his forehead.

"Moreover," Post continued suavely, "my obstinate manner that people like Picket kindly construe as honesty separated me from the rest. So, I was alone, a solitary hiker—"

"Sob, sob," whimpered the book reviewer.

"On that mountain. William Blake had assured us of its capaciousness but I could find no space for myself. So then came power by way of Governor Lyon and with power the temptation for revenge, but well ... you understand."

It was not a question and his dark eyes took on a peculiar flow, as if the sun about to disappear behind the Catskills had ignited the whites around the pupils. Abruptly, he grunted and stood up and strolled to the banquette to prepare more cocktails. The book reviewer impatiently played with one of his tubular crutches, tapping its rubber tip against the flagstone. A large tanker, the superstructure twinkling with numerous lights, passed downriver, resembling a small city that had somehow come loose from the shore above us, being carried off by the current.

"This river," the author was saying as he stirred the rum and lime juice, "runs in my blood—dare I say our blood? We can't seem to get away from it. Molly and I made love along its length in that first campaign. We knew every little cove and harbor of it. Lyon was making his carefully contrived public appearances from the battery all the way up to Lake Tear of the Clouds, where it starts. We embellished every ceremony with a private celebration of our own. Naturally, I was unaware of his plans, this madness now called the Self-Propelled Expressway—the very matter that has brought you here to us.

"The meeting with Taylor that Sneat has urged me to tell you of took place during the first campaign. A night in October. A large parking mall had been dedicated in Harlem. One of Lyon's foundations had cleared several blocks of tenements; he just bought them up and tore them down, to create the huge parking lot. This private venture clearly became a model for the first Perpetual Parking Plaza he was to create when he became governor. The media made him the colossus he became—private citizen Lyon answering the need in Harlem for more parking space."

"Of course, reducing the living space also reduced the number of car owners who needed parking space," Sneat suggested with a winning grin. He wiped his cocktail glass with a finger and put the finger in his mouth to suck.

Leo Post considered his cohort for a moment and then continued. "The suggestion was floated that such a man as Kimball Lyon could be the leader New York needed in these times of continual emergency. He met a crisis straight on and with common sense. In any event, Molly and I wandered away from the lights and the crowd during that first parking-lot dedication. If we were observed, our pairing off was put to the fashion, ratified in the social notes of newspapers and magazines, of bourgeois daughters running wide-nostrilled and sprung-eyed with mongrels and half-breeds before returning to the proper husbands chosen for them by their own kind. Indeed, for a time I identified with and even felt sorry for those poor louts tuning up the frissons of their fine-boned mistresses unaware they were being used to store up fantasies these women could play back later in a lifetime of conventional nights."

"I dare say," Sneat said, and burped. "But surely, Leo, you did not put yourself in the same category with these professional roosters."

"Well, at first, I considered that I might be nothing more to Molly than a safe adventure, an experiment before she joined the garden parties. Moreover, I was a change from her last lover, a construction worker from Queens, if only because I could tell the dessert spoon from the soup spoon. But I was almost in the same category.

"Certainly, my modest achievements, my small fame as a word maker, would have got me an invitation to her wedding. I'd be another in line to kiss the bride adieu, perhaps lingering just a little at the corner of her mouth. You see, there were the rumors about my birth, my background—was it Africa? Italy? No one considered Armenia—when was Armenia ever considered? An older man with a young woman had become the novelty of the age as well. But the substance of my déclassé allure lay in my persona of a writer, an artist, in the classic posture on bended knee before the patron class. Foolishly perhaps, I saw myself as the troubadour, the scribe, even the jester—part of the court but never one of the family."

"What you are saying," his companion interrupted, "is that she hadn't screwed a writer yet, and you were a variation."

Leo Post jumped up and took several steps away to face the high hedge. Anger crackled in his eyes. He took a deep breath, then slowly turned back to us. He even emitted several bark-like guffaws peculiar to the males of Hudson River families. Hah-hah-HAH!

"What would I do without you, Pick," he said. "My very own blue pencil. Now, where was I?"

"You and Molly Lyon were strolling down Riverside Drive on a warm October evening. But while you're up—" Pick raised his empty glass. Post carried it to the bar cart and prepared another drink as the book reviewer continued. "You were talking about her attitude toward you, how she thought of you, but what we are more interested in—" he paused to include us with a wave of his hand, "is what you felt for her. Was she just another conquest? True, a rather glossy number, but how did you feel? You've talked at length—at great length, I might add—of the high-charged atmosphere around her father, the smell of money, the seductive

accoutrements of power; could not some of that euphoria become
a fever for the daughter?"

"Yes, yes—all too true, Pick." Post served the fresh drink.
"But if we try to define love, to separate it into its many compo-
nents and qualities, then it becomes something else. A sophist's
puzzle. Love is the color of light, a total spectrum; to analyze it is
to break it down into ordinary colors."

"Oh my, Leo," Sneat cackled into his daiquiri. "Sometimes
you say things that make me wonder if Khalil Gibran didn't finish
his tuna on toast in the drugstore and then sneak up the stairs of
the Chelsea to play moving finger with your high-born mama."

The author threw his head back and joined the critic in unre-
strained laughter. Their eccentric commonality was momentarily
revealed. It had become dark on the terrace.

"Well, as to my feelings," Post resumed in a serious tone. He
had sat down and sipped from his own glass then carefully placed
it on the table next to him. "Beyond the sexual deliciousness,
beyond her being the daughter of the next governor, beyond the
compelling allure of her face and figure, beyond the grace of her
manner—beyond all those elements, something else overwhelmed
me as we strolled down Riverside Drive." He abruptly stopped
speaking as if looking for the right word in the hiatus. Finally,
with a shrug indicating the choice was not completely satisfying,
he offered, "Concern."

"Concern?" The book reviewer had become round eyed, his
mouth hung open, a fine line of saliva dribbled from his lower lip.

"I know, the word is inadequate, but it's all I can come up
with. As I walked beside her, keeping my eye out for urban guerillas, she held my hand in her long, capable fingers. The expression
of her face had become sad. The design of her dress exposed the
sensuous elegance of her back. My eyes were teased to that spot
between her shoulder blades, that area which by its own vulnerability demanded a kiss.

"It struck me that she bore within herself a defenselessness
that invited more serious wounding. Call them what you will—

fate or her birth's circumstances—a shaft of incident had been loosened already to pierce that hidden spot in her soul that would kill all imagination and wonder—all passion and responsiveness—making her into a beautiful mannequin to be exhibited on important occasions. How she was going to spend the rest of her time on earth became important to me as we strolled through the night. I was determined to challenge that destiny. I would put her out of the path of that arrow."

"Stout fellow," Pickett Sneat hurrahed, rapping his metal cane against the stone terrace. "I couldn't have said it better and there's a pity."

"Mind you," Post sternly demanded our attention, " I was not thinking of myself as being part of her future—"

"Of course not, you just wanted to tinker with it a little," Sneat observed in the dark. "Some of that crypto-liberal fingering."

"—I had the sudden desire to make her future more extraordinary than the concretized protocol that awaited her. Presumptuous to a fault—I readily admit. But love can clothe itself with such sweet arrogance.

"In our idyll along this river, Molly had shown me flashes of her brilliant mind within its approved matriculation. An adventurous spirit charged with a passion to climb Himalayan heights rather than the carpeted stairway of a charity ball. The good works of some well-meaning organization would only brick up the magic of her mind.

"'What will you do?' I asked her.

"'What will I do?' It seemed I had been the only one to put the question to her—beside herself. She had turned away, mouth pursed. 'What will I do? I don't know what I will do.'

"She had looked into the glare of a streetlight overhead. The large eyes glowed, and the long throat arched back. She slowly shook her head without an answer.

"'Perhaps I'll go back to school,' she said. 'Maybe I could teach, maybe I could study something interesting.'

"'Maybe you could race cars,' I offered half-seriously.

"She shrugged and laughed with a charming embarrassment.

'It's just a hobby. I couldn't really compete in the big races.'

"'Why not? What's stopping you?' I asked, and her breath caught on a spur of recognition within her. She smiled and squeezed my hand.

"Just at that moment, over her bare shoulder, I caught sight of several shadowy figures moving stealthily in the small park. Taking no chances, I took her by the arm and we moved away briskly. Footsteps hurried after us. It was not very late, but the neighborhood had already locked up; the streets were deserted. We were alone—save for our pursuers. The Soldiers and Sailors Monument was at hand, and I reasoned its small foyer would grant us a strategic place for a defense. If you are familiar with its architecture, you'll remember its narrow aperture would force our assailants to attack us singly. We rushed up the steps to this small foyer and, with the iron grill of the locked entrance at our backs, waited for the footpads to make their move.

"'Oh my, Leo, I'm frightened,' Molly whispered. I comforted her and mentioned that I possessed a black belt. 'Not of them,' she said, impatiently waving aside my credentials, 'but what am I supposed to do with myself? Will you help me? Will you guide me, *mon professeur*?'

"If our assailants had attacked us at that moment," Leo Post continued, with a tug of his shirt cuffs, "they would have easily overcome us, for we had fallen into a passionate embrace that took all of our attention—oblivious to everything but the joint thudding of our hearts. However, they had passed on to attack easier prey—an aged veteran of our country's triumphs over tyranny. The poor fellow's screams as he was maimed tempered our pleasure somewhat, but what he was doing in the park at that time of night is also questionable. However, at this point in my narrative I appeal to your discretion to ask for no further details."

"However indeed," Sneat interrupted. His harness squeaked as he turned and leaned toward us. "You might be interested to read a passage in an early bit of Banal smut. The scene has been changed to Grant's Tomb rather than the Soldiers and Sailors Monument, and the heroine employs the iron grillwork of the entryway for some rather ingenious leverage."

"No more," Post warned his colleague sternly. "It should be noted that such passion was not unknown to us. It can be said that in that alcove of the mausoleum, raised to honor the victor of Vicksburg and other engagements, we raised an awesome parapotamian paroxysm."

The cripple muttered, "More of your adolescent boasting."

"After we caught our breath," continued Post, "I told her of my mixed parentage, the backstairs childhood in the crumbling Leek mansion—just over there." The author had pointed across the river in the darkness. "Her cat's eyes still swimming with the pleasure we had shared went wide as I unveiled the history. Nor did I hide from her the hazards of my father's Phrygian blood; the fierce pride that ran in my veins from the Artaxian throne that, when insulted, responds with a fury known only to the damned and outnumbered. I made it clear to her that I was not just another political huckster drawn into her father's fiery orbit, and she realized that I was sufficiently prepared to fulfill her most profound enthusiasms."

"Stout fellow," his colleague exclaimed, once again rattling his cage.

"Her arms had gone around me, and she nodded, then nodded once again. She would risk all. So we hailed a taxi, and this is where Mr. Taylor enters our story."

"Not my story," Sneat said glumly.

"We paid little attention to him at first," Post went on, "but as our pulses calmed, certain details of the cab became apparent. A horse's head had been mounted on the hood. Pistol grips for door handles. Inside, small louvered doors screened the passenger from the front seat, and the fold-up seats—this was a vintage Checker—became small saddles complete with pommels and stirrups. The latter became clever accoutrements for further dalliance— our encounter at the Soldiers and Sailors only filing the edge of our desire."

"Spare us, Leo, please spare us. Keep that salacity of yours for your pulp inventions." The other tapped his empty glass against his metal harness, but the author ignored the signal.

"We had recovered our senses once again, as the driver turned onto West 23rd Street. We passed the Chelsea Hotel, and Molly's lovely eyes, deepened by the intensity of our lovemaking, turned down sadly as she heard of the event that took place in room 242. We passed the automat where Gaius O'Malley lost his hand in a pie window, and then farther downtown, a turn around Gramercy Park. The driver was having trouble finding the restaurant I had called out to him."

The heavy rumble of a powerful diesel engine made all discourse impossible. Through the wall of privet, the shape of an oceangoing tug could be made out, going downstream, and its throbbing engines accompanied an overpowering stench of putrescence and offal. Post and Pickett quickly pinched their nostrils, motioning us to do the same. A flock of scavenging gulls wheeled above the garbage scow, and the steady progress of the tug could be judged by their swoop and spirals as they fed, their wings catching the last gleams of the fading day.

"That's the evening run," Post explained, holding his nose. "The garbage barges from the Tri-City going out to sea. There." He released his nostrils, and the widely spaced apertures seemed to spread apart even wider. "Wasn't so bad today, was it, Pickett?" The other shook his head, still breathing through his mouth. "Well, now, where were we?"

"Gramercy Park," the book reviewer replied, taking a deep breath.

"Yes, and we passed the first apartment building in Manhattan. Oliver Hereford lived there. How quaint to remember his charming little stories about the world ending. Further, the corner where Luke Barnett kicked Horace Liveright in the behind. Thusly, I attempted to entertain Molly with my ragbag of footnotes and anecdotes, and we had just crossed Second Avenue when she suddenly sat up and looked through the rear window of the taxi. She rapped on the miniature swinging doors and told the driver to stop. To back up.

"'Look—' she said to me and pointed at the façade of a derelict brownstone. A small sign on a ground floor window announced *Capt. Charlie's Tattoo Lounge.*

"'What do you have in mind?' I asked. Her flights of fancy were sometimes bewildering.

"'I want to mark this evening—' her mouth said deliciously into my ear, '—Mark this evening and myself so that we will become indelible—'

"It was an astounding pronouncement in the back of that taxi and one that made my Khaldian lust rise. Had we not just parked at the curb, I might have taken her there on one of the jumps in the Turkish fashion. Near the building's entrance, about a dozen members of a motorcycle gang lounged on their gleaming machines, caressing the throttles and resembling a brood of mechanical roaches chewing up the autumn night. A pall of fumes festooned the air. I told our driver to wait for us.

"Inside, Molly confronted Capt. Charlie calmly and with the self-assurance of the heiress she was. Then, with a kiss on my cheek, she disappeared behind a sliding door. The weasel-like countenance of the artist-in-residence regarded me with a bold amusement, then followed her and pulled the door closed.

"I reviewed the dreary selection of magazines on a table—you know the kind—but I was too tense to read anything. What was happening to my beloved behind that closed door? The screech and rattle of the motorcycles just outside on the street. The seedy atmosphere. My cell phone had become lost during our gymnastics in the alcove of the Soldiers and Sailors Monument, and there was no instrument in this room. A buzzing had commenced on the other side of the sliding partition. Was there a back door, a rear exit? I had thoughts of her being drugged even as I inspected the well-thumbed issues of *Creative Mechanics* on the table—Molly kidnapped and held captive in some abandoned skating rink in the Bronx. Brutally used by hooligans.

"A half hour had elapsed as my imagination tortured me. The buzz in the other room continued. My shirt was wet with perspiration. Suddenly, the outside-hall door was opened—footsteps hurried near. The waiting-room door was flung open, and there stood the man we have come to know as Taylor. He said he had overheard the cyclists talking of taking over the tattoo parlor and performing the dark deeds I had been imaging.

"'I got my rig around back,' he said. His lips hardly seemed to move as he spoke in even tones. His eyes shifted around the room.

"'You get the lady, and I'll cover the rear.'

"And saying this, he pulled back his suit jacket to reveal the Colt .44 holstered on his hip. A pearl-handled Smith & Wesson .38 double-action swing-out, reputedly a favorite of Wild Bill Hickok, was tucked into his belt. He slipped the heavier revolver from its holster and spun the cylinder several times.

"'What is your name?' I asked him.

"'I am the man they call Taylor,' he replied through close-set lips. He inspected the waiting room once more. He had hefted the Smith & Wesson in his left hand while holding the forty-four in his right.

"Outside, the frenzy of the motorcycles' engines had increased, roaring to a climax. Then the screams began behind the sliding doors. Molly's voice, but whether in agony or terror I could not tell. I rushed to the doors, the man called Taylor stepping behind me, guns ready. What an extraordinary sight met my frightened eyes!

"The craven wretch of the tattooist was bending over the near nakedness of my beloved. She lay on a sort of operating table, her succulent loins exposed and her slim thighs raised; feet fit into accommodating stirrups. The wretch crouched between her outspread legs, his face level with the femoral junction. I was stunned. I heard the click-clack of the man called Taylor's revolver behind me. The crisp, coppery curls of her *mons veneris* were gone—that feathery adornment that I had fitted to my forehead more than once to play the feasting Iroquois—all gone. She had been shaved clean! And this vile fellow was engraving something on that sweet flesh, in the upper corner of that divine dimple—the purplish burr of a blossoming leek."

"On her snatch—her snatch!" Sneat shouted. The steel framework that contained him pinged and vibrated. He could be heard sucking air and spit. "Oh, she was screaming all right, but in terror? Hardly terror. She was getting off from that electric needle."

"Now Pickett—now Pick," Post responded in a soothing manner. He had risen as if to quiet the critic, then turned away.

"'We have come to defend you,' Mr. Goody-good said.

"'It's not that,' she replied. 'I'm coming. I can't stop coming.'"

The book reviewer had shouted the last sentences, and his left leg suddenly snapped out stiffly before him. His molluscan corpus quivered within its metal shell as he continued to laugh and choke on his laughter. The reflective pose of his colleague seemed to inflame even more glee.

"It's always astounded me that you know that detail," Post said as Sneat's strangled chortles subsided. "Your imagination is compelling," the author said dryly. "In any event," he continued, "there was a sudden commotion at the front door. Wood splintered and the stomp of heavy boots. The motorcycle gang was attacking. The tattooist, already alarmed by Taylor's pistols, became terrified by the entrance of the leather-jacketed hooligans. Yet, artist that he was, he pleaded for a little more time to complete his masterpiece—could we hold these tartars at bay so he could complete the articulation of the blossom?"

"Hah!" Sneat snorted.

"Taylor, guns drawn, faced down the ruffians in the waiting room. Quickly Capt. Charlie finished his work and Molly, still shivering and weak from the ordeal, rose into the safety of my arms. I dressed her, then step-by-step we retreated behind Taylor's defense out the back door. They rushed us as I fumbled with the door's lock. Taylor began firing, the muzzles of his weapons spitting out blue flames of damnation."

"Blanks!" His colleague pounded the pavement with his crutch. "He only had blanks in those guns. Reminiscent of some of your prose, old bean."

"Yes," Post seemed to agree. "A man after my own heart. He continued to fire at the advancing mob. Startled by the cannonading explosions and the clouds of acrid smoke, some of them tripped over their companions and were taken to have been shot. The rest turned and fled. We made our escape in the waiting cab. Taylor, his seasoned eyes surveying the area, adroitly leapt into the driver's seat and spurred us away.

"Some of the streets in that neighborhood were under repair and became two closed-off play streets and a one-way thoroughfare. We came full circle to find us again before Capt. Charlie's Tattoo Parlor. The gang had regrouped, saw us coming, and like a troop of demented Cossacks jumped upon their motorcycles to give chase. With a deafening roar the machines spun off their stands. One went directly across the street to crash into a delicatessen, and two others collided with a dreadful wrench of metal and screams. A third bucked up the steps of a brownstone to disappear down its hallway. Each came to a similar end, raising the suspicion that its rider had never operated the motorcycle but had only gunned its engine as it sat upright in its stand. One, perhaps ridden by the pack's leader, overtook our taxi, but roared past as if unable to stop, out of control, toward the East River. Its rider raised one leather-clad arm above his head in what could have been a frantic farewell.

"And this is how we met the man called Taylor. He drove us to this sanctuary that night, and he's been here ever since." Leo Post had been neatening up the area, putting different bottles and items back on the bar. He took our glasses. Sneat seemed to have fallen into a doze. "Well, now. Shall we see what little delicacy our very own Lucy has created for us?"

LATER THAT EVENING...

The discourse of the cocktail hour prevented I, B. Smith, receiver of believable stories, from meeting with Sgt. Anderson in the kitchen as planned. When we accompanied the dinner party into the main chamber of the castle, the undercover state policewoman was putting food on the table. The damp wood that had smoldered in the hearth this morning had caught fire. Its small blaze provided little warmth, but only emphasized the enormous gloom of the place. Several lizards enmeshed in the ivy that had crept up the walls witnessed our entrance. It had become very dark all of a sudden, for when the sun went below the profile of the Catskills to the west, it seemed to pull down a great shade on the Hudson Valley.

The river also was making adjustments, preparing for night—a changing of the guard of life and habit. Even noises had been modified, as if the current had floated the sounds of day downstream. The thick tangles of underbrush and scrub trees on both banks absorbed sound, but happily, the brisk whirr of cars moving across the Expressway a few miles south threw an audible line to us, so one did not completely feel adrift on this vagrant isle.

Four places had been set at one end of the large commissary-style table. Books, papers, stuffed birds, and other paraphernalia had been pushed aside for the place settings so it seemed this tidal wave of materials and trash was about to engulf the man called Taylor who already had taken his place. He sat slightly stooped, long arms pressed between his knees, and regarded the space bracketed by knife and fork with a morose expression.

Leo Post positioned Pickett Sneat's wheelchair and then, with an offhand gesture—approximating a shift of shoulder—directed us to a chair at his right. We waited in silence for the meal to be served—the forlorn hoot of an owl the single commentary. As has been suggested, Leek's Island was not an abode of small talk but an establishment of long and supposedly meaningful narratives. Taylor's stunned attitude seemed fixed. Sneat shifted in his metal contraption, his pink-rimmed eyes glancing to Post and then lifting to a point in the blackness near the high ceiling. Post pulled at his cuffs and realigned the dinnerware several times. His mouth worked soundlessly as if rehearsing the lines of a new account, as if an amusing anecdote had just been remembered for our file.

Or it could have been the expression of a dinner host who knew what was about to be served, for just then Sgt. Anderson, in her disguise as the Negro cook Lucy, crashed backwards through the door in the plywood hoarding. One of the hinges came free. On a large tray she carried several smaller trays, each compartmentalized and steaming with pre-processed victuals.

"Ah, there," Post sniffed with appreciation. "What's this you have for us, Lucy? It smells like *daube de boeuf à la Provençale*."

"We had this last night," Sneat grumbled.

"And the night before," Post reminded him cheerfully. "A good thing never tires."

Meantime, Lucy, a.k.a. Sgt. Anderson, slithered the rectangular metal trays around the table as if they were cards being dealt.

Her sullen expression was a masterpiece of personification. In fact, her immersion in her role was so profound we were unable to catch her eye before she stomped back to the kitchen. Post had finished off the meal with an efficient use of cutlery, but the man called Taylor slurped and scooped up his food, the fork held in his fist. He shoveled the meat and vegetables into his mouth held almost at tabletop level. A driblet of brown gravy descended his chin.

"Ahem... Mr. Taylor," Post gently admonished him, and the taxi driver wiped his face.

The man's clear eyes were set far apart and carried a strange distance within them, as if their focal length had been fixed long ago while looking into a measureless vista. His hair was uniformly black, apparently dyed. Every move he made was accompanied by the wrench of leather of the wide gun belt and the heavy holster strapped to his thigh. Empty. He had polished compartments of the metal serving plate with a piece of bread and a furtive glance toward Sneat's plate. The book reviewer had taken only a few bites of the meal and pushed the rest away. He observed the man called Taylor's interest with an expression that contested contempt with compassion, and the latter attitude succeeded for he nudged the tin toward the ersatz Westerner.

"More snoops, Mr. Taylor? Did those fisherman show up again?" Post asked.

"Nope," replied the cowboy between gulps. He gripped a fortified dinner roll and scrubbed the aluminum tray as if it were a piece of silver plate to be polished.

"It's out of season, isn't it?" Sneat asked. "Fishing."

"Yup," Taylor answered.

"Quite," Post agreed. His eyes encountered Sneat's for a moment, then fell upon us. "Are you expecting any companions, more investigators?" We assured him we were alone.

"Ah, well, poaching is a sacred tradition—an old American custom, starting with that first heath hen. The sacred right of the hunter." The author had pushed aside his prefabricated tray as if the meal had abruptly become distasteful. He carefully placed his arms along the edge of the table, hands cupping his elbows.

"As you must realize, Pick, our guest is here because of those ads we bought criticizing the Self-Propelled Expressway."

"You mean that you bought," the book reviewer shot back. "You ignored my warning, but your vanity is overpowering."

"Yes, I confess to that," the author replied amiably. "But are we to allow the world to become absorbed by the Expressway without a whimper of objection?"

"Too late for all that," Pickett Sneat replied and sucked some food trapped in his front gat-teeth. "An empty protest—always post facto, Leo. Too late, too late."

A brooding misery suffused Leo Post's expression, and the dark eyes seemed to review his colleague. The earlier contentions that had marked their exchanges had cooled in the evening draughts that came through the enormous windows on the riverside. Their manner suggested a wary, stiff cordiality.

"It began so simply," Post said. "Probably DeWitt Clinton introduced the idea, digging the Erie Canal. Every governor since has wanted to build something, modify the landscape. The urge goes with the office perhaps. However, when Kimball Lyon came along, there wasn't much left to build. The capital had been transformed into that glass-walled mirror of greed, a target of opportunity. More than enough stadiums. Shopping malls abounded. What could he build? Then inspiration struck— parking lots. It was an idea that met its time. The threat of terrorist attacks obsessed every city planner. In Lyon's genius— I can recall those discussions we had on into the early hours—the idea was to give the terrorists nothing to attack. Just pave it over! Brilliant, you must agree, and simple as so many great ideas are. He took the old green- belt concept that zoned an encirclement of farmland around a city so as to retain its rural character—a remembrance, if you will, of our agrarian origins but one that had become littered with frozen custard stands and yoga spas and gutted public phone booths—Lyon translated this postulate into more concrete terms."

"A pretty turn of phrase." Sneat smacked his lips and then raised his voice, "And it only cost a few billion!"

"Ah well, Pickett, when you have leaders who are also passionate devotees of the arts, the cost of government becomes
meaningless because every project becomes a work of art and
therefore priceless."

Post paused to realign the aluminum dish before him, a visual
representation of his thoughts being so ordered. "Let's say this is
the city of Albany—the capital. Here's the Hudson River along
its eastern area." He traced a line on the tabletop along the right
edge of the plate. "This catsup bottle down here, south, used to
be the community of East Delmar. Thence, moving clockwise, we
come to Voorheesville—this saltcellar—Guilderland, the pepper,
and on around through the peanut butter or Watervliet and then
rejoin the river to the south at Loudonville. A full circle. The mustard pot will do nicely for this juncture.

"As you know," he swept aside all the positioned condiments
as he went on, "this has become the area of the Perpetual Parking
Plaza—a cement and macadam belt ten miles wide that completely
encircles the capital city except for the natural boundary of the
Hudson River. Governor Lyon was always annoyed that the river
interfered with his plans for a 360-degree paved encirclement of
the capital, and in fact there had been some talk of re-routing the
river eastward so it ran along the foothills of the Berkshires, but
the technology of the time did not match the splendor of that vision. Paving the river over was also not within the expertise of
the period. This incompleteness—untidy was the word that often
came to Lyon's lips—of the project remained a source of frustration for the Governor, though he put a good face on it. Leaving
the river untouched, he claimed, was his subscription to environmental issues.

"Of course, the plan was strongly criticized in editorials and
in public arenas, for it meant seizing by eminent domain all the
communities in the way of the project—seizing and leveling them.
Some nine hundred square miles of backyard barbecues, cul de
sacs and school-bus stops—all gone. Lyon shot back that the
towns were only elaborate bedrooms that could be set up anywhere,

and the outcry was the usual objection raised by the ignorant and shortsighted when faced with a genuine example of creative genius."

"Tsk, tsk," Sneat admonished. "You are trying to separate yourself from that opinion. You are the classic example of a cultural elitist in league with a political elitist."

"Oh, come now," the author replied rather huffily. "History has proved him right. No terrorist has attacked a square foot of the Perpetual Parking Lot."

"But do you never feel a second of guilt for that displacement, that destruction of all those towns!" The book reviewer's face had grown red, and he picked up the catsup bottle and shook it in his colleague's face as if he were confronting the author with the entire disenfranchised population of East Delmar. He seemed ready to jump to his feet and lunge at Leo Post, but of course he could not do so.

"Of course," Post replied with a muted voice. He had become meek, seemed humbled by Sneat's attack, and their exchange resembled a well-practiced ritual, a change of season. "But the techniques of government can become the ultimate purpose of government, and I became a victim of that phenomenon." He shrugged and stood to attend the fire in the hearth, adding more wood to it. "Of course the senators and assemblymen from those particular areas were particularly upset. We had eliminated their constituencies with one swoop of the governor's pen. And they had no recourse, for they no longer represented anyone—the logic had been breathtaking.

"Also incorporating techniques of his predecessors, Lyon created the State Parking Authority, which was answerable to no elected official except him and could take over the areas needed by eminent domain, issue its own bonds to support the endeavor, and these bonds, in turn, proposed a high rate of interest paid out of tax monies that no one really noticed, and the bonds were bought by banks and corporations that would construct the Plaza. The displaced legislators were all appointed to serve on the Authority at no reduction of pay for, to be realistic, who would know better about parking in the area that, say, had once been the town of Guilderland than the legislators who had once represented Guilderland? You see the brilliance of the conception."

The table responded to Post's point in silence. The man called Taylor dozed in his chair, chin on chest. Pickett Sneat had stared upwards as if searching for some argument in the darkness of the high ceiling. No noise came from behind the kitchen partition; Sgt. Anderson a.k.a. Lucy was biding her time.

"Simple—direct and—efficient," Post had continued, each word pushed into the air by the tip of one finger. "Only the Hudson River denied Governor Lyon the circuitry that would have capped his achievement, the completeness, the rounding of the idea."

"And no expense spared," Sneat said as if he had just come on the words. "The Perpetually Being-Paid-For Parking Plaza is its correct title. It might be remembered that the Lyon fortune was amassed by employing Ben Franklin's concept of compounding interest. One of Lyon's ancestors, a contemporary of Franklin's, had established trust funds that continued to compound interest, growing larger and larger. The Governor had simply translated this concept to the funding of the Plaza with the taxpayer continually paying off the interest on the bonds while those that had bought them—figure out what family banks were involved—cleaned up on the ever-expanding principal. *Das vaz kapital*, baby!"

"Oh, Pick, that fantasy doesn't do you justice," Post said with a pained expression. He crossed his long legs encased in black knee socks and leaned back in his chair. He adjusted his shirt cuffs. "It just doesn't illustrate Lyon's administrative genius. For example, his idea to do away with the legislature entirely as a fiscal item of the annual budget. Multiply several hundred legislators times their salary of ninety thousand dollars each—not to mention printing expenses, light bulbs, and the continuously wasteful miscellaneous—and you have only one argument that made sense to the voters. He called it a Proposal for Unicameral Government

—that had just the right sound to it, don't you agree? Opposition raised by hotels and restaurants and bars in Albany, who would suffer considerable losses were there no legislators in town, made Lyon back off.

"The Self-Propelled Expressway was a direct result of the Perpetual Parking Plaza; one followed the other naturally. I remember Lyon telling me about this next idea on the night that dear Pickett here received the National Letters Award from the Pegasus Society. A momentous evening all around."

"You are too kind," Sneat sighed.

"The Governor and I were driving down from Albany for the ceremony in New York City on the Taconic Parkway. You'll remember that example of automotive deployment was built by FDR when he was governor to facilitate his own tripping between New York City and Albany. Roosevelt had been an inspiration to Lyon. In any event, Kimball Lyon was to be the main speaker at the Pegasus Society's banquet, and a group of his poems had been printed in the program. It was part of the deal," Post said, with a sly smile that suggested his own part in the deal.

"Taylor was up front, at the wheel of the limousine, and as expert a driver as he was, he could not avoid some of the bone-jarring potholes on the crumbling highway. It had been an acceptable practice to permit older road systems to deteriorate so incoming administrations could build new highways, thereby satisfying both labor unions and the suppliers of raw materials. However, the repetition of these new constructions annoyed Lyon's sense of neatness. Why not, he asked me during that evening drive, initiate a road system that would never be completed—that would always be under construction and so, for all practical purposes, could never deteriorate because it would never be finished? A particularly vicious jounce over a rupture in the parkway's pavement bounced the Governor off his seat as he made this point.

"The technical means to achieve this perpetuality had just been incidentally realized during the Protective Defense Scrimmage in South America. We now recognize that such exercises are naïve ventures in hemispheric defense. Those who wish to challenge our way of life need only to get on the subway or charter a plane—attacking Bolivia, for example, is not in the contemporary terrorist's songbook," Post said with an ironic laugh. "However, America's rapid response in those war games was credited to the development of the Mark VIII Earth Modulator, that self-propelled thingamajig that could clear and grade land, fell trees, and lay concrete, all in one smooth operation. You will remember the Brazilian rain forest was transformed into an efficient and sparkling airdrome in a matter of weeks. That and the other airfields this powerful machine constructed in what had been the primitive wilds of Paraguay, Bolivia, and Argentina, practically overnight, were credited to our Western Team's ability to control the goal in Antarctica and therefore win the Scrimmage. The French, as usual, were overly concerned about aesthetics and lost the game. Well, you know all that."

"Another example, if I might interpolate," Pickett Sneat had roused himself importantly, "of the horrifying result that is often produced when artistic genius is frustrated—not recognized. That is what we have been talking about, is it not?" he asked sternly of Post. "The Mark VIII was actually the invention—unintended or not—of a sculptor from Topeka, Kansas. Homer Gladewart. He suffered years of rejection by galleries and museums and eventually lost his mind. In a frenzy of anger, the poor fellow welded all of his creations together and motorized the whole construction with solar panels he had originally used to power various water organs that tooted selections from Victor Herbert. He became a victim to his own genius. As it crashed through the walls of his Brooklyn studio onto Flatbush Avenue, Gladewart was crushed to death and never enjoyed the fruit of his ingenious grafting." The book reviewer had begun to laugh, and hiccups punctured his mirth. "More dis-(huc)-cerning minds saw how the sculpture could be a-(huc)-dapted for the war (hick) games and put to (uck-hick) use."

Leo Post moved swiftly to his colleague and gave several smart raps on the top of his head. The whacks interrupted the spasmodic cycle that had overcome the man, and his eyes rolled up toward Post in gratitude.

"Yes, true," Post agreed as he resumed his chair. "The artist's fate today is not oblivion—how sweet that would be, actually— but appropriation; to be perpetuated in wallpaper design, deodorant commercials, kitchenware, and in the case of Gladewart, laying down mile after mile of the Self-Propelled Expressway. That night Pickett Sneat was honored, Governor Lyon revealed to me his idea for building a road that would never be completed. I can still see him moving excitedly around the passenger compartment of the limousine as we bounced over the broken pavement of FDR's earlier experiment in mass transportation. I can still see him, perched excitedly on one of the jumps, his little feet dangling on either side. To make it short—"

"Oh, please do," Sneat interjected.

"—a corporation controlled by the Lyon Foundation bought up several of the Mark VIIIs in surplus depots after the South American Scrimmage, in which the machine had already demonstrated its versatility, to create the Perpetual Parking Plaza. Staff technicians had adapted several for the task, running six of them abreast to obliterate the town of Guilderland in one morning, grade the entire area, and lay down a smooth surface of concrete before nightfall. But painting the white lines that designated the million or so parking stations seemed to be beyond the contraption's capabilities. There had been snide editorials in some of the press about the Mark VIII being unable to do this simple task, and the Governor's opposition licked its chops. I remember him leaning toward me in the limousine, tapping my knee, and squinting to signal a joke on its way.

"'The simple fact of the matter is, Leo,' he said, in that peculiar drawl, 'the Mark VIII can paint the white lines, too. It can be programmed to do almost anything except make ice cream. But to paint those white lines by hand provides thousands of jobs. Painting them by hand'—here he tapped my knee again—'also gives the whole project a sense of individual, native craftsmanship. It gives people a sense of participation. Also'—he squinted again—'as soon as the job is finished at one end of the Plaza—up in Watervliet—it will have to be started all over again in Delmar. Whole families at work, generation following generation, painting those white lines—' The scope of the effort even seemed to amaze the Governor, and he paused to contemplate the enormous prospect his genius had produced. Then, he winked.

"'And as Jack Keats said, a thing of beauty is a job forever.'"

Post's reputed gift for mimicry was evident in his telling, for he had reproduced the late Governor's speech pattern, inflection, and emphasis with an exacting mastery. He had continued in his normal voice.

"A chill went through me as I regarded this minute monster perched on the limousine's jumpseat. But what could I do? Not only had I become his closest aide, but I was about to become his son-in-law as well—and I wanted nothing to come between my adorable Molly and me. The more he talked of his plans, the more desperate I became. He talked of using atomic engines that would drive the machines forever. They would lay down expressways across the state back and forth, up and down, paving over the entire landscape. His squinty little eyes became inflamed with the vision as we passed the Tappan Zee Bridge. How incongruous to hear his mad scheme as we drove to the occasion that would honor your work, Pickett."

"What a glorious night that was, too," the book reviewer said, and then with a smirk, added, "That was the night of our wager. Do you remember, Leo?"

Sneat's remembrance drew a pained expression upon Leo Post's face. He stood and walked into the shadows at the far end of the long room. Despite his somewhat careless, even seedy appearance, he was still an impressive figure. Something frightening in the man also had been brought to the suave surface of his usual aspect, and for one moment this curtain of civility had been thrust aside to reveal the violent nature behind. His figure was dimly limned in the chamber's obscurity, and his hands reached high to grasp the sculpted adornments above the darkened hearth so it appeared he was hanging from the mantel. An owl signaled the changing of the night. Then, Post turned back to us, the urbane composure restored as if the rage that had driven him away from us had been drawn into that lightless premise.

"Well now," Post said jovially, rubbing his hands together. "On with the show." Taylor returned with a film in the afternoon mail. We had ordered it from the Archives. "Mr. Taylor, let's run the film." But the chauffeur was fast asleep. "Mr. Taylor," Post said again, louder, but no response. "Taylor!"

"DRAW," shouted Pickett Sneat, and the man they called Taylor jerked to his feet as if pulled on string. In one smooth motion he was standing, his right arm outstretched and the six-gun gripped in his hand. The hammer had been cocked and his cool eyes sighted down the revolver's barrel. Pickett whooped and rattled his metal harness as the cowboy looked sheepishly but good-naturedly around. He returned the pistol to its holster as Leo Post put an arm around him.

"There, there, old friend. All is well. Would you be good enough to set up the screen and run the film we received today?"

The man called Taylor went about answering this request soberly, unfolding a small motion-picture screen and setting it on the floor against the near wall. Meanwhile, the author and book reviewer had become silent and seemed to observe a cool politeness between them. Post had dragged his chair beside Sneat's wheeled apparatus so the two would view the screen from the same vantage, side by side, but with several feet between them. Taylor had unwrapped the film canister and had fixed the reel on the antiquated movie projector. He threaded the film through the gates and lowered the kerosene lamp. The motion picture was an excerpt from an ancient newsreel, similar to those that were shown in movie theatres of yore.

(CLOSE-UP OF POWELL LOMAS) *Hello again, America, Powell Lomas reporting. Here's a strange story for you...*(OA OF PRETTY STEWARDESS CARRYING A STUFFED PIGEON INTO A COMMERCIAL AIRLINER. LOMAS

VOICE-OVER) ...*Martha, the passenger pigeon, flies again! This time—first class! All the way from Washington, where she's perched in the Smithsonian Institute, to San Diego, California,* (CLOSE-UP... STUFFED PIGEON WIRED TO A PERCH ON A SMALL BRANCH, AND HELD IN LAP OF PRETTY STEWARDESS WHO SMILES INTO CAMERA) *where she will help the San Diego Zoo celebrate its fiftieth anniversary. Only a small flight for Martha and her kind when they flew by the billions all over America— thousands of miles—but now no more.* (PLANE LANDING. PAN IN AS DOOR OPENS AND PRETTY STEWARDESS STEPS DOWN STAIRS FROM PLANE HOLDING PIGEON IN ONE HAND) ...*She was named after our very first First Lady and was the last of her species, dying in the Cincinati Zoo in September of 1914 at the ripe old age of 29.* (PRETTY STEWARDESS HANDS BIRD OVER TO A ZOO OFFICIAL) *Another example of our difficulty living with our fellow creatures on the planet. But the folks in San Diego hope to make Martha the guest of honor at their celebration. The guest of honor. When she died in 1914, the Cincinati Zoo officials packed her in 300 pounds of ice and shipped her to the Smithsonian, where she's nested ever since. But not this week.* (CLOSE-UP... PIGEON, HEAD AND GLASS EYES) *this week... the passenger pigeon takes to the skies...over America once again!!* (HEAD OF LOMAS...MUSIC UP AND OUT—LOMAS FADES OUT)

*

5

4

3

2

1

(BLANK   SCREEN—OVEREXPOSED   COLOR
FILM—CLOSE-UP ERECT PENIS THRUST INTO A
VAGINA. FEMALE APPARENTLY IN SUPERIOR POSI-
TION. PENIS IS THICK AND HEAVILY VEINED AND
GREATLY DILATES LABIA—VOICES OVER). *Ugh..uh...
agh...ahh..agh...ugh...ooh...ahh..oh...oh* (MONS VENERIS
SMOOTH AND HAIRLESS AND BEARS A SMALL PUR-
PLISH MARK. PARTICIPANTS PAUSE TO RE-INSERT
MALE ORGAN THAT HAS SLIPPED OUT.)...*hurry up....
yes...oh yes...agh...ah...of...ugh...ohhhh* (DURING CESSATION
TO RE-INSERT PENIS, PURPLISH MARK IDENTIFIED
AS A TATTOO OF A SMALL BURR-LIKE BLOSSOM.)

"LIGHTS...Give me some light!" It was Leo Post's strangled
cry. The man had leapt to his feet and ran to the table. Turned up
the wick of the kerosene lamp. "What villainy. You villain. You
vile bastard!"

"It wasn't me, Leo," the book reviewer shouted as he cowed
within the metal framework of his wheelchair. "I swear, Leo—I
know nothing of this."

The man called Taylor had stopped the film. The book reviewer spun the wheels of his device frantically and sped away from
Leo Post's anger. The writer's fists had raised and his face gone
dark. Sneat took the turn at the fireplace on one wheel and circled
back toward the table apparently out of control. "You must believe
me," he cried out desperately. He could not brake his apparatus
as it brought him back within the author's range. "How could I?
When could I have spliced that film on to the newsreel footage?"

The question stopped Post but did not soothe his anguish. The
long, aristocratic face had become bleached, the eyes like pieces of
jet, and he turned on the man called Taylor. But the simple fellow
stood dumbly by the projector, tears glistening on his cheeks—
clearly innocent of such foul behavior.

"But who would have done such a thing?" Post asked as bewilderment replaced his anger. "Who?"

No longer in danger, Sneat's cocky manner reasserted itself.
He idly pushed himself around the table and came to face us, I,

B. Smith, monitor of evidence. "But you have been exposed now, have you not?" Sneat said to Post. "You might as well confess it all now." There was no friendliness in his tone of voice, and he evidently was waiting for Post to say something. The author had clasped his hands and raised his large head. Eyes closed, he had turned toward the long row of windows and looked into the darkness outside. "Very well," Pickett Sneat said and turned back to us. "I will do the job for you." He moved even closer to us.

"That was no accident in the Woodlawn Cemetery of Elmira, New York, which took his wife's life. It was a planned murder. He killed her. He killed his wife, Governor Lyon's daughter, and there's the man"—he skillfully wheeled the chair in a complete circle to point at the man they call Taylor—"that's the man who did the job."

LATER THAT EVENING...

I, B. Smith, solemnly affirm this report to be a fair and actual account of all that has transpired on Pijon Island, commonly known as Leek's Island; said island to be situated mid-channel of the Hudson River, approximately forty miles south of the port of Albany and five miles north of the Poughkeepsie-Elmira Access Spur of the Self-Propelled Expressway.

WHEREAS the lapidated ruins of a castle, thought to be uninhabited, are actually the domain of several persons: NAME-LY (1) one Leo Post, né Leonard Leek, alias Len Banal, a writer and formerly chief advisor and son-in-law to the late Governor Kimball Lyon; (2) one Pickett Sneat, a book reviewer and literary figure, a National Letters Award winner and best known for *The Art and Craft of Reviewing*; (3) one man called Taylor, formerly a performer in rodeo sideshows, whose horse was apparently destroyed during an urban riot; (4) one Sergeant Lucille Anderson, BCI, New York State Police, who has infiltrated this household disguised as a Negro cook and part-time masseuse using the name of Lucy.

MOREOVER, certain revelations have been noted in the course of this investigation; Olivia Leek, heiress to a distinguished Hudson River family, did murder her lover and the father of the aforementioned Leo Post, né Leonard Leek, alias Len Banal, said murder occurring in Room 242 of the Hotel Chelsea, New York, New York—a previously unsolved homicide. Victim was Emil Nalbandian, a minor player of cards.

IN ADDITION, testimony has been given that the immense construction projects initiated by Governor Lyon were the result of his love and practice of poetry that had been frustrated by an alleged literary establishment as personified by Pickett Sneat. And that this same group were known to slant reviews to advance their own careers, and if this dishonesty was wittily confessed in subsequent publications, then these dissertations often won prizes for the honesty of their revelations.

FURTHER IT IS SAID that several tons of black powder have been stored in the cellars of Leek's Castle by an ancestor of Leo Post who, under the pseudonym of Len Banal, writes superficial pornography and that he currently claims to be engaged in research on an extinct bird, AND THAT, after a highly publicized romance and marriage serialized in tabloids and femme-slicks, said Leo Post did murder his wife, Mary Ellen (Molly) Lyon, daughter of the late Governor Kimball Lyon, AND THAT the man called Taylor was employed in this felony; THAT FURTHER Pickett Sneat was an accomplice.

SUBSEQUENTLY, I, B. Smith, a guest and witness, was invited to the rooms occupied by Pickett Sneat for the purpose of taking testimony on matters related to the murder of the aforementioned Governor's daughter, Molly Lyon. Keeping her disguise intact, Sgt. Anderson had just installed the book reviewer in the large four-poster bed situated in an alcove of his apartment. The metal harness stood emptily near the bed like the husk of a crustacean, its soft meat scooped out. The man's round and rascally face peered over the voluminous quilt within which Sgt. Anderson had swaddled him, and the undercover policewoman left the room in the discreet manner of her role—Lucy on tiptoe. She covertly winked.

The faded plush of the bed's canopy suggested the pinkish ambiance of a nursery. By contrast, the man's voice rumbled from within the mounds of soft feather ticking to make for an odd nursling, tucked in and cozy. He spoke without notes.

"Etymologically speaking," he began at once, "Smith must be the beetle of all names; there are so many of you. Or maybe I should say entomologically speaking; you are the bug of all names, so numerous as to become anonymous. You are a bug, of sorts, are you not, and so appropriately named? Over there," a shift of his eyes directed our attention to an antique tape recorder on a table. Stacks of tape spools rose next to it. "Over there are the voices of many Smiths and all of them reading their own poetry. They had turned to poetry in prison when they had been forced to exchange their common name for uncommon numbers. Identification has always been an issue for poets.

"But you're not interested in that bit of literary toying, and by training you are urged to look for motive in a crime—if not in a poem—for the logic of passion. Permit me to advise you—it would be a waste of your time to review my background to find some past event that would explain my present behavior, and do put away any speculation that some rude interference pulled me off the tit of life so that my nature, collicked to a fault, became permanently angered and programmed, if you will, to destroy Leo Post. Not at all. I am that monster born of Post's own genius; we are inseparable—I am cousin to the phantom brute who pushed Foucault before that delivery truck. I was created to hate Leo Post on sight, that's my role—all of those qualities that made him instantly loved, immediately admired, unquestionably respected only turned up the heat in my spleen. It was only fair after all—to even the account.

"And if you could have seen him in those days, the handsome arrogance of his entry into a room as if he owned everything in it and as if none of it—none of US—was worth more than the few pennies that always jingled in his pocket—always just a few pennies. I never once saw him pick up the check. He was an easy companion to the rowdy fellowship of professional athletes, while in other surroundings, could throw off an analysis of Aristophanes that made the Greek's importance to contemporary thought irrefutable. One evening at Ruby's—a dive frequented by the intelligentsia—I once saw him produce an off-the-cuff rendition of *Oedipus Rex*, taking all the parts and in the original Greek. His blind scene, staggering around the saloon, brought sobs from the breasts of the most hardened of sophisticates, and Katrina Patoux, her own Jocasta yet to make her immortal, went on her knees to embrace his feet. Needlessly to say, they left together at the end of the evening.

"I could go on." Sneat's round head rolled back and forth on the pillow. "Scrubwomen adored him. Cabbies of every nationality talked familiarly with him, and he often answered them in their native tongue. He had turned down the presidency of several universities and was an ex officio member of the Foreign Policy Committee. He had the ear of foreign ministers and, to be vulgar but accurate, the twats of every glamour queen. Women poets courted him, and the fairest anthropologists invited him on digs. Can you wonder, can you WONDER why…" The book reviewer's anger overwhelmed him, and he pulled the damask counterpane over his head to as if to smother his fury.

"However," he continued after several deep breaths, "until that night of my award, my only feeling toward Leo Post was an idling scorn, a bemused contempt for his manner, his poise. He was likeable enough, certainly had done me no harm—after all, I existed because of him, didn't I—and oftentimes his courtliness and awfully good manners could be rather droll. Quaint, if you know what I mean. He was fun to tease—I had already played my little joke on him as to Kimball Lyon's book of poems. I had convinced him to puff a review of that tripe, believing he was pro-

tecting the citizenry from Lyon's madness. Then, because of that...
BECAUSE OF THAT... he became the Governor's aide. THEN
HIS SON-IN-LAW..."

The man's face had become tomato red, and he once again
pulled the covers over his head, gasping and choking. The whole
bed quaked with the tremors of his suppressed anger. The heavy
quilting made it impossible to discern the man's attenuated limbs
and body within so that the head on the pillow, uncovered, pink
and sweaty, appeared like something contrived by a conjurer.

"At the Academy, I had just been wheeled on stage to receive
some light but altogether just applause and had begun to greet
some who came to shake my hand." Subject relived the moment
and smiled sweetly, nodding left and then right on the pillow.
Abruptly, the expression changed. "A flurry of noise rose from
the rear of the hall, and the applause—appropriate and properly
contained—became a wild clamor. Shouts and squeals. Governor
Lyon had walked in though he could not be seen in the crowd, but
his place was made clear by the tall advisor who followed him. Leo
Post. For whom this acclamation was being made, since Lyon was
too short to be seen. It was a moment almost ludicrous for Post
pushed through the thronged elite. His manner resembled that
of a Great White Hunter resolutely threading his way through the
jungle, preceded by his pygmy gun bearer.

"His dark eyes flashed as he so very graciously shook hands
with both cheat and genius, scoundrel and saint. He made no difference, don't you UNDERSTAND," the critic screeched, out of
control, "NO DIFFERENCE. He treated everyone the same."
The man's tone had dulled.

"As I watched him move toward the stage, sometimes holding
the Governor above the crowd so the politician could wave and
blow kisses, the sour wad of undigested anger clogged my throat.

"Understand, I had lied and cheated," the book reviewer continued piteously, "worked hard to bear false witness at fifty cents a
line. Here I was after years of planning and scheming and with—
to put it in a crude figurative—the best greased bum in the criti-

cal fraternity—on MY NIGHT! MY NIGHT! And then enters
Leo Post who had dropped into the pie without the slightest im-
propriety. Leo Post with all those family backgrounds that he so
charmingly dismissed—BUT he had them to dismiss—and who
could write so well about almost anything, who was handsome, a
holder of several athletic records, a man of action and renowned
lover and he could WALK... HE COULD WALK...

"Then to top it all," Sneat continued after gulping and swallowing his rage, "he married the Governor's daughter. All that
money and all that. ALL that," he smacked his lips obscenely. "Do
you understand? Post has only told you the obvious things about
Molly Lyon: her beauty and charm, the flare of her mind. And, as
he said, he did urge her to take seriously this feel she had for fast
cars. Just prior to their elopement, she took second at Le Mans.
Moreover, she was something of a mathematics prodigy, and with
the guidance of a Nobel laureate who played squash with Leo, she
reworked some of her undergraduate papers, and she delivered one
of these before the Dublin Institute, 'Another Look at the Schro-
dinger Equation.' Friends in the field tell me it had no little effect
on quantum mechanics.

"In addition, she was a superb cook—Marcella Hazan was said
to ask her advice on certain pork recipes. She whipped up clothes
of her own design and was rumored to be fantastic. FANTASTIC
IN BED." The visage on the pillow had turned purple, a sputter-
ing image that disappeared beneath the counterpane that for several moments resembled one of those topographical models meant
to suggest the tremors of an earthquake. The convulsions grew less
violent and finally subsided and he uncovered his face, gasping for
air. The reddish fringe of hair was plastered to his brow. A flutter of wings beat against the shuttered window, followed by the
shriek of a small animal—then, silence.

"Not even the amplification system worked for me that
night," Sneat continued mournfully. "When I was pushed to the
microphone to make my acceptance speech—a gem, if I do say so,
of clichés and plagiarisms that would please without offending—

some wires crossed to obliterate the room with horrendous feed-back. It could not be corrected. Only poets and other writers in the room—not a single electrician. So the plug was pulled, and only those in front heard me; the rest looked to Leo Post for cues as to when to applaud, to laugh, or snicker. So, I even owed him the manufactured approbation of the assembly.

"During the reception, Governor Lyon pushed me into a corner, saying he never properly thanked me for my review of his poems, *Sunspots*. Then he talked about his executive order reinstituting executions and the possible effect of a death sentence on art and say-gee-whiz wouldn't that make a dandy study? Something that would make someone like me really famous if I had the right backing like, say, a little stipend from the Lyon Foundation?

"'Betcha there are some humdingers locked up that are dying for expression,' he said, squinting up at me and giving that famous wink of the right eye. I told him I had several projects in progress.

"'Whatta they pay you?' he asked and finished his champagne. He balanced the flute on the back of one hand, a trick to distract me. So I asked if I would have to live in the prison.

"'I hear the grub's pretty good,' he replied. I countered that I could not be bought so easily, and if a genuine contribution to poetry would come of it, then, given the right conditions, I would consider the idea.

"'Sure, pally, sure. Here's the foundation application. Just fill it in. Be sure to spell your name right. It's a matter of form—this form.'

"He always carried applications with him. He had picked up the trophy just awarded me.

"'That'll look neat on your mantel. We had a bunch of them made up for that TV quiz show one of my outfits sponsored. Can't remember its name. Was you on that show? You look familiar.'

"I told him no. Post had joined us in the meantime, congratulating me with a warmth and sincerity that soured my spleen even as I found myself taking his hand with an equal fervor—like a giddy schoolgirl. You see the vicious encirclement around me.

Lyon had departed to inspect a portion of the Long Island Rail-road as members of the Pegasus Society enveloped us to gush over Leo Post. They ignored me, of course. They questioned Post about Molly, about the Governor's re-election, about his new book *RFD, The Loves of a Rural Postman.* I was pushed to one side, jostled and leaned over by the reigning matrons of the Society, my face on a level with and unable to avoid their musty pubes because of the heavy tribute to my ambition that lay in my lap—The National Literary Award. You talk about irony!

"It was at that exact moment," the book reviewer continued, "that I promised myself to find some way to punish Leo Post for his goodness. His openhearted benevolence that forgave my false-hoods, his indifference to my meanest, most slimy instincts—his very charity sucked up the atmosphere in which I could breathe, purifying it as trees give back oxygen.

"And just as this smothering press of his admirers was about to overcome me, he bent down and suggested we leave, find a place we could talk. Imagine turning his back on this claque that a gen-eration of Whitmans would have groveled in the grass for. Post's every act of kindness toward me became one more faggot laid upon the pile I prepared for him.

"The man called Taylor drove us across town to this appalling place called Ruby's with dreadful food and the atmosphere out of *Lower Depths.* Thieves and pimps drank and chatted with scholars and society belles. Movie people and bond salesmen. The stench of clogged urinals hung overall. The place had become the watering hole of the intelligentsia, and every item on its faux Chinese menu tasted like the next. Leo Post greeted one and all as equals, never lowering himself but somehow raising each to his level.

"I see you are becoming restless, and I will come to the point. The wager. You have asked about the wager between Post and me. I hadn't forgot but you must allow me a bit of narrative. I've been locked up on this island with people who know only one story. I had hopes for Lucy, fresh tales of life as a minority; the black expe-rience relived—oh, the dire deliciousness of it! But whenever we are alone and I try to question her, she begins to pummel me and all discourse becomes impossible." His pink-rimmed eyes turned piteously. He took a deep breath.

"Post was so full of himself that night as we sat at a corner table of Ruby's. He boasted of his inamorata. How Molly did this. She was the best at that, the greatest of all. And her loyalty to him above all else—how true she was in this time of casual encounters. More than lover, more than wife—she was his perfect mate, his ideal friend. I can still hear the Hudson Valley accent put upon the word—fra-end.

"Such goodness is always boring—no one wants to hear of it or be near it. To be stuck at a table with it in a crummy restaurant is surely to be stuck in a ring of hell. So my idea for revenge slowly blossomed as Post went on and on. If I could plant the seeds of doubt as to his wife's loyalty in that seraphic soul, then what viperfish weed would take root? It's a familiar device. I've never claimed to be original. Gently I lofted certain speculations about her past—one or two of her affairs were common knowledge. That matter with the German aerialist team, for example. Post only smiled and turned aside these slanders with that gesture of good fellowship that only drove the spike of my malice deeper into my soul.

"Surely, I said to him, the sultry greasiness of a pit stop during the Peoria Three Hundred could generate a sensuality that would be uncontrollable—that would overcome the woman's dedication to him. Consider the pace of the competition, the rough usage of those hard-muscled mechanics as they took off parts and fitted new ones together, measured, inspected their dipsticks and inflated the tires. She was a hot-blooded, well-seasoned female who, by his own boasts, was ready for play on every occasion. But Post laughed loftily, amused by my imagery, and his very appreciation of my language inflamed my hatred even more.

"Well, where was she tonight, I asked him? Perhaps enjoying a reunion with an old paramour. Wasn't the prime minister of Finland in town for the United Nations session, and there was that story about the two of them held hostage in a sauna by Lapland extremists. Post gave my implication one of his University Club ha-hahs. He looked down on me with an amiable contempt.

'You must remember,' he lectured me as he raised the slim cigar he favored then, 'that faith and trust create an impenetrable shield against such silliness. For Molly to be unfaithful,' he continued as he flicked some cigar ash my way, 'would be like day becoming night.'

"'But she's an independent, adventurous woman!' I persisted, wondering how long a lever it would take to turn his world on its axis. As I spoke, a good-humored scorn for my words came into his dark eyes, and with a patrician indifference, he turned his face to one side.

'My dear fellow,' he murmured, 'my Molly would never be unfaithful.'

"Never? I challenged him. The pulse in my throat fluttered birdlike.

'No, never,' he answered, suddenly serious. The eyes had lost their softness and become obsidian.

"And though I knew my next words, could already hear them in my head," the book reviewer went on, "my lungs seemed to collapse, and my vocal cords had stuck together. These poor limbs you see screwed tight and imprisoned in steel seemed to lift as light as the tobacco smoke rising above Ruby's bar—my blood tingled with refreshed circulation.

'Wanna bet?' I asked.

"Leo was about to answer me when the front doors of the restaurant crashed back and the subject of our discussion swaggered in, flanked by members of the Hartford Harridans. She was, you may remember, the general manager of this professional women's basketball team, and they were on their way to the national championship. The loose-limbed hilarity of these young women, the sparkle in their eyes, personified their victory on the boards. The place roundly cheered them. These stunning jockettes, if I may coin such an appellation, were in great contrast to the anemic bawds and frivolous nymphs dabbling at their plates of Ruby's high-priced chop suey, the usual sorry handmaidens to be found around the altar of Kultur. The appearance of these champions was reason enough for celebration. All of them were well over six feet—Molly Lyon looked petite in their midst—and they moved about the restaurant clapping hands to backs with the graceful poise of the prime athletes they were. Several picked up one of the waiters and playfully passed him around. More than one dribbled basketballs as they sipped sugary concoctions. Their faces shone with a scrubbed radiance where no dissemblance could adhere.

"But moving through this exuberant pandemonium, clearly a single-minded devotion determining her stride, was Molly Lyon Post bearing down on our table. She approached with a long-legged, liquid lope, her Persian cat's eyes fixed on Leo. She cut through the crowd at the bar as if they did not exist, as if she were homing in on some radio signal sent out by the man in the chair next to me. She stopped beside him, but he did not rise.

"'You are splendid,' Leo told her. And she was.

"I remember the maroon blouse she wore, cut like a Cossack smock, fastened tight at the wrist and belted low at the waist. Black tights and thigh-high floppy boots of gray suede. Her dazzling hair fell loose upon her shoulders.

"You would expect a passionate embrace at this point," the book reviewer continued. "Certainly the patrons at this seedy watering hole did so as they raised their drinks in salutation. I certainly wouldn't have minded seeing a little schmoochy-feelie," said Sneat, and immediately looked a little embarrassed. I, B. Smith, knowledgeable in public morality, gave the man credit. "Not so," he had continued. "As if to deny us such a voyeuristic treat, and clearly pleasuring themselves in that denial, Molly simply took Post's left hand between her hands, looked deeply into his eyes and, bending over, lightly brushed her cheek against his. The ordinary hubbub was restored."

A tremendous blast boomed from the river as a large tanker passed the island. The noise had interrupted Sneat. The ship's wake crashed against the old fortress walls and trembled the paving stones beneath our feet. As the vessel continued downriver, a final apostrophe to its passage was marked by a piece of coping above the interior courtyard as it plunked into the basin.

"And what do you suppose this glamorous pair talked about?" Pickett picked up his narrative. "You might expect profound explorations of literary matters—how about difference, fear, and creation in belles-lettres? Or maybe an analysis of some new theory of the universe—how it all began and how it will end? Or a hot pepper-play of words on the unassailable quality of color—does it really exist or is it only a value our eyes put upon an object? How did civil liberties become equated with anarchy, for example? Can you guess?" He did not wait for an answer but went on; the circumference of his face seemed to square off, become angular as his voice imitated the nasal hauteur of Leo Post.

"'Looks like you're celebrating a victory,' Post said to Molly Lyon.

"'They were super tonight. Came from behind at the half to take it 107 to 103,' she replied, taking a chair and crossing her elegant long legs. The slithery sound of her hosiery caressing beneath the table reminded me of the torture rack that encased me.

"Eventually they remembered me as I toyed with my soggy egg foo yung. Molly reviewed the menu with the pink, damp, open-mouthed wonder of a child. Her upper lip was full, almost a pout, as it covered a slight overbite.

"'What will you have?' Post asked her. He suggested the rice noodles with mushrooms and shrimp.

"'No, just a couple of spring rolls would do,' she replied.

"Molly had crossed her legs once again. You know that silky sound almost nearly stopped James Joyce's career dead before it began. In a story called 'The Contrast' in *Dubliners*. He had to change it or the printers would not print the book. Too sexy for them. Look it up," the book reviewer advised us. And waggled his chopsticks. Post wanted to order cider. He was beaming with good-heartedness.

"'Yes, a pitcher of cider will do nicely,' he says.

"'I don't care for cider,' I say. 'It makes my stomach sour.'

"'What?' He pulls up as if offended? 'Come to Ruby's and not have the cider?'

"I rattled my braces menacingly but who attends a book reviewer's voice? Post has leaned on the table, a bland smile on his aristocratic puss. 'You have to drink the cider,' he said. 'Ruby makes it herself in an old cider mill she owns upstate. It used to belong to Dutch Schultz.'

"'Who was Dutch Schultz?' asks Molly.

"'Bless that sweet ignorance,' Post says as he nuzzles the golden hair around her ear. She pulls away to look upon him with the adoration a pupil gives a master, a pupil waiting for further instruction. She could have had great athletes for lovers. Prime ministers and clowns—not to mention a select list of literary culturists. It came to me in a flash that the source of her fascination was Leo's overwhelming store of trivia.

"'Dutch Schultz,' he accounts, taking another puff of his cigar, 'is an old folk hero who was assassinated just a few blocks from where we sit. He was sitting at a marble-topped table of his favorite café when two former associates, also in the cider business, walked in and shot him in the middle of his knockwurst. I mean as he was eating the sausage. One used a Smith & Wesson .38 caliber Police special. The other weapon was a Browning, .44 caliber revolver made for the British Army in World War I that, in fact, still bore the crest of the 32nd Royal Fusiliers stamped on the frame just aft the cylinder. How Schultz's assailants got these particular weapons, I could tell you.'

"And for a terrible moment, I thought he would," Pickett Sneat snapped. The round head had rolled from side to side on the pillow, a definitive show of impatience. "But the woman's green eyes had nearly crossed with attention.

"'And they killed him?' she asks.

"'Oh, quite,' Post replies. 'But not on the spot. Schultz didn't die immediately. He managed to crawl into the lavatory to expire on the floor of the middle stall—one without toilet tissue and with a large amount of graffiti on its walls. He took to his grave many recipes that might have gladdened the heart of a true ciderist. In fact, a contemporary copy of *Smart Set* contains a eulogy in Alexandrine meter by a talented lyricist of that day; sadly, not talented enough to escape oblivion. And so it goes.'

"And so it went," Sneat complained from beneath the counterpane. "I had to endure nonsense like this for the next hour, unable to get away. My lack of mobility gave me little choice but to witness the grab bag of Post's mind dumped on the table. My lust to bring the man down had momentarily cooled, and Molly Lyon had become rather ordinary. Any woman who could be entranced by such *petite merde*, to use some of the French linguistics, was no prize—not at table anyway." The man paused to roll his eyes roguishly. "However, the evening ended rather gaily—the three of us in good spirits as we left Ruby's. The star center of the Harridans, a wholesome young woman—all seven feet of her—smelling of wintergreen but with armpits still redolent of her Nebraskan childhood..." The book reviewer stretched in memory of the moment, and his tongue lolled at one corner of his mouth. "Where was I?" Sneat asked us after a moment of arousal.

I, B. Smith, eager for him to make his point, mentioned the party leaving the then-fashionable restaurant on the Upper East Side of New York City. Records indicate Ruby's has subsequently been paved over as part of the Harlem Perpetual Parking Plaza.

"Yes, this charming athlete folded me into the back of the Governor's limo but not before Leo put his mouth close to my ear.

"'I'll take that bet,' he whispered.

"Truly I could not have cared less at that moment, for I had begun to prepare myself for entering prison the next morning to take up my obligation to the Lyon Foundation. I was to begin my research and recording of data surrounding the effect of the death sentence on the creative faculties. Moreover, it seemed unlikely that I would encounter the Posts again. My challenge had only been part of the banter common to places like Ruby's. But Post had taken it seriously."

He paused as if to recreate the moment in his memory. The tip of his tongue poked out from clenched teeth. A rumbling began deep in his throat, and his round head rolled back and forth on the pillow, and his rabbity eyes fixed upon us.

"What happened next was the purest chance—the best turn of a melodrama. A year after that evening, I was interviewing a prisoner about to take his place in the electric chair. You must understand how emotionally draining this experience was—how to sift the genuinely talented from the pile of those who merely wanted to tickle their egos before being executed. A sort of ultimate frisson.

"I remember his number but not his name." He feigned an apologetic expression. "Number 62890 was a sly-looking fellow, and I could tell from the moment he entered the interrogation room that he didn't possess a shred of talent. I was ready to dismiss him immediately when he began talking about certain pictures in his possession that might be of interest to Governor Lyon. He had calculated that my Lyon Fellowship had put me close to the Governor, so clearly I was being inducted into a conspiracy.

"And what were these pictures? you might ask." I, B. Smith, auditor, had said nothing. "Perhaps you will guess when I tell you that the fellow had been a tattooist before being arrested for the murder of a series of beauticians. Yes, he was the very artist who had engraved the Leek blossom on the high-class tundra of Molly Lyon." The invalid's head rocked upon the pillow with a suppressed glee, and his tongue was clamped between his teeth. He smothered the fit with the counterpane and then emerged huffing and gulping as calm was restored. "That's how I know details of the operation that only someone present in that dingy office could know.

"Apparently, No. 62890 also aspired to a career in photography; and while Post and the man called Taylor confronted the motorcycle gang, he snapped some pictures of his masterpiece to add to his portfolio. He told me he wanted to be recognized as a realist. I ascertained his motive at once—in return for these pictures I was to get the Governor to lift the death sentence, a laughable idea but the man was desperate. I played along with his fancy, for though my rancor with Leo Post had been somewhat assuaged by my time spent in prison, this turn of events—recognizable to all of us in literature—pricked the jealous boil of my subcutaneous ire. I convinced him I would be part of his blackmail in return for the pictures, and the day before he was screwed into the socket he told me of the pictures' whereabouts—in a coffee can buried near his old tattoo parlor.

"The fellow made an unseemly racket and mess on his way to the chair, claiming that he had been betrayed, that his work was not given its due, and that there were sides to his personality that had some merit. The usual list of desperate appeals common to us all. But I had the pictures and the film." Sneat smacked his lips. "But they were different from what I supposed.

"The photos were similar to the images in the film clip we saw this evening—probably stills taken from that same extravaganza. I assume that Molly Post returned to his backstreet studio for more modeling, perhaps that one exposure on that humid night had loosened lasciviousness in her nature she could not control. She had the presence, being the Governor's daughter, to obscure her face, though the mark of the leek clearly identified her. Not so the bemused expressions of the several men who performed with her—who worked like maniacal carpenters over the sawhorse of HER BODY." The man's voice scaled out of control, and his figure beneath the bedclothes spasmed. He coughed, captured his demeanor, and went on. "Indeed, to continue this figure of speech, one photograph indicated one of these busy miners—I make no apology for mixing the metaphor—had ceased operations in the upper mine to take core samples in the arroyo just below. I rather like that," he complimented himself.

"I couldn't believe my good luck when I received a message from Leo Post—using the official letterhead of his office—inviting me to contribute an essay for the program celebrating the opening of the Poughkeepsie-Elmira spur of the Self-Propelled Expressway. He thought he was doing me a favor, extending his patrician largesse to this poor cripple of a book reviewer, throwing a copper to the beggar at the back door. Little did he know. He asked for something on Mark Twain since Twain is buried in Elmira, New York—and how absurd can history be—*just a couple of hundred words since you're on the Lyon payroll already* was his tone of voice. Oh, yes, I would give him something, an essay with pictures." He snuggled down into the covers with a self-satisfied sigh. A heavy door slammed shut somewhere below in the castle.

"In the end, I didn't send the pictures with the essay but had the great fun of witnessing Post's face as he looked at them. Lyon had unexpectedly died, choking on an olive pit, though there have always been those rumors of his bodyguards finding him facedown in the damp luxuriance of a naiad from the secretarial pool. But what a triumph to watch Post's face as he saw the pictures of his darling Molly lending herself to the louts from whom he thought he had won her over. Leo thought the envelope contained some suggestions for his funeral oration." Sneat paused to wipe his lips on the sheet.

"Probably only I and Post and a few others knew of the enormous tomb Kimball Lyon had built for himself beneath the Perpetual Parking Plaza. Its cost had been enormous and raised the sales tax several percentage points. Post was to deliver the eulogy as the coffin was lowered into the crypt deep beneath the surface and with parking meters eternally running at every corner of the chamber like those figures on a pharaoh's tomb endlessly hunting and trapping birds. Molly sat at the end of the platform with some officials. Her face was pale and her features drawn by sorrow and fatigue. She had just completed the time trials for the race in Elmira in which she was to lose her life. The Perpetual Parking Plaza was full. Almost a festive atmosphere inspired the throng. I watched the messenger hand Leo the envelope. He recognized my handwriting and cast a regal wink of appreciation my way. Ah, how sweet that moment lies in my memory. Leo Post poised on the fulcrum of his destruction. What a moment of power—I held the man on my hip.

"He had opened the envelope and looked at the contents. The long, elegant face went gray. The eyes became dead. He was waiting for his introduction, sitting down, but his whole frame seemed to sag, pushed him down and off the chair so he crumpled to the ground. A groan of sympathy escaped the crowd, for they assumed the full weigh of his grief over his mentor's death had just then overwhelmed him. The man introducing him quickly ascertained Leo's condition—he was now openly sobbing—and deftly rerouted the ceremony around him. Molly knelt to inspect and comfort him. Oh, what a lovely scene I had created." The book reviewer chortled and gurgled and started an uncontrollable coughing fit that took several minutes to abate.

"But Post struggled from her embrace, as if she were something contaminated, and rose to his full hauteur, his face stony and the dark eyes like beads of onyx. I had won. I had won the bet! I looked around fully expecting to see all the parking meters waving their red flags. VIOLATION—VIOLATION—VIO-LATION." The paroxysm of coughing overcame him again, and the bed shook. He pulled at the counterpane and his countenance purpled.

"You know the rest," the man resumed after a moment's recovery. "How Molly Lyon was killed in Elmira a few days later, completely annihilated during the premier run of the Pough-keepsie-Elmira Five Hundred, later to be renamed the Mark Twain Five Hundred. Her car went out of control on a hairpin turn in the Woodlawn Cemetery only a little distance from the old riverboat captain's final anchorage. Her car was completely demolished when it crashed into the stone side of a mausoleum erected by a minor industrialist, a manufacturer of soap dispensers. The Moroni Special was consumed by a fire that left nothing. Nothing. But I tell you, it was no accident. It was a murder and one conceived by Leo Post and executed by the man called Taylor.

He must have done something to the brakes. But now, you know," said Pickett Sneat, and lifted his head from the pillow to fix his eyes upon us. "Now you know, and you must do your duty. I won't mind being in prison again, this time on the other side of the bars. There's a kind of comfort in that solitude. My real work may yet be done there."

I, B. Smith, duly recording this material, became aware of a disturbance in the chambers below. It sounded as if the Romanesque table and chairs of the dining room were being moved about, accompanied by shouts and a clamor of orders. Hurried footsteps neared us, and the apartment's door was thrown open. Leo Post, wild-eyed, his wine-colored dressing gown ripped, stood in the doorway.

"We have been seized," he announced. "Terrorists have taken the castle. Taylor was overcome, and Lucy is being held hostage in the kitchen."

"Terrorists, you say?" his colleague asked.

"Armed vagrants. Guerillas. We saw them earlier. Those three men we saw earlier. We thought they were fishermen." Leo Post had strode to Sneat's bedside and was endeavoring to lift him from the bed. "Let me put you into your chair. I need you to negotiate with these thugs."

"Leave me alone," the man shouted, his voice climbing. He pulled the covers over his head.

"Old friend, you must help me protect the pigeon papers. As a scholar, you must rise to this threat—" A gunshot boomed deep in the caverns of the castle, then Post continued. "You as a scholar of Americana."

"No, no! Leave me be. It's all your fault," Sneat fumed. "I've told this interrogator everything. Your time is up, Post. You're finished," shouted the critic.

"Your pardon, gentlemen all," a voice said softly but no less commandingly. A tall youth wearing a bright yellow cap stood in the doorway. A small automatic rifle was slung over one shoulder. Dark glasses shielded his eyes so it was difficult to identify the curve of his lips as a smile or a sardonic grimace. "We shall require the presence of everyone below."

"But ... what ... are you going to do with us?" Pickett Sneat asked.

"Take me," Post said, advancing arms outstretched. "Spare the others. They are of lesser importance..."

"Did you hear that, did you hear that?" the book reviewer inquired of us.

"And they have done little harm," the author continued. As he spoke, the terrorist had slowly swung the muzzle of his weapon so it pointed directly at Post. I, B. Smith, holding my breath, heard the stones of the vaulted chamber creak under the tension. Then the armed intruder assumed his former nonchalance and re-shouldered his weapon. He walked toward Post who still stood, arms out, a figure of sacrifice. With a manner that in earlier times would have been called cheeky, the assailant picked a small piece of lint from the lapel of the writer's dressing gown. He smoothed down the nap of the material.

"And what harm have you ever caused?" he asked Post evenly.

Early the Next Morning...

"Imagine that flight of swallows raising Aurora from her bower." Leo Post, clad in his red velvet dressing gown, gestured through the open casement windows toward the river. "Imagine those two dozen swallows to be millions—millions, and you have an idea of the awesome effect of passenger pigeons when they lifted from a forest."

We had been assembled in the long gallery by the youth in the yellow cap and his two accomplices. These last two could be brothers for they resembled each other by their lack of distinction rather than in sharing a characteristic. Even as Post spoke, the two young terrorists stood by the immense fireplace, on either side of the mantel, to resemble figures that had been restored to the Romanesque design. They seemed to be unarmed unless the hand-sized portable radio one of them carried could be considered a weapon, tuned to a continuous weather station.

Yellow Hat casually handled the automatic rifle and then slung it on the table when he assumed Post's large chair. The man called Taylor stood motionless and looked toward the river, the holster strapped to his thigh, empty. Pickett Sneat, slumped in a catatonic trance, feigned or real, seemed to have become smaller within his metal harness so that the bands of steel looked loose and outsized. I, B. Smith, the keeper of this record, observed these proceedings from an appropriate distance.

"Please continue," the terrorist said with a wave of hand. The morning light silvered his glasses. Earlier he had questioned Post about the stuffed birds on the table, and the author, requiring little persuasion, had commenced his lecture. He took a deep breath and continued.

"There is probably no more complete record of a species becoming extinct than that of the passenger pigeon," he told us. His eyes had passed over our assembly and then swept up to the ceiling. "The first descriptions of the bird go back to 1524 and Cartier's account of a flock over Prince Edward Island. There is considerable reportage prior to Cartier's in different Indian scrolls and records. But, from 1524 all the way down to 1914 and the last bird, named Martha, who dropped off her perch in the Cincinnati Zoo one cloudy March morning, there is a consistent, verifiable record. Year after year, like the daily hospital record of a declining patient, a meticulous register of *Columbia migratoria* was kept. Where their great flights took them, their routes, the quantity of mast they consumed, how they mated, the path laid down across the countryside of their bluish-white excrement, the cries they made—everything down to Martha's last feeble cry as she toppled off her roost. I should mention that her cage in the zoo had been roped off during her last months so that curious crowds would not press too close. She had a weak heart, not unusual for a pigeon in her twenty-ninth year."

"What are you telling us?" Yellow Hat interrupted, his voice airily amused and sardonic. He waved the automatic rifle toward Pickett Sneat. The two accomplices leapt to this command and wheeled the book reviewer against the wall, next to the author.

"No, no," Sneat screamed, suddenly awake. "Do something, Leo. My best work is still before me."

"I am talking about *Columbia migratoria*," the author persisted with a reserved sangfroid. He squeezed the bridge of his nose, the gesture of a patient instructor before dense students rather than someone staring into a gun muzzle. "I am talking about a bird that no longer exists," he continued amiably. "The bird of liberty, not the eagle but a pigeon. A dead pigeon, as the story goes, long dead and once dead, no constitution or legislature can bring it back. A dead species cannot be revived, be cloned.

"You see, their great number astonished us from the beginning; their quantity was continually measured, estimated, and wondered at. Even the estimates of their number became valuable, entities to be stolen as was the case with Audubon—but I'll get to that later." His voice became sad. "All along, it wasn't their number that was important, not their quantity, but their quality. Measuring them, marking the dimension of their existence, we destroyed them." In a flourish of defiance, Post turned his back on our captor.

"Did they fly east and west or north and south?" Yellow Hat asked, leaning forward.

"North and south," replied Post as he watched a cargo ship pass silently downriver, largely driven by the current. Clearly, the author was in a reflective mode. "You may find it difficult to believe, but I once had a love whose quality could not be measured, and I made the mistake of trying to characterize that love, translate it into a rational order—to quantify it."

"Professor!" Yellow Hat was on his feet suddenly, pulling back and releasing the bolt of his weapon. Click-clack. "You are becoming a bore. We can't tolerate bores. Right, boys?" His two cohorts nodded, folded their arms.

"Please, Leo," Sneat squealed, eyes closed, fists drumming the arms of his chair. "Tell them something interesting. Make it new, for God's sake. Give them a good story, and they'll leave us alone."

"No chance of that," replied the young guerilla. He had leveled his weapon at something outside the window and fired several rounds just over Leo Post's head. The blast was deafening in the stone chamber. Then he laughed, his harlequin expression a disturbing contrast to the blankness of the dark glasses.

The sounds of the gunfire echoed and re-echoed through the castle's halls and chambers, and Sgt. Anderson, as if summoned by the racket, stepped from behind the screen of the kitchen area. She carried a tray with a coffee decanter, mugs, and a plate of freshly baked biscuits. She was barefoot and had apparently only been given enough time by our assailants to pull on a brief tunic. She placed the tray on the table with an odd servility, as if the militant posture of before only came with her booted disguise.

"What's that I smell?" Sneat lifted his round face and sniffed.

"Our dear Lucy has whipped up some fresh biscuits," Leo said happily, and poured himself a cup of coffee. "And I spy a jar of gooseberry jam as well. Good show, Lucy, keeping the morale up." But the woman had turned away. The terrorists served themselves, the two accomplices stuffing biscuits into their pockets as if for later consumption. Being the only persona in the room who knew the woman's true identity, we hoped Sgt. Anderson might affect some act to free us, but the brevity of her costume offered no concealment for a weapon. Perhaps she had put something in the biscuits.

"Very well," Yellow Cap addressed Post. He munched on a biscuit heavy with jam. "We'll give you a bit more time, but you must keep the narrative interesting. No moralizing or personal reflections. No theories; we've had enough of them. Keep it amusing. Keep one incident falling upon the next. String one trivial bead after another until you have an ornament than can be worn or tossed aside with no great loss."

Yellow Hat had risen to his feet as he gave these instructions, his insolence underlined as he turned his back on Post to look closely into Sgt. Anderson's eyes. Without her boots, her stature had decreased, so she had to look up into the terrorist's face. He stroked her cheek softly with the back of his fingers. They passed over her neck and beneath her ear, down to the smooth sculptured plane of her shoulder and then back up again. I, B. Smith, a keen observer of this behavior, admired the demeanor of our associate in police protocol, for she gave no hint of the disgust this abuse must have produced in her. She was a great credit to the discipline taught by the New York State Police Academy. As she continued to endure Yellow Hat's familiarities, one large toe lifted and curled over the large toe of the other foot.

"All right," Yellow Hat said, waving his associates back to their posts by the immense hearth. "Let's hear more about these clay pigeons." He resumed his place at the head of the table, casually slinging one slender leg over the chair arm. Sgt. Anderson stayed close by but avoided our meaningful look.

"Clay pigeons." Leo Post took a step back as if struck, almost falling over the stone window. The words had metamorphosed to actually strike him, it seemed. "How close you have come to the truth. A wing-shot to continue the word play. Clay had to be substituted for flesh and feather because eventually there were no real birds left to use as targets. I had an ancestor, Capt. Ira Leek— a resident of these very halls—who in his lifetime accounted for 28,000 pigeons—and that only in contests, not in the field.

"But I am getting ahead of the story. The Indians hunted them, using nets. They were a natural food supply, but our native citizens did not want to destroy them. Some early French explorers of this New World were put to death by the Indians for killing pigeons during the nesting season. An early form of conservation, you might say; a primitive but effective game law as well as a collision of magic and technology. That weapon you threaten us with is the result of a culture that uses explosives to propel lead pellets at other beings. In another culture that same combination of phosphates and saltpeter had been used to make magical fireworks."

"Wandering again, Professor. You're not being specific," Yellow Hat reproached him gently. He finished the last of a biscuit and almost delicately dusted his fingers against a napkin while his other hand absent-mindedly stroked the bare thigh of Sgt. Anderson as she stood beside his chair. "If you're not going to give us a story without these digressions and curlicues, we might as well complete our mission."

"For God's sake, Leo," Sneat complained, his body retracting within its cage, "cut the modernist crap and give us the fact."

"Facts, you want facts," Post replied, drawing himself up. "Very well then. In March of 1883, my ancestor Capt. Ira Leek was traveling to Milwaukee, Wisconsin, aboard the Red Diamond Express of the Richmond & Minneapolis Railroad, a company incidentally that Lucius Beebe said offered the best dining service on the rails. It was from one of these praised diners that Capt. Leek leisurely sauntered, playfully jostled and staggered by the play of the train's trucks over a roadbed that had been dedicated, at the Richmond end, by one of Henry Clay's sons.

"Capt. Leek had just consumed a very worthy breakfast consisting of Roanoke ham, grits, three poached eggs, potatoes tarragon, two peaches, and a cup of warm barley water. The service by the several black waiters—all of whom went by the name of George—was superb, as Beebe noted in his journals, and the eggs were only a few hours from the hen. As the Red Diamond Express roared through Paris, Kentucky, in the dark hours of morning, the eggs were picked up with the mail sacks as the train hurtled down the tracks at speeds exceeding one hundred miles per hour. In the history of the line, not a single egg was ever broken in the breakneck transfer."

"Just a minute," Yellow Hat commanded. A newsbreak crackled ominously by the hearth—something about a refinery being blown up in Texas?—but I, B. Smith, focusing on the immediate situation, did not register all the details. "How do you know all these details—your ancestor's breakfast and the rest?" Sgt. Anderson continued to patiently endure the terrorist's casual, impersonal handling. "We want nothing but the facts; not any of that embroidery for which you have been unduly merited."

"Capt. Leek kept extensive diaries," the author replied. He had sat down on the stone bench beneath the casement window. "And I am preparing you for some of the material to come, which is extraordinary but true. I'm afraid you must also humor a lifelong passion for seemingly irrelevant data that does—after testing, fitting, and collating—assemble into a coherent picture. Before I was nine, I could give you the batting averages of every player in both leagues. You would be wrong to construe the virus of imagination flushed out by the dark Armenian blood that courses in these veins as a proclivity for fancy. Not so. It's just I never wanted to discover how things worked, never took a clock apart, but would spend hours studying the movement of its hands, what the different placement of its hands mean. It's an arbitrary assignment, isn't it? What is time and where is it? When the library clock strikes three, how does that calculation relate to the books on the shelves? How about at four o'clock?"

"Oh, Leo!" his fellow exile rattled his harness. "You're borrowing from yourself. That's part of your acceptance speech for the Pulitzer-Jones."

Yellow Hat looked unconcerned and had even strolled away, down to the end of the chamber to confer with his associates. They left the room, the forecast of a disturbance off the coast of North Carolina trailing behind them. We assume the terrorist was directing them to different posts within the castle as the rest of us were bound and made helpless by Post's narrative.

"What you are saying," Yellow Hat said on his return, "is that you put the stuff of your dreams on the waking world."

"Exactly," Post replied. He had come to his feet, his complexion pinking with excitement. "That's it exactly."

'That seems to be a luxury ordinary folks can't afford," the handsome guerilla said. He has resumed his chair next to Sgt. Anderson and leaned forward to kiss her full on the mouth. Her police discipline masked her response to this gross familiarity, though her hands clenched and relaxed. Our captor had continued. "Facts have a way of burglarizing the house of dreams..."

"A sentimental image, " Sneat growled.

"...indeed, the world around us is nothing but fact that we have inherited and refurbished." From the courtyard below came a communiqué describing a depression moving into the Mississippi Valley.

"Yes, but in freshening these facts," Post countered with visible energy, "they become fiction. When we say we have discovered this feature or that aspect of the world, what we have really done is to define an illusion born in our dreams. Even Descartes, you remember, said an angel in a dream brought him his theory on analytical geometry."

"You make it sound like the world is a big yard that we sniff about like dogs, looking for bones we have buried and forgotten," the young man said. Sgt. Anderson had sat down on the floor; the short skirt of her costume had ridden up a supple length of honey-colored thigh. I, B. Smith, a duly qualified observer, file this commendation of the New York State Police's physical fitness regimen.

"And why not?" Post asked, even more agitated. "The fallacy engendered by the Christian egocentricity promotes the belief that human beings can remake the earth to order. But it's the other way around—the world could survive very well without humans. We are in temporary residence only."

"But what would happen, professor," Yellow Hat said casually as his fingers moved comb-like through the brisk blackness of Sgt. Anderson's Afro, "if this transference of dreams you posit creates a misrepresentation—also a picture. Does that ever happen?"

"Yes. A nightmare," Post said and turned to the window behind him. It was now full daylight, and the sun had dispatched the residue of mist that had yet dressed the river's surface. The slack water had begun to whisper a change in direction.

"All right—enough," Sneat boomed. "Let's get back to the Red Diamond Express just pulling into Milwaukee with Capt.

Ira Leek aboard, savoring his breakfast and feeling a particular affection for the Negroes who had served him—all of whom were called George."

"Thank you, Pickett, for putting us back on course," Leo Post said sincerely. "George, the Pullman porter, was making up the Captain's berth as the sportsman stood to one side. He enjoyed the last of a Havana No. 12, made especially for him, and he became aware of an unusual haste in the porter's service, an unduly quick dispatch of the crisp linens and blanket that was untypical of the behavior for which the Richmond & Minneapolis was noted. Moreover, the porter looked about him and over his shoulder with that walleyed expression so affectionately a part of the literature and lithographs of the period. Clearly, the man was frightened or disturbed by something. 'George,' my ancestor addressed him, 'there seems to be something bothering you.'

"Parenthetically, I should note that a small number of these porters were also called Sam—or Sambo, to use the affectionate diminutive—as well as a sprinkling of Roberts could be found pouring coffee in the diners. It was an example of renaming an entity being put to one's personal fancy."

"The dream world coloring the actual, you're saying," Yellow Hat said with a smirk. The dark lenses of his glasses winked like semaphores in the clear morning light.

"Quite so," agreed Post. " I will not attempt to reproduce the porter's speech in his reply, but I can assure you it was studded with the quaint idioms of that day that were given him to pronounce in the pages of popular journals. In essence, he told my ancestor that additional cars had been added to the train during the night; one in Lexington, another in Cincinnati, and a third in Vincennes, and so forth, so by morning the train was about six cars longer when it pulled into Milwaukee. The occupants of these cars were professional pigeon-netters.

"It seems that a great flock of passenger pigeons had nested in a large forest near the small town of Mauston, Wisconsin. The railway freight agent of that community had telegraphed the good tidings. Tickety-tick-tick-tack. One afternoon he had watched the sky darken as millions of these handsome creatures winged low over the village and the brown fields of early spring to glide into the oak forest. They festooned the yet-bare limbs with their flat, shaggy nests; a crowding, cooing, preening foliage. Tickety-tick-tick went the telegraph key—come and get them.

"Word had passed—perhaps by one of the dining-car staff—that my ancestor was on the train, and the coaches for the netters in the rear forwarded an invitation to Capt. Leek for him to join them. In just the previous year, he had established his reputation as a pigeon shot in a three-way match with Brewer and E.D. Fulford in Chicago. There had been an immense coverage of the contest in the *Police Gazette*. Capt. Leek had killed 100 pigeons without a miss, using his second barrel with 'marvelous effect,' reported the *Gazette*. The élan of his stance at the stand and the commanding timbre of his voice when he ordered a bird to be released were noted by the *Appalachian Sportsman*. So, the assembly of netters and sportsmen on their way to Wisconsin where the pigeons were innocently and unknowingly nesting welcomed this paragon of pigeon shooters.

The next morning in Milwaukee this jolly convention boarded a special train that had been put together with coachers for the netters and two boxcars for their equipment and supplies. The railroad credited the costs for this special train against the profits it would receive from freighting the results of the hunt. According to my ancestor's journals, the journey was most felicitous. Talented musicians were among the group, and these men had brought their guitars, banjos, and mouth organs. Old camp songs, reminiscent of the recent Civil War battlefield, were spontaneously joined. Fine bourbon was passed around, stories swapped, and the good-natured manliness of the occasion started many life-long relationships down paths of amity.

"Capt. Ira Leek, upon request, readily demonstrated the proper stance for making a good wing shot: left foot slightly advanced, right foot as a brace, and left hand advanced to the tip of the fore end—the gunstock not at the shoulder but halfway between elbow and armpit. Therefore, should the bird fly either right or left, the right foot is used as a pivot to swing the body around. Capt. Leek was easy to talk to, it was generally agreed, and found to be a good fellow in every respect.

"This happy fraternity of sportsmen plied the famous marksman with questions about the same creature they trapped in quantity that he shot in quality. Should the shotgun barrels be choked or not? What is the optimum distance for a clean kill? What effect has the Parker trap had on the sport of pigeon shooting? Is it true that clipping the toes off the bird will make it fly like a rocket when released from its trap? And then there were inquiries about different personalities. Does Brewer actually wear that derby throughout the whole match or just for the picture in the *Police Gazette*? Had Capt. Leek shot against this new man named Bogardus? When Annie Oakley and he, Capt. Leek, held their famous match in Seneca, New York, did she actually kill her first fifty birds shooting from the hip? And then, Capt. Leek, just between us, you know, well—later on—you know—a good sport, was she?

"By the time this special train, this comradely caravan, arrived at its destination that afternoon, the small town of Mauston was humming with preparations. A tent city had been raised along the rail spur because the number of netters and the attendant curious easily tripled the town's population. Several boxcars were already parked on the freight siding, and their cargoes of barrels and salt were unloaded and stored in another large tent set up behind the station. Probably the same station agent whose talented tapping on the telegraphy key had alerted the netters also supervised how this camp and processing site was organized. He was a small, wiry man with sandy hair and cool blue eyes."

"One moment, professor." Yellow Hat held up a hand. "Those details bother me."

"Well, then, will you allow me a green eyeshade pulled low over the brow, shirtsleeves snappily served by a pair of plain elastic

garters, and the open front of a black vest kept together by the
heavy gold vine from which hung the thick fruit of the trainman's
gold watch, thack-thopping in one pocket?"

"Yes. Those details, trite as they are, are acceptable because
they are so familiar," the young man replied with a slight smile.

"Heavy wagons," Post continued, "crashed back and forth
through the town drawn by teams of horses whipped this side of
madness, while—dodging disaster in this hurly-burly—small boys
ran on errands, each one breathless with the certainty that the success of the whole enterprise depended on his agile legs. On the
appeal of the station agent, probably after winding and checking
that heavy watch, the town's one bank closed down for the next
couple of days so that the tellers could help with the bookkeeping
and accounting at the site—the freight agent issued special chits in
lieu of currency for those citizens who ran short during the trapping. More netters and some journalists including reporters from
the *Police Gazette* and the *New York World* arrived on the evening
train just as a string of silent and sealed freight cars pulled in from
the north to be shunted to the spur near the granary. A glistening patina of frost covered the sides of this new train for its cargo
was ice, blocks of it cut from the still frozen lakes of Canada. This
gathering of contingents from different points of the compass was
all pulled together by that thin wire strung on poles. Tap-tappety-
tap—come and get 'em.

"I must mention the very large tent erected behind the station
to be used for processing and packing. And just across the tracks—
and it would always be across the tracks, wouldn't it be? —another
sort of processing plant had been set up by a group of amiable
young women, finely feathered themselves and making the characteristic cries of the species. They had arrived from Chicago on the
noon train. At the same time, spiritual values were not neglected:
the Bible Institute of Cairo, Illinois, established a tidy mission
that served soup and other forms of spiritual sustenance to the
harmony of a barbershop quartet—each one a divinity student—
who raised at different intervals a repertoire of familiar hymns.

Andrew Carnegie was reported to ship in a load of books, but we know this report to be untrue—the man never supplied any books, but only the shelves to support them—so we may assume the canny industrialist made an offer of a library building to the town of Mauston, but whether the inhabitants supplied any books I cannot say.

"Therefore, in a matter of forty-eight hours, the summarized weight of Western Culture followed the tracks into this small prairie village in Wisconsin, drawn along those steel rails by that strange rasp of wires overhead and the flutter of wings in a nearby forest. What was the lasting effect of this *blitzkultur*, one might ask?"

"Nobody asked," Pickett Sneat muttered.

"True. The Bible Institute, after the hunt was over, pulled up stakes and wandered away in the manner of a vagrant faith, satisfied with the comfort and salvation it had temporarily provided. Their number had been increased by a dozen or so converts. Several of the young women from Chicago packed away their gaudy plumage and remade their gowns to wed into the community to become eventually the stern great-grandmothers whose tintypes marshal local mantels today.

"Jo Jefferson detoured his company of *Rip Van Winkle* that had been playing Minneapolis to give a special performance of his classic on a stage improvised in the grange hall above the pharmacy. This show took place after the grand dinner sponsored by the newly formed chamber of commerce on the final evening of the netting. Capt. Leek was the guest of honor and told many a humorous anecdote about shooting pigeons.

"A widow's son, a good lad who helped his mother with the washing and ironing by which they earned their keep, was chosen by the famous actor, Jefferson, to fill in for one of the several parts required by the play's crowd scenes. For example, that moving moment when Rip returns to the village tavern to find it no longer called the George III."

"Surely, one of the more significant epiphanies in contemporary drama," Sneat said out of the corner of his mouth. "Not since *Oedipus Rex,* etcetera and etceteras."

"Of course the rest is history," Post continued, unrattled. "Struck between the eyes by the light of the Fresneled lenses, that boy left Mauston, Wisconsin, to become one of the great matinee idols of all time, one of David Belasco's more lustrous stars whose performances in such American masterpieces as *The Wreck of Old No. 42* and *Warrior Wears the Silks* are now legendary. I am talking of course of Templeton Drew."

"Stop!" It was Pickett Sneat and on his feet. He had somehow suspended himself on a pair of steel crutches that pushed his shoulders above his ears as he awkwardly and probably painfully scraped and dragged himself across the floor toward Leo Post. He shouted into the author's face. "My God, must we endure this endless trivia, this picked-over bag of literary lint? To think of my campaign against the long narrative and now to be forced to hear this yellowed patchwork."

Yellow Hat had sprung to his feet, and Sneat's outburst fizzled into a garbled gurgle deep in his throat as the terrorist pushed the muzzle of his gun into the pudgy belly of the book reviewer. "We know of your different campaigns, Mr. Sneat, that furthered your career more than they extended the boundaries of art. I suggest you resume your place." And saying so, Yellow Hat helped back to his wheelchair, tottering the man as if he were a heavy armoire being shifted across the floor, rocking him back and forth from one foot to another, one crutch tip to another. Then, he folded him back into the steel chair.

"At the same time, Professor, if you could give us this account with a minimum of gratuitous details, it might sharpen our interest. Brevity and wit, if you remember." He sauntered back to the chair at the head of the table and picked up a biscuit and swabbed it through a pool of cooling sausage gravy and ate it. He smacked his lips and gave Sgt. Anderson a thumbs-up sign ostensibly to approve of her cooking. The undercover policewoman grinned and modestly looked away.

"Come, come," Yellow Hat commanded off-handedly. The mirrored glasses swung around so the panes doubled the image of the writer, arms across his knees and head lowered. "We are in Mauston, Wisconsin, on a morning in March of 1883. Proceed."

"It's not that easy, or else this tale will become just one more numbers game. We are possessed by numbers. We have become saturated with the accounts of fires and hurricanes, bombings and mass slaughters and random devastations—I fear my story will be too familiar. You will excuse me from dressing my family site in gaudy details—my effort is to make the account unique." Post stood from his stone bench and strode to the end of the room as if to choose the blackened mouth of the cavernous hearth as the backdrop for his next installment.

"Figures like 25,000 dead only whet the appetite for 44,000 lost, and this number makes us hungry for, say, 500,000 annihilated, which gives us a taste for six million exterminated. But we can do better." The expression in the dark, soulful eyes was countered by the smile on his face. "We have the know-how to do better. The bloody multiplication, this deduction *ad extincta* becomes greedier even as it chokes on the zeroes it consumes. Humans become bored with their own evil and practice self-astonishment by quantification. The algebraic x is the first dehumanization epithet in the language.

"I've always been perplexed by those writers who hold up one disaster as being more significant, more worthy of their attention than another. To compare one atrocity with another is rather sentimental, don't you agree? And to do so becomes a part of the mechanism as much as that first twist of a thumbscrew. What I am getting at..."

"Yes, please get at something," Sneat interjected, then quickly darted a look at Yellow Hat.

"...what I am saying," Post continued, " is that I could tell you that at the end of the Mauston hunt, it's been estimated that two million pigeons had been trapped, killed, and iced or salted down and packed off to market. This does not include the great number, nobody knows how many, that were left to rot on the forest floor or gobbled by pigs that local farmers turned loose in the wood. Pigs in the wood. The figure of x.

"Nor, in another attempt of accuracy, does that number include the 550 birds, ultimate specimens, that Capt. Leek paid to have captured alive and unharmed, then shipped to the grateful membership of the Dexter Park Sportsmen's Club of Providence, Rhode Island—a gift of his appreciation for the warm reception given him earlier that year. All of the birds survived the trip in good shape, taking about three times longer by train as it would have taken them on their own wings; that is, if they flew west to east. The club's secretary wrote Capt. Leek a note of appreciation for 'the most challenging birds at twenty yards we've ever released, flying straight and clean. You provided us a splendid afternoon.' Again numbers on a splendid afternoon."

"Very well," Yellow Hat said genially. "Tell it your way."

Leo Post stepped away from the hearth, taking one, then two, and then a third step toward us. "It's all there," he said, waving one hand at the pile of papers and books on the long table. "Capt. Leek's journals, newspaper reports, historical surveys; I have added nothing, no exaggerations, for the sums were already made and with exactness." He had returned to the hearth and looked down into its depth.

"The next morning, the small army of netters left town on greased axles, the horses' hooves muffled. A small rise several miles down the road gave an excellent perspective in all directions—one vast wheat field. The first shoots of wheat delicately tongued the crisp air of dawn. To the southwest lay the edge of the forest, thick and wild with large oaks and softer woods, sycamore, dogwood, some spruce and elm, naturally. Tendrils of partridgeberry encircled the tree trunks, and from their prospect, the hunters breathed the sweet winery of honeysuckle that matted the forest floor. Lady's slipper was in bloom, lovely as any jungle orchid, and deeper in the woods the ghostly stems of Indian pipes glimmered in the perpetual twilight. Extending some twenty miles, this forest was only a remnant of its original spread across the prairie and gave the impression to some of the assembly of a huge stage set with the thick vines of wild grape hanging from trees resembling cables to raise or lower scenery. Pull on this bunch of vines here and a Moorish marketplace would be revealed. Tug here and a pharaoh's court is reproduced. That sort of thing."

The author's mood had visibly changed, for the black eyes twinkled with good humor, as if the mere act of storytelling had cheered him up. The man called Taylor had just brought in an armload of kindling and laid a fire in the great hearth. Post watched his aide for several moments and then turned to us.

"Captain Leek always carried two shotguns in his personal luggage, but he did not have them with him on this morning. Perhaps Wisconsin had a law that forbade carrying such armament. For example, New York state passed a law in 1862 that prohibited the discharge of any firearm one mile from a pigeon nesting. Progressive journals and certain conservation organizations had hailed the legislation as a measure to preserve the pigeon though later it was disclosed that the strongest lobby for its passage was financed by the wholesale poultry industry. In effect, the New York state law allowed the professional netters and trappers—like those who had paused on this prairie levee in Mauston—to go about their work in peace and safety without risking injury from a stray shot." Post paused as his mouth curved into the mask of a silent laugh. He sat down on the window sill. The funnel of a tanker passing downriver crossed the windows behind him.

I, B. Smith, attempting to record everything, noted Yellow Hat's relaxed pose in the chair, though it was impossible to tell if his eyes were closed due to the mirrored lenses of his glasses. The kindling, better than yesterday's wood, started a fire quickly, and flames leaped in the stone hearth though its contribution was more cosmetic than comforting. As if responding to the agreeable crackle of the wood, the terrorist stretched his long legs and resumed his idle caress of Sgt. Anderson's ear and neck.

"Suddenly," Post continued, "the pale dawn sky went black, as if one of those early photographers had fitted a cap over the lens of heaven. An eerie sound swept over the assembled hunters, like that of a gale invisibly roaring down the countryside, but not a blade of timothy, not a finger of new wheat had stirred. The sound crammed into their ears, a fearful scream that made some of the horses rear and look wildly about for the destruction that was surely just upon them. Close to a million pigeons had risen to take wing from the forest; an awesome and perverse leave-taking. The birds formed a gigantic, sensuous column high above the woods and the hunting party, then became a gigantic blot that swept in a wide flank across the sky at a speed well above sixty miles an hour. In their passage they seemed to polish the morning sky brighter.

"No—I anticipate your question—they had not been spooked by the men poised on the hill, the cart horses impatiently pawing and stamping the earth. This flight was a normal feeding procedure, for the passenger pigeon almost never ate and nested in the same place. A fastidious bird. Quite often, as in this situation, the feeding ground would be at some distance, and for this flight of birds their destination was a near-primeval beechwood one hundred miles to the east. These were the males who had just taken off, leaving the females to tend the nests, for they took turns, and the males always took their feeding shift before noon.

"The small army of hunters had quietly moved off the road and into the fields, a flanking maneuver across the wheat field toward the forest. We can assume," the Postian profile had lifted haughtily, "that the farmer who owned that field was fully compensated for the damage done his crop; even that he shared in the profits from this work, since his grandfathers had cleared and pushed back the wilderness to set the trap that was about to be sprung.

"Now more tents were erected for dormitories, for a mess hall, a small infirmary and, at a suitable distance, an orderly network of latrines was dug. The establishment of this camp was under the supervision of a retired master sergeant of the U.S. Cavalry, a veteran of the Indian Wars who had made the claim, in a notorious memoir, that he had advised Custer to leave his troops' sabers behind on that fateful trot to the Little Bighorn River. A questionable claim perhaps, but it should be noted that the chiefs of the Sioux Nation were to posthumously adopt him, giving him the name..."

"Stop it! STOP IT," shouted Sneat, his face turned purple. "No more footnotes, Leo."

"Yes, quite right," Post replied, looking chastened. "Forgive me, Pick." The author stood and turned his back on the chamber to look at the eastern bank of the Hudson River now fully detailed by the midmorning light. "These digressions, these footnotes as you call them, only delay the simple story of the slaughter about to happen. As if this event could be postponed by such extraneous tidbits. Perversely, the strategy is similar to the ancient Egyptian idea that a comfortable and salubrious time in the afterlife could be achieved by the numberless times those happy events were pictured on the tomb walls. So, maybe, if I do not tell the central truth of this hunt, but talk around it, give extraneous data, its existence in our path will become parenthesized, if not erased."

"LEO," bellowed the book reviewer.

"Yes, yes," Post nodded and pulled the robe's sash tighter around his waist. He took a deep breath. "Other tents were erected, and in these were long tables, piles of gunnysacks and barrels. Bags of salt. Almost every woman from Mauston and many from neighboring villages were there, sleeves rolled up and heavy canvas aprons tied snug. Their preparations done, the professionals determined the first sweep in the forest had to commence before the male birds returned. While the camp was being established, the hunters had fastened large nets between the trees—purse nets they were called, and they were aptly named. Large iron pots were set up over fires and had commenced cooking their stew of sulfur. Long limbs were prepared as poles.

"Above them, the saucer-shaped nests of the pigeons clotted the branches of the trees like fungus growths, and though it was too early for spring to have leaved the forest, the great number of nests was enough to subdue the light, making the men's work below difficult. They stumbled over obscured roots, caught their feet in tangles of honeysuckle and wild grape; saplings slashed their faces. They cursed. In numbers—yes, their number is also important—about a half million pigeon nests had been fixed high above them and each one with a fuzzy squab in it, some of them curiously observing the preparations taking place below.

"These small pigeons, their crops swollen with the food their parents pushed down their throats, were the objects of these feverish preparations. These downy fledglings had caused the freight agent to sit in his cozy office and finger the telegraph key to set off a transcontinental caucus. The delicacy of squab. It was a favorite dish of Diamond Jim Brady when he dined at Luchow's. The Prince of Wales used the fastest warship of his mother's navy to transport iced kegs of squabs to the royal table during the Silver Anniversary. 12:47 P.M. The appetite for these succulent birds never wearied but increased worldwide as techniques to process and transport them improved. Adult pigeons were also trapped for market, and though tougher and gamier, they brought a better price than chicken. The flavor of the flesh was also improved when birds were caught alive and fed a diet of certain grains before being prepared for the family table.

"From their nests fifteen feet above, the fat little squabs watched all the activity below, their black bills turning back and forth as their soft beasts pressed excitedly against the coarsely woven mat of twigs. They would be about a week away from their first flight, and the irises of their eyes were still hazel colored, not the bright orange of the adult female birds who had now set up a dreadful racket—screeching, flapping their wings and whizzing through the trees like gray-feathered missiles. Audubon, if he can be relied upon, reported these birds retained some of a vestigial coo, employed only in moments of courtship, but their great number demanded a sound that could be heard over the din of their own assembly so the millions of them raised a full-throated keeck-

keeck, keeck-keeeck that miles away resembled the roar of a great cataract—a Niagara on the prairie.

"Their best defense was their dung. It would have routed any ordinary woods rambler who might have stumbled on their nesting ground, for it fell in a steady bluish-white rain. But the professional netters were prepared. Each wore a leather or cloth helmet, and an armor-like suit of sackcloth protected them from the drizzle of excrement. Heavy boots were also necessary, for in some places the stuff covered the forest floor several inches deep.

"Did anyone give a signal? Did anyone stand at the edge of this near primeval forest, and—when all was ready—blow a bugle? Did anyone vault into the crook of a tree, raise his cap and shout, 'C'mon, boys—c'mon?' My ancestor does not mention any such command, but perhaps the mayor of Mauston raised and dropped his handkerchief. Perhaps a flare was struck. I want to think that someone said something, gave the order rather than that the slaughter commenced unbidden, anonymously and casually.

"In any event, those nests within fifteen feet of the ground were pushed over by long poles, and the nurslings would drop into the netters' gunnysacks below. Sometimes the men would miss catching them, and the little birds so fat and tender would burst apart on impact. Of course, this happenstance would render them quite useless. The large pots of sulfur were cooking and sending up choking fumes to those nests beyond the reach of the poles. Unable to fly yet, the small birds would try to escape the reek and wobble out of their nests, take one or two steps along a weaving limb, and then tumble to the ground.

"But the great number of them could be prepared for market with almost no effort; there were few feathers to pluck. Most important was the removal of the crop, for if this pouch in the neck were not removed, the undigested food it contained would spoil and make the bird unpalatable. This stage was easy to accomplish because their flesh was so tender, butter-soft, that the head and the crop could be pulled off in one easy gesture. The size of the crop was often equal to the body of the squab. Local schoolchildren who had followed the netters out of the village became very accomplished in this technique and were paid a penny per two dozen headless squabs delivered to the processing tents set up in the fields. A boy could hold the small bird in the left hand, then grasp the base of the neck between the fore and index fingers of the other hand—much as one might hold a cigar. Then, scissoring the fingers together and pulling away with a motion much like setting a top spinning, the neck would be separated from the body, smoothly and all in one motion, giving the young pigeon only time enough for the briefest of startled squeaks.

"The larger birds required more work. Imagine millions of these adult birds dipping and sweeping through the forest on eighteen-inch wings, the lavender-ringed eyes targets where terror scored. The passenger pigeon was a very communal bird; yet, each pair of adults tended only a single egg, taking turns on the nest, until the squab took wing. But now, on this March morning outside of Mauston, Wisconsin, thousands of female birds became aware their nests were empty, that their offspring had tumbled below to be gutted and packed in ice by the mothers, grandmothers, aunts, and cousins of the children who pulled off the squabs' heads.

"The females frantically sought another nest to tend, another squab to care for, only to have the same calamity happen again. The nest would be shaken violently, tipped, and the fledgling would disappear into the heavy smoke below. The adult birds would scold and screech warnings as the doughy occupants of the nests stepped onto wobbly branches to escape the smothering smoke— one step and then two on those short red legs that were not even very useful in the adult bird. Then gone, down the little nestling would fall into the waiting hands of the netters.

"As you can understand, all their natural instincts were turned around and thwarted. They confronted an unknown, a force that choked them, destroyed their nests, set up a clash of drums, pots and pans—a shouting din that almost drowned out their own cries. Unlike us, they had no memory of previous slaughters— they would not remember this destruction done them—so this attack was as strange as it was terrific. The full-grown birds went berserk.

"It became hazardous for those netters working in the gloom of the forest floor. They slipped and fell in the muck and slime created by the thick layer of dung. Thousands of birds began to fly blindly, hysterically among them, seeking their young at full speed in and around the trees at ground level. Some smacked into the solid oaks, others would collide with netters, knocking the men down. These fellows would laugh good-naturedly as they got up, scrape off the bluish excrement and return to their work. The air whizzed with crazed birds, and now the purse nets were sprung.

"The pigeons flew straight into them, so fast and in such numbers that the huge nets quickly resembled colonies of bees working about a gigantic comb. Mostly, their heads and necks would be thrust through the webbing of the nets, facilitating their wringing and decapitation. Again, the entire crop had to be removed, but because they had not recently fed, this part required little attention. However, the bleeding, feathered carcasses were shoveled on waiting carts that would transfer them to the wagons pulled up at the edge of the wood. Then the quivering cargoes were hauled to Mauston and the processing tents where the town ladies removed the feathers, gutted the innards, and packed the birds into barrels of salt or ice. The netting found its routine, and a continuous line of farm wagons shuttled between village and forest that reminded some veterans of the recent Civil War of the flight from Savannah after Sherman's pillage. So several published interviews reported. The townswomen could not keep up with the seemingly endless supply of raw goods, so large pickling vats were set up, and load after load of birds were dumped into these enormous containers.

"In the village the sound of the hunt was like the rupture of a huge dam that had just given way. Farm animals became restless in their pens and stalls; some broke their restraints. Cows upset milking pails and forced their stanchions. Chickens fled their roosts. Dogs barked and barked and barked; they could not stop barking. Pigs stepped mindfully in their wallow and waited.

"Then those in town saw a black cloud take shape in the sky, on the horizon, like a storm front moving in but from the east— unnaturally. The male pigeons were returning from their feeding grounds to take their turns minding the nests and to feed the squabs from the mast partially digested in their crops.

"Did anyone think it beautiful, an awesome spectacle as Wilson described it almost a century before or as Audubon and Burroughs recorded similar flights? The birds flew very high, gradually descending as they neared the nesting ground they had left several hours before dawn when all was well. The netters working on the ground were experienced from previous hunts and became aware of the males' arrival because of the doubling of the commotion in the forest, by the greater number of pigeons flapping about their heads."

Leo Post paused. A small sailboat, its mast stepped on deck, moved downriver as the cough-coughing of its auxiliary engine nudged the late-morning haze. Everyone seemed asleep or stunned, as if a spell had been cast upon the castle and its occupants. I, B. Smith, a keen observer in most cases, wondered if Yellow Hat was only pretending sleep behind those large sunglasses, to tempt one of us to try to escape so he could use that automatic weapon. Pickett Sneat was the first to show signs of recovery. The metal husk that enclosed his body creaked as he drew a deep breath, and his eyes popped open almost audibly.

"Well, what then, Leo?" he asked with uncharacteristic interest.

"Oh, more of the same—more of the same," Post responded. "Three days and three nights, the slaughter continued. The male birds became crazed by the unknown terror that had confronted their mates. Where were the offspring they had left at dawn? Where were their mates? And something else. Whenever the adults exchanged places on the nests they would touch bills. It was the slightest of contacts but to be denied this slight caress of their beaks, with the females already dead and being processed, drove the male birds mad.

"These powerful, beautiful birds had come the distance from the swamps of Louisiana to this forest in Wisconsin to bear their young. They had made similar flights for hundreds of seasons, nobody knows how many seasons, and they would make a few more until that thin wire looped around telegraph posts grew tighter and tighter, and until the great hardwood forests disappeared altogether. Indeed, that wood outside of Mauston resembled a theatrical rendering of Hades those three nights—something a touring stock company of *Dante's Inferno* might try to improvise.

"The pots of bubbling sulfur cast a hideous glow, half-illuminating the vine-draped tree trunks. Monstrous shadows of hooded figures passed among the convulsive carcasses of the doomed— methodically separating heads from bodies. Several of the netters had been overcome by the noxious fumes of the sulfur and had been removed to the tented infirmary. In fact, the congregation of netters had been so exhausted by the first day's netting that they had to work in shifts thereafter. The flock turned out to be larger than they had been led to expect.

"Meanwhile, the men of Mauston had replaced their wives in the processing tents so that the women could return home to feed their own offspring and tuck them into bed with a story. The men had rolled up their sleeves and plunged into the work, speculating on the effect of this unexpected bounty: how Mauston would benefit, how they would use the extra income.

"All in all it had been a profitable interlude. The freight agent in Mauston signed a loading receipt for 1,500 barrels shipped by special train on only that first evening. Each barrel contained about thirty birds."

"Just a moment, Professor." Yellow Hat had raised a languid hand. "That shipment only accounts for about 50,000 birds. Earlier, you had put their destruction in higher figures. What happened to the others?"

"Thank you for bringing up this issue." Post made a slight bow. "We can only make an account of the birds shipped. These netters had professional reputations to maintain; they were supplying markets that had become very particular as to the quality of the product, so only the best of the squabs and birds left Mauston. All others, and these were in the majority, had become too mangled or spoiled in the process of their capture or too befouled, the rose-colored breasts and powerful wings encrusted by shit."

"Ugh," Pickett Sneat erupted heavily, and his volleyball of a head rolled from one shoulder to the other.

"So the greater number of the birds in this hunt were left on the floor of the forest," Leo Post continued after studying his audience for a brief moment. "Except for closing the school and one or two business places, the routines of Mauston continued undisturbed by the holocaust occurring on its outskirts. The *Mauston Star* of that week (circulation 365—'With Malice Toward None') carried the usual number of birth and death announcements. An excursion to Menominee Falls by the Lutheran Sunday School was reported. Oliver Simms Rutledge, one of the leading orators on the Chautauqua circuit, had agreed to speak at the town's Fourth of July celebration. Marsh's Dry Goods and Variety announced the receipt of the latest style ladies' hats from Boston along with the most recent patterns from *Harper's*.

"A local grain merchant predicted bumper crops of wheat and oats nationally and suggested that local farmers might have to take less for their production. So much for the front page.

"On an inside page, an Indian uprising in the southwestern territories was reported. But most of page two was taken up by a reprinted article from the *Kansas City Times* that suggested it was not Jesse James who was killed reaching for the family Bible in that bookcase in St. Joseph, Missouri, but an unidentified, unlucky wallpaper hanger. Also, a full account..."

"Mmmmmm-gwan." The agonized groan erupted from Pickett Sneat, who twisted in his chair as if open flame had been applied to his extremities.

"Sorry, forgive me," apologized Leo Post and turned to the window. "What I'm saying is only a few items concerning the pigeon hunt made the paper. A brief mention of the flock sighted and that the station agent had alerted the world. Another insert boxed

neatly and on page three of the four-page edition announced that
Mrs. Avery Mueller had given birth to a girl while plucking pigeon
feathers in the large tent near the railroad station. Labor had come
on suddenly, and delivery was made on a spare table away from
the activity—plenty of hot water was already available. To com-
memorate the occasion, Mr. and Mrs. Mueller named the baby girl
Dove."

"Oh, my," Sneat laughed. He switched his eyes toward our
captor who also had smiled.

"That evening," Post continued, the long features of his face
animated and the dark eyes flashing, "that first evening, the off-
duty shift of netters were the guests at a barbecue sponsored by the
local grange. They scrubbed the odors of their day's labor, splashed
Lucky Tiger on their hair, and were generally reported to be good
fellows—modest of manner and easy to talk to. The tent of wom-
en across the tracks also did a brisk business that first night—their
customers probably still reeking of barbecue sauce—for apparently
the lust of the kill had prompted another sort of rage. Reportedly,
these practitioners of the amatory arts worked tirelessly through
the night and had invented by early morning a new technique appropriately called—pulling the crop. Some years later, one of these
woman became the manager of Chicago's famous Everleigh Club
where she introduced this maneuver, a sleight-of-hand one might
say, with considerable success though the historical origins of the
method had been forgot."

"Oh for God's sake." Sneat threw up his hands. "If we're going to go on with this lecture, I must have something to eat. Isn't
it lunchtime? What sort of mess that wench might throw together
no longer matters. I'm starving."

"An excellent suggestion, Mr. Sneat." Yellow Hat stood up,
offering Sgt. Anderson his hand to help her rise from the floor.
"In fact, our subterfuge as fishermen was not completely an empty
camouflage—we had some luck this morning. We did not come
empty-handed to your confinement, and this wench, as you call
her—your language struts the paralysis of your soul—has prepared

the fish well." The young guerilla had accompanied the police officer to the entrance of the kitchen area where he kissed her on the lips. She disappeared behind the partition humming.

Yellow Hat paced off the distance between himself and the book reviewer. The man was visibly frightened and looked away toward the fireplace until our captor had forcibly turned Sneat's face to meet its doubles in the mirrored sunglasses.

"Of all those here, I want your blood the most, Mr. Sneat," Yellow Hat said in a low voice. "You are to be civil and generous these last few hours. Do you understand?"

"Now, now," Leo Post said soothingly, striding to the side of his colleague, and this gesture seemed to mollify our captor. Yellow Hat smiled, gave the book reviewer's cheek an ominous pat, and then walked toward the man called Taylor.

"And who's this Texas Ranger?" he asked, though his scornful tone offered an amused lilt.

"Mr. Taylor has been my confidant and associate for several years," Leo Post offered.

"Bodyguard, chauffeur—" Yellow Hat completed the curriculum vitae as he stood next to the man.

"Well, yes," Post agreed.

"—faithful servant, loving lackey, willing to comply with all your master's orders. Isn't that so?" The man called Taylor stared at the young guerilla, the large Adam's apple slowly working up and down the long neck. "Have we ever met, Mr. Taylor? You look very familiar to me. Must have been all those TV dramas of how the West was won."

"Possibly you have seen Taylor before," Post interjected. "He was world famous for his rope-throwing and equestrian feats in the better rodeos. He appeared in numerous television commercials. You might recall the most memorable of these—he's leading his horse through a desert."

"Where is that horse, Mr. Taylor?" Yellow Hat inquired.

"He's passed on," the man called Taylor replied and looked down at the floor.

"Ah, too bad. And who is this we have here?" The terrorist had come to us, looked into our face as if we might be something hanging on a wall.

"From the agency investigating Leo," Sneat said quickly, "who has written one-too-many Letters to the Editor. Tiresome bore with all his righteous quibbling. The new Acts of Civility make excesses like Post's liable for prosecution, and they have tracked him down. So we are all now under surveillance, thanks to him."

"This may be more quibble in your view, Pickett, but the actual reason for this investigation is my objection to the extension of the Kimball Lyon Self-Propelled Expressway across 23rd Street in Manhattan, and that objection is precisely if not cleverly connected to what I've just been talking about."

"Oh yes, the pigeon hunt," Yellow Hat said, moving away

"Yes, in Mauston, Wisconsin. 1883."

"How much more is there?" The terrorist had sunk into one of the armchairs and stretched out long, booted legs.

"Well, we've only just covered the first day and night. The netting went on for two more days and nights."

"Kill me," gasped Pickett Sneat. "Do it now, I beg of you, I cannot sit through more of his narrative." As the man spoke, the armed youth casually let the muzzle of his weapon drift to aim at him directly. Sneat swallowed his protests and rattled his metal harness.

"Well, if you insist," Post said graciously and bowed slightly. "On that second morning in the forest outside Mauston, a new sound greeted the dawn—the ring of metal striking wood—the thwack of axes chopping trees. Most of the nests within reach of the poles had been tumbled; most of those enveloped by the fumes of burning sulfur were empty. But there were a hundred thousand or more at higher elevations—at the very tops of the trees—that had not been affected. The little squabs huddled cozily in these and waited to be fed. So, the trees had to be brought down to maximize the profit of the expedition. Axes and saws flashed in the early light, and great oaks and ancient spruce fell to the ground.

"Some villagers described the sound of the operation in terms of cataracts of water, a storm at sea, and we might wonder if these same auditors imagined the wrench and splintering of these huge timbers to be the noise of ships breaking up on a shore. One after another bark was imagined sent to destruction on a rocky coast, hulls ripped apart and proud spars snapping in two on that dreadful landfall—a flotilla, indeed a whole armada coming to grief upon that Wisconsin prairie."

"But wouldn't the objects of this hunt be mangled by this method?" our captor asked.

"Many of the squabs would be made worthless by the violence of their fall, but many, many more remained marketable. Moreover, the parent birds would follow their young down to the forest floor and were then netted, large numbers were merely swatted out of the air with sticks as they flew dazedly in thick clusters. A subsequent issue of the *Mauston Star* reported one youth used his mother's rug beater with deadly effect.

"And so on into the night and the next day. Some objections were now being raised as to the dimensions the netting had begun to assume. What had originally seemed to be a gift of nature was becoming a horrible spectacle. An editorial in the *Chicago Sun* criticized the netters for their wasteful methods. 'Surely a more humane method—one that might even be more productive in its operation—can be devised to harvest these birds.' Residents in Mauston grumbled about the rowdies and layabouts that had accompanied the netters beginning to pester the community. Moreover, the tented brothel across the tracks had begun to be visited by townsmen, respectable husbands and family men tempted by Big City debaucheries. They had been gripped by their imaginations overnight. Aggrieved wives passed around petitions. But the long freight trains continued to ease into the station, all bells and whistles, and then depart, their wheels slipping up to speed under their heavy cargoes of packed pigeons, gathering momentum and direction toward the world market. The filigrees of steam spun from the wheels of those Baldwin giants hooked the station, the village, the fields and wood into a giant crochet whose pattern could never be undone."

As reported earlier, the great willow trees that rose outside the casement windows masked the river view, so that the morning garbage scows from Albany caught the assembly off-guard, and the stench was overpowering. The flotilla of waste passed downriver swiftly on the outgoing tide and the river's current, the accompanying tug saluting Leek's Island with a perky toot, but not swiftly enough; the assembly was drenched with a putrefaction so loathsome that I, B. Smith, not a novice to purulence, noted the resemblance to mortal corruption.

"They're an hour late," Post said as he pinched his nose and checked his watch. Sneat also held his nose tight, and his eyes bulged. One lifeless leg lifted from the floor as if inflated by the noxious reek. "Must have been an unusually large dump in Albany last night," Post speculated nasally. "The legislature is in session." Our captor had become pale and coughed several times, obviously overcome by the odor. Had the company not been similarly affected, it would have been a good opportunity to overwhelm him. But it was not to be.

"Let's wind this presentation up before lunch, Professor," Yellow Hat ordered crisply, standing and taking several lungfuls of air. "There can't be much more to tell."

"Not much more that would not be repetitious," Leo Post agreed. "Earlier, I told you of the banquet hosted by the chamber of commerce when the netters arrived; now, another feasting was taking place in the wood, in the dark but not silent. Hogs grunted and squealed in the slimy dung that covered everything as they rooted out the carcasses of mangled pigeons. The birds, coated by their own excrement, were gobbled up by the pigs like schoolboys munching on sugarcoated raisins."

"Aghh," Sneat spat. "There's no need for such imagery, particularly just before lunch. You are a boor, Post. You always were a boor."

"The following morning, the netters and their friends boarded several Pullman parlor cars that had been waiting for them on a siding since midnight. Most of the men had not slept, for the farewell festivities had been continuous, so they dropped like stones into the thick upholstered chairs and lounges of the special cars. The tents had been struck and packed up, the temporary latrines limed and filled in, and the entrails and wastes from the processed birds had been dumped in a marsh outside of town to become the nesting place of several swarms of maggot flies.

"It had been a good hunt, all agreed. Profitable. Nearly six thousand barrels of premium squabs had been shipped out in those three days, and the price in Chicago currently brought twenty-five dollars per barrel. Moreover, several thousand crates of salted birds plus those that had been pickled were also shipped out. Additional profits were realized from the byproducts, for example, feathers for ticks for the summer homes of the better families. It took the plumage of one thousand birds to make one tick.

"Going toward Chicago, the trains passed the forest that lay south of the village. It appeared as if a tornado had ripped through the stand. Ravaged, oaks a hundred years old or more had crushed and splintered younger trees as they lay under their tremendous size. All rested where they had fallen in a tangled mass barely accessible to squirrels.

"Most of the stand forest had been scorched by the sulphuric inferno and would remain leafless and barren, but in all this devastation there were still nests that had not been disturbed. Unbelieveable but true. They had been constructed too far from the eye of the hunt, too deep into the forest to make it worth the effort to ravage them, and so several thousand fledging birds miraculously survived the onslaught. Normality returned to the village of Mauston: children went back to school, daily chores resumed, and business as usual was restarted. The station agent once again leaned back in his chair, wound his watch, and waited for the two scheduled trains that stopped in Mauston—one a milk train and the later one of salesmen and young people leaving their native hamlets for the bright lights of Milwaukee."

"Ah, the poor dears," Pickett interrupted, wiping his nose. "That migration of innocence, riding to its corruption."

Post regarded his associate with a careful eye, searching out the man's attitude—scorn or sympathy—and apparently finding neither but only a rhetorical fanfaronade, he continued soberly. "All would be peaceful at night, though someone's dog might bark far, far away."

"Now I must object to that image," the book reviewer exclaimed. He had rattled his chair. "Dogs barking in the distance— how many times do these canine yaps and croons interrupt the silence of an innocent narrative. They have to be muzzled, Post— penned up if you will. Send them off with the weather."

"But how else to describe silence—silence falling over a neighborhood or a town—but in terms of the lonely yelp of a mongrel."

"It's the same dog and the same *woof-woof,* and I'm tired of it," his colleague replied and looked around the chamber for support. Yellow Hat seemed to be asleep. The man called Taylor stared out the window. Sgt. Anderson, in her persona as Lucy, studied the embroidered pattern of a tea towel.

Leo Post had also taken a similar poll, then shrugged and continued. "About a week after the hunt was over, the villagers were startled by an eerie sound from the woods. It resembled the great sigh from a huge beast. Perhaps some unknown monster had been startled from its spellbound slumber by the slaughter and now stumbled through the wood and toward the village enraged at being dragged from its enchantment."

"One moment, Professor." The young guerilla had not been asleep, but had leaped up. "We're getting into areas of speculation, don't you think? First that the villagers might imagine such a monster—a post-Freudian figure of guilt obviously introduced by you as narrator. And secondly, how are you privy to the monster's feelings? He might have been very pleased to be up and around once again—brought back from a long night of dreamless boredom. Enchantment, with all its pleasures, implies a loss of freedom."

"Quite so," Leo Post agreed as his black eyes scrutinized the terrorist. "Well, then, what the villagers heard was the flight of pigeons leaving the forest—the thousands of them that had survived the hunt. They were taking wing and continuing to Canada. By now those squabs that were yet alive had made their first headlong pitch from their perches to discover their wings. After that initial winging, the muscles in their backs rapidly grew strong, and with only a day's practice, these fledglings could fly as swiftly and as far as their parents. Suddenly, some predetermined signal had gone off in two hundred thousand birdbrains, and they all rose from the forest as one. Naturally, this estimate would include a great many adult birds with no young to care for. The villagers and farmers around Mauston watched and remembered. A hurried recess was declared in the schools so children could watch and remember. The station agent crooked his head out the bay window of his office, wound his watch and remembered. But the pigeons did not remember. Already they had no memory of the decimation of their flock, and though some may have felt odd—they had no young to escort north—by the time they crossed the border, the instinctual but unidentifiable sense of loss would have been erased by the demands of survival. So they climbed in a glittering, raucous column in the morning light, leaving the blackened wood as if it were an untouched wilderness—thinking nothing was wrong, remembering nothing had gone wrong. At an altitude of a thousand feet, they formed their characteristic wave, not quite a mile wide now, and swept north to be out of sight and sound within five minutes. At the last, they were seen to be a thin gray mark penciled along the horizon, and then that disappeared, erased by distance to foreshadow their eventual rubout."

As if commanded by some aptitude peculiar to her, Sgt. Anderson had begun to set the table for lunch, and she was assisted after a morose hesitation by the man called Taylor. The undercover police office placed a vase of white and purple lilac that grew wild over the island in the center of the table. She seemed to take uncharacteristic pleasure in arranging the long stems of the blooms. Her velvety brown eyes passed slowly over the guerilla in the yellow hat.

"Mr. Post," she announced in a voice as smooth as buckwheat honey, "Mr. Post and gentlemen, if you will take your seats, lunch will be served."

I, B. Smith, no stranger to haute cuisine, was impressed by what Sgt. Anderson brought to the table. Two large fish lay on a metal platter, garlanded with aromatic strands. The policewoman then placed a small saucepan over a portable alcohol stove.

"Can it be?" Post had sniffed the air at his place, the large head thrown back as nostrils and dark eyes widened with anticipation. "Can it be?" he asked once more, and then applauded as the sauce in the small pan erupted in blue flame. Sgt. Anderson poured the flaming contents over the fish. "It is—it is—"

"It is what?" Pickett Sneat asked, pulling away from the blue flames Sgt. Anderson ladled over the fish.

"Lucy miraculously presents us with a *loup au fenouil, flambé*," Post replied. "A marvelous fixing of bass. Fennel seeds, salt, and pepper, a little peanut oil on the outside of the fish and then bake in—what would you say, Lucy, about a 400 degree oven?"

"That'll do it," she replied thoughtfully. "Bake for about a half hour."

"Then before serving," Post continued enthusiastically, "a mixture of cognac and more fennel seeds are flamed and poured over the fish. Too bad our cellar has no Muscadet to serve with it. My apologies, sir." He had turned toward Yellow Hat who sat at Post's right elbow. "The wine cellar of this castle was never of much distinction, and there's nothing in it now. Well, not to drink anyway," he said, looking toward us with a meaningful smirk.

Employing a large spoon and fork, Sgt. Anderson served the fish, deftly separating bone from flesh, dressing each portion with melted butter—and all performed in a manner that credited her training at the New York State Police Academy. A green salad accompanied the dish.

Post approved of the meal with a vocabulary of gurgles, lip smackings, and sighs as each morsel passed his lips, but consumed the meal straight on, as if it were no different from the bowls of oatmeal served up earlier. Yellow Hat, with a graceful precision of knife and fork, rather delicate for a terrorist, sampled the recipe, nodding approval. Sgt. Anderson seemed especially interested in his good opinion.

It is right to report that this meal occasioned the first conversational blackout since our arrival at Leek's Castle. The only intrusion was the hyper-excited voices from the transistor in the garden below, where Yellow Hat's companions stood guard. Apparently, they had brought their own rations. Once, maybe twice, Leo Post seemed on the edge of a comment, only to be silenced by the delectable repast that passed his tongue. In little time, the two large bass were reduced to bony cartoons, and the author-turnedpolitician pushed his chair back from the table and gave a final flourish of napkin to his mouth.

"Splendid," he complimented Sgt. Anderson. "Absolutely splendid, Lucy. Don't you think so?" The book reviewer had fallen into a semi-doze within his metal harness. In fact, a torpor seemed to have overcome the whole company, I, B. Smith, notwithstanding, nor did the cat-like vigilance of our captor seem immune to this lassitude.

"There is a river haze this time of day," Yellow Hat said as he stood slowly and moved toward the open casement, "a haze that blurs the lines, softens stones, and laves all harsh projections. We are lulled, and something is set in motion by this river tunneling through the mist of noon that pulls us with it, a yearning for the perpetual turning in our veins. Let's take a brief recess; Mr. Sneat is already leading the way. But be warned—any attempt to leave the island will meet with unpleasantness. My companions, as you hear them in the garden, will be on guard. Mr. Taylor, please assist Mr. Sneat to his rooms. Mr. Post, we will assemble here later. And Lucy," the guerilla took Sgt. Anderson by the arm, "please come with me."

Later That Afternoon...

I, B. Smith, a duly appointed informant, had fallen asleep while thumbing *Stella's Phallus*, the pornographic trash available on the bedside table. Pseudo-sophisticates may be amused that this smut was written by Leo Post under the pseudonym of Len Banal, but we note on the record that this material is the sad evidence of the degeneration of one of the great minds of our time. The object of our perusal was to find further proof of his opposition to the proposed extension of the Self-Propelled Expressway.

However, we must regretfully report that our efforts revealed nothing relevant to Post's motivations, nor to the circumstances of his wife's death. In fact, the monotonous descriptions of the depravities that composed the aforementioned book, *Stella's Phallus*, had put us to sleep. For the record, it might be important to summarize some of these outrageous events. On pages 71-75, the heroine is being held captive in the weight room of the YMCA on West 23rd Street in New York City. Incidentally,

said facility is directly across the street from the Chelsea Hotel. In the novel, the Y is used by a secret association of wealthy
sportsmen as a place in which to indulge their salacious whims.
In the course of these four pages, the heroine is made to submit,
not altogether unwillingly we must state, to a series of encounters
with a band of strolling gypsies, three damson plums, a souvenir
from the World's Fair of 1939, a vacuum-cleaner salesman and his
machine, a dozen blue- point oysters and the swarthy brute who
opened them, three coins from a fountain, a plumber's friend,
a light at the end of a tunnel, a dusky child of nature, a roll of
thunder, a boatload of trouble, a piece of the True Cross, a former
member of President Nixon's inner circle, a bullet bitten, a Gold-
wyn Girl from the West—and this is only a partial list.

The rumbling passage of a tanker in the river woke us. We
cannot estimate the length of our recess, and since the window of
our room faced east, the chamber was in shadow as the afternoon
sun was now over the Catskills, so our sleep-matted eyes did not
immediately make out the figure standing next to a heavy bookcase. It was the man called Taylor.

He posed with one hand hooked on the gun belt aslant his
hips and gazed with a faraway look at nothing in particular. His
head was slightly tilted, and his eyes glinted mischievously. We
cannot say how long he had been standing here, and he resembled
one of those lifelike cardboard cutouts stores use to feature a product. When he noted our waking, he became quickly animated.

"Shucks," he said, "I hadn't ought to have bothered you none."
His sidewise glance was charming, a primitive nobility in his manner. "I figgered to just set up here a while 'til you sawed your wood
so that we might shoot the breeze some about this accident of
Molly Post's."

I, B. Smith, attention quickly alerted, prepared to accept
some testimony. But he motioned us to follow him out of the
room, using an elaborate sign language probably learned from
the Native Americans once featured in the Wild West shows that
followed the regular circus performances. He led us on tiptoes

through the humid hallways of the castle, pausing to carefully edge around doorways. A part of the castle's masonry plunked into the lagoon outside and other splashes and gurgles intimated the seepage that was overcoming the structure. We had come to an unfamiliar part of the castle, a tower in the northwest corner of the citadel which we approached single-file across a crumbling redoubt. In the tower we found ourselves surrounded by piles of magazines that rose from the floor like moldy stalagmites. Closer inspection identified them being of hobby interests, and the highest stacks were built from old issues of *Popular Mechanics* and *Mechanics Illustrated*.

"Mr. Post was real good to me," Taylor muttered, these surroundings clearly setting him at ease. "He fixed me with a good job after Tony, the Wonder Horse, was killed, and he gave me a safe place for these magazines." As he spoke, his arm swept over the collections piled high in the room. "I put together that little ferryboat you took over to the island the other morning from plans in one of those *Popular Mechanics*. Those years with the circus and the rodeo, the usual pastimes were poker and bourbon, and I wasn't partial to either. So, I read these magazines, and then after I read them sent them to a cousin in New Jersey to keep them. But he ran out of room, and just about then I had met Mr. Post and he gave me this place to keep them." As he spoke, the man called Taylor led us through the maze, *une collonade des journaux* as Leo Post might say, to a stone stairway that serpentined around the tower's wall to the top. We climbed this spiral stair cautiously, aware that the man called Taylor might be following an order from Leo Post to hurl us to our death. Case closed.

We were led through a small door at the top and into a circular room that was carpeted with more copies of *Popular Mechanics, Home Craftsman,* and the *Serious Hobbyist*. Missing tiles contributed to a gaping hole in the roof that had been patched by translucent plastic to improvise a sort of skylight, and directly beneath this opening was a curious contraption of wire, paddle-wheels, and hinged-out riggers. The telescope we had seen him using earlier was nearby.

"Haven't finished it yet," the man called Taylor said with some apology. "Got the idea from one of—" He looked about the cluttered floor for the source of his inspiration. "—well, one of them. The idea is to use sunlight to generate electricity. I've always been handy, and Mr. Post set up this workshop so I could try out these ideas."

Evidence of the man's hobbies cluttered the space, some recognizable—such as an automatic picnic table with a sudden-shower preventer—but others lying about like discarded puppets. However, what was clearly his masterwork took up one half of the room. The invention was part bed and part kitchen cabinet and featured lockers (with various doors and shelves) on either side of the sleeping area. Reading lamps thrust out from the carpentry like the necks of geese caught in a trap. A dictionary stand pivoted on one side, and three accordion-like shelves pulled out from the headboard to support a small television set, a radio, and a rather sophisticated audio resource unit. Reaching over the head of the bed and down to what might be the lap level of its occupant was an electric griddle, while a small but serviceable refrigerator was fitted into the cupboard on the right. With obvious pride, the man called Taylor touched a button on the control panel, and a self-contained and automatically sanitized toilet emerged from the left side of the bed frame.

"If you need to," he offered and seemed slightly disappointed when we declined. But he had continued the demonstration of his invention by pressing another button to pull out a small but complete workbench from the opposite side of the bed frame, as if to counterbalance the waste facility. Within this castle on this island on the Hudson River, the man had created another island for himself.

This brief review by no means registered the contrivance's complexities—there were many more levers and buttons on the control panel, and the whole contrivance seemed to hum with the possibilities of an isolated life. And other examples of his creativity drew our inspection. Upon a freeform table cut from thick Lucite rested an ingenious lamp in the design of an old-fashioned water pump—pushing the pump handle up or down activates the light. Several screens of painted plywood, each with scrollwork and cutouts more intricate than the next, stood here and there. Near the room's small hearth was a heavy vase of cement decorated with bottle caps from Orange Crush soda embedded in the mortar. A stuffed red-tailed hawk suggested his self-taught taxidermy, while suspended from the ceiling in flight more credible than the hawk's was a large-scale model of the *Spirit of Saint Louis.*

An odd juxtaposition was crammed into one corner, beneath the window—the Golden Gate Bridge created entirely from toothpicks seemed to offer vain help to a highly detailed model of the *Titanic* sinking in a field of plastic icebergs. The expressions on the faces of the ship's orchestra playing their last benefit were particularly noteworthy.

In this amazing debris of homely inventions and scaled-down icons, one exhibit stood out in its authenticity. It was a large framed photograph hung above the fireplace showing a handsome black horse rearing on its hind legs with the man called Taylor in the saddle wearing the costume of a rodeo and waving a white ten-gallon Stetson above his head.

"That was my horse," he told us, noting our interest. "A wonder horse—smarter than me. All over now. Here, let's sit a while." He invited us by kicking in our direction a cushioned seat made from a barrel. He stretched out on a crude chaise put together from several orange crates, each of his motions accompanied by the comfortable creak of leather. The empty holster was strapped to his right thigh, his countenance parallel with the holster.

"Mr. Post says I'm to tell you about Miss Molly's accident, since I was there on the spot." He looked down at his large hands for a moment. " 'Cept it didn't happen that way—I guess you figured that out. Funny how the gentlest of beings will rear up and kick to death their own kind. Seen a mare rip apart her foal for no good reason.

"Course, you might say, Mr. Post had a reason. You know about that already. When Mr. Sneat showed him those pictures, he just went crazy. It was like some part of him had been withered by a bolt of lightning. I found him one evening down in that room with all the pictures, taking apart and cleaning that shotgun that had been his great-granddaddy's. He told me he was planning to make one last wing shot with it to bring down a mollymuck that was hanging round his neck.

"Seemed like a dangerous sort of target," the former rodeo star continued, "and I tried to persuade him not to try. But he was determined to do in his wife, talking crazy about his family name, about his being betrayed. Then he came up with the idea about using the Mark Twain 500, the car race, and he had talked me into it before I could say *heck*, I owe him a lot, you see."

The man called Taylor's eyes, reflecting the limitless light of a prairie, looked into ours for a moment. He smoothed down the straight black hair plastered to his skull. Then he rose and walked to an imitation pirate chest against a wall. From it he took a coil of rope, a lariat, and expertly worked a loop into it and began to twirl this circle above his head like a humming halo.

"It always eases me, 'specially when I'm jawing, if I have something to keep my hands busy." He had passed the spinning rope down, over, and up his body several times, moving rapidly so it appeared his whole figure was being encased in a cocoon. "This here one," he explained while completing an intricate maneuver, "is called the double-eight rollout. You don't hardly see anyone doing this one anymore. Well, now where was I?"

We reminded him he had introduced the Mark Twain 500 into the evidence. He had begun to throw and retrieve the whirling lariat in small circles straight out and back from his waist, and apparently was able to collect his thoughts.

"Miss Molly was a crackerjack driver. She had this special car made for her, and I had helped her with some of its design, getting ideas from some of my magazines. I was her chief mechanic.

"You might remember that first race was to celebrate the opening of the new spur of the Expressway from Poughkeepsie to Elmira and also a memorial to the Governor, her father, who had just passed on. That's now called the Mark Twain 500, but this was to be just the first run-through." He had returned to the rope trick that used his torso as an axis for the lariat's continuous gyration. The supple strength of his wrist amazed us.

"You might remember that first run was also to be a memorial to her father who had just passed on, and there's a funny thing there." He had paused to recoil the lariat and then began its last revolutions around his boot tops. "When they put him into the tomb underneath the parking lot he had built at the capital, his casket was over nine feet long, and he was just a little fella too. Never understood why.

"Anyways, we had set up the last pit stop just outside of Elmira, because the final leg of the race was the most difficult, going round and round inside the cemetery where Tom Sawyer's creator had been laid to rest. It was at that point—right at the gravesite—that Mr. Post ordered me to fix Miss Molly's car—loosen the steering and... well, you know the rest." He had let the lariat slip to the floor, a slack heap, and I, B.Smith, a practiced observer, determined him visibly overcome with the recollection of his murderous act. He slowly gathered the stunt rope together as he seemed to reflect on that moment.

"She came down that road, on either side stone markers some as high as a man, hell-bent for election. She was way out in front, leading the pack. I never seen her so pretty when she pulled into the pit, a little smudge of oil on her nose only making her prettier. She was a handsome woman, don't you know, and nearly as tall as me. She eased out of the car's cockpit and pulled off her helmet. Her bronze hair let loose. I never seen her so happy. As we serviced the car, she kept talking about how she was winning this race for Mr. Post, and how they would have a big celebration afterward. Her eyes were lit up, and looking and listening to her, I came to the sense that it wasn't true. I mean about those pictures."

The man called Taylor had begun another slow demonstration of his rope handling. "But what if it was true? I asked myself." He had settled the rope deftly over a large concrete jug by the fireplace. "How many times have I seen a wild stallion keeping company with a whole troop of mares and hadn't I seen the other too—a free-roaming female leading a canyon of studs. No bolt from the blue came down on them. Also, remember, I'd lost my horse because of my foolishness, shot out from under me, you might say, and here I was supposed to do in another fine animal, a blue-ribbon specimen, who had only been behaving like one of God's creatures."

The lariat had snagged on the handles of a plywood armoire in the corner, a rough representation of the Queen Anne period, and he interrupted his narrative to fetch the collapsed rope.

"Well, to cut it short, I just couldn't loosen that steering column." Soberly, he had proceeded on to other variations. "The folks at the Kansas City American Royal used to think quite highly of this routine," he said as he rotated the large loop vertically and stepped through its encirclement neatly and then back again as if through a large looking glass as the frame of the rope whirred around him.

"Anyways, I got to her behind a family plot with several large grave markers and told her about what was afoot—what had been afoot—and it was almost as if I had killed her there on the spot. The look on her face. I gave her the truth, how I was supposed to jimmy the car and get herself killed. I had to shout all of this in her ear because of the noise of the other racers coming up on us. She was sipping a bottle of sody. She couldn't lose her lead; you could see that about her, even though I had just told her her husband wanted to kill her. She was a true sportsman. Sportswoman. She handed me the bottle and kissed me on the cheek, jumped into her car, fastened her helmet, and was gone in a blast of the four hundred horses under the hood and a burst of gravel from under the car's wheels. She pulled off. That was the last I was to see of her." As if to accompany this voice, the sad substance of its message, he was now turning the rope in those slow figure eights at boot-top level.

"Yep, I know what you're going to say," he went on with a nod of the head. "How her car did crack up anyways, how it had left the road and smacked onto the side of a mausoleum and exploded. The tomb belonged to a family that had provided the city of Elmira with a school for the blind. Molly was so far ahead of the pack that no one was near to help her out of the wreckage. The racecar exploded, and all that was left of her was a small gold nugget that the police said was a gold chain that Mr. Post had given her. The accident took place a half mile from the finish line. She had been on her way to a world's record for a 500-mile contest. She must have grown careless, her mind distracted by the terrible information I had revealed to her, but Mr. Post thinks her death was caused by the tinkering I had been supposed to do to her car. He never knew the difference, and if truth be told, it seemed all the same to me; that I had done what he wanted anyhow."

I, B. Smith, becoming cramped by my position in the barrel, had risen and received the last of Taylor's testimony standing by the window near the ersatz pirate chest. This window was set high in one of the two towers of the old castle and gave a remarkable perspective upriver, exposing the lacework of bridges that looked ready to close up the open seam of the Hudson River. The Catskills, to our left, had grown blue in the afternoon hour and the Taghkanic hills, on the right bank, undulated beneath the oblique illumination of the failing sun. But below, an even more curious tableau had just terminated. A flash of color caught our eye such as that made by a goldfinch darting in and out of the dense growth. But it proved to be the bright headgear of the young guerilla, our captor, as he bent over the supine form of Sgt. Anderson. They had secreted themselves in the core of what had once been a maze of thick privet, now overgrown and untrimmed; however, our perspective high in the tower compromised the privacy of their innovative siesta.

Sgt. Anderson lay on her back fully exposed like a strip of the rich, black veldt of her ancestors' Africa. Yellow Hat, his back to us, knelt beside her and partially obscured our view of her Congo regions, so to speak. Certain motions of his arms suggested he worked to repair his costume, buttoning his shirt and so forth; however, we witnessed enough to substantiate the magnificent benefits Sgt. Anderson had received from the physical training program of the New York State Police Academy.

The secret agent lay with left arm bent to pillow her head while revealing a well-formed *teres major* whose supple anterior and posterior folds lifted the muscles and tissues of the *pectoralis major* to even greater prominence than we had observed earlier. At the apex of this conformation glistened a cusp of vascular material the color of polished mahogany. The svelte plain of the lumbar plexus descended smoothly into the *rectus abdominus*, a charming vista only matched by the luxuriant landscape that dipped down from the river's eastern shore.

As if to highlight our comparison, Yellow Hat had leaned forward to mark the agent's *linea alba* with a series of kisses, and clearly not satisfied with this explication, he duplicated his oral argument along the parallel *linea semilunaris* into the femoral conjunction that called forth a proof to his discourse from the manner by which Sgt. Anderson arched her torso as if to partake of the gentle ritual that resembled a seasonal ceremony. The terrorist had concluded his oscular survey at the umbilicus. A punctuation was made here, a reflective pause that lingered to a stop as if he wished to draw from this vestige of a life-support system some particle of nourishment overlooked and left behind to slake a latent hunger.

I, B. Smith, slightly alarmed by this tableau vivant, realized the police officer had exposed her true identity to the armed vagrant, for her agent's serial number tattooed just under the left mammary gland was obvious and in good light. She and the entire operation had been put in jeopardy. However, she stretched on the grass casually, and her right leg raised to put its polished knee into a metronomic movement from side to side to weave a distraction that prevented a more objective gathering of data. This position, knee raised and lazily marking some time known only to her, also put emphasis on the inguinal ligament, but Yellow Hat's position blocked our following the band of tissue to its maximum depth.

Also, after he had completed his review of her rectus, he continued to kneel beside her, one hand bestowing a final blandishment upon her person, and because—as we have stated—his pose obscured our view, our concluding statement must be taken as a reasoned assumption though the circumstances of their proximity favors the suggestion that his valediction was made in the area of Sgt. Anderson's pubic symphysis.

I, B. Smith, a seasoned witness, further affirm that the confession by the man they call Taylor, a party to the conspiracy surrounding the death of Molly Lyon Post, has also implicated her husband, said Leo Post, also known as Len Banal. Our faculties thus employed by these several impressions were troubled by a whirr above our head as the coils of the lariat descended over us. The man called Taylor played no prank or pleasantry on us but had firmly lassoed us as we stood at the window. His close-set eyes were moved even closer together by his grave expression.

"Nobody's going to hurt you," he said. With a few rapid but expert hitches of the rope, unquestionably a technique from his rodeo days, he had completely immobilized us in a bondage as secure as the steel encasement that enclosed Pickett Sneat. "There now," he said, stepping back to admire his handiwork. "Now, I'm going to tell you how I lost my horse." We could not escape.

LATER THAT AFTERNOON...

"I am Sgt. Lucille Anderson, Bureau of Criminal Investigation, New York State Police, and you are all under arrest.

"Let me advise you of the constitutional rights still permitted you and that everything you say or have ever said will be held against you."

The policewoman had resumed her costume of crossed bandoliers and white boots before we had been assembled in the dark portrait gallery of Leek's Castle. An ivory-handled knife was stuck in the black halo of her wooly hair and the official badge of her office glinted provocatively over the left pocket of her blouse. Her voice was crisp, businesslike, each word rising to the vaulted roof of the chamber.

I, B. Smith, still bobbined by a skein of lariat, expressed hearty appreciation for this turn of events, expecting to be freed as rightful order was returned; however, Sgt. Anderson ignored our comments and left us trussed and helpless next to Pickett

Sneat, similarly but gratuitously discomforted. We could only wonder that some breakdown in communication, or perhaps an interdepartmental feud, had caused the police officer to ignore our authority.

"Excellent, excellent," Leo Post almost sang, and clapped his hands. He regarded Anderson with a bemused affection. "I knew from the first that you were something special. A special agent! How marvelous. How per-fect-ly marvelous." He stretched out his pronunciation as the policewoman waved a small machine gun in his direction and Post obeyed the gesture and sat down on one of the several ottomans made of elephant feet. He winked toward Pickett Sneat.

Our host was dressed in the dark blazer, flannel pants, and glowing white bucks he had worn yesterday morning when he had greeted us at the island's landing dock. With an elegant flair, he adjusted the cuffs of the worn jacket and tugged at the knees of the shapeless trousers, as if this attention would renew the garments' long-lost crispness. The ersatz cowboy squatted on his heels beside Post and stared at the hide of a Bengal tiger, now a rug.

"Well, old fellow." The author patted Taylor on his shoulders. "It looks like we've come to the end of the trail." The man called Taylor nodded silently and continued to stare into the glass eyes of the tiger as if the reflections of old campfires might still flit within them.

Only Yellow Hat seemed indifferent to Sgt. Anderson's announcement, and we had to assume, with the clarity of hindsight, that the interlude in the maze we had witnessed earlier had given him a particular status vis-à-vis the policewoman that would also explain her possession of his weapon. The guerilla casually made a thoughtful perusal of the different portraits that hung in this vast chamber, in the manner of a tourist on holiday. His companions outside had disap-peared, and their radio had fallen silent. We feared they had escaped the island to gather fellow terrorists to storm the castle and overthrow Sgt. Anderson's effort to restore law and order.

"What are the charges? Why are we arrested?" Sneat's voice boomed and echoed within the stone-walled chamber. The book reviewer had suddenly come to life after a somnolent interval, and his freckled face was set in a mien of unnatural glee. He resembled the frozen grimaces on the animal heads that hung from the walls around us. "What are the crimes we are alleged to have committed?"

"In your case," Sgt. Anderson replied smoothly as she turned to confront him, "the charges are perjury, bearing false witness, and falsification of evidence."

"Oh dear, is that all?" he replied as a jack-o'-lantern smile lit up his features. He took a deep breath, and his face purpled. "Guilty!" he exploded. Then shouted again, "Guilty!" The fringe of red hair trembled on his forehead. "Actually, I've already confessed. Surely you know my prize-winning collection of essays *The Art and Craft of Reviewing.* It's a full-length book, and in it I have voluntarily admitted these crimes of lying, misrepresentation, purposeful sentimentalism. It's the old custom, isn't it—once confessed, guilty no more." He looked about us, avidly sucking matter down from his sinuses. "And the royalties keep coming in. The public adores liars who confess.

"Moreover, I've never claimed to be a critic, though there have been times when I have been forced into the posture." His round face worked to achieve a modest cast. "I am but a humble book reviewer. Listen to my program on public radio. Some of the best minds of our time have written an occasional crooked review. What's the harm—who's going to buy the book anyway? I've never claimed to be brilliant—let the light shine where it doesn't. My ignorance is tantamount—I admit it."

"Come now, Pick," Post chided his associate with a genial affection in his eyes. "You're being way too modest, though your pledge of ignorance does sometimes resemble a fetish." The author kicked and rolled an elephant foot over to Sneat's chair and sat down beside him. It was an obvious display of allegiance. "Indeed, I recall you commenced all of your reviews with a statement affirming your ignorance of the subject at hand."

"Exactly." The book reviewer nodded, his complexion pinking once again. "One had to be careful of patronizing the reader, of seeming to know more than he or she. Mostly she." He giggled. "You find it in chapter three of my little tome—create the illusion that reader and reviewer learn about the book simultaneously."

Both men seemed to have forgotten our present circumstances and continued their discussion even as I, B. Smith, endeavoring to identify our official capacity, rapped against the tabletop for attention. Sgt. Anderson ignored our motion as she lounged in one of the high-backed Italian Renaissance-style chairs, the automatic weapon held across her lap. She placed one leg over the chair's arm and clocked the colloquy with the swing of a white-booted foot. Her racial origins set her apart from the rest of the company, as did her gender, and it occurred to us that she might take this opportunity under the guise of official duty to exact retribution for the injustices sustained on both levels over an immeasurable span of time.

"Something I've never told you," Leo Post hunched toward his colleague with a chummy intimacy, "but perhaps this is the time for frankness. I never believed that pose of naiveté—especially your attitude toward fiction."

"It has always been a struggle to reconstruct reality and still be interesting." The book reviewer had placed his fingers together, tip to tip, as he reflected. "The new genre—Especially Original Non-Fiction—is an attempt to address the problem of making mundane histories interesting, and if a little imagination is required here and there to grease the acceptability of an awkward objective, then it is the quality of the lubricant that becomes important and not its usage."

"Ha!" exclaimed Yellow Hat from across the chamber. The militant had paused beneath the enormous portrait of Major Burtis Leek (1803-1852), the supposed hero of Black Hawk's Rebellion.

"In any event, this discussion is old stuff and *réchauffé*," Sgt. Anderson proclaimed.

"Very good," Post commended her use of language. "Very good indeed. And of what crime am I accused?"

"Murder—the destruction of a rare gift."

"Oh, well," the author replied. He had sagged on the hassock as if his own limbs had been filled with sand. "You refer to my talent, and I must plead guilty as my colleague has just done. It's no justification, but there was so much raw material at hand, the refinement seemed unnecessary, and for a long time, that was true. A continent of images surrounded me, like prairie flowers, while others felt fortunate to find a single blossom above the timberline, a flower to be cherished, pressed, and lovingly taken from a journal's notes now and again. The abundance seeded my prodigal ways; my dissolution was born of rapture." Post had spread his arms as if to implore sympathy.

"Just admit it," his colleague interrupted impatiently. "Cut to the chase. You were a fool in love."

"You lay too much importance," Post said reprovingly, "on the natural selection of the indiscreet."

"But to lay on what fool?" asked Yellow Hat. He stood before a Leek family portrait, circa late nineteenth century. "The laying of a fool grants little distinction."

"Quite so," Post agreed, glancing curiously at the guerilla who was still examining the painting. "But if fools be inferior they must, by definition, lie beneath others."

"That's a trifle," Yellow Hat replied.

"To call me a fool is to trifle." Post's dark eyes had become luminous.

"Stop, stop," Sneat exploded and rattled his metal harness. "What is this—some kind of third-rate Shakespeare festival?"

"Sit down, Mr. Post," the policewoman ordered. Her own restlessness had become apparent. "Whatever you're talking about has nothing to do with the felony with which you are charged."

"I am fully aware of the charge," the author said, resuming his place on the elephant foot. "I have been trying to sugar the rankness of the charge, to put the monster into domino."

"Will he never cease this rhetorical flimflam?" the book reviewer asked.

"I claim all responsibility," the author had continued. "All others are blameless. My good companion, Mr. Taylor, had nothing to do with the event. He cannot be charged."

"The man called Taylor will be charged," the policewoman replied. "He is guilty of promoting a lie."

I, B. Smith, a captive audience in the truest sense of the word, had just heard the complete circumstances surrounding the destruction of the bogus cowboy's horse. Consequently, what sympathy we may have had for this ingenuous fellow had been spent, and we were not unhappy to see him caught in the net thrown by Sgt. Anderson. The man called Taylor looked unmoved by the accusation, squatting in the same butt-on-boot pose as before. We wondered if the muscles of his legs had atrophied.

"Permit me, dear Lucy—dear Sgt. Anderson—to raise a defense of Mr. Taylor." Post was on his feet once more and took two steps toward the policeperson, though he seemed to address himself to Yellow Hat. The guerilla-terrorist had moved farther along the gallery and had stopped before the formal portrait of a woman. The figure's elongation, an exaggeration of the Leek length, suggested the brush of a Whistler.

"One man's fraud is another's myth," the author continued. "Every American boy had the same dreams as Mr. Taylor had. His only crime was that he successfully lived out his dream." The author stood, one foot slightly advanced before the other, left hand in the blazer's side pocket. From outside, a continuous sound of water splashed against the stone bulwarks to lead one to believe the island was sinking into the Hudson.

"Imagine a childhood of Saturday matinees starring Ken Maynard, Buck Jones, and the immortal Johnny Mack Brown. Alas, I see those names mean nothing to you. Well, then, does anyone remember Tom Mix? Surely his monument still stands on Route 66? Consider Zane Grey—*Tales of the Bar-X* and *Bunkhouse Romances*. Wild Bill Hickok, Wyatt Earp, Buffalo Bill, Bat

Masterson, Pat Garrett, and Billy the Kid. As a boy in Paramus, New Jersey, there was always a sunset that the young Taylor could ride into. A water hole to defend and a six-gun to confront. Every pulp story from his neighborhood newsstand took him closer to that frontier where fantasy passes into myth—the territory always ahead."

"You'll permit me a personal observation, Mr. Post," the policewoman interrupted. She had brought her feet primly together and leaned toward him with authority. "These myths you extol are the exaggerated tales of oppressors, told at the historic expense of minorities and the underprivileged."

"I cannot dispute your contention, dear Sgt. Anderson," Post replied. "Accept then that I but describe the corruption that influenced the man called Taylor. He only played predicate of the subject you have mentioned. The abundance of targets in that hunt in Mauston, Wisconsin, in 1883 is related to the myth of the great hunter. They couldn't miss! What the man called Taylor has done is to excerpt and refashion the good part of the myth; should he be blamed when his re-creation calls up the sordid part of the story? He has renewed a subject that had ceased to exist. That's it." Post held up a finger. "His attempt to renew an extinct species should at least claim your praise, and he is not an oppressor, no threat. He only had blanks in his gun, only ornaments of his fantasy. Those in your weapon are real."

"Oh, this is old stuff," the policewoman said with a shrug that pulled our attention to the badge that decorated her bosom. "Let's return to the facts. Mr. Taylor, you are charged with the murder of the late Molly Lyon Post by the means of disabling her car. You have taken a life rather than renewing it."

I, B. Smith, having witnessed Taylor's contradictory testimony, was surprised he made no effort to defend himself against this accusation. Instead, he looked at his employer, the author Leo Post, and then toward us, I, B. Smith, a professional spectator, as if he had more to fear from these quarters than from the police. In any event, the breathy signal from a large boat passing the island would have made any vocal response inaudible.

This pause in the interrogation also made room for deliberation. Should we put on the record now Taylor's previous testimony, or should it be withheld for our own departmental purpose? It must be kept in sight that our prime responsibility was to investigate Leo Post's conspiracy to thwart the extension of the Governor Kimball Lyon Self-Propelled Expressway and not alleged foul play during the Mark Twain 500. So, the remarks made to us by the man called Taylor seemed of smaller importance, and we remained silent. And he seemed relieved.

"Take me." Leo Post spoke softly after the vessel had passed upstream. He had stood and placed a hand on his employee's shoulder. "I am the only guilty party here."

"Loyalty is very important to you, Professor." It was Yellow Hat who spoke from the far fireplace. In the failing light of the portrait gallery, the militant's dark glasses were even more opaque.

The tensions of the last several minutes seemed to have unstrung Pickett Sneat even as he was confined by his metal fittings. His head rolled from side to side, and he slumped in the wheelchair. Spit drooled from his pink lips. Above the fireplace, directly over Yellow Hat, the portrait of a woman seemed to be illuminated by some trick of the artificial lighting. The luminous eyes painted on the canvas appeared to move as if to follow the conversation.

"Taylor's loyalty has been absolute," Post was saying.

"Who is this? There's no nameplate on the frame." Yellow Hat stood back to look at the portrait.

"That is my wife."

"Dead?"

"Yes, dead."

"Did she love you?" the guerilla asked.

"Perhaps. I do not know." Post's composure had begun to fray like the cuffs of his dark blazer. His fingers counted the brass buttons—one was missing.

"Did she never tell you she loved you?" the terrorist persisted.

"Yes, many times."

"You did not believe her?"

"Yes—no." The author sat down on the large hassock, unconsciously aligning his white buckskins with the metallic toenails of the elephant foot. "Like Robinson Crusoe, each of us looks for a footprint in the sand, some evidence of a companion. If by the rarest chance, one is discovered, we cannot resist placing our own foot into the mold. We cannot believe the footprint is one of our own, so we destroy it."

"Love, then, was a stranger at this table," Yellow Hat observed.

"LOVE WAS A STRANGER TO THIS ISLE..." Sneat's booming baritone vibrated within the chamber. The melody of his song suggested Thomas Campion.

LOVE WAS A STRANGER TO THIS ISLE,
WALKING HERE AND WALKING THERE;
YET, LIFE'S ANTICIPATION ALL THE WHILE
IS TO SHARE...

The critic's round head fell back, his lips pursed and eyes half-closed as he readied another stanza. Yellow Hat had approached us, moving with a graceful menace similar to the stilled suppleness of the white panther that crouched in the hearth. In the ecstasy of his inspiration, Pickett had continued to croon.

OH, LOVE, A STRANGER TO THIS ISLE,
FRAGILE FOOTPRINTS IN THE SAND,
WE TRACE THEIR PATH, OUR OWN EXILE...

Though he sang the last line of the quatrain, we could not hear the words above the terrific explosions of gunfire that obliterated everything. Yellow Hat had raised the small machine gun from Sgt. Anderson's grasp and stood squarely before the book reviewer, firing point-blank. Enrapt by his own burst of lyricism, Sneat was unaware he was being fired upon until the bombardment eventually demolished his concentration. His eyes widened, and his body jerked in concert with the machine gun's blasts. Despite the steel fittings that held him together, his whole being vibrated under the fearful tattoo of the weapon like a dry leaf in a gust.

It was all over before any of those present could react. I, B. Smith, immobilized by the coils of the lasso, was unable to interrupt the assault. The unexpected suddenness of the guerilla's attack, the realization of what had been a constant threat since Yellow Hat's arrival, the assassination of one of the culture's more important book reviewers—the computation of these different assessments added up to a catatonic condition.

The clips of the automatic weapon had emptied, and the final brass cartridges looped into the air to fall tinkling on the stone floor. Yellow Hat abruptly about-faced and walked away from the still figure of Pickett Sneat. He tossed the weapon casually into Sgt. Anderson's lap as he passed her. The police officer, like the rest of us, seemed unable to respond to what happened. The man called Taylor stood like a statue, his hand fixed above the empty holster on his hip, and Leo Post—his oratorical pose frozen—was the first to recover.

"Good Lord, Pickett!" he cried, rushing to his colleague. He turned furiously on the guerilla who stood at the high windows that faced the inner lagoon. "You are no better than those you say you wish to bring down," Leo Post shouted at the obscure figure. "For a song. A song? My God, what a rack, what a bed we have made up for ourselves. If we don't fit one way, we can fit the other, but guardians like you will make the adjustments—in parts. Questions that cannot be answered will not be asked. Behavior that cannot be predicted will be eliminated. A species that cannot live behind bars will be extinguished. The pilgrims wore many colors, but the rest of you introduced black and white."

"You are babbling," the terrorist replied and pulled the brim of his hat lower. "What I have just done is to get at the truth."

"Truth!" Post exploded. "The vilest lie is truth. Truth's victims litter the fields of our sad history."

"But you have taken life, Professor."

"I admit to murder, but done in rage, in lust, with an animal's honesty, but not committed to satisfy an abstract argument, a cold doctrine of right and wrong. Punish me, if you wish, but forgive the truth of my nature."

"No other creature requires or asks forgiveness," Yellow Hat replied. "Why this exception? Simply because you may feel a little bad about your act—after you've done it. You have forgiven the wrongs he has committed against you." The terrorist spoke as he moved away from the windows with an insolent gait.

"A plagiarism or two, what do they matter?" Post counted on his fingers. "Conspiracies foisted by inconsequential journals. A jockeying for position at the front table of Ruby Foo's—I forgave him these amusements long ago. They do not merit his destruction."

"But what if he wronged you for more than these paltry offenses?" The guerilla had moved close to Post and placed a hand gently on his upper arm. Were it not for the dire circumstances, his gesture could be seen as affectionate. "What if his envy of you, his innate jealousy and unbounded evil, worked to destroy something you loved more than life? Would you forgive him this?"

"But I wouldn't kill him," Leo Post replied quickly. He regarded his double reflection in Yellow Hat's dark glasses. "Yes, I would forgive him. Yes."

The author and the terrorist seemed linked together, as if woven into a single image by invisible strands and on the verge of an embrace. Then, the militant spun on his heels and in one step was beside the book reviewer's wheelchair. He shook Sneat's shoulder.

"Wake up," he commanded, though his voice was amused. "You have been forgiven all." He walked away, and casually stroked Sgt. Anderson's cheek as he passed her. The gesture further supported our speculation of a conspiracy between the two. "You see, Professor," Yellow Hat remarked airily over his shoulder, "Taylor's guns are not the only ones that contain blank cartridges."

Pickett's eyes snapped open, and he smacked his lips several times. He wiped away a milky glob that had collected beneath his round nose. "Well now," he said slowly. He seemed to relocate himself and looked around the room with a haughty expression. "Members and friends of the Pegasus Society—it is my honor to introduce Reuben Slate, who—"

"None of that—" the terrorist interrupted from the far window.

"Pickett, old fellow." Leo Post had taken his startled colleague by the hand. "It is so good to have you back with us once more." Pickett Sneat blinked owlishly and took us in as the numbing effects of his trauma gradually wore off.

"You have been born again, Mr. Sneat." Yellow Hat's voice came lightly from the obscurity of the darkening windows, for the sun had passed over the Catskills. "You have been renewed."

"Yes, yes. That's right, renewed," agreed Leo Post, clapping his colleague on the shoulder. "Think of that, Pick."

The book reviewer did seem to contemplate the idea, nodding his head, and finally said, "So what? I'm still anchored in this contraption. Nothing's been changed."

"But perhaps other weights have been cast off," the terrorist told him. His silhouette appeared against the leaded panes of the windows. "Perhaps they lie heavier than those braces."

The book reviewer continued to blink, to wipe his nose, and to look intently at each of us. His expression was a mixture of puzzlement and curiosity like that of a beast whose keeper has accidentally left open the door of his cage—should he risk the unknown freedom outside or remain within the security of the cell? His hands gripped the armrest of his wheelchair.

"Come now, Mr. Sneat," Yellow Hat's voice coaxed. "Post says he will forgive you everything, whatever it may be."

"Everything?" the man asked slyly.

"And anything," Post replied, patting his shoulder.

"How I despised you," Sneat said, tears spilling down his face.

"I know, I know," the author soothed him.

"You were never touched by the wickedness around you," Sneat complained. "By the deceit and disloyalty. You had some kind of condom pulled over you that protected you from the virus of our infection. Every one of us plotted and schemed, but not you, and the irony of it all closed in on me when those heavy steel doors of Sing Sing clanged shut behind me, making me a prisoner twice over. Now that I had become a Lyon fellow," the critic addressed us, "where had all my perjuries and double-crossings got me but in prison to make those silly-ass recordings of *Last Words: Poems from Death Row*. A clumsy title but it was at the time all we had to work with. And just to satisfy Kimball Lyon's crazy hypothesis and to further create confusion in the liberal community who could never resolve the Governor's fervid advocacy of the death penalty with his generous patronage of the arts.

"And there you were, Leo Post, so deserving of misery—if even just a little misery. A small nick in your ineffable poise. If praise and fame can be doled out for all but the right reasons, surely wretchedness and pain can be similarly administered."

Pickett Sneat had clearly recovered the full measure of his spite. His Halloween expression, part demonic, part comical, illuminated his features as if from a candle within his head that he cocked this way and that with an assurance of his audience's complete attention. At a signal from Leo Post, the man called Taylor moved a floor lamp to the chair where Sgt. Anderson lounged. It was a slender invention with a frosted spheroid shade reminiscent of Gropius and the middle 1920s. It threw an encirclement of light around the immediate area but gave small illumination elsewhere in the chamber.

"Did you have any feeling for those men you recorded?" Sgt. Anderson asked.

"Nothing, of course," the book reviewer replied. "I did think that most had been tricked and tripped up as much as I had been. But so what else is new? Anyway, recording their frustrations and anger helped pass the time before the final lights out. It was that

appeal for immortality that snags all of us, and theirs was imminent. I suppose you could find a pathos in that."

Sneat had pulled himself upright in his chair with great
effort and continued. "One fellow particularly I remember. He
went by the name of Capt. Charlie. That was his pen name. Get
it—pen name?" The critic had begun to giggle and lost control of
his sinuses. One leg snapped out straight as he continued to choke
and gurgle on his own effluent. Sgt. Anderson rose quickly and
administered several restorative cuffs to the man's head and then
wiped his nose clean.

"Well, now," Sneat said, blinking his eyes and looking around
his audience. "The fellow came to me as No. 62890, a convicted
murderer with dirty fingernails. A repulsive little man. He admitted to no ability with words, whining that his talents were visual.
Specifically as a tattooist. He knew of our association, Leo, and of
course knew about Molly Lyon. He wanted to make a deal. You
can guess the rest of it."

"Poor fellow," Leo Post said, resuming his place on the elephant foot. "How desperate he must have been."

"That's all you can say?" Sneat asked. "Knowing you as I do,
this example of your manor-house benevolence still surprises me."

"Continue, Mr. Sneat," Yellow Hat's voice commanded from
the darkness of the far hall. "There is more, is there not?"

"No. 62890 told me about Leo and Molly coming to his tattoo parlor, and that's how I know certain details about that cli-
mactic session. Is that a pun in the making?"

"Not close," said Post.

"I spare you the details the slavering wretch put upon the
scene, but to be brief, he hoped to trade this information for a
commutation of his sentence to life—wouldn't it spare the governor a little pain if these pictures of his daughter's privates adorned
by the Leek family *motiv* were done away with—yes, he had taken
pictures—"

"The villain," growled Yellow Hat.

"—and like all those consumed by prurience, the fellow was a
prude himself and reasoned that anyone as high-born as your wife,

Leo—the governor's daughter—would do anything to avoid this exposure of her whim—or should I say quim?"

"None of that, none of that," Leo Post admonished his associate.

"But how could he know?" his colleague continued. "The antics of heel-clacking heiresses tumbling with assorted taxi drivers were yet to be filmed and distributed to every schoolboy."

"Yes, he was ahead of his time," Post said soberly. "And what a time it is, too."

"Quite so," the other man smirked. "But I was not to tell him differently but played to his lewd Puritanism. Over and over, he repeated for my amusement the features of your mistress's nether configuration and, if you don't mind my saying so, Leo—since she is no longer with us—I may know as much about that spot as you do." A muffled gasp came from the darkness at the end of the hall. "Hearsay, of course," Sneat added, but smacked his lips and grinned widely.

"In any event, the man's desperate imagination was easy to feed. Yes, of course, I told him I could get his sentence commuted to life in return for the details, and is that such a serious offense— giving another hope? False hope, you say? Isn't all hope false? Think of the organizations created for such enterprise." Sneat shrugged as no one answered him. "I could not get him clemency, I told him, but perhaps a transfer to a more luxurious confinement, if he could reproduce the design his electric pen had made and its exact location. What happened to the pictures he took? you are about to ask. He bartered them in the early years of his term for cigarettes and extra scoops of Jell-o and they had been passed around the prison community for solitary amusements to the extent that the images had become worn and ill-defined, resembling the shadows in a dry ravine west of Topeka, Kansas."

"I cannot bear more of this," Leo Post said, rising to his full and dignified height. His demeanor was the tattered shred of a pose that the old *Time* magazine once described as Post-Toasty.

"Wait," Sneat commanded. "I'm just coming to the best part. Taking pen and paper, he quickly drew the subject from memory, no doubt a recall enforced by feverish refreshments of the image made in solitary confinement—?"

"Enough, enough," Post pleaded.

"—and ultimately he fell at my feet as the erotomania induced by his own drafting seized him, and he had to be dragged back to his cell frothing and in obscene pantomime to conclude his demented frenzy in enforced privacy. So, I forged the photographs that have become collector's items. Through my membership in the Pegasus Society, I met a young woman, a recent graduate of a writing program, who was willing to duplicate the mark of the leek on her own person, and for further consideration—the publication of a chapbook of her earnest verse by a small press in North Dakota where I had some influence—she struck various poses before the camera with a couple of young men recruited from the waiting staff at Ruby Foo's. These were close-ups, of course—no faces shown," he giggled, showing his gapped teeth.

"How could you involve innocents in your foul play?" Post demanded.

"Nonsense," Sneat snapped. "They thoroughly enjoyed themselves. The young woman became a star, leaving behind her ordinary iambics for glory on the silver screen, such as we saw last night. And, while we're on the subject, who was it here who spliced that footage onto the old newsreel?" The book reviewer scrutinized the figures huddled about the glow from the floor lamp.

"You handed those pictures to me," Leo Post said softly, "at Governor Lyon's funeral. I could not get up from my chair. The media attributed my stupefaction to grief for Kimball Lyon."

"How I pleasured in that moment," Pickett Sneat crooned, and sucked air in through his teeth and rattled his metal fittings. "To catch you up twice with one shot, Leo. To puncture your idyll with the Lyon princess and at the same time to sink your buoyant goodness, wired to the corpse of the tyrant king. Unexpected dividends."

"But why? Why?" Leo Post asked, his lips trembling. "I never wronged you."

"Never," Sneat agreed. "On the contrary. One unkind word, the merest slight at a social occasion, anything like that would have saved you from my wrath. Some called my style 'parsonage prose' but you commended its 'delicacy,' cited its 'suppleness.' You defended me when certain pages called me 'the establishment toady' and that a careful reading of my reviews revealed an infectious self-deprecation that only enforced the ruling point of view. No, there was nothing between the lines, Leo." Sneat's voice had become gentle. "Nothing but the desire to make it. Then there was the time Roland Castle attacked *The Art and Craft of Reviewing*. 'As an evaluator of literature, Mr. Sneat is more currier than courier,' he wrote. I rather like that phrase, and he was right. He was right, Leo."

"He was a joskin," Post said severely.

"And you beat him up." Sneat began to titter. "You tracked him all the way out to Long Island, walked into his composition class, and punched him in the mouth—all to defend my reputation." The book reviewer had become convulsed by laughter.

"He deserved a good thrashing," Leo Post said, taking a military posture and tugging at his cuffs.

"But why, Leo? Why? Because I couldn't do it myself? Because I'm a cripple and can't get out of this contraption, can't stand on my own feet and deliver the blow? Now we're coming to it—why I have hated you all these years. Why I concocted those pictures to string you up. You had made yourself my protector. You were being kind to a cripple. A cree-PLE." The book reviewer's voice had risen out of control, his eyes popped from his face which had become tomato red. I, B. Smith, unable to help, thought he might throw himself from his wheelchair.

"What some may think is villainy," he went on, "is really retribution for all the kindnesses shown me—from opening a door to opening a conversation. And you were the worst, Leo. Nothing I had ever done in my life justified your attacks of goodness. Nothing I had ever said, nothing written, merited your praise and your centering me in the canon the way you have. Synthetic diamonds in platinum settings—that's what you did. Your influence got me the Barnaby Prize, not the value of my book. It was on your recommendation that I was named a Lyon fellow. And why did you do these things?"

"Because—"

"Yes, because—"

"Well, I've heard you say many times that a basic rule of book reviewing is to reward those who have had some unhappy circumstance of birth or life."

"But not me. NOT ME, " Sneat shouted. His eyes had twisted shut and his fists pounded the arms of his wheelchair. When his eyes opened they glistened from tears as he looked up at Post. "That only applies to others, Leo—not me," he said brokenly. "Surely, there was a small scrap of achievement, a notable paragraph even, that could be legitimately praised?"

"Of course, Pickett—your book on—"

"No—no—no," he shouted. His head shook violently from side to side and his mouth twisted as if he had tasted something bitter. "Don't you see, Leo, I could never believe you now. More than my legs have become paralyzed; these steel fastenings have worked deep inside me."

"Poor Pickett," the author mourned.

"Stop that. Stop it! Your pity only tightens the screws. If you are determined to grant indulgence, permit my frolic in the fields of treachery."

"You realize, Mr. Sneat," Sgt. Anderson spoke plainly, "that your narrative makes you an accessory before the fact of the murder of Mrs. Post?"

"No matter," responded the book reviewer. "I've already spent most of my life in prisons of one construction or another. Naturally I regret the loss of such a fine piece of—" his pinkish mouth pursed and moistened, "—such an extraordinary person as Molly Lyon. But that was not my doing. Let the record show who it was. I did not suggest the act to Leo the Good." Post groaned and sank to the ottoman, head in his hands.

"Is that true, Professor?" Yellow Hat's voice came from the darkened end of the gallery. "After all this wretch has said, are you still able to forgive his evil?" the guerilla asked casually. Post, hands covering his face, merely nodded his head. "You say nothing," the terrorist pressed his query.

"Subject has signaled the affirmative by a head movement," Sgt. Anderson stated. The portrait gallery had become completely dark save for the circle of illumination cast by the floor lamp, and those of us within its radiance resembled a group of survivors of some fearful tragedy. We huddled while outside this strange camp's perimeter. The glazed eyes of the Leek ancestral portraits seemed to glow. The glass eyes of the stuffed animals continued to watch us patiently with timeless confidence.

"How is it you are able to forgive this villain but the same benevolence is not granted the victim whose only mistake was to trust you, to love you?"

"I cannot make it clear to myself," a shaken Leo Post replied. "Violence is in my blood; to kill is part of my heritage. The cold, two-dimensional betrayal I thought I saw in those bogus pictures preyed upon my mind, obscuring all other perceptions. Anger was a feckless keeper that played upon the doubts I had kept locked up. The loins are more prone to injury than the mind," Post said and gripped his brow.

"You really want me to record that statement?" Sgt. Anderson inquired. She repeated his language—loins more prone than the mind? —but her question was ignored.

"What you—Leo Post—having doubts?" the voice of Yellow Hat mocked. A moon had just edged over the Taghkanic Range.

"Yes." Post stood up, clasping his hands. "If freedom means that one is never sure his actions are correct, then to be loved only makes one question if he is worthy of love. Well," he spoke to Sgt. Anderson, his voice neutral of emotion. "There was the age matter, you know. I was somewhat older than she, and there was the anxiety that always accompanies a man to the bed of a younger woman. Then there was her brilliance, not just in appearance but her mind, her appetite for life and adventure. How embarrassing to stumble on a hike in the Adirondacks, or to sense she was holding back her pace, moderating her step as I wanted her to scale the heights—"

"Listen to that poop-diddle, Lucy," Sneat interrupted. "I mean, Sgt. Anderson. Hear that prose, those sentiments. Can you not believe my attempt to destroy Leo Post might be considered a civic duty?"

"Perhaps, Professor, you had other doubts." Yellow Hat's voice had come from another direction, near the stone bench beneath the casement windows. "Why did you marry the Governor's daughter?"

"You expect me to say—to be near the Governor, near the source of power. And I'll say that. Yes, I'll say that. Who among us has not been attracted by power? Who would not want to whisper into the ear of the most powerful man in the state? Of the country, perhaps the world? Molly and I discussed this possibility—the heat of that allure passing on to her."

"And your observations—the two of you?" the terrorist asked.

"Basically, that someone had to advise him, and it might as well be me."

"Surely you were the most qualified—your knowledge of pigeons, for example," Sneat observed with a poker face.

"Something like that," Post murmured. "The fact that Molly was Kimball Lyon's daughter was pure chance."

"Completely pure," the book reviewer said with a wink toward us.

"All right." Post's manner had coarsened. He raised one fist in the air. "Yes, I sometimes wondered if her lineage made a difference. Consider my position: halfway in, halfway out of the Establishment. I was a unicorn looking for a maiden's lap where I could rest my head."

"There's a couple of extinct species for you," the book reviewer snorted.

"You must understand the attraction Kimball Lyon had for me when he offered me that position. And to be with his daughter for only a few moments answered any misgivings I may have had for my motives. But those pictures you showed me—those pictures."

"They really did the trick, didn't they?" Sneat rubbed his hands together gleefully.

"In the field of betrayal, only deformed weeds will grow." Post spoke as if he were alone. "It is an ugly and self-accusing crop. I told myself she had committed these acts because I am too old for her pleasures. This is her revenge for my whimsically suggesting how fortunate she was to be Governor Lyon's daughter. Her unfaithfulness, so obscenely pictured, was to retaliate for my attitude to her father's vulgar, ostentatious ways. Hers too, for that matter, before I changed her and she was paying me back for changing her, for making her unique, too singular and thus vulnerable. I had made her foreign in her own habitat.

"Sitting in the hot sunlight falling on the Perpetual Parking Plaza, half-hearing the introductory speakers at the Governor's bier, my mind boiled with uncertainties. Reason was stifled. Rather than answer these questions sensibly, some maniacal impulse forged by the day's heat and the devils summoned by those pictures demanded I eliminate the agent of these misgivings. So, you see, dear Sgt. Anderson, my love became a monster— ungainly, illformed and with zoological errors that could not be tolerated. A hegira. Pickett's malicious joke is only that, and cite Taylor only for his blind loyalty. But as for me, my crime is the rankest. I destroyed a species."

"Are you telling us, Mr. Post," the terrorist said, approaching the light, "that you pardon Pickett of all his evilness?"

"Yes."

"That you assume responsibility for Taylor's misplaced loyalty?"

"That, too, yes."

"That you cite your own vanity, plead guilty to eccentric arrogance, an unbridled careerism, and admit to the cardinal folly of reducing love to a measured phenomenon?"

"However you wish to say it," replied Leo Post with a despondent throw of his hands. He sank upon the hassock to become a piteous figure, suiting the worn elegance of his apparel.

I, B. Smith, witnessing this startling transformation, noted the expression of the man called Taylor. His eyes had become glassy like those of the stuffed tiger at his feet. He half-rose in a trance. Sneat had begun to jabber and whimper. He drooled uncontrollably. What prompted their expressions stood behind the chair where Sgt. Anderson sat. It seemed that Yellow Hat somehow, within the cover of darkness, had lifted down from the wall above the mantel the large portrait of Leo Post's wife, and for some fancy had carried it to our group as the author gave his testimony. In what appeared to be a cruel joke, a sadistic ploy of the terrorist, this image of the slain woman was suspended in the darkness just beyond the circle of light, like a new sun in the empty waste of the universe.

The visual power of the painting overwhelmed our senses, especially when the green eyes of its subject seemed to move, looked to the right and then the left to encompass our stunned assembly. We credited this phenomenon to the skill of the artist. But the eyes had moved. The generous mouth smiled, bringing a cry from Sneat and a profound sigh from Leo Post. A slender hand had materialized out of the darkness to magically fluff and arrange the reddish gold hair that—it was now apparent—had been concealed beneath the yellow hat.

"Perhaps then, *mon professeur*," Molly Lyon Post said with the same sly insouciance we had come to recognize in Yellow Hat, the terrorist, "it might be possible to renew a species."

SOMETIME LATER

"What will we do with What's-His-Name?" Pickett Sneat asked. His tone was neutral, casual.

I, B. Smith, now girdled in hemp rope, had been put at the head of the procession that had made the rounds of the fortress ruin. This review had commenced in the portrait gallery, where Molly Lyon had revealed herself three nights before, and terminated in the reception hall overlooking the river.

Hundreds of candles illuminated this spacious chamber where we had first interviewed Leo Post, thinking our investigation complete. The candle flames turned the limestone walls similar to the velvet lining of certain jewel caskets, and more candles burned on the high mantel, along the window casements, the chair rails, and the long commissary table. Post had produced these wax lights from a storehouse of used military equipment, calling our attention to them—as if they were the selections of a rare wine collection—saying they were the last of those tapers that had brought a modest cheer to dugouts in trenches of World War I. Their cumulative flickers could fill a reservoir of light that nearly reached the high-vaulted ceiling.

Our host continued to rummage through a pile of old clothing, sometimes holding up a garment to measure it against an imaginary model. A patina of mold covered the cartons that had contained these rags, suggesting their storage was the same damp, underground compartments that had held the candles. Mrs. Post and Sgt. Anderson also poked through the used apparel. The man called Taylor had disappeared.

"Let's see what we have here," the author said, pulling and snapping twine that secured a large carton. "My ancestor, an American sentimentalist, went bankrupt collecting the stuff of old parades, old ceremonials, and reviews. He was ahead of his time."

"Costumes," Molly Post exclaimed as the box was opened— more uniforms from different wars. Her enthusiasm for masquerade did not surprise us—she still wore the heavy boots, breeches, and rough shirt of her guerilla disguise that had fooled us with its impression of a militant youth. But now, she was unmistakably a woman, and we cannot explain this duality. The particular pigeon-toed, loose-kneed carriage that had given a flair of arrogance to her role as a terrorist now suggested a touching vulnerability.

"What are these?" Sgt. Anderson asked suspiciously, wrinkling her nose.

"They look like infantry capes from the war with Mexico," Post replied. He extended a heavy blue garment in the air and shook the dust from it. This practical gesture was reinvented, as if a whimsical aside, into several graceful *doblandoes*.

"Olé," cried his wife and clapped her hands.

"Not for this girl." Sgt. Anderson shook her head disdainfully. "This musty imagery is not for me. Also, we had no business being down there in Mexico in the first place."

"Come, come, Lucy." Leo Post chuckled and his eyes glinted. "It's never been required to agree with the war in order to wear the uniform. Quite the contrary. Taylor has gone for more finery, and perhaps he'll return with a period more agreeable to you."

"I doubt it," the policewoman replied, no longer undercover, and looking darkly.

"How does this work?" Molly Post asked. As she twirled, the long officer's cape flared from her figure, and the deep cowl of the cloak framed the fall of coppery hair, the flash of her extraordinary eyes.

"I think we should decide about Smith right now," Pickett Sneat said, casting an anxious glance toward us, firmly restrained.

"Splendid," Post told his wife. "You look splendid." He leaned toward her, and their lips met briefly. "Don't worry, Pickett. All in good time. Here's Taylor with more."

Called by that name, the man staggered into view, peering around a large stack of boxes he clutched in his arms like an old-time railroad engineer leaning from his cab. He bumped against the end of the long table, stumbled, and the tower of cartons began a parody of the arcing dénouement of a clumsy juggler. With a muffled gasp, Sneat spun his wheels to get out of the way of the collection before they crashed to the floor. I, B. Smith, authority outraged and insulted, memorandized that this Taylor had been in costume from the start, and that his disguise had been completed by the inclusion of an antique pistol. The weapon was snugged into the leather holster strapped low on his right thigh.

"Good man, Taylor," his employer complimented him. "Now kindly conduct Smith to the head of the table. Put him in my chair, for he is to have the seat of honor now."

"*Dominus festi.*" Molly Post snapped her fingers. "Our Lord of Misrule."

"Quite so," Post nodded.

"Master Fuck-Up," Sgt. Anderson contributed, a smile tempering her usual solemnity.

"Even that," Post nodded.

"Perhaps, even our Precentor?" Pickett Sneat suggested.

"You're going to risk a song again, Pick?" the author asked the book reviewer.

"Well, I never got to finish my song, if you remember," he replied with a degree of petulance.

"My apologies for that," Molly Post said. The long cape graced her stride as she moved toward the book reviewer, her hands those of a supplicant. Even so, the cripple cringed in his wheelchair as if he still feared her earlier pose of a terrorist.

"You were cruelly used," the woman said gently, her hands now resting on his shoulders. "But it was all I could think of doing to commence our reunion, to restore us each to each."

"But in the middle of my lyric?" Sneat complained.

"Who ever gets to finish his song?" Leo Post said from the pile of used clothing.

"I hope we don't fall into such sentimental postures?" the book reviewer asked sourly. He shrugged off Mrs. Post's hands. "You always had a tendency toward sentimentalism, Leo, trying to stretch the truth over some idealistic structure much too large for verity to cover. And besides," he pivoted the wheelchair like a top, "this Smith worries me. He's witnessed much too much raw data and undigested gossip. All this information might be dangerous in the wrong hands."

"Agreed," Leo Post replied. "And there's more data to come. Molly has yet to tell us her part. But we will always be surrounded by Smiths—they are like beetles. Everywhere overhearing our confessions, registering our resignations. They have been born to hear us out. Ah." The author interrupted himself to dart into the pile of clothing. Something had caught his eye. "Here's an item for you." He emerged with a tricornered hat. His elbow polished its tarnished gold trim and, with a flick of a finger to its cockade, he presented the hat to his colleague.

"I don't know if it's exactly my style," the book reviewer said and looked hesitantly around the assemblage, then abruptly clutched the hat and placed it on his head. A toothy grin broke open his pumpkin face.

"Of course it is your style," Post assured him. He had stepped back to inspect the effect of the headpiece. "The conviction of authority, the impulse to redraw the lines and then appropriate—the imperialism of having the last word. It's all there."

"Authority and mental instability all worn at once—is that what you're implying, Leo?" he said with a mad gleam in his eye. The author merely employed his typical sang-froid and turned away.

Meanwhile, I, B. Smith, a sworn witness and fully bound, had been trundled to the high-backed chair at the end of the table by the man called Taylor. Sgt. Anderson and Molly Lyon Post continued to open the cartons of old clothing, holding up and discarding the different pieces of the shabby inventory.

"There's nothing here for us," the police agent announced with a scowl. "These uniforms are all men's." She shook out the battle jacket of a five-star general.

"Here." Post motioned to her. "Bring that here—just the thing for Smith." Both arranged the jacket about our torso, and Post rubbed the tarnish from the circlet of stars pinned to the shoulders.

"Look at all those medals," Sgt. Anderson exclaimed. I, B. Smith, a common auditor for the people, had been much decorated.

"An extraordinary hero," Leo Post observed. He ticked off the different honors pinned to our chest. "Silver stars, orange chrysanthemums, purple hearts, black crosses, golden elephants, red banners. We are honored to serve you, sir." He stepped back and snapped to attention to salute us crisply and with some mockery. The others followed his gesture—even Sgt. Anderson, a graduate of the New York State Police Academy, we are sorry to report. Naturally, we were unable to return the salute.

"Hee-haw—hee-haw," brayed Pickett Sneat, and the exaggerated correctness of his salute tipped the tricorn lower on his brow.

"What are these?" Molly Post exclaimed. "These aren't so bad, we could wear these." She held up for Sgt. Anderson's opinion a pair of voluminous pajama-like trousers of faded scarlet. A short blue jacket was part of the costume.

"The uniform of the Zouave," her husband explained. "Originally they were Berber tribesmen recruited into the French army to keep order in their African colonies. In our Civil War, volunteer regiments composed of New York City firemen adopted this uniform, for reasons I cannot recall. In any event, that war was different from what they had supposed—they had not dressed appropriately for the occasion. The baggy trousers proved impractical in the mud of Chancellorsville, and the crimson fezzes were a convenient target for sharpshooters." As he spoke the author held each article aloft. Sgt. Anderson took them one after the other and then retired behind the curtained alcove by the fireplace.

A large fire had been set in the cavern of the hearth, for a nippiness had fallen into the Hudson Valley. The kindling that the ersatz cowboy had collected had dried out, and a torrential blaze quickly warmed the room. The Posts, husband and wife, emptied more containers and bags. Molly in her Zouave costume looked fetching.

Tunics, blouses, pants, map cases, trench tools, hats, belts of all kinds, puttees, boots, helmets with goggles. "The famous Belgian Third Motorcycle Brigade," Post instructed us. "They wore these goggles." Overseas caps, combination knives-screwdrivers-awls-dented-canteens (several with bullet holes through them), neckerchiefs, K-rations, cartridge packs, USN underwear, sashes, cavalry breeches, canned water, dress blues, forage caps, bell-bottomed pants, assorted corks, trench periscopes, sets of celluloid wing collars, insignias and chevrons of all kinds, life jackets, charts, tent poles, officers' gloves, heavy coats, one parachute unopened—a huge pile of surplus stuff from earlier wars dumped into one dun heap—a glint of button or wrap of braid here and there.

"Why, Leo." Pickett Sneat wheeled about excitedly, his eyes a child's at Christmas. "You never let on you had these goodies. We could live here for years." He had just retrieved a tin of chopped beef and reviewed the label.

The chamber had become an eerie arena, antique remnants strewn as if left on an old battlefield—the uniforms of ghostly casualties. Molly Post played among these abandoned items, finding a white sailor's hat or a collapsible telescope. Her vitality imbued these pathetic remnants with a false quickness, such as a child playing among fallen leaves might impart a temporary life to the dried-up foliage.

Similarly, the woman had affected the demeanor of her husband as if her reappearance from the dead had restored him, for there was suppleness to his movements that suggested a reversal of time. The obsidian eyes sparkled, and when the couple spoke to each other, their faces leaned inches apart, their expressions eager and intense.

"Here, try this on," she said, tossing him an olive-drab vest. Or, "How about this?" as a sword sash arced high and fell. Or, "It was made for you," and a campaign hat saucered the air. "You may fire when ready, Gridley," she said as she held up a fully epauletted coat. "The Yanks are coming!" A Sam Browne belt chased after a steel helmet.

Leo Post stumbled and fell, rose to fall again, tripped up by the surplus stuff around his ankles. Sneat raised the tricorn hat from his head and waved it in jubilation. "Hurrah, hurrah," his voiced boomed and echoed in the chamber as he celebrated this shadow parade. Post staggered drunkenly as he pulled on the different garments, hats and tunics, blouses and pants, until he wore so many layers of material that nothing more would fit. His final investment was to bandage his legs ankle to knee with the khaki-colored puttees of the World War I doughboy. Then he stood at attention, a veteran of assorted conflicts in uniforms scavenged from the different battlefields and looking somewhat like an un-baked pastry.

"Fantastic," his wife applauded. She lay in a drift of dusty uniforms, her remarkable eyes in slits as she observed her husband. Her portrait had faithfully reproduced the feline cast of those green eyes; however, the painter seemed to have spent the veracity of his brush upon them, for the rest of her characteristics had been embellished or modified to accord an idealized version that was not hers.

The portraits of Post's ancestors faithfully recorded every wart and wen, every fold of flesh and deranged stare that the naïve limners of the time felt bound to duplicate, but the post-society painter had sought to glamorize Molly Lyon Post and had erased or mollified certain defects, and in doing so had lost the splendor of the original that lolled on the pile of surplus stuff in the center of the chamber.

The fine blade of her nose had been dulled, smoothed out, possibly for fear the narrow bridge would suggest meanness; consequently, the voluptuous flare in the wide-set nostrils was missing—the conflict between sensitivity and sensuousness.

I, B. Smith, not an art critic—but I know what I like—also noted the demure dimensions of the subject's smile, perhaps meant to suggest an enigmatic persona. The full traverse of the mouth had been reshaped to minimalize the teeth that gave her actual appearance an appealing frankness. One by one, the different features given the subject of the portrait would never be included in a hornbook for apprentice portraitists, but assembled in the living mask, the aggregate imperfections fêted life and joy.

"Do you know what all this reminds me of, Leo?" the subject of the portrait had just asked. The generous mouth had just proffered a dazzling smile. "That night in the clothes closet when we met."

"How so?" the author wondered.

"All those clothes scattered about, boots and shoe trees. Don't you remember?" she asked, rising from the heap to perch on her knees.

"Of course I remember. How could I forget?" Post replied.

"What's this? A clothes closet, you say?" Sneat interjected.

"It was just after my review of his poems had appeared—before he became governor. Lyon had invited me to dinner as an appreciation of my review." Post adjusted the close-fitted dress coat of a captain, USN, circa 1900.

"You were leaving," Molly Lyon Post recalled." I was showing you to the door. The cloakroom was dark, and several coats had fallen to the floor. A pair of galoshes, I remember." Her voice became weighted in reverie.

"An unbelievable mess, I remember," Post added, and sat down in the clothing beside his wife. He had removed the heavy dress coat and fanned himself with a campaign hat bearing the device of the U.S. Seventh Cavalry.

"Father had thrown a tantrum earlier that day," Molly Post said. "Whenever he became especially angry, he always raged in closets, ripping things off their hangers and kicking shoes about. I don't remember what had so angered him this day, but it was a safety valve for him. Probably saved the taxpayers enormous hardships. Now I remember." She turned to Post. "One of his poems had been rejected by *Tractor Age*."

"They were always a hard market to get into," Post observed. "The editors especially finicky." Then he leaned toward his wife. "But it was pitch black and I had to search the closet floor to find my coat. I was on my hands and knees like this." He assumed the position. "Then I smelled your perfume and realized you were also on the floor, feeling around for my coat."

"Well, after all, it was a closet in my house. I knew it better than you did."

"Side by side," Post reminisced.

"What sort of a coat?" Molly asked, her hands pulling through the old clothing.

"A black wool chesterfield with a velvet-lined collar. It had been made for me by—"

"All right, all right," exclaimed Pickett Sneat. He spun his wheelchair around impatiently. From the edge of the surplus junk, he viewed the couple sporting in the middle of the piled rubbish with the wistful look of a boy left out of a swimming party. "What happened next?"

"I've already mentioned how she appealed to me at dinner."

"Only then," the woman said softly.

"So there we were on the dark floor of a closet. An errant ray of light struck the gold earring of her right ear—you wore your hair swept back that evening," the author murmured in said ear. He reproduced the style briefly by pulling back her hair and holding it at the nape of her neck. "Just so," Post said. "The reflection was like a signal, a beam sent out to guide me through the darkness to the delicate fold of flesh just behind the ear. I lost control," Leo Post said softly as he leaned toward his wife, mouth pursed and eyes half closed. His lips sought the referenced location.

"You kissed me then without warning," Molly Post gasped as she felt his lips. The book reviewer had begun to sniffle and whimper, and his hands drummed the metal framework of his wheelchair.

"Then—and then"—Post murmured into the golden tresses of the woman's hair—"you turned very slowly—very carefully—and very precisely—fitted—your lips—to mine." The couple knelt knee to knee and lip to lip to create this original embrace with a few embellishments not available then. For example, as their mouths joined, Molly Post slowly peeled off the gold epaulettes from the left shoulder of her husband's uniform, and then both of them abruptly disappeared as they fell into the mound of military surplus material.

"What—hey, wait a minute," shouted Pickett Sneat. His face became red with anger. "Come back here," he cried, and looked ready to launch himself from his contrivance.

"How do I look?" Sgt. Anderson had returned. She had changed her costume. The Zouave pantaloons emphasized the police officer's length of limb, and her admirable chest development was set off by the parenthesis of the open vest. "Where is everybody?" she asked, seeing only the book reviewer present.

"They're in there," he told her, nodding toward the surplus goods that moved with a peculiar undulant wave that lapped the outer edge of the pool of clothing. "Get them out of there," he pleaded.

"No kidding?" Sgt. Anderson responded. She seemed delighted. "That's cool."

"No time for these little pranks," Sneat growled and wheeled partway around the moldy conglomerate, peering into its tangle to locate the self-interred couple. "Leo, come out. Much to do here. Smith must be disposed of. Be realistic, Leo. Help me, Lucy. Where's Taylor?" But the man called Taylor was not present, and Sgt. Anderson ignored him.

Just then, the Posts surfaced with flushed faces. "Really, Pickett," Post admonished his colleague. "You must control yourself."

"Control myself," he replied with a governed humor. "What were you two doing in there, replaying that first tryst?"

"Not at all," answered Molly almost primly. "That business on the closet floor was only a little skirmish. The first full engagement took place in a small inn near Hillsdale, New York."

"Yes, the Mount Phudd Arms," Post said with suppressed relish. The couple sat on the bank of the clothing. Pickett leaned toward them, and Sgt. Anderson, in her new costume, placed a hand on the back of the book reviewer's chair. They resembled a group of hikers resting for the final ascent.

I, B. Smith, confined to the large chair to which I had been bound, was totally ignored and was therefore able to make these observations. The manner and tone of voice Leo Post used to announce the name of the small inn—the site of their first intercourse—played down its importance, which gave it more significance, and an undeserved notoriety. This was the sort of verbal indulgence practiced by intellectuals and literati of the previous era. Details, minute as they were unimportant, were assessed a value far beyond their actual worth or societal pertinence so that the public's patience was tried with the endless revision of their personal lives. So the introduction of a small village in upstate New York and a quaint local inn—

neither of which exist anymore—was considered more important than any effort to restore and maintain community standards.

"Yes, Hillsdale is no more," Post continued. He slowly adjusted and tightened a puttee on his right leg, setting off the shape of his calf. "When the Harlem Valley Access was built as part of the Self-Propelled Expressway, most of the villages in that area were obliterated. But what a charming afternoon," he reminisced and looked toward his wife. She met his gaze.

"It was autumn," Post continued. "Leaves played mellow villanelles of light upon the lapstraked walls of village cottages. Streams were low and blazed with mica and quartz, the rubble of an old empire. Cows strung homeward in the late hour, returning to their barns full of grace and milk. A lone tree, an oak or branching sycamore, stood sentinel on a vantage point, while in the distance the soft underbelly of a hill sunned a pubic patch of fir. We were nervous and drunk with each other."

"Do you remember what I said?" Molly Post asked her husband. She turned to him. "After we had found our room, closed the door and pulled the curtains—"

"Of course I remember," Leo Post said. He lay back into the jumble of old uniforms, eyes half-closed. "You were undressing in the small bathroom, the door partly open; I waited in the calico-curtained bedroom on a creaky four-poster and you said, 'My breasts are smallish.' I've always wondered why you said that."

Molly Post hugged her husband, who had planned her murder, I, B. Smith, a stickler for such details, must let it be remembered. The woman shook the man playfully but let his question go unanswered. She had begun giggling, and her breath caught on an outcrop of remembrance. She fell back into a pile of navy jumpers as a throe of delight possessed her. "Then you said," she gasped, "you said, well, they're bigger than mine." The recall was a nutrient to her amusement, and her laughter bloomed. Sgt. Anderson, gripping Sneat's wheelchair, bent like a reed under a gust of her own merriment, and the book reviewer even hooted and gagged. Post looked at each of them.

"But that's true," he pleaded. The company only laughed harder.

"You see what it is about him?" his wife said raggedly. "He always tries to find the happiest interpretation." She kissed him full on the mouth. "You are the original happy ending." And they kissed once more.

The couple fell back into the mound of remaindered material, arms and legs entwined. The puttee on Post's right leg had come unwound as they rolled about. All at once they sat up, he helped her to her feet, and they promenaded to the far end of the chamber, hand in hand. The long piece of material from Post's leg trailed behind them, a sort of soiled festoon, to snake around and through the curtained portal next to the hearth, still trailing them long after they had disappeared through the arras.

"What?" Sneat had regained his voice. "What?" he said again, blinking his eyes and looking about like a forest creature snared in a patch of sunlight. "Where did they go? Post!" he shouted. Sgt. Anderson spun his chair 360 degrees. "Don't do that," the book reviewer commanded irritably. He vainly sought to brake the wheels, but the police agent was too strong for him.

"C'mon, Sugar," she said, propelling him toward the same exit, and then they disappeared.

I, B. Smith, a helpless witness, was left alone and immobilized in the portrait gallery. But a metallic clicking near the fireplace suggested we were not entirely alone. The man called Taylor appeared from behind one of the high-backed chairs that bracketed the hearth. He edged himself cautiously into view as if he was emerging from a prairie defense, and his right hand dropped to his hip, then rose smoothly. The old pistol miraculously grew from his fist, its hammer drawn back, the mechanism cocked. Then he carefully unarmed the gun and holstered it in a single swift process that was repeated again. And again and again while his clear eyes sought targets in the shadows of the immense chamber. Outside the windows, the lights of a large tanker slid by, going upriver, like the forlorn skyline of a small city that had been cut adrift. Its crew was completely unaware of the drama taking place in the derelict castle they passed.

A LITTLE LATER

"CONDUCTUS AD PRAN—DI—UM," Leo Post solemnly intoned. He led the group back into the chamber single file, and the others hummed an unintelligible response. Their clothes had been rearranged, as if they had exchanged costumes, swapped hats for cloaks, on the other side of the archway for another round of a parlor-game conspiracy.

Post now wore the long mantle that had covered his wife, while she reappeared in the baggy pants and skimpy vest that had partly covered Sgt. Anderson. The brevity of the new costume confirmed the modest appraisal she had given earlier of herself. I, B. Smith, a casual student of such matters, must report that the pinkish pommes that bobbed within the scanty vest, nodding, as it were, in a violescent shadow original to the post-impressionist palette, were as deliciously firm as the most perfect Northern Spy.

"CONDUCTUS AD PRAN—DI—UM," droned Post.

"COM—MESS—SHIN—" his offhand acolytes responded.

"CONDUCTUS AD PRANDI—IUM," the author implored again.

"COMMESSATIO—COMMESSATION—CO—MESS—SA—SHUN," his flock hummed.

"What's on the menu, Lucy?" Post asked, rubbing his hands together. He had fitted the tricorn hat on his pink dome and set it at that dignified angle given to our Founding Father breasting the Delaware. "This must be a feast."

"Well." The black woman poked into the junk on the floor and then held up an olive drab can. "I see that we have a whole lot of this stuff." She read the label. "U.S. Army—vanilla-flavored tapioca pudding."

"Phooey," Sneat spat. The tassel of a fez played about his snout, and he swiped at it several times as if it might be a fly.

"Don't be scornful, Pickett," Post chastised him. "That substance was one of our secret weapons in World War II."

"We also got some sausage left over," Sgt. Anderson had continued. "There's lots of apples, butternuts, and hazels."

"And cider," Post contributed to the list, his eyes bright.

"Only cider?" Sneat asked.

"The *vin du pays*," Molly Post said. She had settled herself on the coulee of castoff clothing, supporting herself on one arm in the odalisque attitude favored by XIX century soft-pornographers. The man called Taylor had tiptoed, spurless and silent, to perch on the edge of the long commissary table. Post took a position on an upended ammunition box and pulled the voluminous cape around himself.

"Well now, Molly," the author began, "it's time we heard from you."

"Just a damn minute." Pickett Sneat waved his hand. "There's something peculiar about all this."

"What could that be?" Post asked blandly, inspecting the material of his cloak as if to discover an embarrassing stain.

"This!" the book reviewer shouted, his face the color of the fez on his head. "She's supposed to be dead." He pointed at Molly Lyon Post. "Then she comes back from the dead—incidentally a death you tried to arrange—and it's as if nothing happened. It's all tea and cakes. Hello, luv, have a nice trip?" The book reviewer had improvised a near-perfect imitation of Leo Post's Hudson River Valley accent down to the oscillation of the jaw.

"You know what I think?" he continued and swung around on his wheels to address Sgt. Anderson. The policewoman had been gathering up the little green cans of tapioca pudding and held them to her bosom. "I think Post knew she was alive all along. I think he put those ads in the paper not to defend the city against the new highway but to draw her out of hiding, to lure her back. But you didn't figure on attracting B. Smith also. Come, fess up, Leo."

"If you say so, old man," Post replied. With the great cloak gathered about him and the tricorn low on his brow, Post reminded I, B. Smith, an amateur student of history, of that dark trial at Valley Forge.

Sneat continued to stare at Leo Post with an expression that toyed with comprehension. Sgt. Anderson spoke to the man called Taylor, but we were unable to hear the exchange. "What was it?" the book reviewer persisted. "A little group session meant to get me to reveal how I had tricked you with those staged photos?" Molly Post laughed softly. "What's funny?"

"Perhaps it's Smith." The woman pointed a slender finger in our direction.

"Smith?" Sneat's brow wrinkled.

"Yes. Maybe we're part of a report that Smith must submit to the authorities—a manufacturing of data—prerecorded and notarized. That's already in some file and prepackaged." She came toward us, utilizing the same loose stride that so intimidated the company when she wore the yellow hat. "But who will believe him, even if he posts an affidavit?"

"Quite so," Leo Post said with a snap of certainty. "It's natural for you to want everything to be reasonable and orderly. Your natural instinct is to gouf a narrative, to replace its natural foundations with diagnostic blocks. It's what you do—your whole life has been dedicated to seeking perfection—the perfect novel, the perfect poem. The templates of perfection hang in your head, and your reputation has been made by fitting these patterns upon the perfect failures, failures at perfection, that have passed across your desk. Of course you have never found a perfect fit. You have become famous pointing out our omissions, our near-misses and imperfect inventions."

"Why do you say it would be a frivolous quest?" Molly Post had put her face close to Post's, as if in her myopia she hoped to see the answer take shape on his lips.

"Because it would be a useless perfection. As extinction is a factor of survival, so intolerance is a measurement of perfection."

Sneat rattled his chair's fastenings, and his expression spread apart with exasperation. "Well, what then?" he asked. "What are we to do?"

"We must return to the city," Post said, leaning over to kiss his wife. Her arms lightly scarved his shoulders. "Our retreat here has come to its end. We return to challenge the Self-Propelled Expressway. We look for a miracle."

"Miracle, indeed," Sneat muttered scornfully.

"Yes, a miracle. Here's one miracle to begin with," Leo Post said and kissed his wife. "Haven't you noticed how everything is better after she has returned? She is our sunny season, our best change of weather. She is the tolerance that eases our passage through the dreary forecast."

"Get back to the city?" Sneat had asked. "Now?"

"We cannot whine like schoolboys about the day's assignment," Post replied. "If we are to survive, we must share our lessons, do them together. Those pigeons in Mauston had existed because of their vast numbers, and we have the same instinct to live together in large numbers."

"It seems to me they were easy targets because of their number," his colleague said.

"They had no memory of past disasters, and so they were without defenses against their current threats. They could not adapt. They became less able to live together and to survive. We face a similar threat, another traffic jam. But we are the traffic, and the city is the solution. And we have memories."

"Screeching at each other over our own din?" Sneat ruminated. "Nesting on top of our own dung?" His wheelchair abruptly turned full circle, he rolled toward us, and skidded to a halt. One finger aimed at us. "What of this Smith? Isn't he the product of urban conglomerate?"

"Just the opposite," Post replied. He adjusted the tricorn and rose from the mass of used clothing. "Smith represents those agencies that suspect the city, who are intolerant of the municipal species. They would like to eliminate the languages spoken in the side streets. They want only one language spoken—so much easier to control. Tyranny requires only one dictionary. Not just the fit survive, but those who fit in."

The author had paused to wipe what appeared to be a feverish brow. Sgt. Anderson had closed her eyes and breathed calmly, and the man called Taylor had disappeared.

"Do you remember Governor Lyon's Committee to Save the Countryside?" Post continued. "It was actually a survey to discover how to maximize the effect of the Self-Propelled Expressway, how to control a troublesome population and make cities part of a homogeneous rural entity. Just as the broad avenues of Paris were created to maximize the use of grapeshot to control a riotous mob, this network of roads would become an endless belt of continuity to effect undelayed transport of security forces to those areas where abnormal irrelevancies might pop up."

I, B. Smith, accustomed as an observer, continued to find ourselves the object of Pickett Sneat's hostile scrutiny. The book reviewer had come quite close, and the rubber-tire wheels of his conveyance pressed us on either side. "And do we leave Smith here when we light out for the city?" he asked.

"I haven't decided yet," the author answered. He was still on his feet, looking down on his wife who, in turn, regarded her hands in her lap. "Your father was a madman, my dear."

"Yes, quite mad," she said simply. "All the controls of the Expressway were entombed with him."

"Which explains why his coffin was so large," the author explained to us, winking. "Only he could shut it off. Get it?" He winked once more in our direction and more broadly.

Russet-haired Molly Post rose from the surf of surplus. "But there's something you may not know, Leo. The official announcement of his death attributed the cause to a colon blockage, but in actuality he had a very bad strep throat. He was so short, the doctors looked at the wrong end."

"An amusing rumor," Post said, "but that wasn't the cause." He nodded into the darkness and the man called Taylor stepped into the light. "You must prepare yourself for some sordid business. Governor Lyon disappeared from a dinner party honoring a former manager of the Catskill-Peekskill Interchange of the Expressway, and the guests all thought he was using the toilet facilities. But Taylor here was expertly and quickly driving him to a rendezvous on the Upper West Side while the dinner party was dabbling its sorbet."

"A rendezvous?" Molly Lyon Post asked, with a slight laugh.

"Yes, a prearranged meeting with a young woman who was the principal manicurist of the barber shop in the Waldorf Astoria—"

"—and noted for her manual dexterity," interjected Sneat and began to choke on his own humor. Several well-placed whacks on his back from Sgt. Anderson restored the man's balance.

"In any event, the Governor reached the apex of his pleasure as this practiced mercenary of rapture was employing a technique called the Scythian Twirl—"

"—Ah, the Scythian Twirl," Sneat murmured with curious affection.

"—and he almost instantly belonged to the ages as has been said of another. The young woman panicked, this response a first in her career, and called the police when Taylor, just outside the door, could have easily handled the situation with his usual aplomb and discretion."

The man called Taylor had stepped forward and lightly touched the brim of his white Stetson. He seemed about to contribute to this history but then shook his head and stepped back into the gloom.

"The manicurist was having difficulty fitting the Governor back into his formal attire," Post continued, "having been something of a tomboy and with no experience dressing up dolls. Two cops arrived and dressed the Governor. By now Taylor was in the picture and finished the job, threw the executive corpse over one shoulder, and smuggled it back into the exclusive suite overlooking the East River and set it on the commode where it was discovered just as the flambeau ananas was served. The press was then notified, and the reporters—curiosity satisfied with the fabrication of the Governor dying at the stool—investigated the circumstances no further."

"All's well but for the cops. They were bribed, of course," Sneat said with a knowing leer.

"Oh yes, them. Fortunately, the manicurist fell in love with one of the policemen—a fellow with ham-sized hands—and the two of them married and relocated to a small town in Arizona with the support of the Lyon Foundation. And the other officer spent the rest of his life trying to publish a memoir no one believed."

"Yes, poor devil," Sneat said. "I remember him showing up at writing festivals, the manuscript in his attaché case becoming more and more tattered. Memoirs had become a dime a dozen by then, and the extraordinary circumstances of the Governor's death at the hands of an unknown manicurist had been outstripped in interest by the fabricated accounts of childhood incest and corruption of

yo-yo championships. But what has your wife been doing all this
time? Here we've been exiled on this fantasy dump of an island and
what has she been doing?" The book reviewer raised a prosecuto-
rial hand at Molly Lyon Post.

As if to defend her, the author raised his wife from the scattered duds and pulled her to him in an avian embrace if not ritual.
The woman's eyes had lowered, and she placed a hand on Post's
chest as if to quell him. "It's time for my contribution to B. Smith's
record." She addressed the book reviewer directly. "Kimball Lyon
was not my father; he was my stepfather."

"Oh, more baloney," Sneat dismissed her statement and wiped
his nose.

"Come now, Pickett," Post said sternly. "Do you think that
little midget, that runt of a Punch, could father this magnificent
creature?" He leaned forward and kissed his wife on the mouth.
Their lips joined urgently as they stood in what looked like the
debris from a costume ball.

"Just a minute—just a minute." The book reviewer spun his
wheelchair from left to right, from right to left. "What's the meaning here?"

"It's all too true," Post said, as his wife adjusted her costume.
She had somewhat tardily become aware of the skimpy vest and
endeavored to hold it together.

"Because his lungs were so close to the ground, Kimball Lyon
suffered a chronic respiratory problem. As a young man he spent
some time in a sanitarium in Arizona."

"Enter a voluptuous nurse," Sneat said out of the corner of his
mouth.

"No, nothing like that," laughed Mrs. Post, the slant of her
eyelids paralleling the angle of her high cheekbones when she
closed her eyes.

"Then a rancher's daughter, thighs hard-muscled from riding
bareback," he suggested with a leer.

"You are quite bizarre, Mr. Sneat," Molly Post said, sounding
as if she had just tapped his wrist with her fan. Of course, she had

no fan. "My mother ran a dude ranch near the sanitarium, and the patients often came over for trail rides and cookouts. She died when I was very young, and I know little about her. Lyon had befriended her and adopted me. It's all that simple," she concluded.

"Thrown from a horse, perhaps?" Sneat offered. "I mean the manner of her death."

"Oh, no," our charming narrator said. "Mother was an excellent horsewoman and a crack shot. A gambling syndicate thought it would be amusing to make her sheriff of the town; however, once in the position she started to clean the place up, including the gambling. A barroom brawl was staged, during which she was shot in the back. It was the only way Mother could be taken." Her eyes shifted sideways to meet her husband's. "I mean from behind," she added demurely.

"Quite so," Post agreed. "And you never knew your father. Perhaps a guest at the ranch, the son of a distinguished family, whose holiday became a romantic interlude. Or maybe a foreign diplomat, enjoying a bit of ersatz Americana. A local knockabout, someone who trained her in rifle-handling as well."

"We're to come to the table." The man called Taylor had interrupted. He had come upon us unnoticed by using the traditional heel-to-toe step that is the quiescent knack of the authentic plainsman.

A Few Moments Later

"A manor house seems to be ablaze," Leo Post said as he guided his wife through the surplus clothing and out onto the solid stone floor of the gallery. He nodded toward the windows where an unnatural glow pulsated in the eastern sky. Night had fallen. "It might be one of the Livingston places or maybe a Beekman or a Bleaker—the old estates are in that direction. It happens fairly regularly now. Well-meaning developers, eager to provide moderately priced housing in historical settings, set them afire to collect the insurance as they clear the land."

"Now this is what we got," Sgt. Anderson announced as she entered. She lifted a large steaming pot before her. The taut position of her arms, raised and spread apart, splayed the US Navy dress coat to effect a thorough *anatomis* such as the moldy husk of a butternut might break apart to reveal the firm sweetmeat within. "There's lots of this tapioca pudding. Taylor is bringing the sausages. Apples are fine, and there's some pears."

"Splendid," said Leo Post, once more rubbing his hands together. The man was of modest gesture. "A classic feast, Lucy.
Come, friends." The company took places around the table while
I, B. Smith, both prisoner and oddly guest of honor, was at the
head of the table. The man called Taylor had appeared with a tray
of sizzling sausages. Plates were distributed, and a sundry service
of cups and glasses was filled with cider.

"Shouldn't there be some sort of invocation?" Molly Post
inquired as she sat down. Her long legs sheathed in the Zouave
pantaloons wrapped around each other with the odd grace of a
flamingo.

"Do us something, Pickett," urged her husband. "Perhaps
something from your anthology of condemned poets."

"That was a mean enterprise, meanly financed and meanly
carried out." The book reviewer sliced the air with his hand. "All
those tapes have been erased," he continued with an unusually
warm expression. "No longer do I have the heart, not the same
heart at least, for such a project."

"What strange effect you have on us." Post nuzzled his wife's
ear. "Are you maid or miracle?"

"Certainly no maid," she replied, "and if miracle, self-made."

"Very well then," Pickett Sneat said with a tremor in his
voice. "Let me propose a toast, a little something borrowed—" he
offered, rising to his feet unassisted. He stood on his own, to lift
a glass of cider. All stood, attentive and solemn.

"What's past is prologue," the book reviewer announced and
drank his cider.

"Well said," cried Post, "though not original yet appropriate.
One island salutes another, is that it?"

And appropriately, a fuel tanker passing upriver unloosed a
blast that rattled the windowpanes and shook loose some masonry
on the upper floors. But the book reviewer was undaunted, and
continued after the evening's quietude had been restored.

"I thought you might make the connection," he said with a
certain modesty and carefully aligned his wheelchair.

"What's Post is often prolonged," Molly Lyon Post remarked and laughed.

"Ah." The author winced with mock agony. "How such a soft hand can twist the knife."

"There." His wife kissed him. "You are healed. All prologue is Post, for if this is Post, there must be a prologue."

"These sausages are getting cold with all this talk," Sgt. Anderson observed.

"Just so, Lucy," Post commended her. "And so, perhaps, is our wit. You keep us on the fire."

"Not always a sanguine endeavor," Sneat growled, "but this tapioca pudding isn't half bad." He took a large spoonful and pushed it into his mouth. The man called Taylor fisted his spoon while Molly Post skimmed the outer edges of her pudding with a delicate swipe. Sgt. Anderson, posture erect, tested the dessert with her fingers. "Did you say this was army rations in World War II?"

"Yes. It says something about a country, I think," Post said, "that sends its men to die on foreign beachheads packing cans of vanilla-flavored tapioca pudding."

"No more of that sort of talk," Molly Post reminded him. "It was probably the idea of someone's mom. Maybe the president's mother—something about the boys having well-balanced meals."

"Let's leave it at that," Post agreed.

"Well-balanced meals," Sneat exploded. "That's one of the worst things that ever happened to this country. Well-balanced meals," he repeated and spat to one side. The freckles across his nose had disappeared into the oncoming rage that colored his face. "Together with a sane sex life!" His teeth ground together.

"Now, Pickett," the author soothed him. Sgt. Anderson put an arm around him, and he was distracted and absorbed by the police-woman's breasts so close to his face. The book reviewer stared at the caramel-tipped spheres and smacked his lips, and the undercover agent seized the opportunity to shovel two spoonfuls of pudding into his open mouth. She delicately wiped his lips with a napkin.

"Thank you, Lucy," Post said. Sneat had shriveled up once again, appearing even more confined to his wheelchair. "Let me propose a Post-toasty," the author said, acknowledging the groans of the assembled group, excepting the book reviewer.

"Here's to Pickett," Leo Post began, but I, B. Smith, a sworn witness, was unable to register the total commemoration due to the sonorous signal of a passing ship that rattled the tableware. Something heavy crashed down near the portrait gallery. And we imagined one of the larger canvasses had been knocked loose. Though we could not hear Leo Post's exact words, the effect of this salutation on Pickett could not be missed. His crumpled limbs expanded, filled out, and the cramped contortion of his disability disappeared as if his body had been inflated by his colleague's words. Even the perpetual grimace softened around its edges.

"I hardly know what to say," he said finally as the company raised their glasses of cider.

"Well, that's the first time," the man called Taylor murmured.

"Listen to Taylor." Leo Post slapped the tabletop.

"No—listen to me," announced Molly Lyon Post.

"Eh?" Her husband leaned back to look at her.

"Yes," she said. "Whenever I've started to tell my story there's been some interruption—costumes and caresses and other diversions."

"You tell 'em, girl," Sgt. Anderson urged.

"And yet, it seems to me," Molly Post made a coquettish bow to the company, "that my story is germane—none of this would have happened if it were not for what happened to me. And yet—and yet—yet." She had begun to look through the pile of clothing near the table, holding up some items and judging others more intently until she chose a long cloak similar to the one worn by her husband. It was butternut gray and trimmed in faded crimson braid. The garment swung over her shoulders and completely enveloped her to cover the shoddy Zouave costume. "Do you think I'm capable only of scattered entries in a girlish diary?"

"Let her speak," commanded Sgt. Anderson.

"Come, Leo," Sneat had joined the petition. "What are you afraid of?"

"And so you shall tell us everything," Leo Post replied, conducting his wife to the table. "Just as your reappearance has commuted our sentence, the story of your exile will signal the end of ours—the departure from Leek's Island that I have been delaying, not the account of your disappearance. Oddly, all this rare junk, this pile of ancestral rubble, has meant something to me, for it once clothed a history that had become obsolete overnight, and though I recognize its poor ashes make a cargo too paltry to ship, there is something in me that mourns its abandonment. Leek's Castle will no more be at this story's end—only a worthy trade for a boy's apple. So set us adrift on your narrative," the author requested his wife. He kissed her eyes, an endearing punctuation, as he let her gently down into her chair.

"Pickett has asked two important questions—"

"—a habit of the trade," the man purred, and looked about importantly.

"—that need to be answered," Molly Lyon Post continued. The candlelight framed her green eyes. "He wondered what happened to my comrades in arms." She paused to pull her hair outside the cloak's high collar. She fluffed it out. "My two companions have returned to their posts as gravediggers in the Woodlawn Cemetery of Elmira, New York. They are simple, goodhearted hobbledehoys, brothers who cared for me when I was in need. You'll meet them again in the course of my story."

"Hobbledehoys?" The book reviewer reviewed the word and shook his head. Sgt. Anderson whacked him on the head with her hand. He abruptly fell silent.

"As to why I returned to this man who had tried to murder me—that is not so easy to answer," Molly Lyon Post said as she lit a new taper. Her large eyes became catlike within the nimbus of the new flame. "A man of passion. At least the Nalbandian part of him if not the Leek, but there was time to think of many things in the cemetery. I wondered if Leo's desire to kill me, fired by misinformation and malicious cartage—"

"Yes, yes," Pickett Sneat said impatiently. But he had blushed and averted his eyes.

"It was a fury," the heiress continued, placing her lips on the author's temple, "a fury to balance the scale. It was that passion, something rare in men today, that drew me back from the grave. Like this candle that draws moths from their safe obscurity. I realized without his light I could only imitate the aimlessness of a crippled cockroach."

"Where's the cockroach?" Sgt. Anderson cried and leaped up. She had picked up a cup as if to defend herself.

"Only a figure of speech, Lucy," Post soothed her. "An urban creature that has survived millions of years, and one we should get to know better."

"Let's get to the race," Sneat advised, "and the accident in Elmira."

"Right," agreed Post's wife. She paused to put her thoughts in order, hands clasped and person relaxed. "Poughkeepsie was resplendent in the morning light," she began. "The Hudson Valley folded sweetly into the furrow of the river, and the Poughkeepsie-Elmira Access Spur was ready to yield its pristine surface to our tire marks. The Catskills defined the morning sky, a purplish line around Aurora's eyes that marked the night's rough usage."

"My word," Sneat wondered, "is this about an auto race or what?"

"You seemed preoccupied that morning, the morning of the race," Molly Post continued, standing behind her husband. She gently massaged the author's broad shoulders. "I put it down to the enormous duties that had fallen upon you since the Governor's death, the transference of power from Lyon's admnistration to his successor. Afterwards, it became clear to me that you were engrossed by another kind of transformation altogether, weren't you?" She bent over him so her shimmering screen of hair fell upon Post's face like a net of woven copper. She swung away and stood apart from the table.

"There were an even two dozen of us in the race." She paced over the flagstones as if to mark where each car was parked. "It was to be a Le Mans start. I had more points than the others, and my only real competition was Grapelly, though Eckelberg would have to be watched. The Moroni was in top condition, thanks to you, Taylor."

"For Smith's benefit, let me describe the Moroni," Post interrupted. "Its body was designed by Tufoli. The motor was a 460 horsepower Paige Warner with six double carbs, fuel injection, overhead cam, after burn and reed rocker arms coupled to a Brunswick transmission. The entire machine was painted a pale lime over which a *millefleurs* had been represented, the predominant blossom being that of the leek." A gasp went up from the attentive audience. "Well, just because it was a racing car," Molly Post demurred, "didn't mean it couldn't be pretty."

"Tell 'em, girl," Sgt. Anderson agreed.

"I remember how you kissed me that morning," Mrs. Post addressed her husband. "I was fastening my crash helmet, and you gave me this offhand, casual peck on the cheek. I started to laugh, for I took it to be a manner of your Leekian cool. Of course it was really the suppression of Nalbandian rage, the Old World dispassionate preparation to punish an unfaithful wife."

"And one," Leo Post reminded her, "who had apparently gone to the trouble of documenting her adultery in living color."

"Yes, that too," Molly Post laughed, her eyes raised. "The indiscretion was as punishable as the fault itself. Well then, we were all lined up in the old Courthouse Square of Poughkeepsie. The engines were warm, the timers ready, the start had been reached. We were using the old-fashioned Le Mans start—running across the track and hopping into the machine and pulling out. This gave me an advantage because, as you know, my time for the 440 at Helsinki is still the record," she said, and made a charming attempt at modesty.

"Indeed it is," Leo Post said proudly, and slapped Sneat on the back. The force of his enthusiasm nearly threw the book reviewer from his chair, but he was secured by the strong arms of Sgt. Anderson.

Meanwhile, Mrs. Post held the heavy cloak together and ran to an empty chair. She jumped into it, smoothed back her hair, and gripped the table edge with both hands.

"Engines roared, tires squealed. A sudden heat flashed in my face, and my spine was compressed against the seat. Power throbbed in my hands. Every cell of my body quickened with the excitement of riding the well-oiled equipment beneath me. We took Mid-Hudson Bridge over the river six abreast like a pack of frenzied beetles. Three cars had stalled at the start and were left behind. I lay halfway back, easy and confident, ready to take the lead whenever I wished."

As if to support her narrative with appropriate sound effects, an empty tanker, its half-exposed screw noisily churning the river, made a thunderous pass of the island. Pickett was enfolded in the policewoman's embrace, eyes closed, his round head lolling to one side. The man called Taylor leaned forward attentively. Mrs. Post's torso canted slightly toward her husband as if thrust by a centrifugal force.

"The long curve near Ellenville had been designed for normal highway speeds but not the terrific rate we were going. I remember my speed was a comfortable 175 miles per hour, but Jones spun out, taking van Nostrand and Ekelberg with him, and apparently so scaring Hewson that he pulled out of the race, braked, and vomited all over his coveralls."

"Poor devil," said Leo Post.

"So there were now fewer of us hurtling toward Elmira.

"The day was faultless and my car was turning over like a sewing machine. The wind polished my face. I teased the accelerator under my foot, trying the enormous amount of power the Paige Warner held in reserve. Spilka could not have noticed—he was always an introverted fellow— but I was singing when I passed his Ortuga II outside of Neversink." Carefully, and never taking her eyes from the center of the long table, Molly Post raised one hand to feel for and then pat the author who sat next to her.

"Singing, my darling, because I knew the race was mine and that I would have the return leg all to myself and that you would be waiting for me in Poughkeepsie to kiss the grime from my face.

"We had talked about supper at a country inn, but of course you were expecting to dine alone, weren't you?" Post hung his head; a hand went to his eyes. Suddenly Molly Post resumed her two-handed grip of the table's edge, her face tightened with alarm.

"Look out," she cried. "A tie rod on Martin's Comanche had let go. He wavered. I saw him frantically trying to control his vehicle, shifting down, correcting the drag, but the car took a slant that he couldn't change. He made a fearful crash into the granite walls that were on either side of us and—oh my, the car just exploded into pieces. I've never seen a car come apart like that, and Martin disappeared in a balloon of fire, and all I could think of was that hard-muscled belly and those thick, capable fingers suddenly becoming ashes."

"Oh, yes, indeed," Post said and gave a curious laugh.

"Grapelly and I now had the race to ourselves. I crept into his slipstream, easing up the RPMs with no loss of speed. His orange helmet moved ever so slightly, but it was enough to give him away—he had spotted me in his mirror. He poured on the juice to move up—topping 185 with a burst—but I was locked onto his tail. So we settled into a groove, a test of nerve. His helmet moved again—I was still in his mirror. I was ready to make my move. My hands, gloved as they were, had become very cool on the wheel, and with just a shade of pressure, I teased my car out from behind and then back close again. He tried to find me in his mirror, his orange helmet spun like a top as he frantically looked for me. When he did find me, I had snuggled under his tailpipes to show him I could go ahead any time. I let Grapelly think about that for a little bit."

"Ah, how cruel," Sneat murmured, but he smiled.

"Our two cars raced as one," Molly Lyon Post continued. I was just three feet from him. We had just slipped over 180. Through the final pass in the Alleghenies, over the Delaware River Bridge, around the graceful radius at Deposit and along the Pennsylvania state line, our cars screamed down the fresh cement of the new expressway as if wired together. Every blistering mile, every twenty seconds, Grapelly became more and more fixed with the idea that he was in control of my car as well as his own. One thoughtless pressure, a split-second blur of concentration, and he would send us both to destruction—or so he thought."

"So you had made him think," Post said with some pride.

"I cannot deny that I had made him drive as he had never driven before. To use the colorful language of the sport, I was crawling right up his ass."

"Make your move, make your move," the man called Taylor urged through tight-pressed lips. "Now!"

"Not yet, not yet," Molly Post replied just as tersely. The knuckles of her hands had grown white as she tightened her grip of the table's edge. "I wanted to test his will a bit more. I had come to respect him—yes, even more than respect. He had given me more of a battle than I had expected, and I wanted to beat him nobly, to pass him and leave him behind gracefully. It would be his decision as to when I would overtake him. And my triumph would sadden me, but it was inevitable. We traveled many miles thus locked together. We shared the one experience on the rim of death, each mile more meaningful than the last.

"The moment of his defeat neared. The towers of Bingington glistened in the clear air. Our two cars drilled down the Expressway like projectiles fired from a gun. My strategy was to take the lead in Bingington. With the slightest of moves, a caress almost, I edged out from behind him." The woman's face seemed to age with the concentration required of the maneuver. Her body pressed against the back of her chair.

"My foot pressed the accelerator, and the Paige Warner responded smoothly. It sounded as if it had enough power for three cars. Our machines were now side by side, wheel to wheel, for I meant to overtake him with a style and dispatch that his courage and skill merited."

"Certainly with style," Post said and looked around for approval from the others. Sneat rattled his chair impatiently.

"At 186 miles per hour, I went ahead and did not look back immediately. I knew he would try to get into my slipstream to ride me out as I had done to him; however I pushed over 190 to put me beyond his car's capability and not to unduly humiliate him; I had beaten Grapelly." Her voice had become hoarse, and she fell back into her seat, exhausted.

"Hurrah!" Leo Post was on his feet. The man called Taylor whistled through two fingers in his mouth.

"Oh, sit down, Leo," Sneat said wearily. I, B. Smith, a dispassionate accumulator of data, noted that Mrs. Post had grown very pale, yet her hands had not lost control of the table.

"As my car zipped through the canyons of downtown Bingington," her narrative continued almost lazily, "I sneaked a look back. He was far behind me and could never make up the distance. It was a Sunday drive from there to the pit stop outside Elmira. I was giggling with anticipation, joyous with my certain victory, and so happy that you would see me coming in first, Taylor. Happy that you would relay that information to my lover. I will never be that happy again. I was in love with the best, and I had just beaten the best."

"Ah, dear," Leo Post said sadly and went to take her hand but thought better of it, for she was still steering the table, the race was yet on, and she required both hands to be free.

"So it was in this jubilant mood that I shifted down and slipped into the pit stop, braked, and hopped out to hug the honest figure of Taylor. And what a magnificent crew you had assembled that day, Taylor. It was a record performance."

"They did a complete tire change, pumped fuel, and replaced the coolant—all in 43.4 seconds." The former rodeo star flushed with the memory.

"And that efficiency also provided the fraction of a second more in which to loosen a fastening in the steering linkage," Molly Post conjectured. "I didn't understand at first what you were shouting into my ear in the midst of the commotion. The excitement of my certain victory, the frenzy of the mechanics, the noise and pace as I gulped down a soda. I looked back on the expressway, prepared to see the red dot that was Grapelly coming on. Then, Taylor, you were beside me, and you shouted—"

"Mr. Post wants me to fix your car," the morose plainsman recalled loudly.

"Well, of course, you were to fix my car, I thought to myself. The man had lost his marbles. Then I looked at your face and saw the tears in your eyes, and the whole meaning became clear. That quick, incandescent passion that had thrilled me so thoroughly in different hotel suites and wayward sylvan haunts had now, for some reason, turned murderous, but why? There was no time for an answer. Grapelly had just appeared on the horizon. There was a race to be won, suddenly heartbroken as I was, but you had not sabotaged my machine. Elmira was where the route turned back to Poughkeepsie, and the actual turnaround pivoted in Woodlawn Cemetery."

"Why there?" Pickett Sneat asked. His gourd-like head rested on the rich loam of Sgt. Anderson's bosom.

"I can give some of the thinking on that," Leo Post suggested. "The Self-Propelled Expressway had begun to receive some mild criticism from certain areas of the intelligentsia. The usual liberal frenzy was smothered in the soft pillow of their ambivalence. Before he died, the Governor was very sensitive to their carping, particularly because the literary review that carried these attacks— and that's to give honor to their dribbles—was one in which he hoped to publish some of his poetry. Consequently, the path off the Self-Propelled Expressway was reprogrammed so that it ran right through the Woodlawn Cemetery of Elmira as a commemorative gesture toward the great man of American letters who was buried there. The race was announced as the Mark Twain 500.

The strategy worked even better than we had supposed—yes, I admit to a modest hand in the planning—for as it turned out, none of the editors of that literary review had known that Mark Twain was buried in Elmira, New York, and the exposure of their ignorance silenced their criticism forever."

"Get back to the race," Sgt. Anderson said. The company leaned toward Molly Lyon Post. Her face had become the color of the gray cloak around her shoulders, and when her eyes opened, tears glistened on the ellipses.

"Leaving the pit," she said softly, taking a deep and ragged breath, "I could hardly see the road ahead. I drove by instinct, and my competitive nature put me in gear. But why had Leo wanted to kill me?"

"Scoundrel," Sneat cried.

"My brain was cramped and threatened to explode within my crash helmet. I needed time to think it through, to discover some innocent event that had turned him to violence against me." She wiped her eyes and leaned forward over the table's edge.

"I was still far ahead of Grapelly. An idea grew within me as I waved at the crowds on either side of the downtown streets. North of the business district, the Expressway follows what used to be Tompkins Street and thence onto Walnut, which leads to the cemetery's entrance. The square stone pillars of the gate embraced me as I entered the necropolis. The road veered to the right and ascended the knoll of the Langdon family plot where the remains of the old raft-dreamer lay. My plan's success depended on the absence of spectators—no witnesses. Only a family of squirrels was in attendance when my car coasted up the rise and I braked. Behind me, downtown Elmira had erupted to indicate that Grapelly had just passed through." The narrator had slipped from the chair, grasping its back and arms.

"At the bottom of the hill was a large mausoleum, windowless and built of huge blocks of limestone. I steered the car in that direction, wedged the accelerator with several walnuts only recently the playthings of the aforementioned squirrels, and quickly released the clutch and leapt away. I had tossed the wedding band you had given me, Leo, into the cockpit."

"How so very sad," the author said and hung his head.

"It was an even grander smashup than Martin's. The side of the mausoleum caved in and the fully loaded fuel tanks bloomed into huge chrysanthemums of flame. The force of the explosions knocked me to the ground—fortunately, because Grapelly screeched by just then but did not see me. I will never forget the gesture he made as he passed the burning wreckage. The intense heat of the calamity had reduced my beautiful machine to the charred framework of an insect set afire by a sadistic child. Grapelly's gloved hand slowly raised and lowered—the salute of one champion to another."

Molly Post had stepped to the window and opened a casement, as if to freshen the air. The night breeze fluttered the candles' flames and perfumed the chamber with the heavy aroma of honeysuckle. A hazy chorus of insects sang to the river's run and an owl in the garden below raised a mournful serenade. The man called Taylor had crumpled seemingly with the car's impact. Post studied his feet. Sgt. Anderson had clasped Pickett Sneat closer as if to protect him.

"And then?" the book reviewer asked finally. His eyes had popped open. "Then?"

"And then, indeed," Molly Post replied almost absent-mindedly. She moved to another casement, released the catch, and swung out the window with an easy grace that reminded us she was the mistress of this castle. "Their names were Curt and Burt, and I could never tell them apart. Not even the portable radio helped because they took turns carrying it. They found me semiconscious. My mind had foundered. The race was over. In my coveralls and crash helmet, they took me to be a man."

"Preposterous," Leo Post interjected and then turned to the group. "Her coveralls were by Schaperelli—pink and with velvet inserts of maroon."

"But these were naïve youths," she insisted, "raised within the gates of the Woodlawn Cemetery by their father, the head groundskeeper, the chief gravedigger. He was a widower himself, and his sons were raised to assist him. Only recently he had been the object of their handling of pick and spade, an expertise he had taught them. So, my sudden appearance on the lawn between the tombstones seemed a happy miracle to them. I was a replacement for the companion they had just lost. They helped me to their abode, an abandoned mausoleum set into a hillock and resembling a cave. It had been fixed up quite comfortably with a stove and cots and, of course, a profusion of cut flowers."

Mrs. Post had refilled her glass with cider and paused to sip some, and her upraised arm lifted part of the cloak to reveal some of her figure. Even I, B. Smith, merely a public auditor, could not understand how her gender might be mistaken.

"So, I became an apprentice gravedigger and helped them bury the dead, as my heart seemed to be buried over and over in the deepest sorrow; the crash helmet was replaced by the yellow hat and the coveralls exchanged for boots, shirt, and pants the boys bought for me in town. With every thrust of the spade, Leo, I reviewed the events of our life; every moment was turned over. How had I wronged you, how had I betrayed you? Earth and more earth was uncovered with no answer appearing. Nothing but clay and the occasional earthworm, sexless as I had become, and moving blindly through the unknown catastrophe that had wrecked my life."

Post was visibly shaken and started to rise, as if to go to his wife, but she pushed him away. "Don't touch me, bastard!" she spat. Her voice was suddenly armed by the militant accent and posture of Yellow Hat. She pushed him away.

Sgt. Anderson had come to attention, roiling the book reviewer's head unmercifully, and her eyes waited upon Mrs. Post as if to receive an order. The man called Taylor sat with his hands covering his face. But the most alarmed by this outburst seemed to be its author herself. She had swiftly turned from us, and the cloak that enveloped her sudden anger trembled as a stage curtain might be jostled during a change of scenery. However, with a profound sigh she turned back to the company, and her expression had become serene once again and beautiful. She smiled to reveal an arc of gleaming teeth. She almost petted her husband.

"Forgive me," she asked, then cradled Post's upturned face. "But a season with the dead has its own effect." She moved to the table and lit a fresh candle and set it in a saucer. "I even thought I had been the victim of a scheme left behind by my stepfather, the Governor, that once set in motion could not be turned off—like his famous expressway. A self-propelled conspiracy. My speculation became bizarre—perhaps my death was to satisfy a pharaoian drama—is that a word?"—she interrupted herself. Author and book reviewer looked at each other and shrugged. "—A crazy ritual Kimball Lyon had designed that demanded I perish with him. In the isolation of that cemetery I even wondered if you had perished as well, dear Leo, forced to perish, to follow the Governor into the underworld as faithful minister and advisor to his court, and I grieved for you, Leo. Grieved for myself as well because I thought I had been left alive and alone. So I thought, clothed in my new disguise as Burt, Curt, and I dug into one world while the transistor radio at graveside rapidly fired accounts of another."

Our storyteller had gone to the far end of the chamber to renew the candles on the mantle. Each new flame lifted more of the gloom in the vast chamber as it burnished the helmet of her hair. With the cloak around her shoulders, she resembled one of those youths made popular by the Post-Raphaelites. "Much of the mystery of my return will be explained," her voice echoed from the hearth, "when I say that Curt and Burt's favorite recreation from shovel and spade was a weekly attendance at a motion picture theatre in the nearby village of Horse Heads, and that this theatre's program was exclusively pornographic."

"Ah," Sneat sighed with closed eyes, "a star was born."

"Another of your creations, Pickett," Molly Post said and laughed. Her voiced bounced against the stone vault.

"My Jenny Hanniver," Sneat said with unusual emotion. "But I had no idea that little bitch would go on to make films. Perhaps she introduced a new fetish to the art with that tattoo."

"And when new concepts were sorely needed," Molly Post said dryly.

"So that was it." Leo Post swung his chair around astutely. "You saw this woman who had reproduced the leek on her person, and you suspected the trick played upon us by this villain here." Pickett Sneat turned and twisted in his metal harness as if it had suddenly become barbed.

"Something like that," Post's wife replied, returning to the table. "But it was not until I had accompanied Curt and Burt to many of these matinees—the theatre offered double and triple features—that I saw my alter pubis. How many couplings, junctions, penetrations, tonguings, and engorgements I sat through cannot be reckoned. The monotonous nature of the act is appalling, you must agree. But Burt and Curt viewed each film with innocent enthusiasm—an innocence they must have learned from the dead. But for me it was a tedious litany of breasts and buttocks, mouths and organs. Endless manipulations and repetitive entrances, droopy exits—we are so very limited in our pleasures. Imagination gives novelty to our ecstasies, for the basic dimensions of the apparati remain the same."

"Quite so," agreed Post.

"Moreover," his wife continued, "we look alike in the close-ups—cocks and cunts have no personalities. To lift my boredom, I would concentrate on the settings of these seedy scenarios. Especially clocks," she said, lighting a last candle. "An infinite variety of alarm clocks appeared on nightstands and bureau tops and bookcases. More formal timepieces topped the mantels of parlors. The prosaic sweep hand of an electric kitchen clock timed encounters between randy housewives and service men— plumbers were the most popular role. In one film, an elegant grandfather clock measured a sequence on a stairway landing, but this film clearly had a higher budget. More common were dashboard clocks, waterproof wristwatches, the clock in the Central Park Zoo—and the chimes of Big Ben in one, but only in the background, a film had pretensions for the comic. The faces of these timepieces were usually more interesting than those of the performers. All hours were portrayed, and only my speculation as to what part of a day—A.M. or P.M.—measured the foreground activity of a particular coupling seasoned the tasteless miscellany. But, those were faces!" Molly Lyon Post laughed and strolled around the table.

"I saw every hour, every variation of an hour, sixty times sixty. The bland creatures dutifully twisting on beds and stairways, on pool tables and in dentist chairs could not match the diversity of those chronometers, their hands moving at a steady pace. Moreover, it makes a girl wonder," she had come behind Sgt. Anderson's chair and grasped the policewoman's shoulder, "it makes you wonder to sit in a dark theatre, the screen rosy with flesh, while surrounded by men sound asleep and snoring. Their blubbery expulsions made a lugubrious counterpoint to the grunts and groans of the enacted sexual frenzies."

"Sad," Sgt. Anderson said and shook her head. "Very sad."

"Perhaps they were as bored as you were," suggested Leo Post.

"Once, a pale Guinevere outspread herself to receive her Lancelot—"

"Rather good, that one," Sneat snickered. "Lance-a-lot."

"Yes, we get it," Post shushed his contemporary. "Continue, Molly."

"The camera had zoomed in on the glistening target just as one of the sleepers awoke to be confronted by a gaping vagina, twenty feet square, and the poor fellow, yet foggy, must have thought the toothless mouth of a monster butterfly was about to engulf him. He was still screaming when they trundled him into the ambulance."

Her audience hooted and gasped for breath. Leo Post pushed his chair back on its legs to free his amusement even more. The man called Taylor allowed himself a thin, tight smile while Pickett and Sgt. Anderson guffawed.

She received their appreciation with eyes closed and a moue of pretty irony on her mouth. It was the expression given to those slant-eyed muses attending Apollo by the Venetian hand of Giovanni Piazzetta.

"But why were they bored?" she asked quietly after her audience had quieted. "My boredom with such fare might be explained by my point of view. I had to accompany Burt and Curt. But we were surrounded by patrons for whom these films were created, who attended them voluntarily only to fall asleep during them. Moreover, there was Curt on one side of me and Burt on the other and both laughing as children might at the disport of seals. A curious response, but they were awake. In fact, their hilarity on more than one occasion brought down the censorious switch of an usher's flashlight to remind us that these films were serious and nothing to laugh at. Nothing to laugh at, indeed," Molly Lyon Post repeated solemnly.

"What has de men folk come to," Sgt. Anderson said with a broad smile.

"You said it, sister," Molly Post replied. "A passionless, drowsy audience for whom the lovely symmetry of the slippery search had been reduced to a boring arrangement of parts sans mystery, sans interest, sans life. That theatre was another cemetery where the apathetic interred themselves. I thought of you, Leo—my little hawk." The couple's eyes met and drifted away. "You were never without passion—in fact your passion had nearly killed me. Curiously, I reasoned your murderous feelings set you apart, a plus mark. Then one rainy afternoon, Curt, Burt, and I sat in our usual seats among the snoozers, and into the action came the actress you called Jenny Hanniver," she told the book reviewer.

"Did she have any talent?" Pickett Sneat inquired. "She had only a few small parts in loft theatres when I met her, roles in post-Platonic comedies. Perhaps you can give us an objective appraisal."

"The role had few lines, you must understand," Molly Post replied. "Her eyes were empty throughout, a characterization that could not be made of the rest of her. During the preliminaries, activities that had become doctrinaire and predictable, she showed no unusual talent. When the basic fucking began, she put herself in a particular position, and it was then I saw the leek blossom on her hairless coign."

"What kind of position was that?" asked Pickett Sneat, his button eyes pressed out and his jaw slack. Sgt. Anderson boxed his ears.

Molly Post was a model of reflection, and then she answered. "It reminded me of that method you showed me, Leo—the one you said had been a favorite of Cheyenne braves and their women while riding to the buffalo hunt."

"I understand," the author said simply and sipped his cider. Pickett Sneat blinked dumbly, looked blankly at host and hostess, and then permitted the policewoman to reposition his head upon her bosom. She gave him a motherly pat.

"The unique tattoo on this particular part of her anatomy was no coincidence," Molly Post continued with a smile. "I knew there was a connection between this actress and the attempt on my life, my exile in a cemetery in Elmira, New York, but what was it?"

Post had risen and approached us. "And in the pictures you passed to me the day of the Governor's funeral, those pictures you passed to me, Pickett, the face of the woman was hidden or omitted and since, as Molly has suggested, *toutes minettes sont gris*, only the artificial could be identified." The author had been checking the knots in the lariat that encircled I, B. Smith, completely immobilized and sworn. Satisfied with our security, the author was about to continue when Pickett Sneat raised a hand.

"Oh, spare us, Leo," the book reviewer implored. He turned from his colleague in letters and implored the man's wife. "I can feel a lecture coming on. One of those circuitous Postian analyses of art and reality. 'Shall we clothe our bare and vulnerable limbs with the false domino of art and so forth and so on'—that's how it goes, isn't it? From your Pulitzer-Jones speech."

"Yes, something like that," Post replied with a certain restraint and fiddled with the sash of his uniform.

"But what's the time frame?" the book reviewer asked. "We need some historical sequence. I've been a hostage on this island, a prisoner of your rhetoric, for how long? Even castaways mark their time on tree trunks, shells—something."

"I'd guess about a year has elapsed," Molly Post told him.

"Do you feel better?" Her husband joined the book reviewer.

"Somewhat," he nodded. "So you spent a year in this cemetery when you saw a film with the young woman I had hired to impersonate you for the pictures I made to trick Leo."

"Correct," Molly Post said as she returned to the high chair.

"Very well. Continue." Sneat looked satisfied and nodded. Post had become disinterested and strolled toward the casement windows that overlooked the river. That had once overlooked the river, but this view was now curtailed by the hedge grown wild.

"The rest is rather simple," the chatelaine continued. "One day, Curt, Burt, and I were preparing the final resting place for a prominent disc jockey. The portable radio blared at graveside. Suddenly—a news flash. The proposed Twenty-third Street Manhattan Access spur was being challenged by none other than Leo Post, confidant and advisor to the late governor. Son-in-law to the late governor. Letters had appeared in influential journals and literary reviews, encouraging opposition to the spur. They caused a furor, and you could not be reached for comment. Whereabouts unknown."

"So you assumed I had come here, to this island," Post murmured, facing the open window. "But you required an accomplice—someone on the inside to help you with certain strategies, such as splicing obscene footage onto a newsreel. Of course," the author said, and turned from the window to regard the man called Taylor.

The former rodeo performer showed no emotion, gave no indication of his feelings. Molly Post had gone to where the ersatz cowboy sat as if to defend him, and pressed the coal black hair of the man tenderly. I, B. Smith, a duly appointed officer of inquiry, must outline the multiple relationships invested in these two actors—woman and man, actress and retainer, driver and mechanic, victim and appointed assassin, conspirator and co-conspirator.

"Forgive his disloyalty," Molly Post pleaded.

"Forgive," Leo Post replied, and the smile on his face told all. "If ever only every man were so betrayed. Oh, happy and honored disloyalty," the author intoned.

"Bullshit," Pickett Sneat said hoarsely. "There's more to explain here. The gun you had, for example. And those two goons— how did you get them to accompany you?"

"Ah, the gun," the woman said with a giggle. "One of those realistic toys sold to children. How it frightened you. And Burt and Curt had a few days off—a spell of longevity had hit Elmira. There was no one to be buried. I told them we were going to a party, a costume party, and were disguised as bandits. Their conditioning by those films prepared them to believe almost anything."

"And I suppose," Sneat continued, "you were able to get some footage of the film featuring Jenny Hanniver from the projectionist of the theatre—through some bribery or other." His eyes widened in a waggish manner.

"That's correct," she replied a little nervously, and moved away.

"What sort of bribe?" Sneat persisted like a prosecutor. "Perhaps you showed him the original of the counterfeited tattoo?"

"Never mind, never mind." Leo Post stepped in quickly. He strode back to the table, his arms outstretched as if to envelop the company in the voluminous cloak. "That's all—"

"Damn you, Leo." His wife spun around, her fury halting him abruptly. "I sometimes think this vaunted magnanimity of yours, this all-forgiving magniloquence is only a device to avoid hearing the ugly things of this world—for some of which you might be responsible."

."Tell him, sister," Sgt. Anderson urged. Leo Post had turned quickly, then spun around once more as if he were trying to throw off a painful wounding. He moved with uncertain steps to his chair but did not sit, only to grasp the back of it and stand winded, eyes vacant.

The angry light in his wife's eyes had become a sparkle of amusement, as a fickle sun might play upon a constant sea. She looped the cape over her left arm in a toga-like fold and stepped jauntily around the perimeter of the table.

"I think I'll leave the nature of my bribe to your besotted imagination," she said with a sly look. "What could it have been?" Her tongue traced the gleaming band of her front teeth. "Probably only coffee and doughnuts brought to the man's lonely cubicle above the men snoring in the darkness below. Or—" she paused and laughed into Sneat's upturned face, "something more substantial. And just to round out this melodrama, how do you suppose Burt and Curt—or sometimes it was Curt and Burt—and I amused ourselves in those heaps of funeral arrangements?" She addressed Leo Post's back as he stood by the open windows. "If they had taken me for a youth, perhaps they took me as a youth."

Post spun around, the heavy cape on his shoulders gyrating dramatically just as a tugboat passed the point of the island and put several toots in his open mouth. But he had continued talking. "—suggest a renewal of a species, renewal of love." His language gradually became understood. "Yet you incite us, tease us to dreadful action. Talk of passion and suffering? What do you want from us, you delectable brigand?" He had taken his wife in his arms; the company looked away, the moment being too profound to view straight on. Sneat fanned his face with one hand.

"I want to stay alive," Molly Post answered simply. Leo Post released her and returned to the table where he picked up an apple and took a bite. "You seem to offer me a choice of being murdered or being loved—or killed because I am loved. Those huge flocks of pigeons that obsess you—was their extinction a measure of their adoration?"

"That wasn't my point." Post shook his head and took another crisp bite of the apple.

"What was your point?" his wife asked and turned to Sgt. Anderson. "I married a hawk and ended up with a pigeon freak."

"Make your point, Leo. Make your point," chortled the book reviewer.

"To stay alive at any price—is that what you want?" Leo Post looked down the long blade of his nose.

"Adaptation is any price," Molly Post countered. "I'm pretty good at adapting, and you'll forgive me if I keep trying. It's part of my nature." Both seemed oblivious to the book reviewer as he crooned to Sgt. Anderson in his mellifluent baritone.

You always hurt—ad—dee-dum-dum,
Thewhan—dum-dee-dum—you love—dum-dee-dum,
Thewhan—dum-dum—yashydenthurt—atallll—

"Not everyone is so lucky to be the posthumous child of an age," Molly Post continued. "You're the only one here who's been called upon to define the citadel of culture, the bastion of taste and grace."

"I don't know what you're talking about," Post said, offended. He finished the apple and threw the core into the hearth of the fireplace. His face had turned red.

"You know, Leo, you know," Molly Post replied. "I don't want to be the last of a species—I'm not built that way. The pride of the dinosaurs, I am not." Her tone was firm but there was an affable glint in her eyes. "Nor do I intend to play Martha the pigeon. Oh, yes, I will take risks and do crazy things, but uppermost in this little bird's brain is a pulse that keeps sending out a signal—stay alive—stay alive."

Post took a deep breath. "Everything has changed then," he said with a certain finality.

"What's changed?" his wife asked quickly and approached him. The large green eyes searched the man's face, a nearsighted attempt to read his expression.

"We have become different," Post said sadly. "You accuse me of a passion that rose to kill you, but that same passion has brought you back even though you fear it."

"Yes."

"Perhaps you find it too risky—love."

"Oh, risky love," Sneat chimed in. "I feel a song coming on." The policewoman put a hand over his mouth.

"Perhaps I should have played along, left you in ignorance. I really don't want to hurt you," Molly Post said.

"You're more honest than I would be," the undercover agent said. "Of course, dissemblance is part of my heritage, my protective coloration, you might say—then there's my professional training." Her voice was as matter-of-fact as a court document.

"I'm willing to take the risks," Molly Post said, ruffling her hair. "I'm willing to risk your passion. After all, life is a matter of alteration, subject to no return." She stopped, looked expectantly at Leo Post's back. The slope of his shoulders pulled back a little. His head raised.

"That sounds familiar," he said.

"One of your own lines," Pickett Sneat told him glumly. "It's from 'Pocahontas, Come Home,' one of the flattest bottles of soda you ever capped," the book reviewer said.

"My goodness," the author said and smiled expansively, clearly pleased by his work being introduced into the discussion.

"No." She palmed him away from herself, almost carelessly. "You have to understand me, Leo. It's not the risks I fear—they make the whole enterprise interesting. More than anyone in this room, I know how close death lies to the surface, and that makes the turf even sweeter. Wait a minute." She furled the cloak around herself. "Remember the Governor's first campaign? That time in Kinderhook. Martin Van Buren's grave?" A saturnine cunning had slipped over the author's countenance that momentarily revealed his Middle Eastern ancestry. "A wild time, wasn't it?" Molly Post prodded his remembrance.

"What was it? What was it?" Pickett Sneat pulled himself erect within his harness.

"Just a small detour into history," Post told his colleague. Mrs. Post turned away with a knowing smile. "A reception was being held in Kinderhook for Kimball Lyon, boring as they all are. Molly and I slipped away to pay our respects to the remains of our eighth president. On the site of his grave, I explained to her the origin of the term *OK*, sometimes spelled *okay* and standing—the story goes—for Old Kinderhook, a pseudonymity assumed by Van Buren as boss of the Regency Democrats of New York. Memoranda or statements prepared by subordinates would be acknowledged by the initials *OK* scrawled on them. This marginalia shorthand of Van Buren's came to symbolize approval and eventually entered the language—all languages—as an expressions of agreement or—"

"Okey—okeh—okeh," Sneat said wearily. "We get it."

Our attention had been momentarily shifted toward the book reviewer so we did not actually see Mrs. Post throw herself into the arms of her husband, but only heard the affectionate gurgle of her laughter and the flurry of the couple's heavy costumes as they embraced, eyes closed. Abruptly, Leo Post pulled away from his wife, interrupting the deep-throated cooing one or both had been making.

"This won't do—I won't do," he said. He walked back to the table, leading his wife, and sat down heavily. Molly Post stood beside the chair. "You say you have returned to risk my passion, and yet there is a difference now between us."

"The difference, *mon professeur*," his wife rested her cheek against the shiny top of his head, and the author was suddenly be-wigged by the fall of her auburn hair. He appeared like the magistrate in a musical comedy routine. "The difference is that I will no longer sit still like your pigeon friends and let you clobber me when your adoration and wonder of me overwhelms you. I can remember my history. Maybe I'll fly back when your ardor cools off—like this time—but maybe not. The difference is I have learned to use my wings—to escape."

"But to extend the metaphor," Post said brightly, "it was I who taught you to fly."

"And to dispose of that metaphor—so what?"

"Hot dog!" cheered Sgt. Anderson.

"But you'd be alone," Post persisted.

"Sure," his wife agreed, "maybe even lonely, but I would be alive, baby."

"Yeah." The policewoman thumped Pickett Sneat on his head.

From the onset of this exchange, I, B. Smith, a careful spectator, had witnessed a pattern of anxiety in the persona of the man called Taylor. This behavior was manifested by the many occasions he took to refer to a large watch he would pull from a vest pocket. As the meal and subsequent colloquy ensued, these time checks occurred with increasing frequency. Apprehension tautened his stoic expression.

"There's another difference," Mrs. Post was saying gently as she stroked her husband's aristocratic cranium. "You no longer awe me."

"There's a kind of freedom in that, I admit. But do I get the idea that you will accompany me back to the city"—he kissed her—"to take a stand with me no matter how futile"—another kiss—"to risk all?"

"My dear romantic," Mrs. Post responded airily. "Of course I am going with you, but with this understanding. If I see that taxidermic look come into you eyes—I'm gone."

"Agreed," Leo Post murmured into her hair and then kissed her on the lips.

Their armchairs creaked and several candles sputtered as the flames drowned in their own wax. Hesitantly, the owl crooned in the garden, and the vines rustled outside. Seemingly immune to the tender accoutrements of this scene, the man called Taylor had once again pulled forth the heavy pocket watch, flipped open its cover, checked the time, and snapped the watch closed. The metallic click startled the entwined couple.

"Excuse me, Mr. Post," Taylor said through tight lips, "but about that fuse."

"The fuse," the author responded hazily. The man was clearly suffused in the deepest of sensations, and his dark eyes turned like great black olives in luxurious oil. A gradual and somewhat frightening transformation began in his feet and worked slowly up his frame from knee to hip and then up the torso to loose its energy at the shoulder. His arms flung out. "The fuse? Zeus betrayed! I forgot the fuse. How much time do we have?" he shouted.

"What—what is it?" Molly Post said. The party had all stood except for Pickett Sneat and I, B. Smith, thoroughly bound and therefore unable to exert my legal force.

"All that black powder—tons of it," Post exclaimed. "No time to explain. I told Taylor to lay down a fuse and a timer to explode after we had left the island."

"But you have explained," Molly Post said, still a little dreamy.

"But we got to talking," the author said with a shrug.

"You mean YOU got to talking," his co-conspirator accused. "There's the danger of a romantic." The book reviewer stabbed a finger in the air. "The windage factor. Ah well." He rubbed his face against Sgt. Anderson's bosom. "It's all over now. Good night, moon."

"We're splitting." Sgt. Anderson wheeled Sneat's chair full circle and pushed him toward the curtained alcove. The stone floor quivered, and a rumbling was heard from deep in the castle's dungeon. The Posts ran after the other couple, pausing in the doorway for the author to shout, "Come, Taylor! Quickly!"

The man called Taylor moved hurriedly to the arch, gave the chamber a last, sweeping scrutiny, and then disappeared through the arras. A scrim of mortar fell from the ceiling. I, B. Smith, helpless at the occasion, awaited the apocalypse.

BEFORE SUNRISE

A huge tanker, loaded to the gunwales and pushing hard against the current, had simulated the vibrations of impending disaster. The magazine of black powder lodged in the bowels of Leek's Castle did not explode, though the antique ammunition retained an essence of its original power sufficient to launch several large, noxious bubbles to the surface of the lagoon, where they burst to defile the morning air with sickening fumes.

The taxi-powered craft bobbed and punched the stone wharf to which it had been tied in the furious backwash of the ship's passage upriver. On the small quay, large amounts of goods from the surplus stores had been assembled, and Leo Post and his guests passed these down to the man called Taylor, who fitted them into the trunk of the improvised ferry. Several boxes were strapped to the taxi's top, and large cargo containers were fixed on the ferry's deck.

The perpetrators to this conspiracy stood in line to pass the contraband along, hand to hand, each person using only one hand as the other was fixed to the nose to mask the putrid odor that had bubbled up from the ruin's nether regions. I, B. Smith, an involuntary witness to these fugitive actions, was overcome by the fetid gasses, and my subsequent report cannot be verified. A peculiar intoxication overcame us to suspend all data evaluation.

"Whew," Leo Post sighed after a deep breath. With both hands, he turned over a carton of biscuits to Sgt. Anderson, who passed them along to Pickett Sneat who, in turn, thrust them at Mrs. Post, who then tossed them down to the man called Taylor. The book reviewer stood in his braces with the assistance of tubular crutches. A fevered excitement acted upon the company with the tempo of a leave-taking.

"And once again, Leo," Sneat's voice bounced off the encircling walls of the castle. "What of Smith?" His question halted the group's activity, and their faces turned up to regard us. We had been installed on one of the balconies overlooking the lagoon and the inner courtyard. "May I suggest his appointment has come to an end?"

"We shall leave him to the elements," Leo Post told his associates. "In short, Smith has done all we have asked and therefore deserves his freedom. Smith will be sovereign of this castle, this island."

"It might even become known as Smith's Island." Molly Lyon Post laughed.

"Why not?" Leo Post agreed, lifting down a sack of cornmeal.

"I've always meant to ask you about the original name of this island," his wife continued as she received a stack of plastic dishes and tableware from him. "Pijon Island. What does that mean in Dutch?"

"Ah, but you see," Post said, not losing his turn in the supply line. "That isn't Dutch. No. This island had been a halfway point, a rest stop if you will, for the Mohawks on the long canoe ride downriver. During one of those riverside exchanges that were the delightful subjects of eighteenth century engravers, Henry

Hudson asked the Indians what they called the island. The natives mumbled something and the ship's scribe took down something approximate to what he heard—Pijon Island."

"And the *j* is silent, of course," Sneat said.

"Of course," Post replied.

"And all this time, I thought it had something to do with pigeons," Molly Post said.

"Not everything has to do with pigeons," her husband said, and handed her a package of fishhooks.

"Well, almost everything," Sneat rumbled. He handed the fishhooks off to Sgt. Anderson, casually kissing her under her left ear. It should be recorded that both women had changed into more practical clothing: pants, layered shirts, and vests. "Indeed, I would make a guess," the book reviewer continued, while making a courtly bow toward Mrs. Post, "that this mission to Manhattan, the whole attack on the Self-Propelled Expressway, has something to do with pigeons. Right?"

Leo Post had started a box of prisms on its way down the line. Reflections of the splintered light dappled the inner walls of Leek's castle as the collection passed from hand to hand, spectra darting and swooping as if the ruin had just become the nesting place of thousands of gaily plumaged birds. Finally the flock of colors was trapped by the man called Taylor and put into a storage bin on the craft's deck.

"He's not going to tell us," Molly Post said.

"He's going to tell us," Sneat assured them. "If he expects us to drift down to the city with him, he will tell us." He passed a carton of tent pins.

Post had just handed down to Sgt. Anderson a carton of tinned liver paste and set himself on a crate of preserved apricots, dusting his hands. The raft bumped and nudged the stone landing.

A rooster crowed in the distance, and a dog barked on the near shore. Birds twittered and called to each other. These sounds, like the details of a large tapestry, placed themselves against the continuous wash of traffic on the Expressway overhead. The author was regarding his companions benevolently as he adjusted the blue silk neckcloth at his throat. He also had changed clothes, wearing the same dark blazer and flannel slacks, the luminous white shoes that he had worn when we first arrived. Each actor had taken a seat on the boxes and crates placed on the dock. The man called Taylor leaned against the fender of the modified taxi, gently rising and falling on the lagoon's swell.

"When Martha toppled from her perch in the Cincinnati Zoo," Post began, "it was reported as the final fall of a passenger pigeon, the solitary plummet of a species that had been brought down by the millions in places like Mauston, Wisconsin. For weeks before her death, her cage at the zoo had been roped off to keep the public at a distance, since she had a bad heart and any disturbance might cause her death. Therefore, that the end of a species was imminent was popular knowledge—in fact, it could be witnessed, observed. The death of a species. It would be an important news story, one would think. However, when that soft body crashed to the floor of the cage, to be gathered up quickly, you'll remember, and packed in three hundred pounds of chipped ice for shipment to the Smithsonian, it received scant notice in the media.

"The date was September 1, 1914," Post said, standing up. He went to a thick, worn portfolio and thumbed through its contents. "World War I had only just begun, and the newspapers were overwhelmed by the reports of the first battles—the beginning of another kind of extinction."

"I feel a parallel coming on," Pickett Sneat murmured to Sgt. Anderson. "As one species expired, another began to kill itself off."

"Yes, I thought of that," the author said good-humoredly. From a mass of clippings he singled one out. "The day after, September 2, 1914, the *Cincinnati Enquirer* carried the story. Page three, the bottom of column two, and listen to this headline— LAST. That's all—LAST." He crooned the word.

"Well, what does it say?" Sneat asked impatiently.

Post began to read the old newsprint. "'Martha is dead. In one great respect she resembled Chingachgook, the last of the Mohicans, for she was the last of the passenger pigeons. No other inhabitant of the zoo could claim greater distinction than she, for during the past 15 years there had been a standing offer of $1,000 for a mate for Martha, but none could be found.' "

"That's part of the trouble right there," Sgt. Anderson interrupted. "Who would collect the bucks for shacking up with that old bird—the buck pigeon or its keeper?" Sneat regarded the police agent with suspicion. Then, he turned back to Post.

"Go on," the book reviewer urged.

"Well, also on page three, for the benefit of those Cincinnati citizens of German origin, was a reprint from New York's *Staats-Zeitung*, regarding the war from the Kaiser's viewpoint."

"Interesting," Sneat said.

"Yes, and there's more," the author said, advancing upon them, both hands full of serpentine slivers of newsprint to look like the head priest of an odd cult. As he had distributed the provisions earlier, he now apportioned the clippings among his friends. "Let's see what else was happening the week of September 1, 1914," Post told them. He handed out some of the reportage to each. "Here's the *New York Times* for you, the *World* for you. You get the *Herald*. And there's the *Tribune* and the *Sun* for these readers."

"We know what the big news was on that date." He resumed his perch on the packing crate. "The German Army was in Belgium and advancing easily into France. But what was the rest of the news on September 2nd, after Martha fell off her perch?"

"Well, here's a long and dreary poem by Rudyard Kipling on the front page of the *Times*," Pickett Sneat said, peering at the yellowed newsprint. "'For All We Have and Are' is the title. You don't expect me to read it, do you—I mean, Kipling after all? The man was in decline in 1914."

"Here's a report of German soldiers cutting off the hands of Belgian boys," Sgt. Anderson said, ignoring the book reviewer.

"But the *Sun* carries an interview," Molly Post held up a clipping, "with Mrs. Benjamin Harrison, the widow of the president, and Mrs. Philip H. Sheridan, widow of the general. Both had just arrived on the *Ryndam* from Germany, and each described the great courtesies and kindnesses shown them in Germany. Fruit and flowers were presented by local *burgermeisters* and the like."

"Seems like the French had made these little steel arrows," the man called Taylor spoke without looking up from his newspaper. "They'd drop them from aeroplanes. These arrows could go right through a man—helmet and all."

"Secretary of State William Jennings Bryan," Post announced in a stentorian manner, "has telegraphed his thanks to General Pancho Villa for keeping things quiet in the State of Sonora." The author paused and added in an undertone, "We're keeping an eye on Mexico. The navy's holding Veracruz."

"And John D. Rockefeller is to get a compromise from the tax collector of Cleveland on the twelve million dollars he owes in overdue taxes." The book reviewer spoke from the corner of his mouth.

"So what else is new?" Sgt. Anderson asked.

"Here's a lyrical note in the *Times*," Molly Post said. "Idlers at the Café Americain on the Boulevard des Capuchins observe a lone aeroplane approach Paris from the south, switch off its engine, and glide down the evening air as the pilot tosses out a bomb from the height of 1,500 feet. It was thought to be aimed at the Bourne and narrowly missed the offices of the *New York Times*."

"*Tant pis*," Sneat observed.

"That was to become a regular evening ritual," Post told them. "Residents of Paris would picnic on the heights of the city to observe the aerial acrobatics of these remarkable new flying machines. *Quel sportif*! But no report yet of Martha and her last flight? Oh, yes, the Cardinals are meeting in Rome to elect a new pope."

"Here's another social note," announced Sgt. Anderson. "The *Times* lists those who have arrived safely at White Sulfur Springs, West Virginia, to take the baths and medicinal waters."

"Behind the big bat of Ty Cobb," Taylor glumly reported, "the Tigers beat the Yankees, 3-2."

"Right. So much for the day after," Post told them, flipping through the bunch of clippings in his hand. "Let's look at September 3rd, 1914." The others made hasty adjustments of their clippings. "Calamitous news," the author exclaimed. "The French have moved their capital to Bordeaux. The German army is closing in on Paris, but the citizens remain calm. The cafés are full."

"Civil libertarians and decent citizens of the world protest the bombing of Antwerp by zeppelins," Sgt. Anderson proclaimed.

"And here's another outrage." Sneat shuffled the strips of newsprint in his hands. "Mrs. George Washington Goethals, wife of the builder and now governor of the recently opened Panama Canal, has been detained and molested by French troops. Mrs. Goethals, a native of Germany, speaks German fluently—which means she speaks English with a thick German accent. But after some embarrassment, she was able to prove her identity and was released. Ruffled but unbowed, I would wager," the book reviewer added.

"After several votes, the cardinals have yet to choose a new pope," Molly Lyon reported.

"The wallpaper hangers have decided to go on strike again," Post said thoughtfully.

"A band of traveling Sioux Indians were badly mauled by a mob in Munich," announced Pickett Sneat. "Seems they were members of a visiting American circus, but some of the populace took them for spies—all that war paint and feathered costumes probably," he said to Post.

"The *Times* does have a report of a death, and that's interesting—it's by a fall, too," Sgt. Anderson said. "A young stockbroker fell from the fifth-floor window of a young lady's apartment at three in the morning after an evening of dinner, theatre, and a round of nightspots. The young lady, according to the coroner's report, said her escort had sought relief from the oppressive heat, had opened the window, and had accidentally tumbled out. Smile-smile."

"Same incident is reported in the *New York Herald*." Molly Post laughed. "In this account she tells the coroner about the heat and how she sat the young man in a chair and loosened his clothes to cool him off and read to him from a novel. She fell asleep reading the novel and woke up to find him gone—out the window."

"What novel was it, do you suppose? Something from England perhaps," Post wondered.

"Or something recommended by Paul Elmer Moore," the book reviewer said, his eyes in slits.

"Moving on," Leo Post directed them, "there was a double electrocution at Sing Sing. Every paper has a story on that."

"Here's an item in the *World*." Sgt. Anderson stood up. "Dateline: Bay Springs, Mississippi. A black man named Mose Johnson was hanged in public for the murder of a lumber company paymaster. Seven thousand people attended the hanging. The main street was turned into a midway, booths and bazaars set up. Picnic tables and barbecues. The paper says that Mr. Johnson was pleased by the turnout, and as the noose was slipped over his head, he said, 'So long, people, I'll meet you in heaven.'"

"The Yankees," Taylor began to read, but was interrupted by his employer.

"Here's what we're looking for." Leo Post held up a small piece of paper. "First appeared in the evening *Post*. Page seven. 'Last of a Winged Race Gone.' It's a small notice quoting the secretary of the Audubon Society on Martha's demise. It says, 'An ornithological wonder of the world is no more.' Here, read it for yourself." The company scanned the obituary in silence except for Taylor, who cleared his throat several times. "All right, Taylor, what is it?" Post asked at last.

"It's the Yankees," the former rodeo star said. "They lost again, 6–5."

"On to September 4th," Post commanded, and the group dutifully rearranged their files.

"It's Pope Benedict XV!" cheered Pickett Sneat, waving his crutch.

"It turns out it wasn't Mrs. Goethals," Molly Post said with relief. "Mrs. Goethals hadn't been to France in over a year, so it wasn't she who was molested by French troops as had been reported earlier."

"The *Tribune* says that the Society of Professors of Dancing has determined the foxtrot and the tango are too difficult for the public to try." Sgt. Anderson read from a news clipping as she rose and began to turn slowly, arms above her head and back arched. The small audience whistled and clapped their hands in tempo with her fast steps.

"Okay," Leo Post said softly. "But there's real trouble brewing in Mexico. Their new president has asked us to pull our navy out of Veracruz, and Zapata is making ominous moves in the south. Concern raises about the trustworthiness of this fellow Villa."

"Here's a certainty," his wife announced. "Prince Frederick William of Lippe shot himself. And we have this shocking news from Lady Randolph Churchill, who has been quoted in the telegram. Seems like his soldiers mistakenly attacked and killed other German troops. He shot himself before his father, the Kaiser, discovered the mistake."

"A note in the *Sun*." Sneat reviewed the clipping in hand. "Lord William Percy, sportsman and naturalist—isn't that a contradiction?" he asked, then continued—"during a field trip in the Yukon bagged a spectacled eider duck. The bird was thought to be extinct."

"Perhaps Lord Percy wanted to be sure of its classification," Leo Post suggested.

"Wait, I have it," Molly Post cried excitedly. "Here it is. Page four of the *New York Herald*, a small note and maybe a reprint of the piece in yesterday's *Post*. It sources the Audubon Society. The last of the wild pigeons that had flown in the millions, it says."

"Right." Post nodded as if he had been proved right about something. "Taylor, how are those Yankees doing?" The man shook his head. "So let's turn to Saturday, September 5th. How's the war going?"

"The Russians are mopping up the Austrians," Sgt. Anderson reported. "Vienna is threatened by famine. Berlin said to be vulnerable."

"The entrance of Turkey on the side of the Central Powers is thought to force Japan to side with the Allies—so says the *Telegram*." Sneat spoke with authority.

"The Kaiser and the Crown Prince view the German army as it launches a huge attack, unexpectedly swings left to bypass Paris," Molly Post read from a story in the *New York Sun*. "Some experts see the maneuver as similar to the strategy by which Grant took Richmond."

"Are the Yankees still losing?" Post asked the man called Taylor?

"To the Senators," the man replied morosely.

"Here's a social note in the *New York Times*." Molly Post leaned toward Pickett Sneat. "The Kaiser's name has been removed from the list of nominations for the Nobel Peace Prize."

"An egregious mistake, no doubt," the book reviewer countered. "But on the business page of the same paper, we read that the Valley Forge Cutlery Company has gone bankrupt."

"But nothing about Martha in the *Times*?" asked Sgt. Anderson.

"Clearly her news didn't fit," Post told them. "Perhaps if Lord William Percy had sauntered into the Cincinnati Zoo and shot Martha off her perch—that would have made the *New York Times*. But for her to simply totter to the ground, the last of the last—"

"Hey, I have it this time," Sgt. Anderson said, a clipping held high about her head. "It's an editorial in the *New York Tribune*."

"And a rather thoughtful piece too, don't you agree?" His familiarity with the articles suggested his preparation for this review of the archive. "The writer suggests the passenger pigeon had become the victim of man's senseless waste and greed and steps should be taken to preserve other wildlife similarly threatened."

"This may be the appropriate time to introduce the casualty lists for the first week in September, 1914." Pickett Sneat chuckled and assumed a forced innocence.

"Irving S. Cobb and other noted correspondents were briefly detained, then released by the German forces. Cobb amused everyone, it was reported, with his imitations." Molly Lyon Post summed up an article. "Who was Irving S. Cobb?"

"On the other hand," her husband retorted, "Walter Lippman is still missing in the war zone, and the Germans have taken Rheims."

"All fronts combined," Sneat announced, "over three hundred thousand dead or wounded."

"—and one pigeon," Sgt. Anderson added.

"*Penrod* has gone into its fourth printing—ten-thousand copies so far." Molly Post thumbed through the newspaper cuttings.

"The German High Command is amused by the state of hostility threatened by the Prince of Monaco." Post let the clipping drop into the wastebin, then also dumped the rest he held. "Well, there's no more."

"No more?" Sneat asked, suddenly alert.

"About the pigeon, I mean," Post told him. "No more news items."

"You mean the death of the last passenger pigeon never made the *New York Times?*" Astonishment had captured the book reviewer's expression.

"Couldn't find room for it, I guess," Post told the group.

"Just a minute." Molly Post stepped forward. Her teeth flashed as she smiled. "Was this baroque survey of trivia to prove that Martha's death in Cincinnati was never reported in the *New York Times*, the paper of record, and so therefore and quite possibly—it never happened?" She looked about the group with a triumphant expression.

"Oh, it happened, all right. It happened," Post assured them with a glint in his dark eyes.

"But she was not the last pigeon," the policewoman spoke deductively.

"Therefore," Sneat continued her cadence, "the *Times* would only consider it as just one more pigeon death and think it unimportant, not worthy of note."

"Then there's that fella in the Yukon that shot the last of the speckled duck." The voice of the man called Taylor startled the group; then he sat down awkwardly on a barrel roped to the raft's stern.

As if this abrupt pause, this aperture in the proceedings, had been waited on, an unearthly sound slipped through the battlements of the old castle. Slowly the sounds assembled into the song of a crewmember of a boat that passed slowly downstream, with the current and outgoing tide. The melody was distorted as the bulk of the ruin eclipsed the passing ship that made the voice incorporeal. The seaman eulogized upland meadows and trackless shores, his voice carried downstream with his bark to be muffled, to disappear, into the morning drisk.

"Ah." Leo Post spoke after a little and sighed deeply. "That's what I will miss about this river. The great contrasts—one minute the foulest of decomposition smothers the senses and the next you are enchanted by celestial music."

"That can happen anywhere," his co-conspirator responded glumly. He walked to the edge of the pier and spat into the water. He moved easily as if his legs were light and the crutches under his arms unnecessary. "Choirs built in a boneyard. A chorus from the garbage dump."

"But singing still." Molly Post jumped up. Her face had flushed prettily. "Singing," she repeated forcefully, and turned to her husband as if for approval. Post nodded and smiled. The couple embraced as an eerie flapping disturbed the calm. A flight of starlings had arrived in the corner tower. "Now, Leo," she implored.

"Very well," the author agreed. "In a memoir he wrote for his family, the remarkable Audubon noted that he netted and carried some 350 live passenger pigeons to England. This was in 1830. Audubon says he gave some of them to the Zoological Society of London, but distributed the rest to different noblemen. The annual report of the Zoological Society for the year 1830 more or less confirms this transfer, though it does not cite the name of the donor. *Columbia migratoria* is listed among the living specimens of the society's collection.

"In 1833," Post continued, "the Zoological Society reports a pair of these pigeons built a nest and bred. A young bird was hatched in sixteen days. Another instance of breeding by a pair of pigeons was accounted in the private menagerie of the society's president. Then nothing more. Either the Society lost its records on these birds or failed to keep a record of them, but according to their librarian, the passenger pigeon appears no more in their inventories."

"So they did not survive," Molly Post said.

"It would seem so," Post agreed, "at least on paper."

"What about the birds he gave to the noblemen?" Sneat asked.

"What about them?" Post echoed his colleague's question as the cunning look of the Levantine suffused his face. Sneat shook his carrot-fringed head. "Yes," the author filled in the book reviewer's speculation. "Imagine a couple of hundred of these birds placed on the estates of the English upper class. Perhaps, Audubon had a presentment of their fate and put some of them on this island, this England, for their preservation. A sort of sanitary exile. Where they mated and nested in the English woodlands."

"Hah?" Sneat snorted. "You've described them migrating thousands of miles. England is but a fraction of that distance in length. Are you saying they flew around its perimeter several times for their exercise?" The book reviewer chuckled and looked wisely at Sgt. Anderson. He had made a point.

"Of course not," Post responded loftily.

"They flew back to North America." Molly Post supplied the answer as if in a trance.

"What?" Sneat cried. "Impossible."

"Yes, and nothing extraordinary in such a feat," Post told them. "There are numerous accounts of similar flights. E.G.F. Sauer in a *Scientific American* of 1958 reports two instances of long-distance flights by disoriented birds. Starlings were removed from their nests near Berlin and released twelve hundred miles away. They flew right back. More pertinent, a Manx Shearwater was taken from its nest on the west coast of England, flown to Boston, and released. Exactly twelve days and 3,067 miles later it was back in its nest in England."

"How do they find their way?" Sneat asked.

"Some form of celestial navigation. Pigeons particularly seem to have an inborn sense of time that accounts for the sun's position. They use it as a compass. Definite experiments indicate migrating birds use the stars at night similarly. And on rainy days? I see the question on your face, Pickett. No one knows that answer, but there are a few theories, and the most acceptable of these suggests that the birds respond to the earth's magnetic field, fix their location and direction by some sense that interprets the varying force of the magnetic wavelengths. Various tests point that way."

"You're saying that the descendants of those birds that Audubon took to England," Molly Post jabbed an elegant finger into the palm of her hand, "the ones he put on the estates of the gentry, are flying back and forth, over the Atlantic, from England to here. But I thought you said they flew only north and south. Not east and west."

"Yes," Post replied with an easy deference. "They probably go over the polar cap."

"THE PASSENGER PIGEON LIVES," Pickett Sneat shouted, his face turned cherry red. His outcry startled a burst of sparrows that peppered the flat morning sky. The book reviewer had even raised both crutch-braced arms and stood unassisted. Convulsive laughter choked him and he had to re-employ the crutches to stake his heaving frame. "What maniacal drollery, Post," he gasped. "What nonsense, what foolish imagination."

"What evidence do you have for this assertion?" Sgt. Anderson demanded. I, B. Smith, the official of record present, file a letter of commendation noting the policewoman's reasoning under stress.

"Well, you will remember that offer of a thousand dollars made by the Cincinnati Zoo to find a mate for Martha?" Leo Post had turned to the policewoman, ignoring the group's whistles and sniggers. "Hundreds of responses. Supposedly passenger pigeons were seen in Texas, in Mexico, in northern Canada. None turned out to be the species. And one response was so fantastic that the zoo authorities never bothered to answer. The lonely and the deranged always answer such inquiries—the so-called nut category—and these responses were promptly filed in that folder. About a dozen pigeon sightings were claimed from the same locale—every spring up until Martha's death."

After what seemed like a serious deliberation with herself, Sgt. Anderson drew a deep breath and asked the question that was clearly on everyone's mind. Even I, B. Smith, usually with all the answers, wondered. "And where were these pigeons sighted?"

"In Madison Square Park," Leo Post said simply. "New York City."

"—and Madison Square Park," Molly Post pronounced dully, "is at the corner of Fifth Avenue and 23rd Street—right in the path of the proposed access spur of the Self-Propelled Expressway." Molly Post laughed and embraced her husband. "My dear ringmaster—it's not the Hotel Chelsea you're trying to save, but the last of this bird."

"Well, keeping the hotel where it is will be an extra dividend," the author said modestly, and looked over her shoulder at Pickett Sneat. He winked.

The book reviewer hung slackly between the pair of crutches so he resembled a large pinkish bat at rest. The police person rolled her eyes and the man called Taylor took in the scene with mouth open. Finally Sgt. Anderson regained her official senses.

"How did you come on this information?" she asked.

"Among the pitiful chattels of my father's estate," Leo Post told them as he lifted from the heap of used material a small traveling kit in dark leather. "Among those items preserved for me by the maiden aunts who raised me was—a paisley scarf." He held the article up. "A gold earring." He continued the inventory from the case. "Assorted small vials of alabaster, smelling of musk and vanilla. A copy of *The Prophet* inscribed by Gibran to my friend Emil Nalbandian—"

"That might be worth a few pennies," the book reviewer figured.

"—numerous invitations to tea parties, the cards scented and properly scripted, a lacquered cigarette box, a well-thumbed copy of Ely Culbertson's *Rules for Contract Bridge*—the chapter on the no-trump bid heavily underlined—"

"Suspicious scholarship indeed," Pickett Sneat muttered.

"And then," Post continued undisturbed, "this book." He held a small volume aloft. "*Rainy Day Projects for Boys and Girls.*"

Molly Post peered at the faded cover. "Oh, Leo, vintage pornography—how quaint."

"No, not the book." The author corrected her sharply. "Not the book, but what it contains, slipped within its pages." He opened its pages and took out several sheets of typescript. "These are carbons of letters, all addressed to the Cincinnati Zoo and all written by the same correspondent. Each one reports the existence of passenger pigeons in Madison Square Park and requests prompt payment of the thousand-dollar reward. Signed by a G.A. Lewis, an old-time resident of the Chelsea Hotel. Lewis was a collector of rare books, and much of his collection was bequeathed to the library across the street from the hotel."

"With the exception of this volume, of course," Pickett Sneat said a little too casually.

"Which the old man, just before his death, gave to his next-door neighbor at the hotel—a young man who had been kind to him, perhaps spoke a few words to him in the dim corridor outside their adjoining rooms. My father. It was Lewis' intention to reward my father with the secret of the pigeons, so that he could claim the reward. The old man had often observed them during his sabbaticals in the park on sunny days. Of course, he had in his collection an original issue of Audubon's *Birds of North America* and made the identification." Post had returned the volume with its inserts to the small case and handed everything down to Taylor, who stored it on the raft.

"I feel a plot coming on," the book reviewer told Sgt. Anderson. "The old man recognizes the bird, verifies its existence by the Audubon prints in his collection, and happily observes the local sportsmen and naturalists who feed them with peanuts and old crusts of Wonder bread. They don't notice the differences from other pigeons—the long tails, for example, and the vivid coloring on the breast, but he does, and now—" Picket Sneat faced Sgt. Anderson. "Post is about to tell us the birds are still in the park."

"Only in season, of course," the author said pleasantly, "and specifically in the vicinity of the statue of Roscoe Conkling." He assumed a statesmanlike pose.

"Who was Roscoe Conkling?" Sgt. Anderson asked suspiciously.

Sneat pivoted about again, a crooked smile on his face. "So you're saying that the Madison Square Park is the spot to make a stand against the Self-Propelled Expressway. Idiot," he fumed at Post. "You and the pigeons are going to challenge that leviathan that Lyon set loose that gobbles up whole villages and complete neighborhoods to leave nothing in its wake but freshly laid cement? Fool," he said, almost to himself.

Post strolled over and placed an arm around the book reviewer's shoulders. The taxi-raft gently nosed against the landing. "Pickett, our mistake was to try to contain Lyon's madness with his own methods. His adoration of power became our affection, too, so we became victims and prisoners of it by the simple act of sharing. His irrational appetite fed on our rational fiber. And all the while we had the antidote, the alternative right before us— you had suggested the cure originally." Author and book reviewer stared at each other—strangers making a common recognition.

"Yes," Post said, as if to encourage the growth of the idea in Sneat's consciousness.

"You're crazy," the other finally said.

"All of that," Post agreed, though he pulled himself away as if offended. His wife had been following the exchange with a quizzical cast in her eyes, and their eyes met. Her long, elliptical eyes blinked. "But singing," the author offered, and his gentle tone yet commanded. He took his wife's hand in his. "You may start the engine, Mr. Taylor," he ordered.

The cowboy-turned-ferryboat-captain disappeared into the car's front, the driver's side, and the engine turned over. "Pickett," Post addressed him. "The nourishment in Tut's tomb is as fresh, as life giving, as the day it was placed there, but the funeral-roasted meats and baked pastries left beside the mummy became dust long ago. You and I," Post held forth his arms, "chose the tangible over the intangible, and when it became dust in our mouths, we blamed the cook—Kimball Lyon."

"You ask too much of me, Leo," the book reviewer said, slowly wheeling himself toward Sgt. Anderson. "The mold that cast me was commonplace, unheroic." He lay back in the policewoman's arms and both regarded Leo Post with dubious expressions.

"Well, then come partway with me," Leo Post suggested. He unbuttoned and buttoned the blazer. "How refreshing to have a little cruise down the river, to drift through the haze, separated at least for a while from the cares of the shore, from the restrictions of the waterline." The taxi's engine continued to gurgle contentedly. The author's somber reflection swept over the balcony where we had just been positioned. Still secured. "In any event, it would be better than staying here with Smith." And the five faces below all turned toward us.

"What's the answer?" the book reviewer wanted to know.

"There is no answer, Pick—that's the answer." Leo Post went to the edge of the landing and pulled on a mooring line. "There are only the same problems and how we adapt to them. Adaptation is the answer; there is no solution. We are sailors on a boat perceiving our destination only as we proceed toward it."

"What's this?" asked Molly Post. Her long red hair swung forward as she stooped to lift a squarish object wrapped in a cloth.

"What is this?" she repeated with a smile that became more generous as she unwrapped the bronze plaque.

EMIL NALBANDIAN
Pioneer of Contract Bridge
Resided Here

"An incidental task." Post dismissed her find, though he looked a little guilty. "Perhaps you might call it an exercise in vanity. I thought when we come ashore in Manhattan, and as we pass the Chelsea, on our way to Madison Park—"

"Oh, get on with it, Leo." Sneat rattled his metal embrasures. "You want to put that marker on the Chelsea."

"There must be a little space left," the author said and looked away.

"That does it," the book reviewer roared. His laughter bounced off the walls of the ruin. "I'll go with you just to see you do that. And I'm a little curious about finding those birds in the park, so I'll hang around just to see how it comes out."

"Splendid." Leo Post clapped the man on his shoulder. "Lucy? What about you?"

The policewoman gently pushed away from her stool. Her face mixed disbelief with temptation. Post continued to speak in a kindly manner. "I know it's not your main interest, but your position as an undercover agent has been blown. You have been compromised."

"I'll go along for the ride, but once we get to the city, no telling what I'll do. You say hope is there, and I've had those expectations every way and Wednesday. But I'll get on board— what the hell, and there's no way of knowing what will happen when I get there."

"I'm with her," Molly Post said suddenly. Her husband looked startled. "No, don't give me that betrayed look," she told him. "I never promised you anything but a little frenzy."

"You said you returned to risk my nature," Post reminded her. He signaled to the man called Taylor to turn off the craft's engine.

The ensuing silence became tense, massaged by the rippling water of the lagoon. A morning breeze played through the vines of ivy.

"Your nature, yes," the woman answered. She had taken up a challenging pose similar to the posture worn by Yellow Hat. "But that monster you and I helped to launch, my infamous stepfather—that's something else." Her finger made Post flinch slightly.

"That's a marvelous idea," she continued, "to confront disaster straight on, confront fate by going to meet it. But whose fate are you talking about? A while back you talked about moving me to one side so the arrow destined for me might miss—"

"But?" Post looked winded and sat down on a box of crackers.

"All you were doing was moving me into a larger target for a more certain disaster and one of your own making." She smiled, but her large green eyes measured the author coolly. "There's something else that disturbs me, too. And perhaps Lucy shares my distrust."

The company waited for her to continue, but she turned away from them to regard the raft and the guileless expression of the man called Taylor. "It's this penchant you have for admiring last survivors—it worries me a little," she said evenly. "That headline you quoted from the story of Martha's death. LAST. You'd like that for your own obituary, wouldn't you? Last."

"Or Post," Sneat offered, and looked pleased with the contribution.

"You picture yourself," Molly Lyon Post continued, sweeping the long lank of her russet hair over her right shoulder, "as the last hiker on the Appalachian Trail, riding the last wagon out of St. Joe, the last train out of Laredo, standing with the last pigeon in the park. Well." She looked to Sgt. Anderson, who had begun to nod. "I have no desire to be the last of anything. It's simply not in my nature, nor am I willing to sacrifice myself, lie down before the Self-Propelled Expressway just to prove how evil it is. Yes, I know—singing." She had silenced his attempt to speak with the rise of an elegant hand. "Singing, that has some appeal. So, I am not optimistic, Leo, but I will accompany you because I love you. I'll sing my little heart going downriver but will freely do so, because I freely love you. However, just because those pigeons may have found their way back to the scene of their disaster, don't assume I'm going to do the same thing.

"Turn the engine back on, Taylor," she said over her shoulder and snapped her fingers. The man obeyed.

"Ah, there's room for discussion," the author said, quickly on his feet.

"Talk, but no hugging," she responded.

"But there's only one place to talk, and that's on the site," Post argued. "This island is fit for reflection only, for storage of old stuff and exiled opinion. We must return to service the argument, renew the illusion, the love, if not the species." Post helped his wife down onto the bobbing raft and turned to assist Pickett Sneat.

"What will become of Smith?" The book reviewer had permitted himself to be placed on the hood of the ancient taxi. Once again I, B. Smith, usually the observer and recorder of events, was made the object of the group's speculation.

"Smith has been joined with the elements," Post explained, "his reward for dutiful service. Already he begins to resemble those abdicant scribes of the gospel, encased in a gothic frieze, hand outstretched and quill at the ready. His accounts to be believed or not." The author had just handed down the policewoman who lightly accepted the courtesy.

"But come, the river waits and adventure beckons," Post said, straightening his blazer. He unbent the lines that secured the raft to the landing. "We are cast off, Mr. Taylor," he declared, and sprang to the deck with agility that reviewed his former prowess on the soccer field.

The taxi's engine quickened, the paddlewheel at the rear splashed the lagoon's water. The craft swung slowly away from the stone landing, and the man called Taylor steered them through the small aperture beneath the portcullis hanging aslant. Taylor had placed a white Stetson upon his head. Pickett Sneat still sat on the hood, the breeze rippling through the ring of pumpkin-colored hair that encircled his shiny pate. The two women stood together, arm in arm. Leo Post walked about the deck, coiling bits of line, securing gear and lashing down crates—the small tasks of leaving port—though the blazer, gray flannels, and white buckskins he wore resembled the costume of a yacht committee-man more than that of an ordinary seaman. Just as the taxi-ferry reached the entrance to the lagoon and then around the outside walls and into midstream, Post commanded, "Give us a song, Pickett."

The book reviewer's deep voice rumbled like distant thunder in the Catskills just behind us. The heavy tones seemed to salute Leek's Castle as the raft passed into the current downstream. After the first verse, the others joined the book reviewer:

Love was a stranger to this isle,
Fragile footprints in the sand—

Some apparatus glinted on the landing below the balcony where I, B. Smith, companion to history, was left behind, as the full sun surmounted the eastern bank. Lying athwart one another, like jackstraws flung there by a child who had passed on to more interesting games, were a pair of metal crutches. The voices diminished as the raft was carried downriver by the current and tide. Shifts of laughter hyphenated the song's lyric.

That followed—followed heart's—exile—
And—ain't that—grand?